D-P Filippi & Silvio Camboni

gregory and the gargoyles

book 3

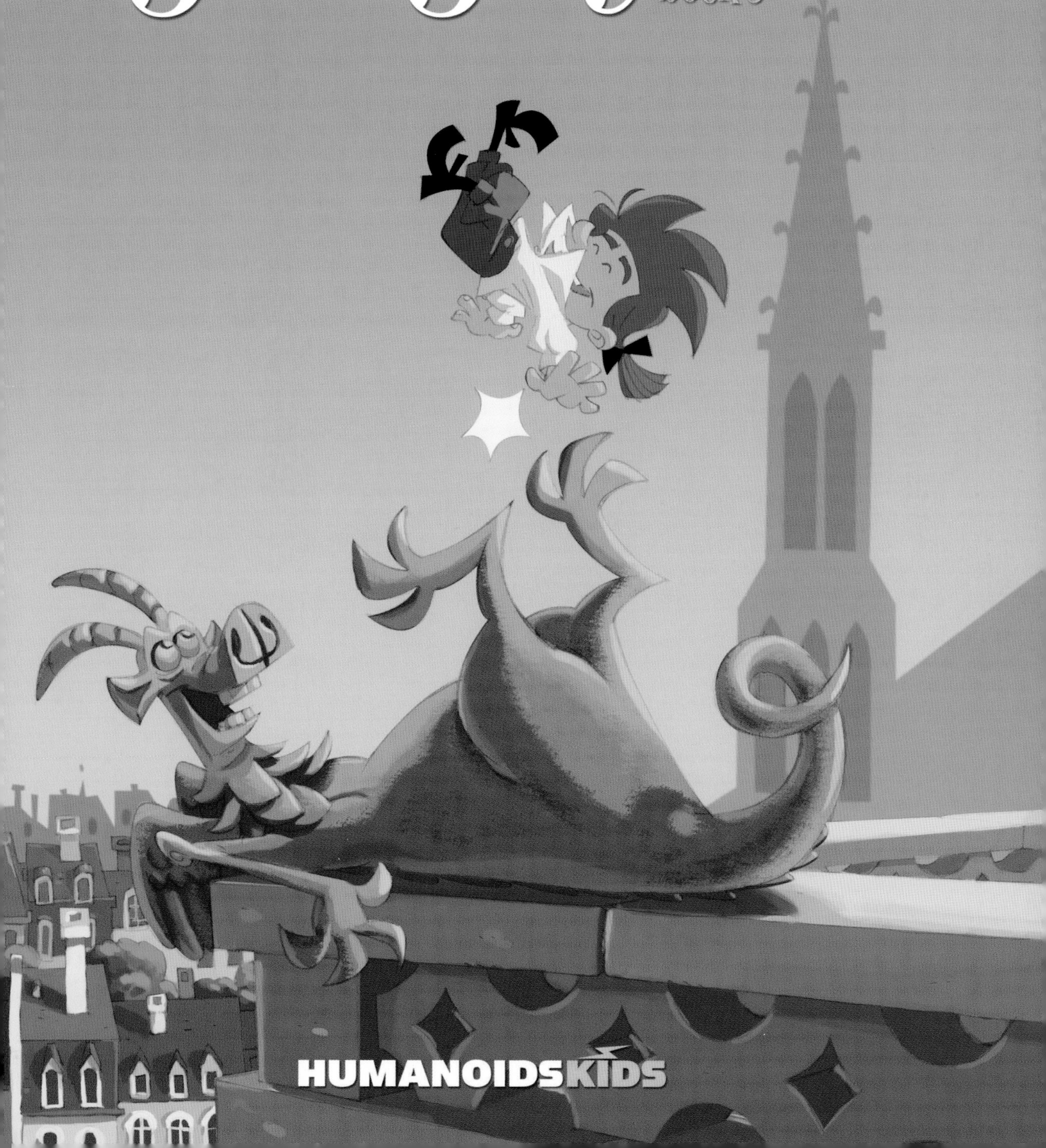

HUMANOIDSKIDS

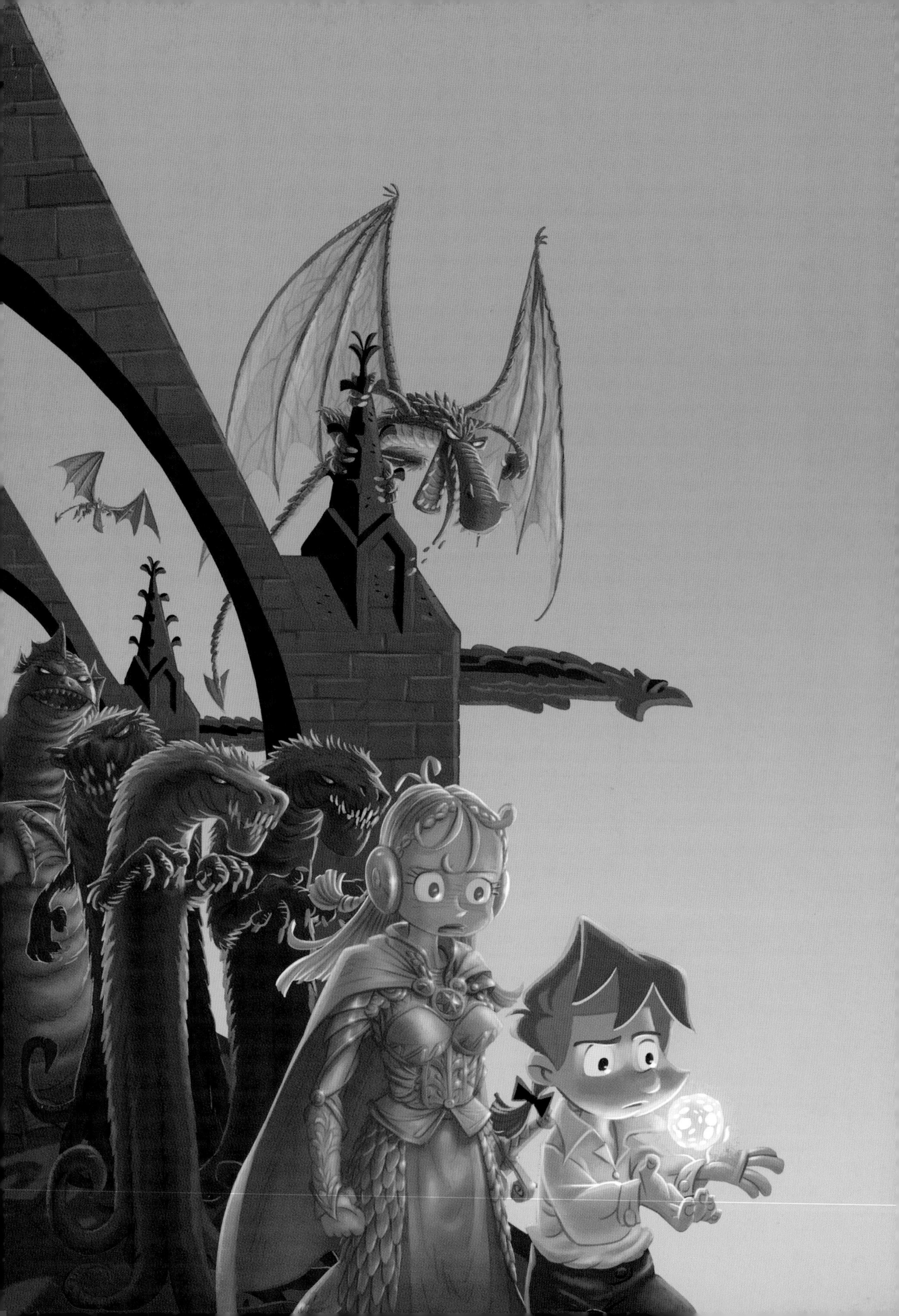

D-P FILIPPI
WRITER

SILVIO CAMBONI
ARTIST

CHRISTELLE MOULART
(PAGES 5 & 6)
BRUNO OLIVIERI
(PAGES 7 TO 52)
**BRUNO OLIVIERI
& RAFAEL RUIZ**
(PAGES 53 TO 98)
RAFAEL RUIZ
(PAGES 99 TO 144)
COLORISTS

*

BLASE A. PROVITOLA
TRANSLATOR

*

JERRY FRISSEN
SENIOR ART DIRECTOR

**ALEX DONOGHUE
& FABRICE SAPOLSKY**
U.S. EDITION EDITORS

**BRUNO LECIGNE
& CAMILLE THÉLOT-VERNOUX**
ORIGINAL EDITION EDITORS

FABRICE GIGER
PUBLISHER

**Rights & Licensing - licensing@humanoids.com
Press and Social Media - pr@humanoids.com**

GREGORY AND THE GARGOYLES: BOOK 3
This title is a publication of Humanoids, Inc. 8033 Sunset Blvd. #628, Los Angeles, CA 90046.
Copyright © 2018 Humanoids, Inc., Los Angeles (USA). All rights reserved. Humanoids and its logos are ® and © 2018 Humanoids, Inc.

Originally published in French by Les Humanoïdes Associés (Paris, France).

The story and characters presented in this publication are fictional. Any similarities to events or persons living or dead
is purely coincidental. No portion of this book may be reproduced by any means without the express written consent
of the copyright holder except for artwork used for review purposes. Printed in PRC.

ALSO BY D-P FILIPPI:

GREGORY AND THE GARGOYLES: BOOK 1
ISBN: 978-1-59465-798-6

GREGORY AND THE GARGOYLES: BOOK 2
ISBN: 978-1-59465-581-4

HALLOWEEN TALES
ISBN: 978-159465-654-5

JOHN LORD
ISBN: 978-1-59465-183-0

MARSHALS
ISBN: 978-1-59465-140-3

MUSE
ISBN: 978-1-59465-038-3

OTHER HUMANOIDSKIDS TITLES:

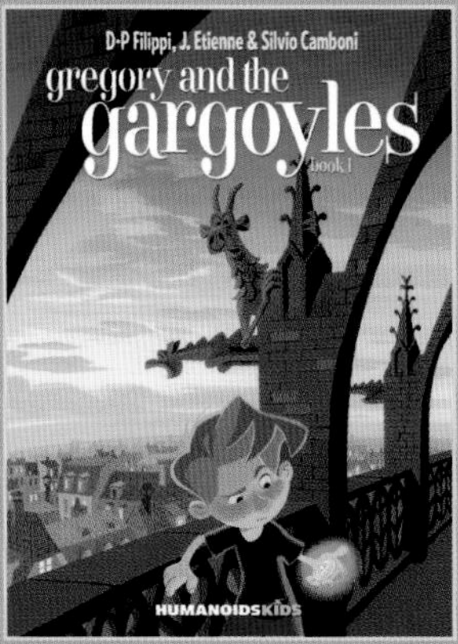
D-P Filippi, J. Etienne & Silvio Camboni
gregory and the
gargoyles
book 1
HUMANOIDSKIDS

GREGORY AND THE GARGOYLES: BOOK 1
ISBN: 978-1-59465-798-6

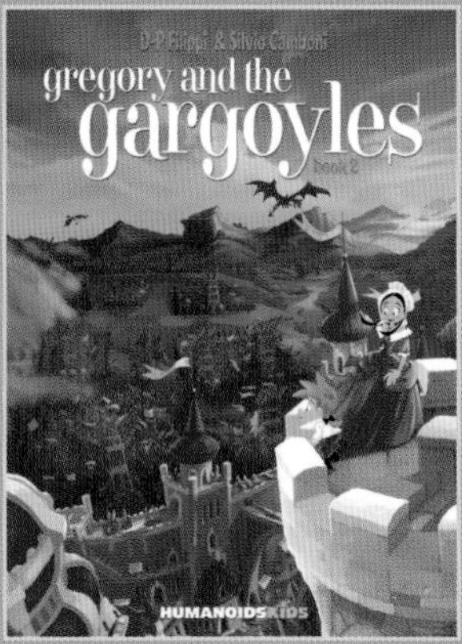
D-P Filippi & Silvio Camboni
gregory and the
gargoyles
HUMANOIDSKIDS

GREGORY AND THE GARGOYLES: BOOK 2
ISBN: 978-1-59465-581-4

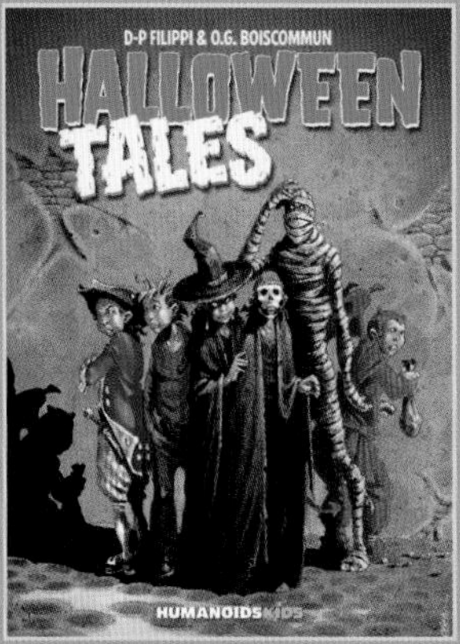
D-P FILIPPI & O.G. BOISCOMMUN
HALLOWEEN
TALES
HUMANOIDSKIDS

HALLOWEEN TALES
ISBN: 978-159465-654-5

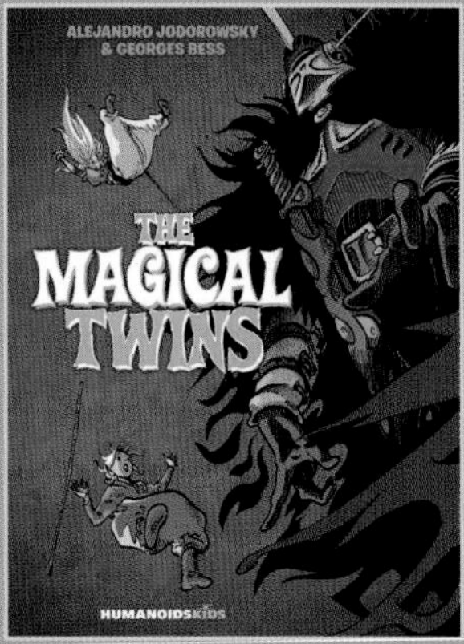
ALEJANDRO JODOROWSKY
& GEORGES BESS
THE
MAGICAL
TWINS
HUMANOIDSKIDS

THE MAGICAL TWINS
ISBN: 978-1-59465-408-4

The Story so far...

Meet Gregory. He's pretty much normal, except that he's a tad lonelier and he daydreams a bit more than the average kid. He lives across from a cathedral with his parents and his annoying sister, whom he can't stand. One day, he finds a magical medallion under the floor in his bedroom that gives him the power to travel back to the 17th century, where an extraordinary destiny awaits him: becoming a magician!

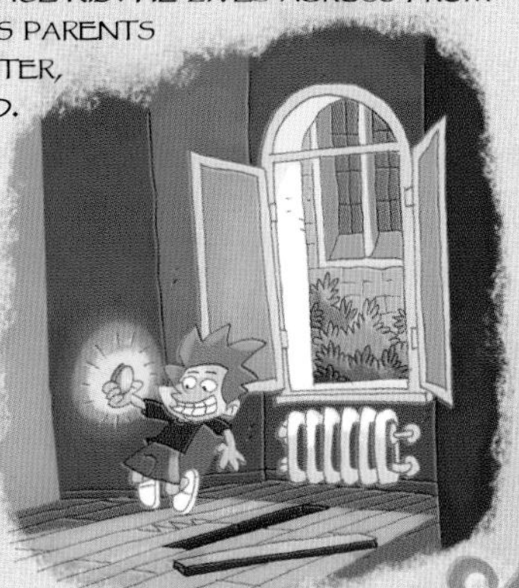

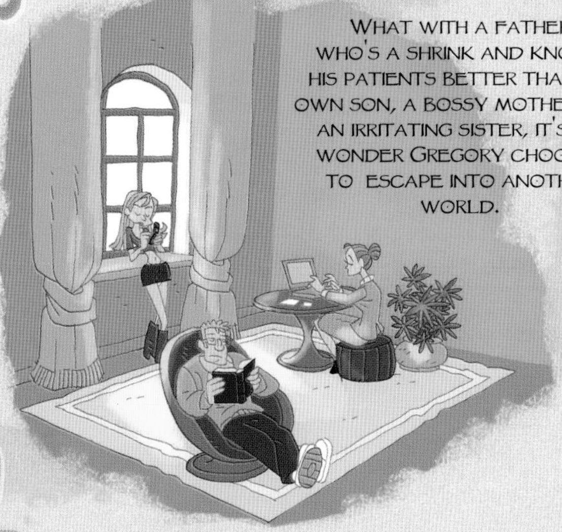

What with a father who's a shrink and knows his patients better than his own son, a bossy mother and an irritating sister, it's no wonder Gregory chooses to escape into another world.

Back in the 17th century, his mom is nicer and more caring, his father is a blacksmith who takes him fishing and treats him like an adult, and his sister is about to be married.

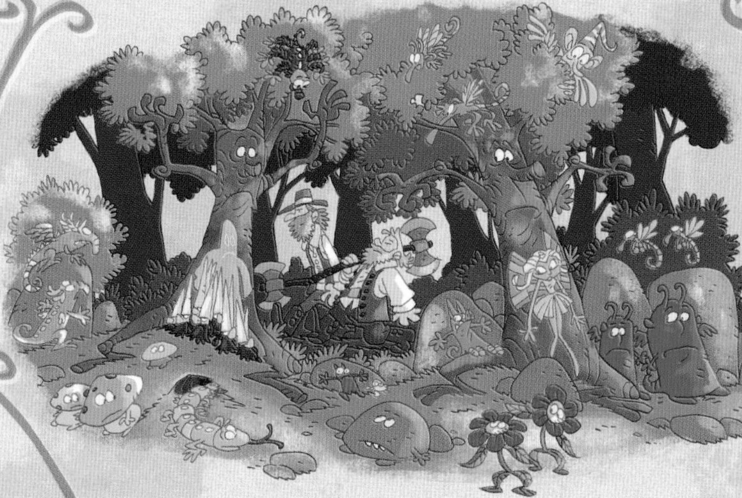

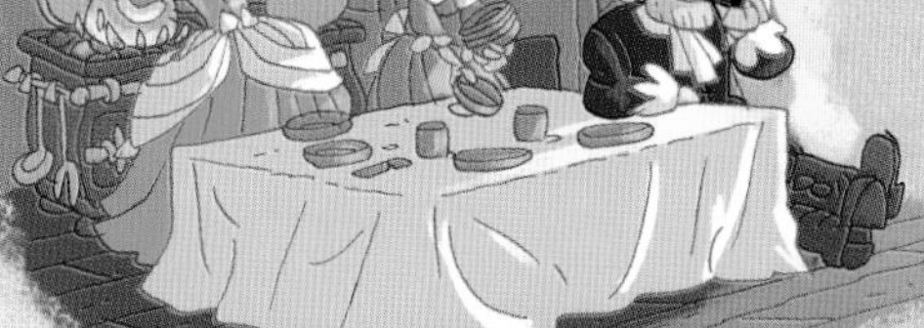

But that's not even the best part! Imagine, if you will, that in those days, magic and magical beings of all sorts still exist and they live right alongside humans.

But, alas, not for much longer, as there are no magicians left to protect the two universes and keep them separate. They all perished during the great conflict with the terrible, fearsome Black magician.

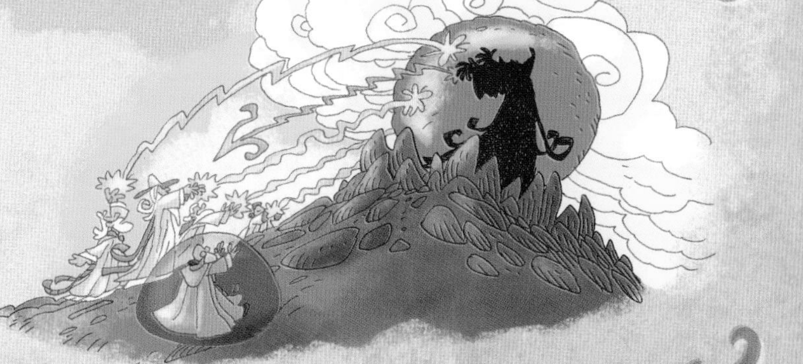

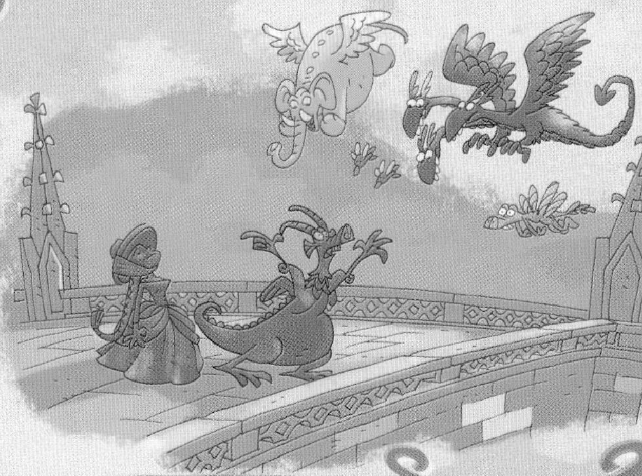

THAT WEIRD-LOOKING STATUE THERE, WAVING WILDLY, THAT'S PHIDIAS. HE'S GREGORY'S GUIDE AND INSTRUCTOR. PHIDIAS AND HIS FRIENDS ALL LIVE ON TOP OF THE CATHEDRAL. THEY ARE THE GUARDIANS OF THE LAST MAGIC DOOR THROUGH WHICH SUPERNATURAL BEINGS CAN ESCAPE. PHIDIAS IS THE ONE WHO TOLD GREGORY HE COULD BECOME A MAGICIAN AND SAVE THEM ALL.

IN ORDER TO DO THIS, GREGORY HAS TO UNDERGO INTENSIVE TRAINING. THANKS TO THE KEY OF TIME, HE TRAVELS BACK TO THE PAST WHERE HE AND OTHER APPRENTICES FROM DIFFERENT TIME PERIODS TAKE LESSONS WITH MASTER WILGUR.

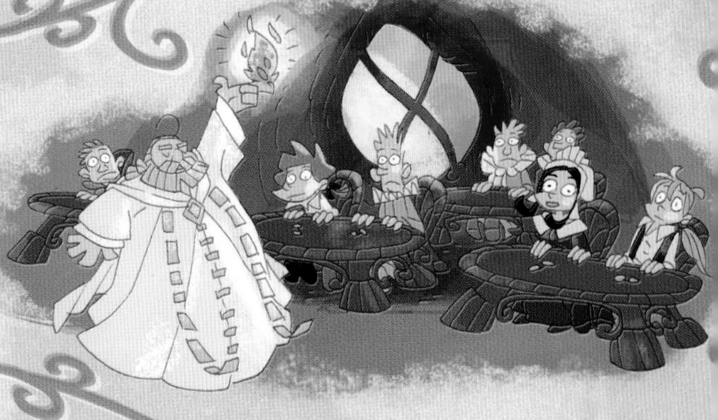

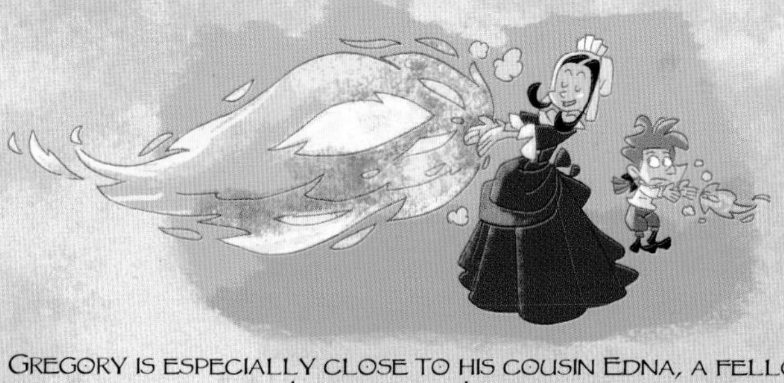

GREGORY IS ESPECIALLY CLOSE TO HIS COUSIN EDNA, A FELLOW STUDENT IN WILGUR'S CLASS. SHE'S AWESOME WITH SPELLS. MAYBE EVEN A LITTLE TOO AWESOME, IF YOU ASK HIM.

EDNA'S MOTHER, I.E. GREGORY'S AUNT, IS AN EVIL BEIN WHO, ALONG WITH A MYSTERIOUS MAN IN A HOOD, SEE TO BRING THE BLACK MAGICIAN BACK TO LIFE, PERHAP EVEN USING EDNA'S BODY FOR HIS REINCARNATION. TO DO THIS, SHE CAPTURES SUPERNATURAL BEINGS AND STEALS THEIR POWERS. NEEDLESS TO SAY, EDNA'S AUNT IS THE SWORN ENEMY OF PHIDIAS AND THE GUARDIANS.

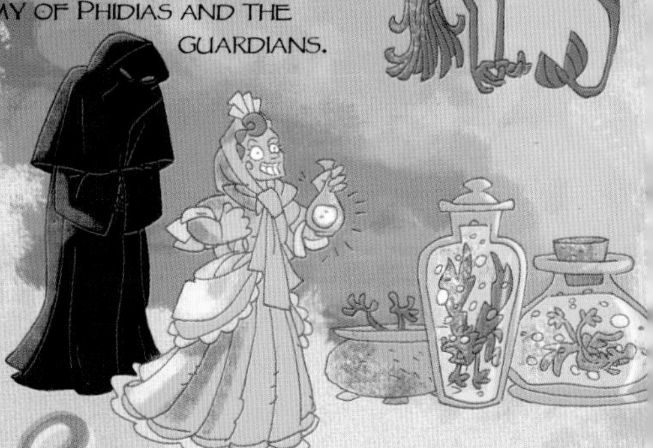

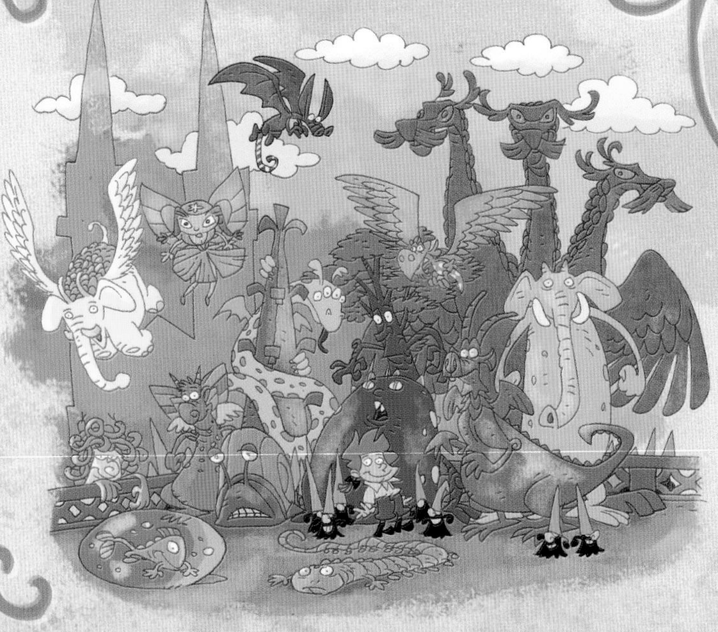

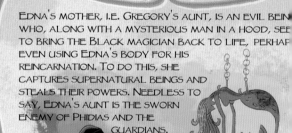

BUT GREGORY INTENDS TO DO EVERYTHING IN HIS POWER TO REACH HIS GOAL. THANKS TO THE MEDALLION THAT ALLOWS HIM TO COME AND GO AS HE PLEASES BETWEEN TIME PERIODS, HE GRADUALLY LEARNS HOW TO BECOME THE ONE WHO EMBODIES ALL THE HOPES AND DREAMS OF THE SUPERNATURAL BEINGS - THE ONE WHO COULD BRING MAGIC BACK ONE DAY. BUT WITH ALL THAT SAID, GREGORY IS STILL JUST A BOY, WITH CONFLICTED FEELINGS...

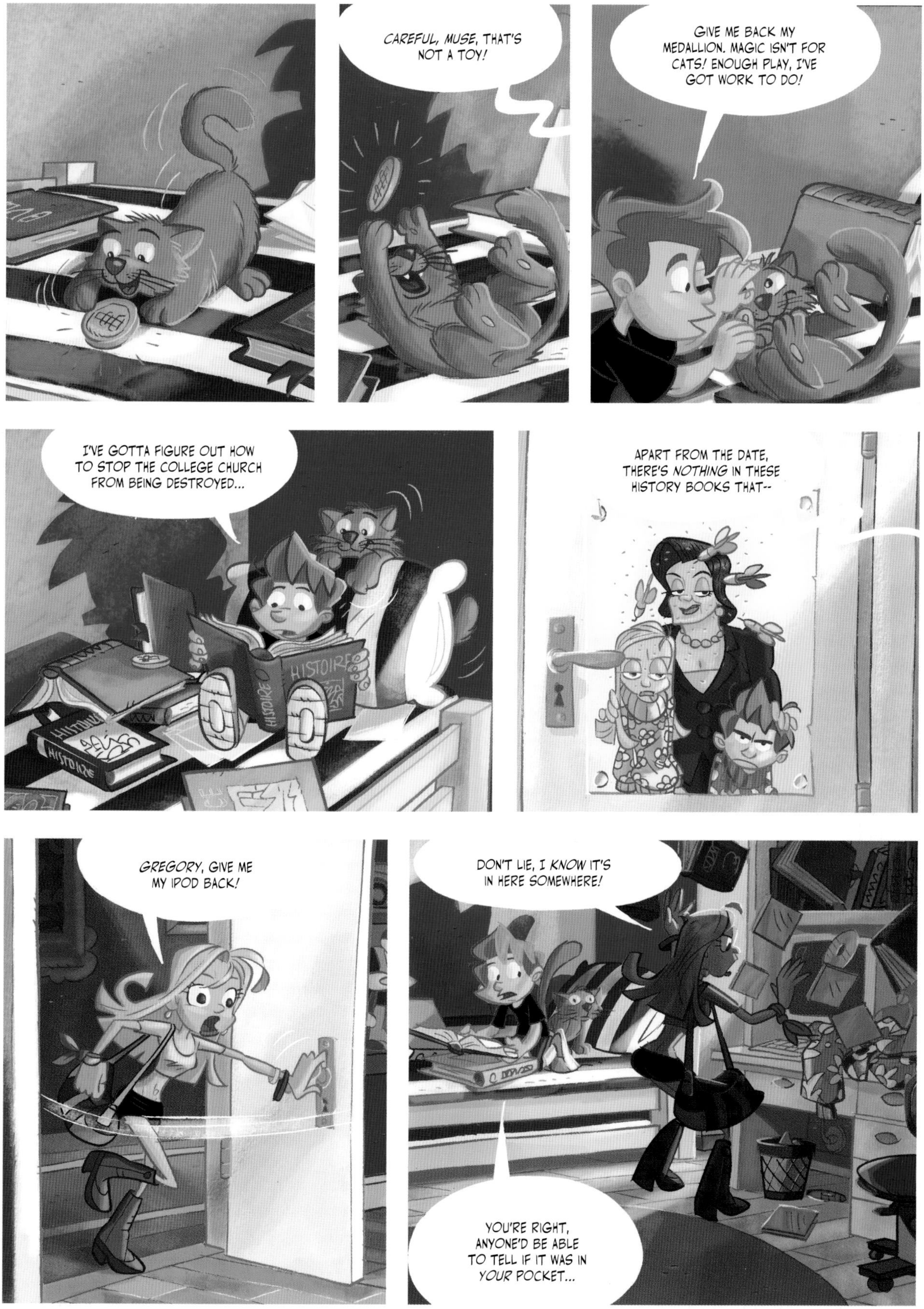
CAREFUL, *MUSE*, THAT'S NOT A TOY!
GIVE ME BACK MY MEDALLION. MAGIC ISN'T FOR CATS! ENOUGH PLAY, I'VE GOT WORK TO DO!
I'VE GOTTA FIGURE OUT HOW TO STOP THE COLLEGE CHURCH FROM BEING DESTROYED...
HISTOIRE
APART FROM THE DATE, THERE'S *NOTHING* IN THESE HISTORY BOOKS THAT--
GREGORY, GIVE ME MY IPOD BACK!
DON'T LIE, I *KNOW* IT'S IN HERE SOMEWHERE!
YOU'RE RIGHT, ANYONE'D BE ABLE TO TELL IF IT WAS IN *YOUR* POCKET...

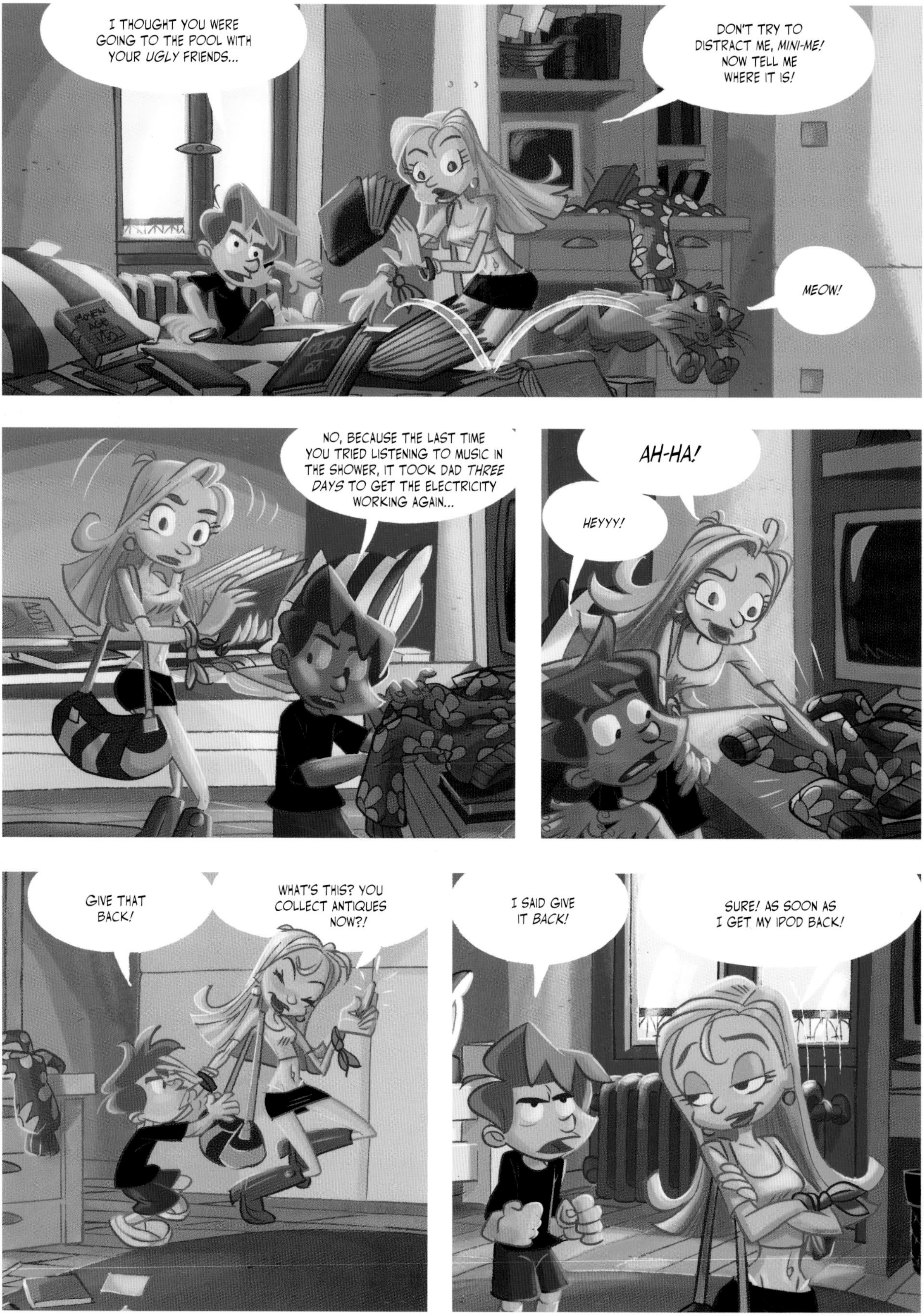
I THOUGHT YOU WERE GOING TO THE POOL WITH YOUR UGLY FRIENDS...
DON'T TRY TO DISTRACT ME, MINI-ME! NOW TELL ME WHERE IT IS!
MEOW!
NO, BECAUSE THE LAST TIME YOU TRIED LISTENING TO MUSIC IN THE SHOWER, IT TOOK DAD THREE DAYS TO GET THE ELECTRICITY WORKING AGAIN...
AH-HA!
HEYYY!
GIVE THAT BACK!
WHAT'S THIS? YOU COLLECT ANTIQUES NOW?!
I SAID GIVE IT BACK!
SURE! AS SOON AS I GET MY IPOD BACK!

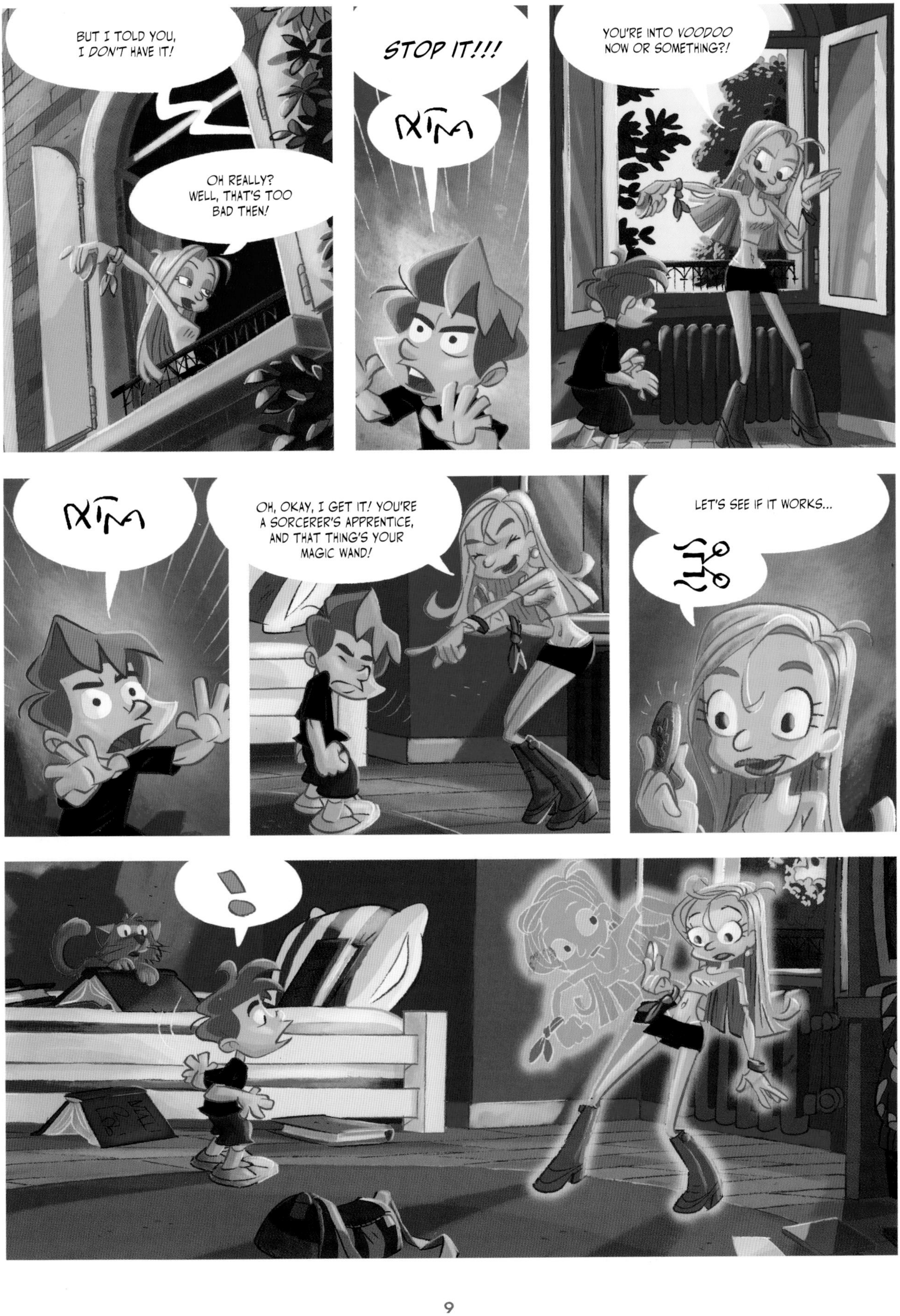
BUT I TOLD YOU, I DON'T HAVE IT!
OH REALLY? WELL, THAT'S TOO BAD THEN!
STOP IT!!!
YOU'RE INTO VOODOO NOW OR SOMETHING?!
OH, OKAY, I GET IT! YOU'RE A SORCERER'S APPRENTICE, AND THAT THING'S YOUR MAGIC WAND!
LET'S SEE IF IT WORKS...
!

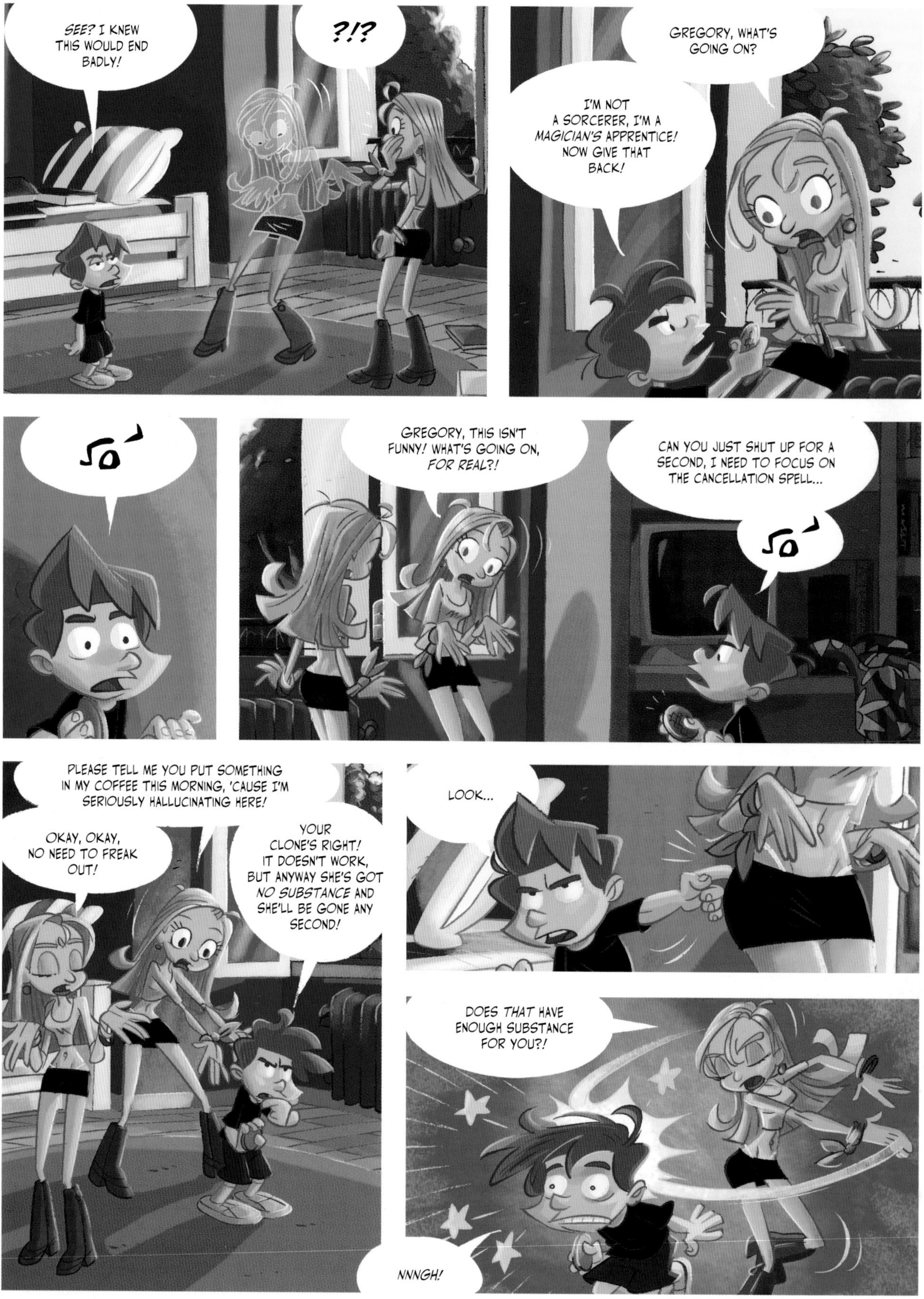
SEE? I KNEW THIS WOULD END BADLY!
?!?
GREGORY, WHAT'S GOING ON?
I'M NOT A SORCERER, I'M A *MAGICIAN'S* APPRENTICE! NOW GIVE THAT BACK!
GREGORY, THIS ISN'T FUNNY! WHAT'S GOING ON, *FOR REAL?!*
CAN YOU JUST SHUT UP FOR A SECOND, I NEED TO FOCUS ON THE CANCELLATION SPELL...
PLEASE TELL ME YOU PUT SOMETHING IN MY COFFEE THIS MORNING, 'CAUSE I'M SERIOUSLY HALLUCINATING HERE!
OKAY, OKAY, NO NEED TO FREAK OUT!
YOUR CLONE'S RIGHT! IT DOESN'T WORK, BUT ANYWAY SHE'S GOT *NO SUBSTANCE* AND SHE'LL BE GONE ANY SECOND!
LOOK...
DOES *THAT* HAVE ENOUGH SUBSTANCE FOR YOU?!
NNNGH!

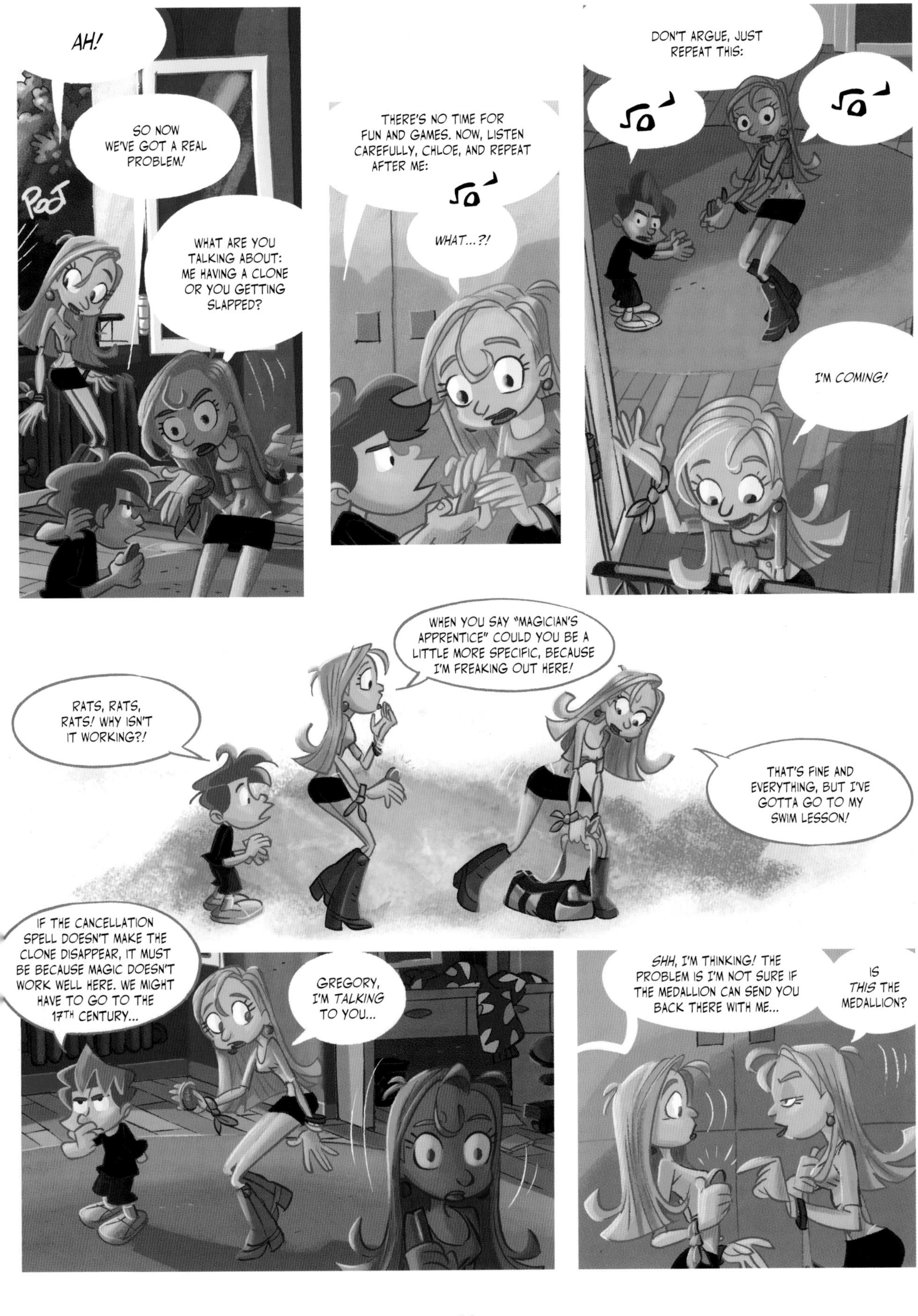
AH!
POC
SO NOW WE'VE GOT A REAL PROBLEM!
WHAT ARE YOU TALKING ABOUT: ME HAVING A CLONE OR YOU GETTING SLAPPED?
THERE'S NO TIME FOR FUN AND GAMES. NOW, LISTEN CAREFULLY, CHLOE, AND REPEAT AFTER ME:
WHAT...?!
DON'T ARGUE, JUST REPEAT THIS:
I'M COMING!
WHEN YOU SAY "MAGICIAN'S APPRENTICE" COULD YOU BE A LITTLE MORE SPECIFIC, BECAUSE I'M FREAKING OUT HERE!
RATS, RATS, RATS! WHY ISN'T IT WORKING?!
THAT'S FINE AND EVERYTHING, BUT I'VE GOTTA GO TO MY SWIM LESSON!
IF THE CANCELLATION SPELL DOESN'T MAKE THE CLONE DISAPPEAR, IT MUST BE BECAUSE MAGIC DOESN'T WORK WELL HERE. WE MIGHT HAVE TO GO TO THE 17TH CENTURY...
GREGORY, I'M TALKING TO YOU...
SHH, I'M THINKING! THE PROBLEM IS I'M NOT SURE IF THE MEDALLION CAN SEND YOU BACK THERE WITH ME...
IS THIS THE MEDALLION?

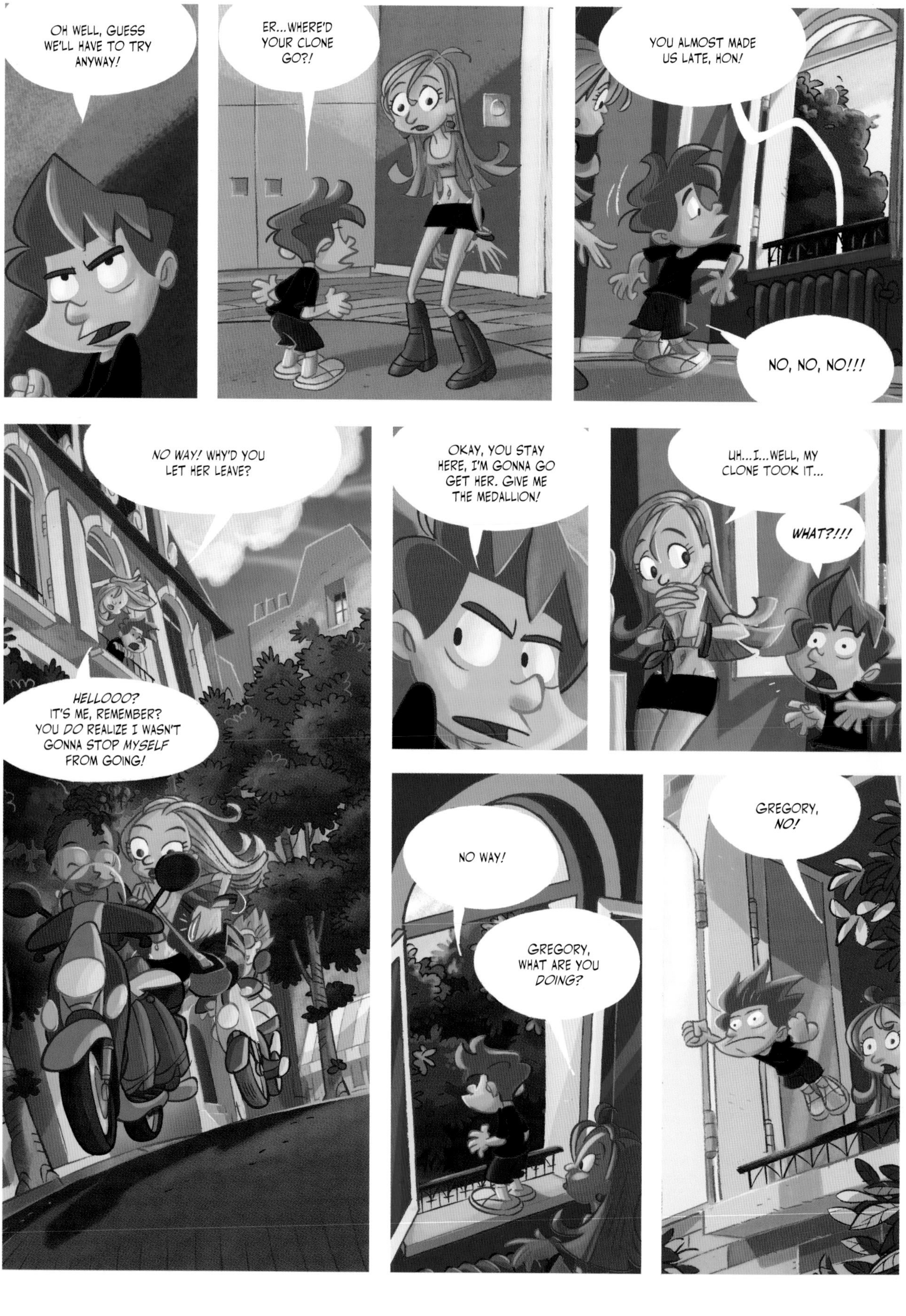
OH WELL, GUESS WE'LL HAVE TO TRY ANYWAY!
ER...WHERE'D YOUR CLONE GO?!
YOU ALMOST MADE US LATE, HON!
NO, NO, NO!!!
NO WAY! WHY'D YOU LET HER LEAVE?
HELLOOO? IT'S ME, REMEMBER? YOU DO REALIZE I WASN'T GONNA STOP MYSELF FROM GOING!
OKAY, YOU STAY HERE, I'M GONNA GO GET HER. GIVE ME THE MEDALLION!
UH...I...WELL, MY CLONE TOOK IT...
WHAT?!!!
NO WAY!
GREGORY, WHAT ARE YOU DOING?
GREGORY, NO!

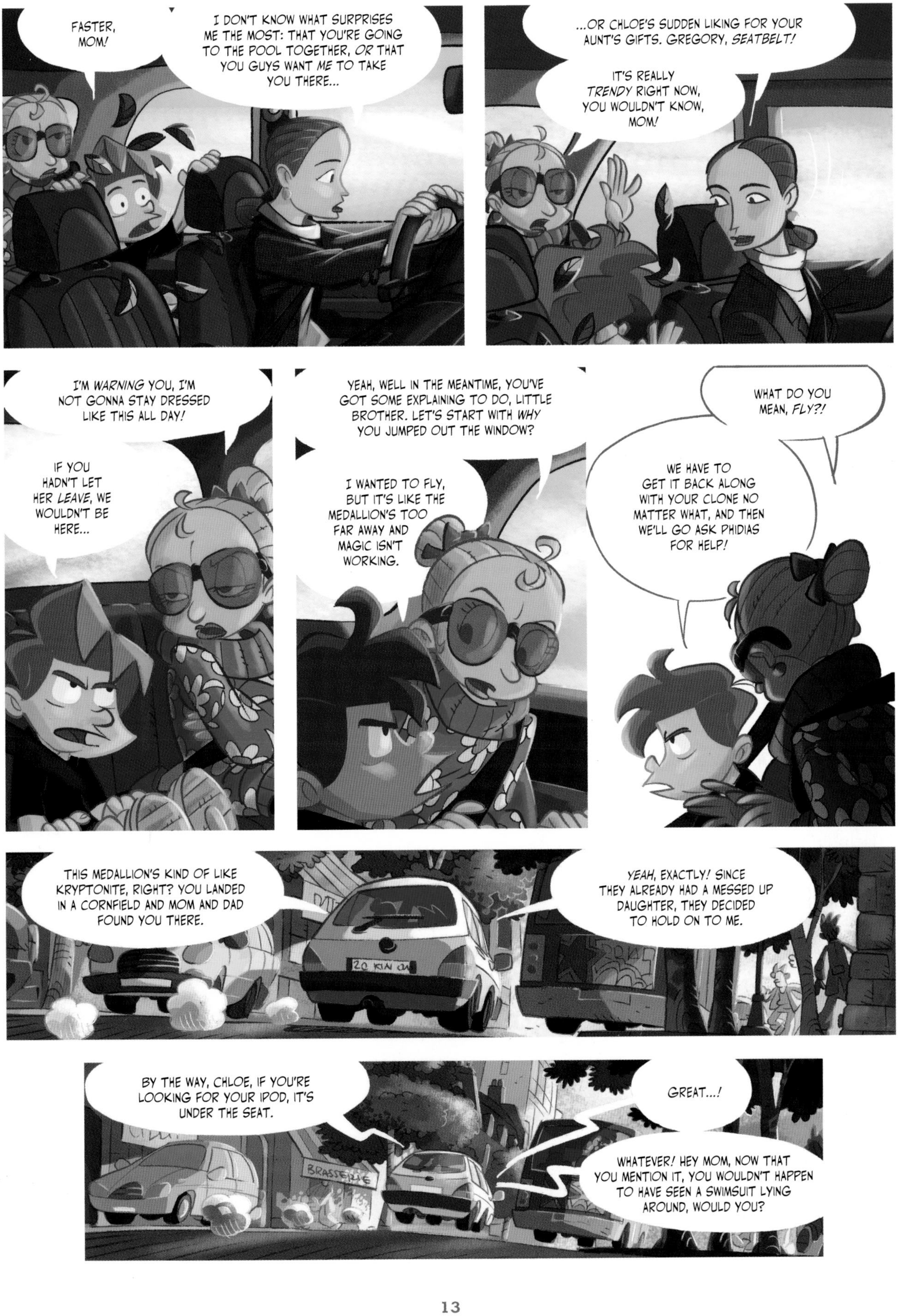
FASTER, MOM!
I DON'T KNOW WHAT SURPRISES ME THE MOST: THAT YOU'RE GOING TO THE POOL TOGETHER, OR THAT YOU GUYS WANT ME TO TAKE YOU THERE...
...OR CHLOE'S SUDDEN LIKING FOR YOUR AUNT'S GIFTS. GREGORY, SEATBELT!
IT'S REALLY TRENDY RIGHT NOW, YOU WOULDN'T KNOW, MOM!
I'M WARNING YOU, I'M NOT GONNA STAY DRESSED LIKE THIS ALL DAY!
IF YOU HADN'T LET HER LEAVE, WE WOULDN'T BE HERE...
YEAH, WELL IN THE MEANTIME, YOU'VE GOT SOME EXPLAINING TO DO, LITTLE BROTHER. LET'S START WITH WHY YOU JUMPED OUT THE WINDOW?
I WANTED TO FLY, BUT IT'S LIKE THE MEDALLION'S TOO FAR AWAY AND MAGIC ISN'T WORKING.
WHAT DO YOU MEAN, FLY?!
WE HAVE TO GET IT BACK ALONG WITH YOUR CLONE NO MATTER WHAT, AND THEN WE'LL GO ASK PHIDIAS FOR HELP!
THIS MEDALLION'S KIND OF LIKE KRYPTONITE, RIGHT? YOU LANDED IN A CORNFIELD AND MOM AND DAD FOUND YOU THERE.
YEAH, EXACTLY! SINCE THEY ALREADY HAD A MESSED UP DAUGHTER, THEY DECIDED TO HOLD ON TO ME.
BY THE WAY, CHLOE, IF YOU'RE LOOKING FOR YOUR IPOD, IT'S UNDER THE SEAT.
GREAT...!
WHATEVER! HEY MOM, NOW THAT YOU MENTION IT, YOU WOULDN'T HAPPEN TO HAVE SEEN A SWIMSUIT LYING AROUND, WOULD YOU?

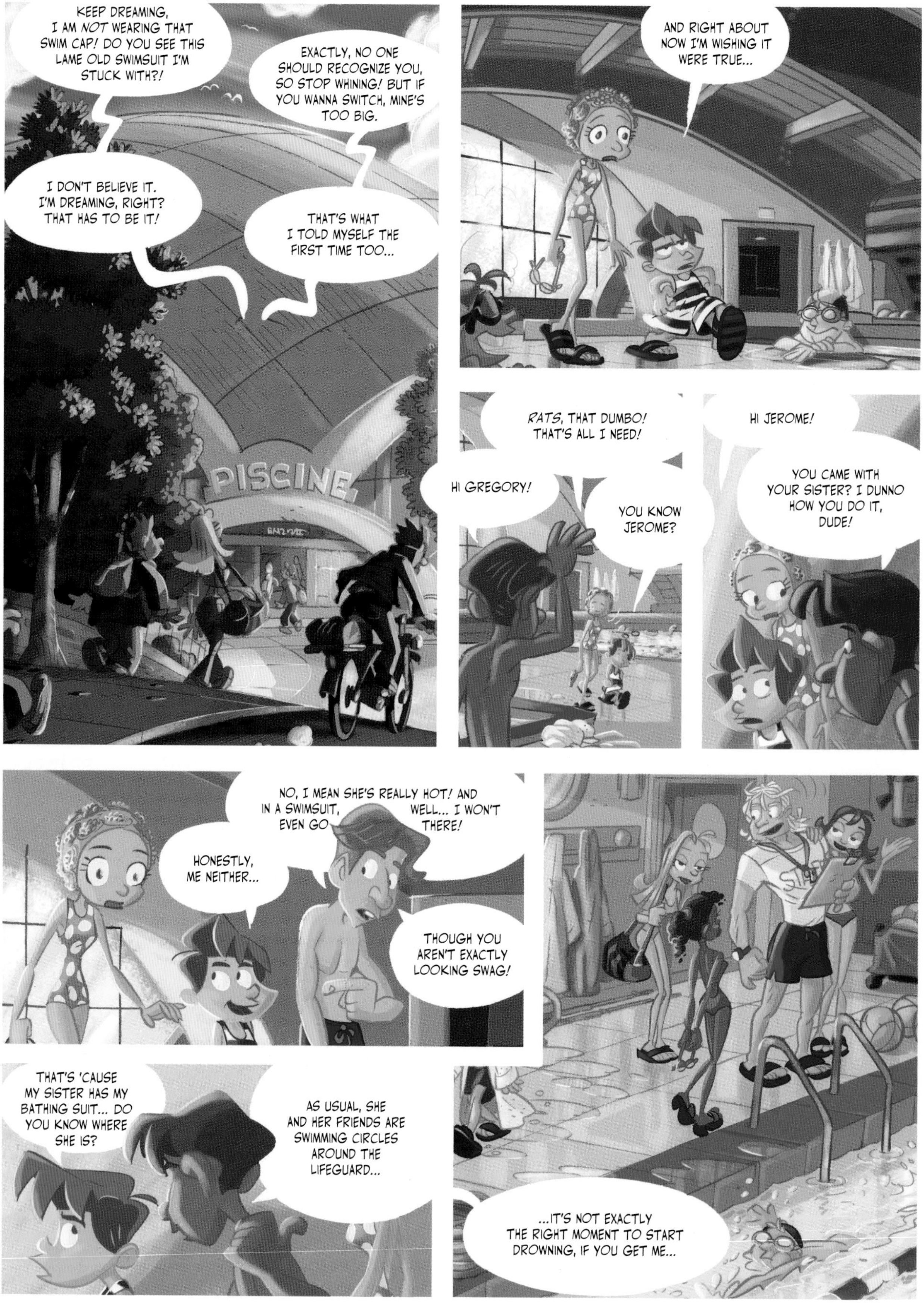
KEEP DREAMING, I AM *NOT* WEARING THAT SWIM CAP! DO YOU SEE THIS LAME OLD SWIMSUIT I'M STUCK WITH?!
EXACTLY, NO ONE SHOULD RECOGNIZE YOU, SO STOP WHINING! BUT IF YOU WANNA SWITCH, MINE'S TOO BIG.
I DON'T BELIEVE IT. I'M DREAMING, RIGHT? THAT HAS TO BE IT!
THAT'S WHAT I TOLD MYSELF THE FIRST TIME TOO...
PISCINE
AND RIGHT ABOUT NOW I'M WISHING IT WERE TRUE...
RATS, THAT DUMBO! THAT'S ALL I NEED!
HI GREGORY!
YOU KNOW JEROME?
HI JEROME!
YOU CAME WITH YOUR SISTER? I DUNNO HOW YOU DO IT, DUDE!
NO, I MEAN SHE'S REALLY HOT! AND IN A SWIMSUIT, WELL... I WON'T EVEN GO THERE!
HONESTLY, ME NEITHER...
THOUGH YOU AREN'T EXACTLY LOOKING SWAG!
THAT'S 'CAUSE MY SISTER HAS MY BATHING SUIT... DO YOU KNOW WHERE SHE IS?
AS USUAL, SHE AND HER FRIENDS ARE SWIMMING CIRCLES AROUND THE LIFEGUARD...
...IT'S NOT EXACTLY THE RIGHT MOMENT TO START DROWNING, IF YOU GET ME...

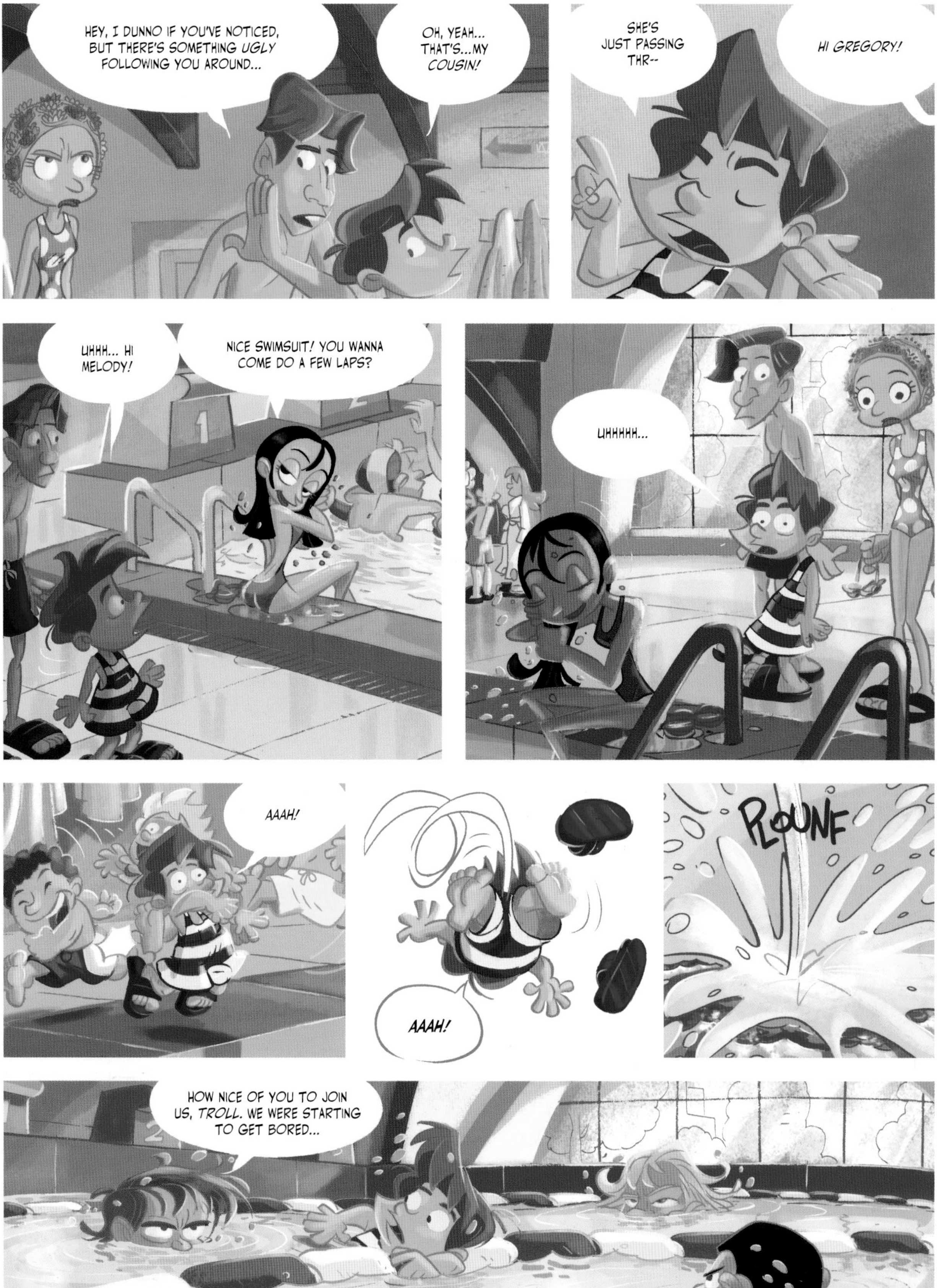
HEY, I DUNNO IF YOU'VE NOTICED, BUT THERE'S SOMETHING *UGLY* FOLLOWING YOU AROUND...
OH, YEAH... THAT'S...MY *COUSIN!*
SHE'S JUST PASSING THR--
HI GREGORY!
UHHH... HI *MELODY!*
NICE SWIMSUIT*!* YOU WANNA COME DO A FEW LAPS?
UHHHHH...
AAAH!
AAAH!
PLOUNF
HOW NICE OF YOU TO JOIN US, *TROLL*. WE WERE STARTING TO GET BORED...

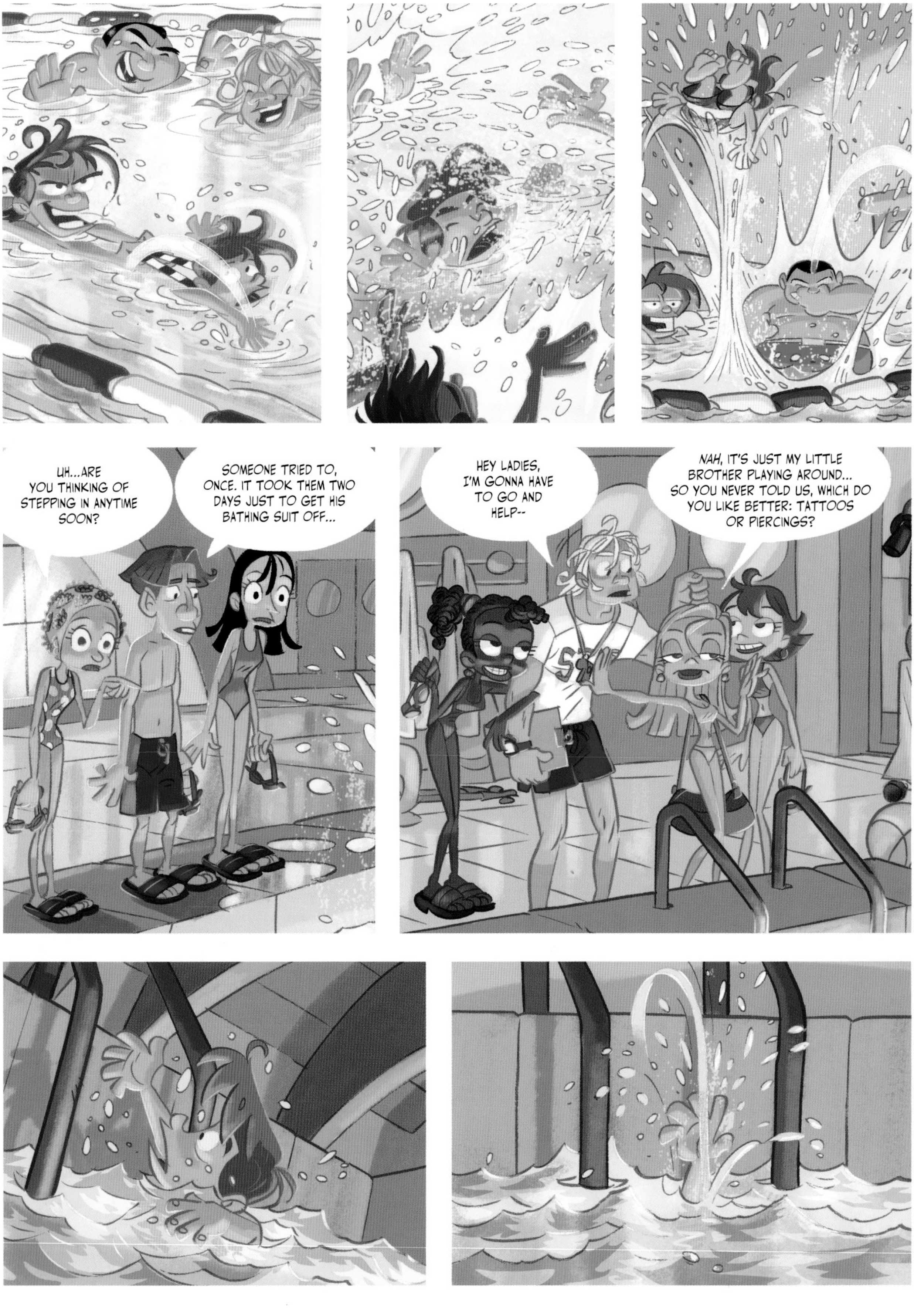
UH...ARE YOU THINKING OF STEPPING IN ANYTIME SOON?
SOMEONE TRIED TO, ONCE. IT TOOK THEM TWO DAYS JUST TO GET HIS BATHING SUIT OFF...
HEY LADIES, I'M GONNA HAVE TO GO AND HELP--
NAH, IT'S JUST MY LITTLE BROTHER PLAYING AROUND... SO YOU NEVER TOLD US, WHICH DO YOU LIKE BETTER: TATTOOS OR PIERCINGS?

HEY! LOOKS LIKE THE MAGIC'S BACK...

YEAH, I CAN BREATHE UNDERWATER! THE MEDALLION CAN'T BE FAR...

NOW IT'S MY TURN TO HAVE SOME FUN!

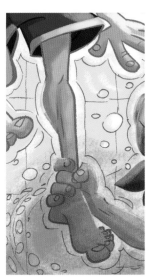

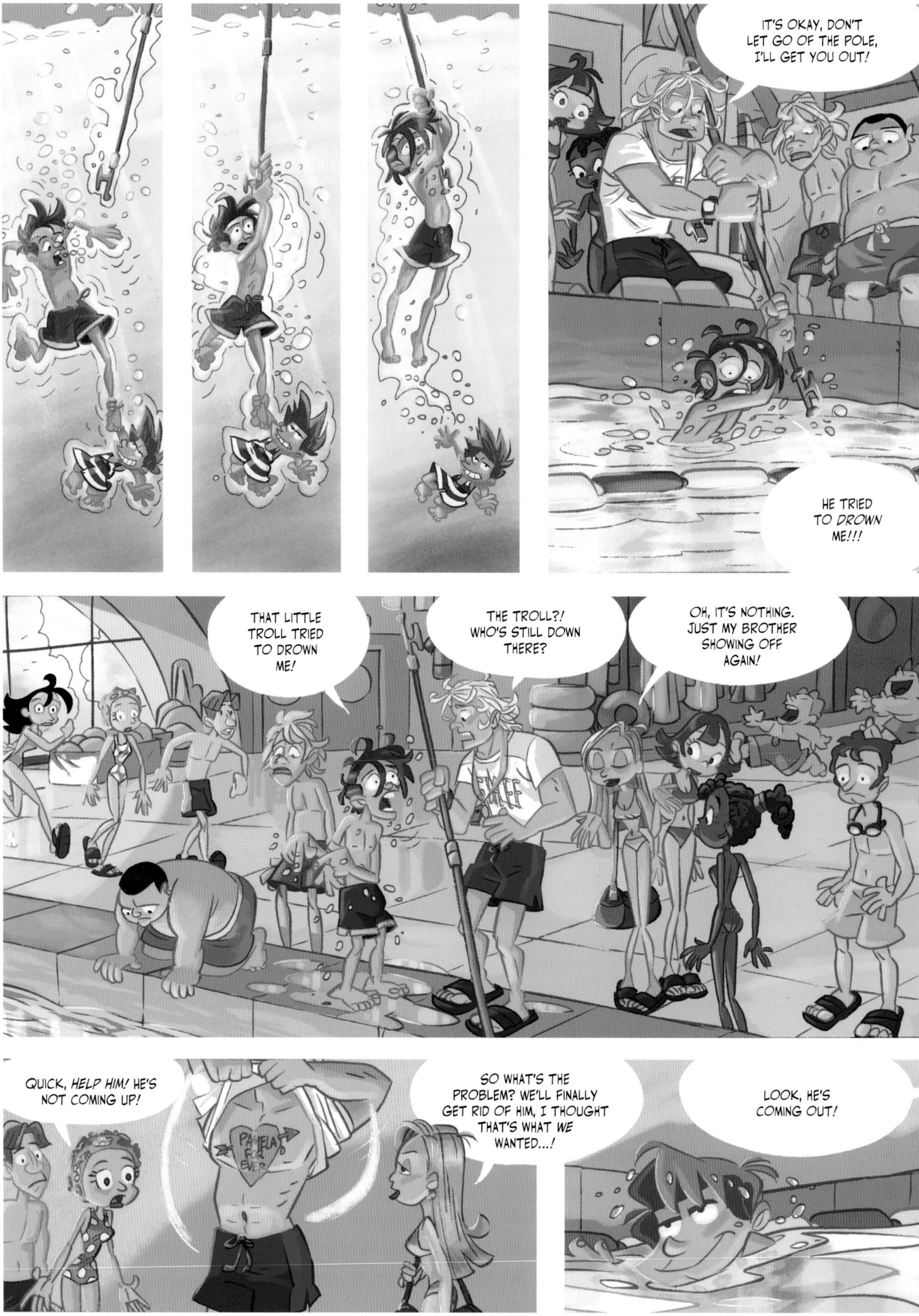
IT'S OKAY, DON'T LET GO OF THE POLE, I'LL GET YOU OUT!
HE TRIED TO *DROWN* ME!!!
THAT LITTLE TROLL TRIED TO DROWN ME!
THE TROLL?! WHO'S STILL DOWN THERE?
OH, IT'S NOTHING. JUST MY BROTHER SHOWING OFF AGAIN!
QUICK, *HELP HIM!* HE'S NOT COMING UP!
PAMELA FOR EVER
SO WHAT'S THE PROBLEM? WE'LL FINALLY GET RID OF HIM, I THOUGHT THAT'S WHAT *WE* WANTED...!
LOOK, HE'S COMING OUT!

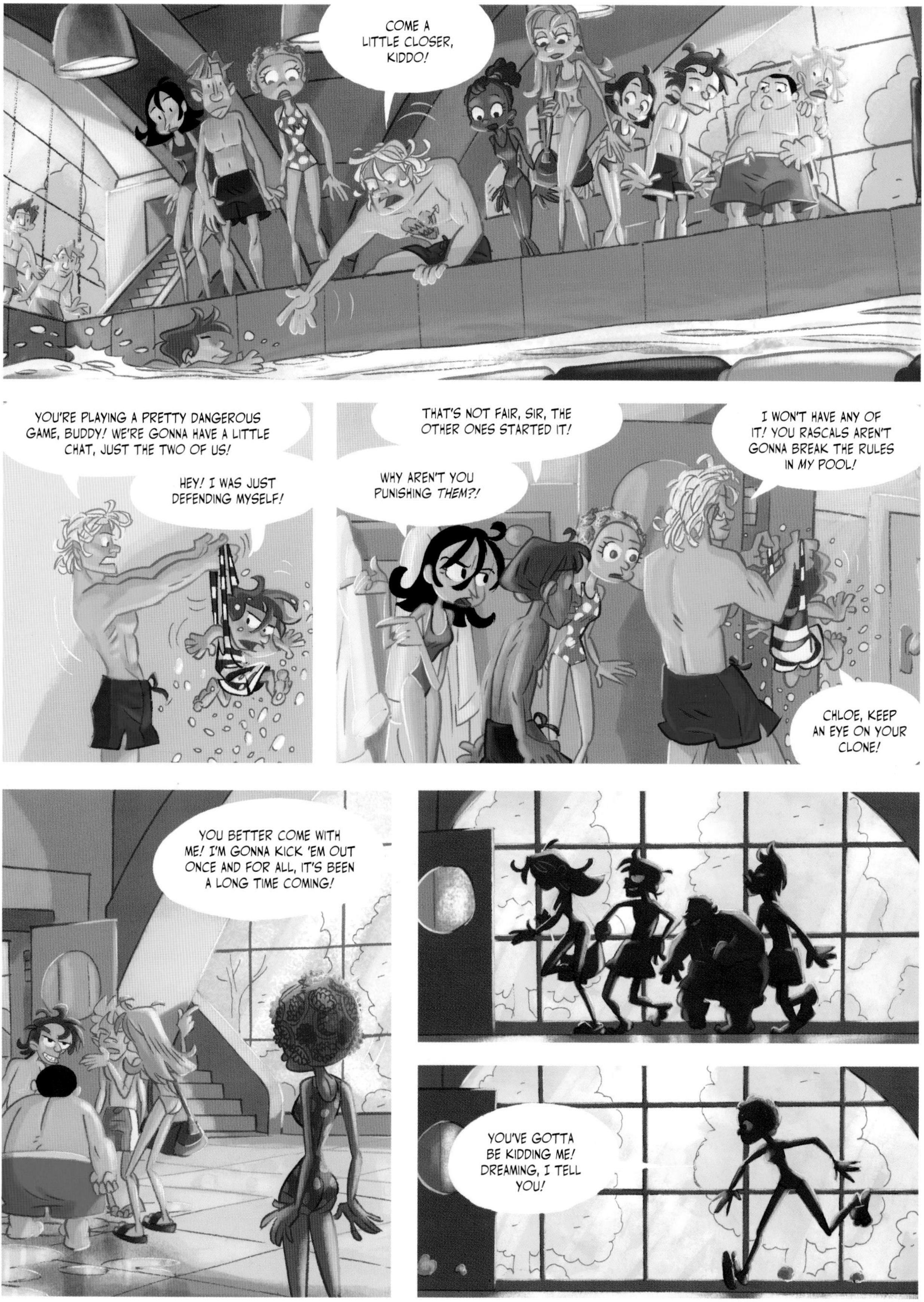
COME A LITTLE CLOSER, KIDDO!
YOU'RE PLAYING A PRETTY DANGEROUS GAME, BUDDY! WE'RE GONNA HAVE A LITTLE CHAT, JUST THE TWO OF US!
HEY! I WAS JUST DEFENDING MYSELF!
THAT'S NOT FAIR, SIR, THE OTHER ONES STARTED IT!
WHY AREN'T YOU PUNISHING *THEM*?!
I WON'T HAVE ANY OF IT! YOU RASCALS AREN'T GONNA BREAK THE RULES IN *MY* POOL!
CHLOE, KEEP AN EYE ON YOUR CLONE!
YOU BETTER COME WITH ME! I'M GONNA KICK 'EM OUT ONCE AND FOR ALL, IT'S BEEN A LONG TIME COMING!
YOU'VE GOTTA BE KIDDING ME! DREAMING, I TELL YOU!

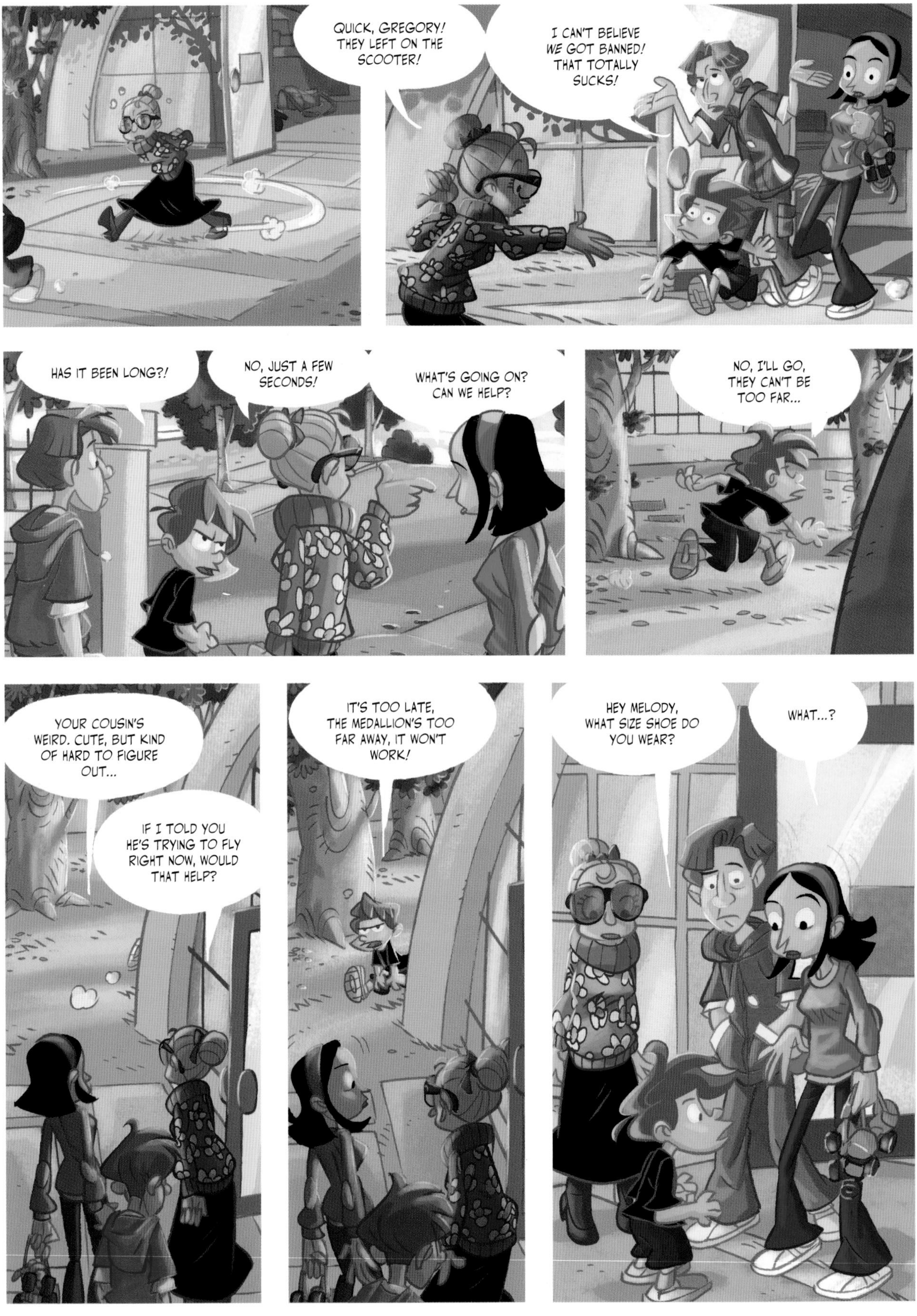
QUICK, GREGORY! THEY LEFT ON THE SCOOTER!
I CAN'T BELIEVE WE GOT BANNED! THAT TOTALLY SUCKS!
HAS IT BEEN LONG?!
NO, JUST A FEW SECONDS!
WHAT'S GOING ON? CAN WE HELP?
NO, I'LL GO, THEY CAN'T BE TOO FAR...
YOUR COUSIN'S WEIRD. CUTE, BUT KIND OF HARD TO FIGURE OUT...
IF I TOLD YOU HE'S TRYING TO FLY RIGHT NOW, WOULD THAT HELP?
IT'S TOO LATE, THE MEDALLION'S TOO FAR AWAY, IT WON'T WORK!
HEY MELODY, WHAT SIZE SHOE DO YOU WEAR?
WHAT...?

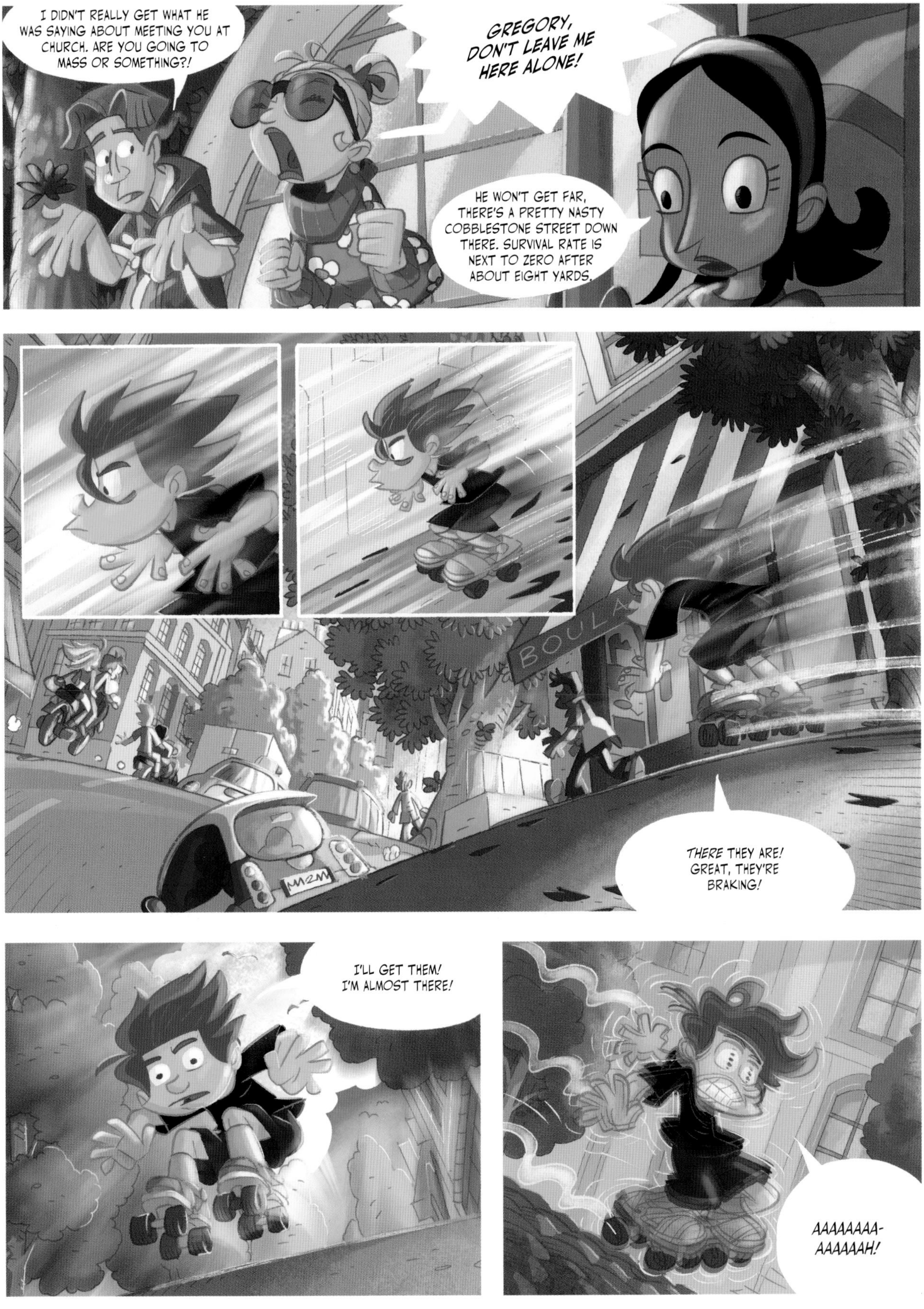
I DIDN'T REALLY GET WHAT HE WAS SAYING ABOUT MEETING YOU AT CHURCH. ARE YOU GOING TO MASS OR SOMETHING?!
GREGORY, DON'T LEAVE ME HERE ALONE!
HE WON'T GET FAR, THERE'S A PRETTY NASTY COBBLESTONE STREET DOWN THERE. SURVIVAL RATE IS NEXT TO ZERO AFTER ABOUT EIGHT YARDS.
BOULA
THERE THEY ARE! GREAT, THEY'RE BRAKING!
I'LL GET THEM! I'M ALMOST THERE!
AAAAAAAA-AAAAAAH!

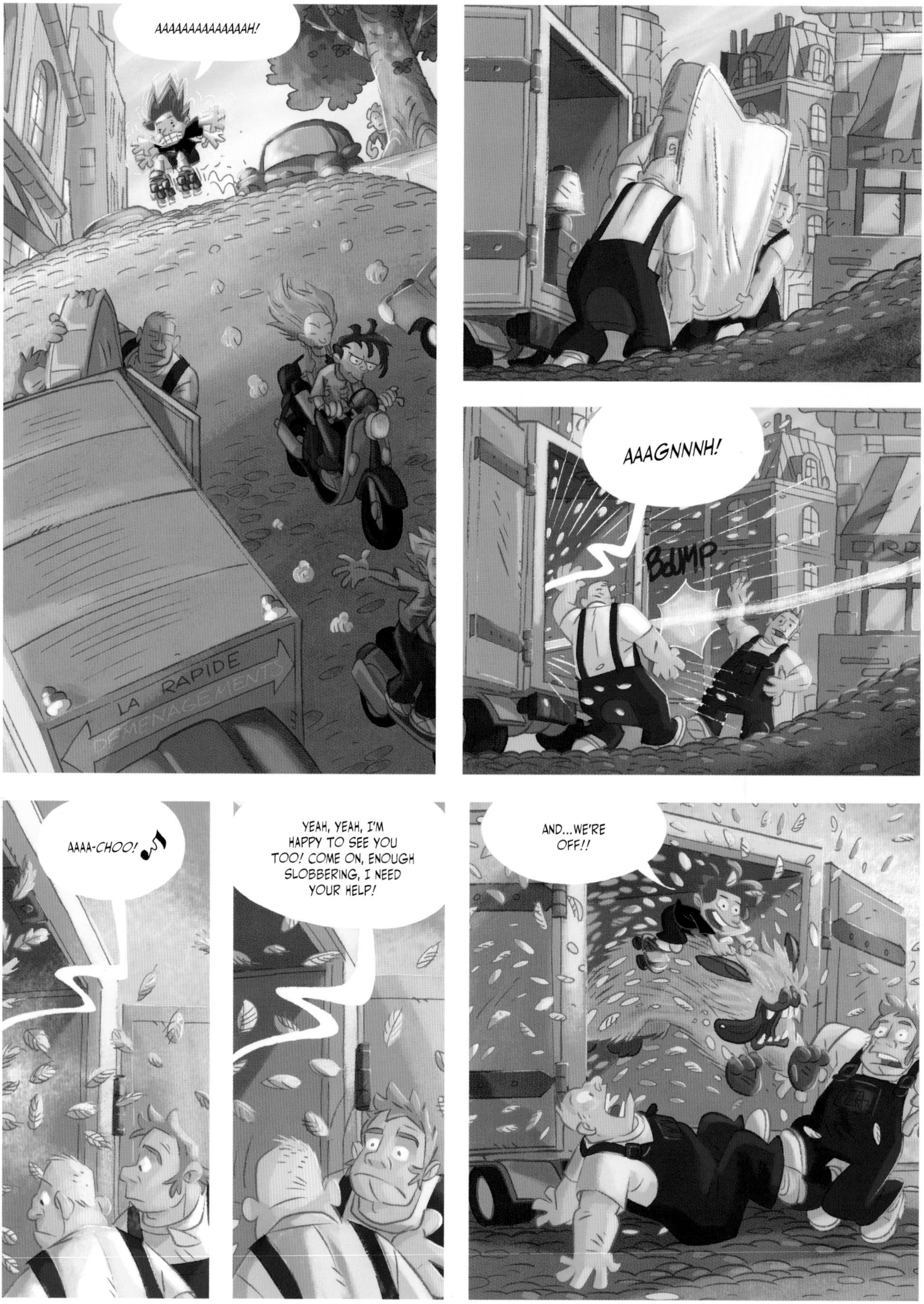

AAAAAAAAAAAAAAAH!
LA RAPIDE
DEMENAGEMENTS
AAAGNNNH!
BDUMP
AAAA-CHOO!
YEAH, YEAH, I'M HAPPY TO SEE YOU TOO! COME ON, ENOUGH SLOBBERING, I NEED YOUR HELP!
AND...WE'RE OFF!!

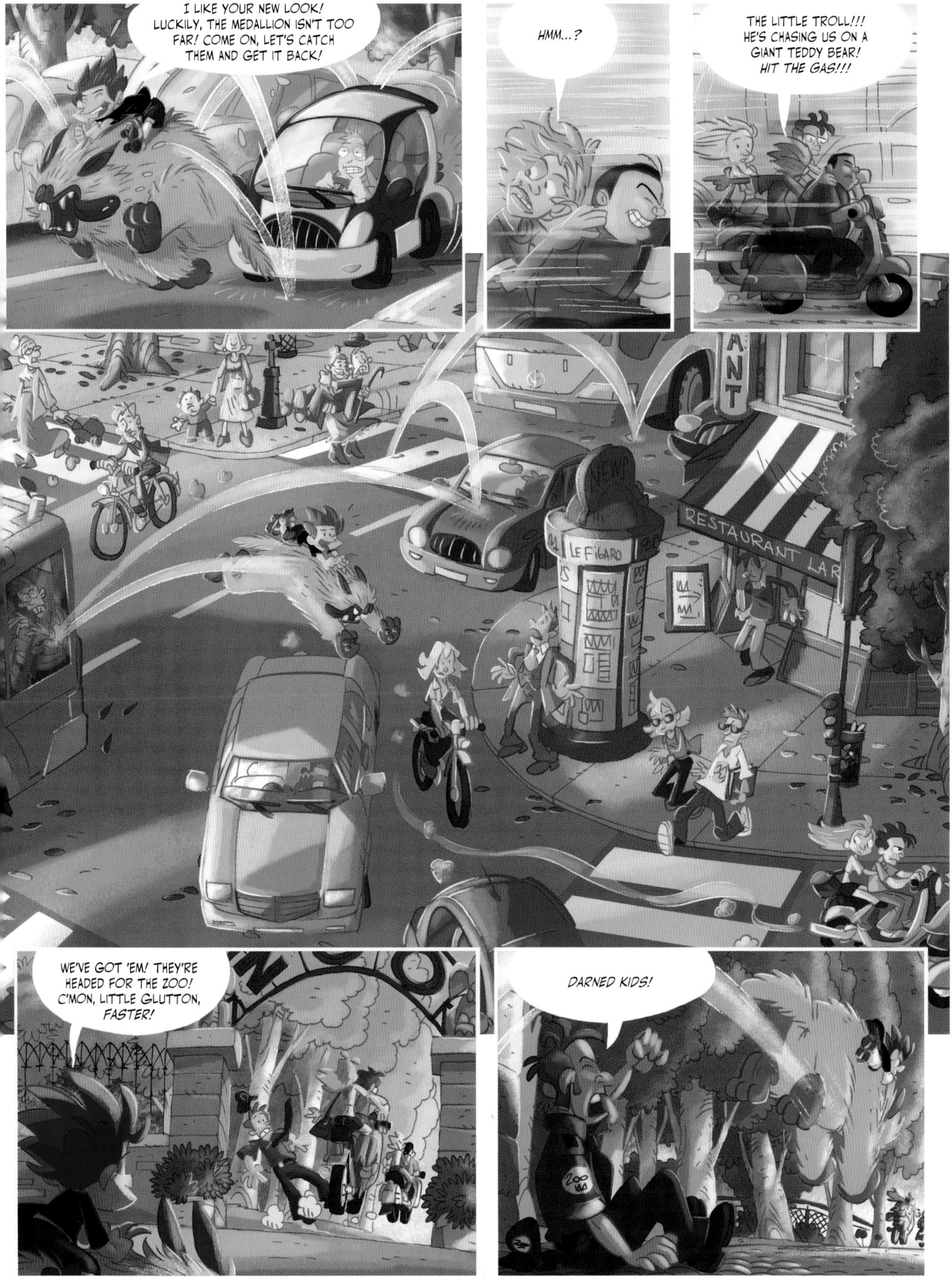
I LIKE YOUR NEW LOOK! LUCKILY, THE MEDALLION ISN'T TOO FAR! COME ON, LET'S CATCH THEM AND GET IT BACK!
HMM...?
THE LITTLE TROLL!!! HE'S CHASING US ON A GIANT TEDDY BEAR! HIT THE GAS!!!
WE'VE GOT 'EM! THEY'RE HEADED FOR THE ZOO! C'MON, LITTLE GLUTTON, FASTER!
DARNED KIDS!

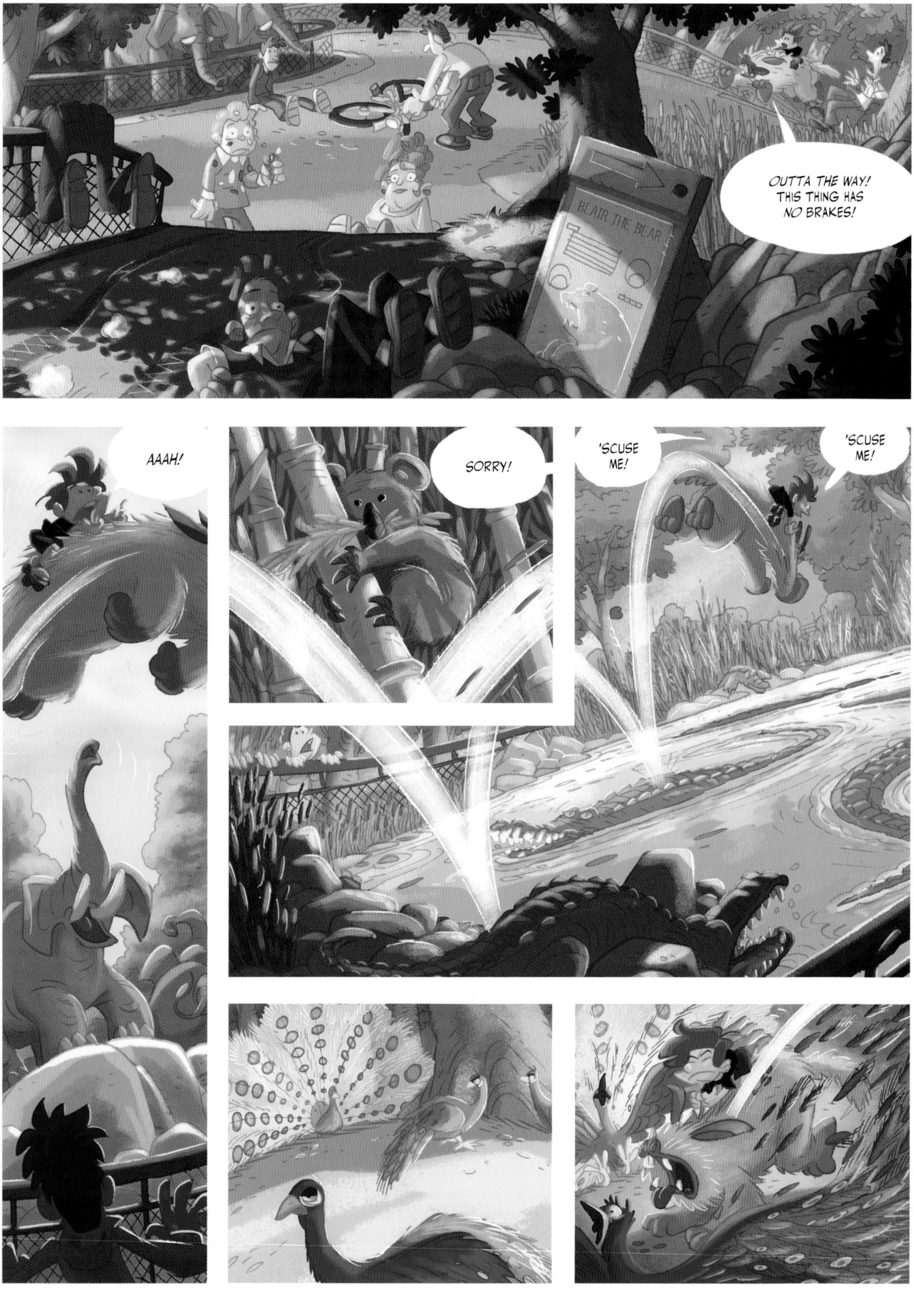

BLAIR THE BEAR
OUTTA THE WAY! THIS THING HAS NO BRAKES!
AAAH!
SORRY!
'SCUSE ME!
'SCUSE ME!

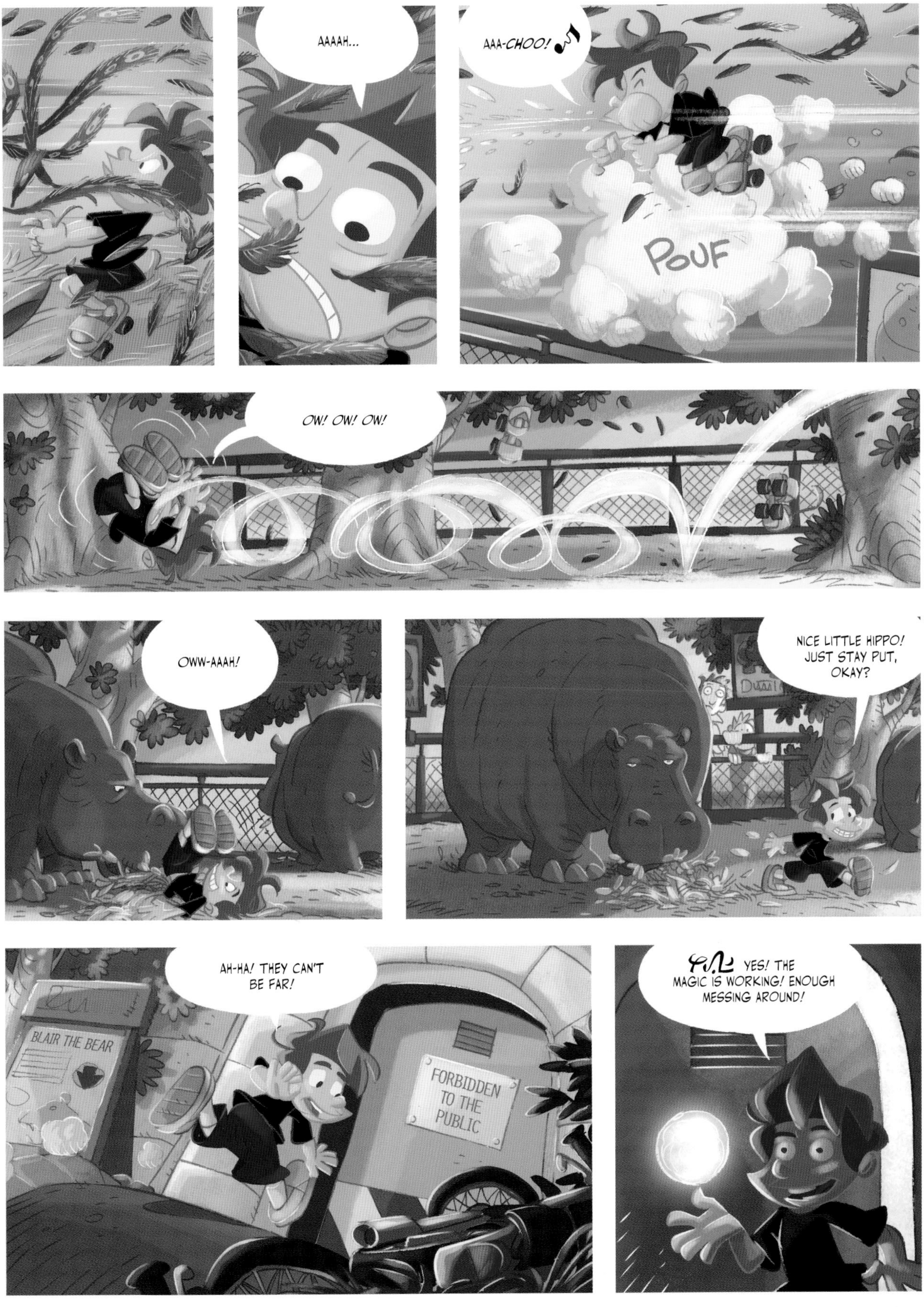
AAAAH...
AAA-CHOO!
POUF
OW! OW! OW!
OWW-AAAH!
NICE LITTLE HIPPO! JUST STAY PUT, OKAY?
BLAIR THE BEAR
AH-HA! THEY CAN'T BE FAR!
FORBIDDEN TO THE PUBLIC
YES! THE MAGIC IS WORKING! ENOUGH MESSING AROUND!

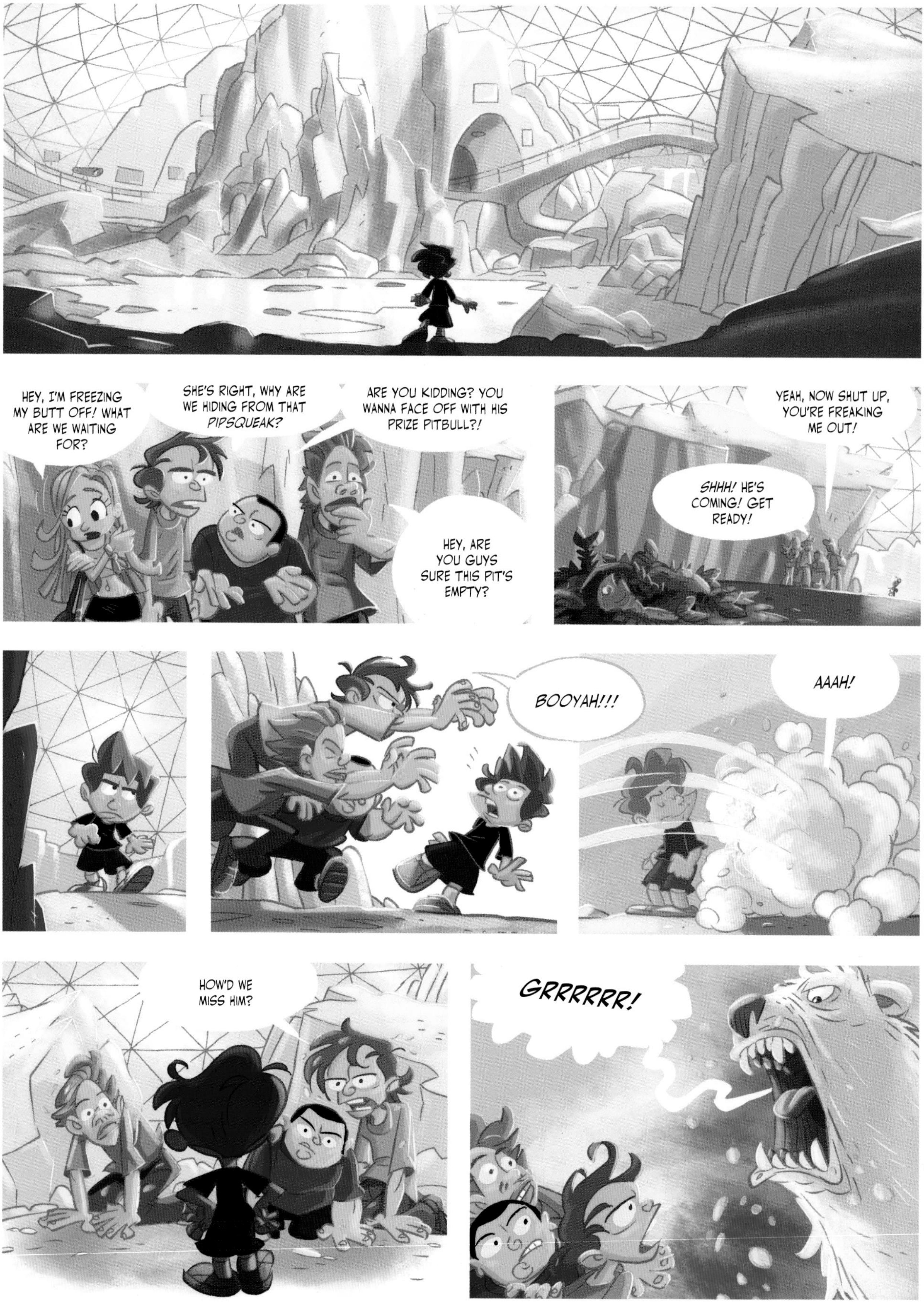
HEY, I'M FREEZING MY BUTT OFF! WHAT ARE WE WAITING FOR?
SHE'S RIGHT, WHY ARE WE HIDING FROM THAT PIPSQUEAK?
ARE YOU KIDDING? YOU WANNA FACE OFF WITH HIS PRIZE PITBULL?!
HEY, ARE YOU GUYS SURE THIS PIT'S EMPTY?
YEAH, NOW SHUT UP, YOU'RE FREAKING ME OUT!
SHHH! HE'S COMING! GET READY!
BOOYAH!!!
AAAH!
HOW'D WE MISS HIM?
GRRRRRR!

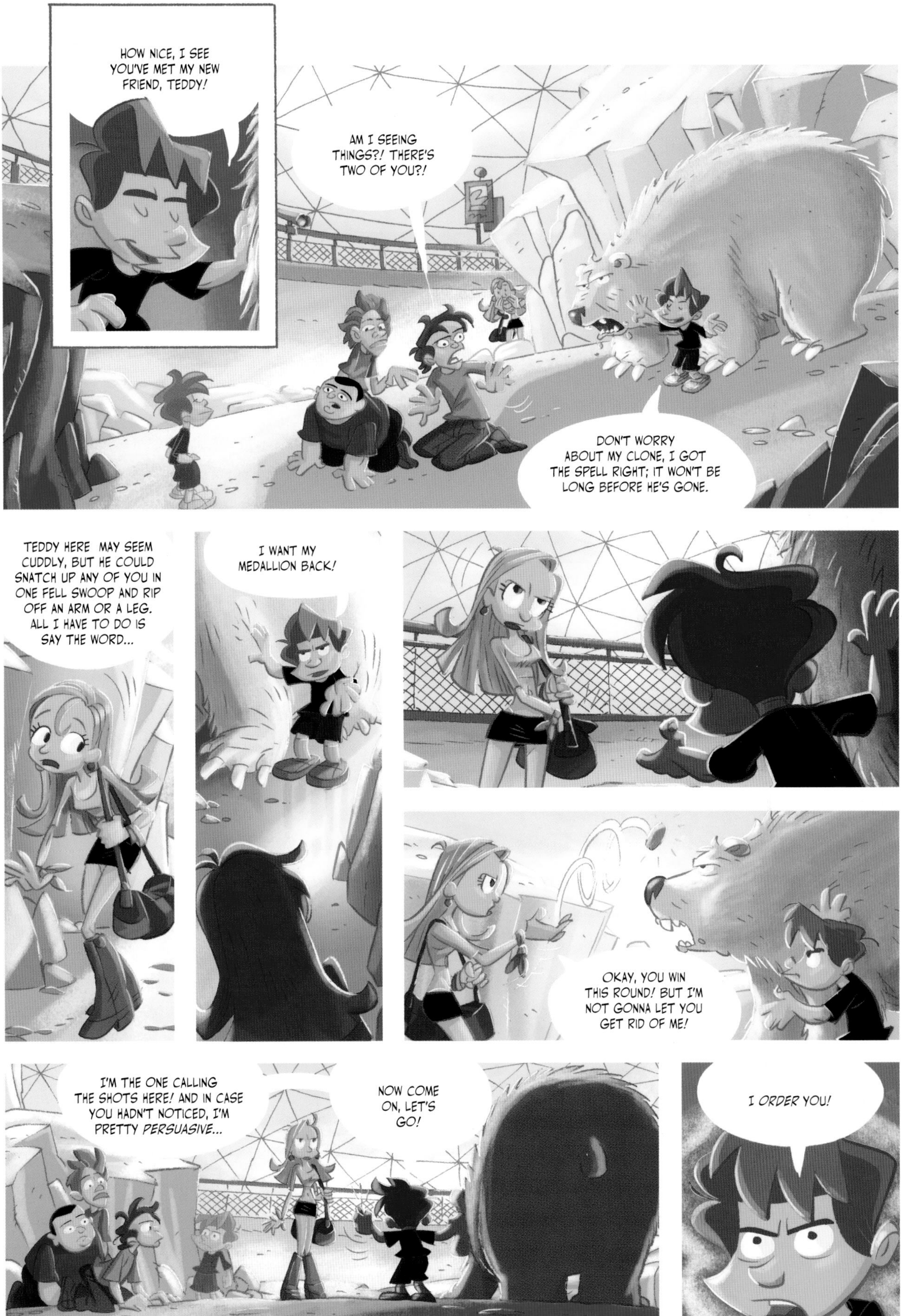
HOW NICE, I SEE YOU'VE MET MY NEW FRIEND, TEDDY!
AM I SEEING THINGS?! THERE'S TWO OF YOU?!
DON'T WORRY ABOUT MY CLONE, I GOT THE SPELL RIGHT; IT WON'T BE LONG BEFORE HE'S GONE.
TEDDY HERE MAY SEEM CUDDLY, BUT HE COULD SNATCH UP ANY OF YOU IN ONE FELL SWOOP AND RIP OFF AN ARM OR A LEG. ALL I HAVE TO DO IS SAY THE WORD...
I WANT MY MEDALLION BACK!
OKAY, YOU WIN THIS ROUND! BUT I'M NOT GONNA LET YOU GET RID OF ME!
I'M THE ONE CALLING THE SHOTS HERE! AND IN CASE YOU HADN'T NOTICED, I'M PRETTY *PERSUASIVE*...
NOW COME ON, LET'S GO!
I *ORDER* YOU!

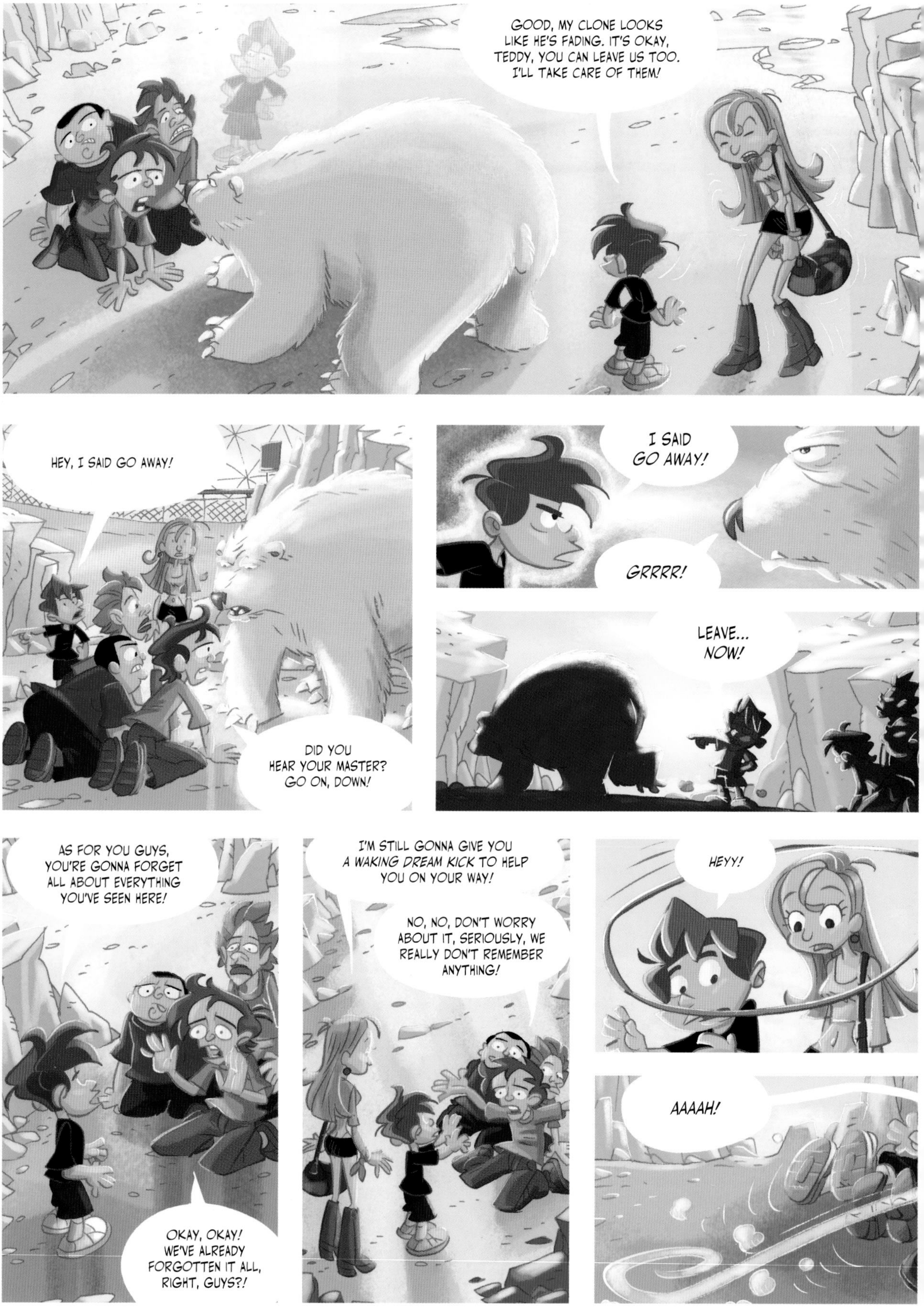
GOOD, MY CLONE LOOKS LIKE HE'S FADING. IT'S OKAY, TEDDY, YOU CAN LEAVE US TOO. I'LL TAKE CARE OF THEM!
HEY, I SAID GO AWAY!
DID YOU HEAR YOUR MASTER? GO ON, DOWN!
I SAID GO AWAY!
GRRRR!
LEAVE... NOW!
AS FOR YOU GUYS, YOU'RE GONNA FORGET ALL ABOUT EVERYTHING YOU'VE SEEN HERE!
OKAY, OKAY! WE'VE ALREADY FORGOTTEN IT ALL, RIGHT, GUYS?!
I'M STILL GONNA GIVE YOU A WAKING DREAM KICK TO HELP YOU ON YOUR WAY!
NO, NO, DON'T WORRY ABOUT IT, SERIOUSLY, WE REALLY DON'T REMEMBER ANYTHING!
HEYY!
AAAAH!

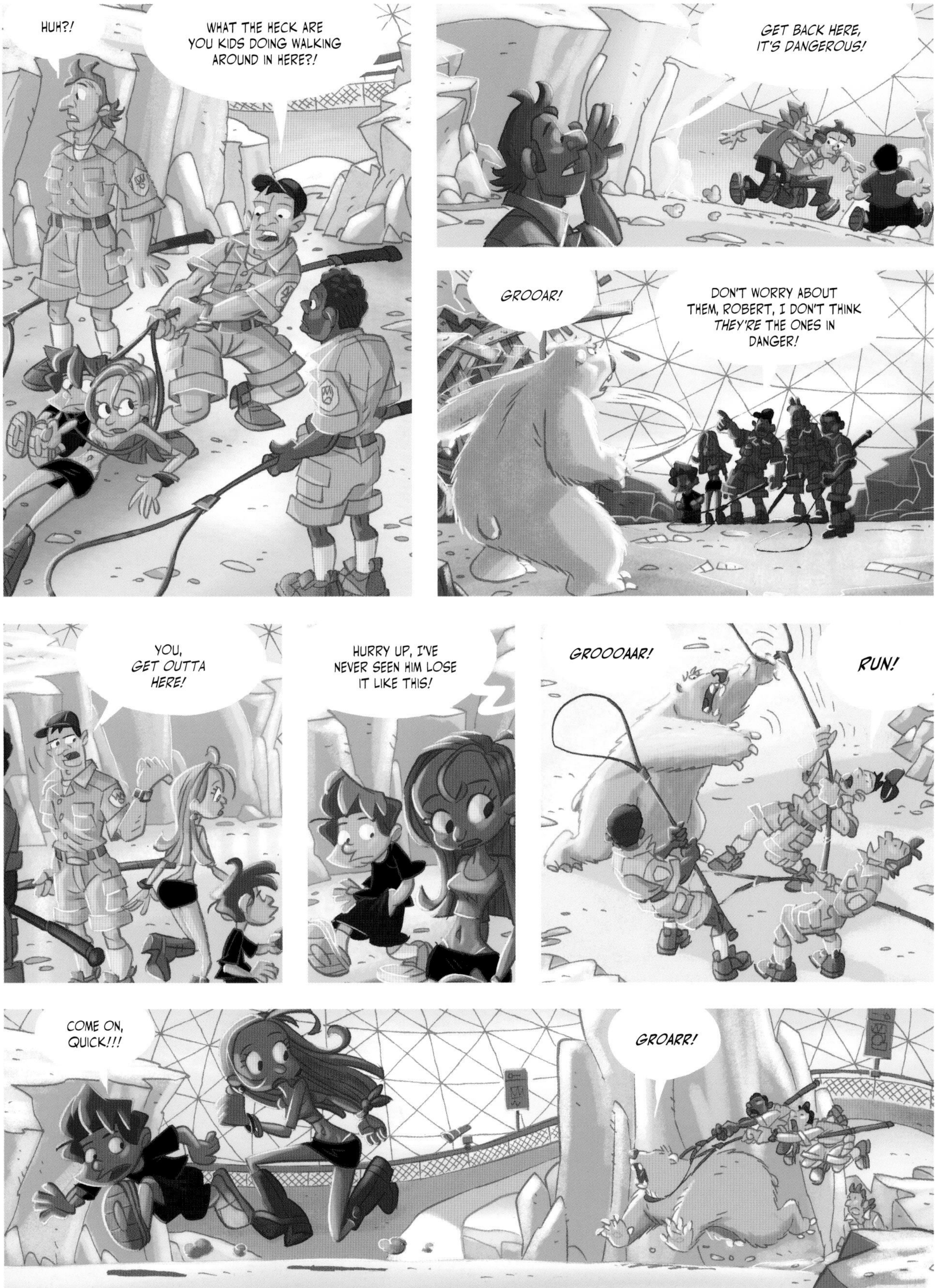
HUH?!
WHAT THE HECK ARE YOU KIDS DOING WALKING AROUND IN HERE?!
GET BACK HERE, IT'S DANGEROUS!
GROOAR!
DON'T WORRY ABOUT THEM, ROBERT, I DON'T THINK THEY'RE THE ONES IN DANGER!
YOU, GET OUTTA HERE!
HURRY UP, I'VE NEVER SEEN HIM LOSE IT LIKE THIS!
GROOOAAR!
RUN!
COME ON, QUICK!!!
GROARR!

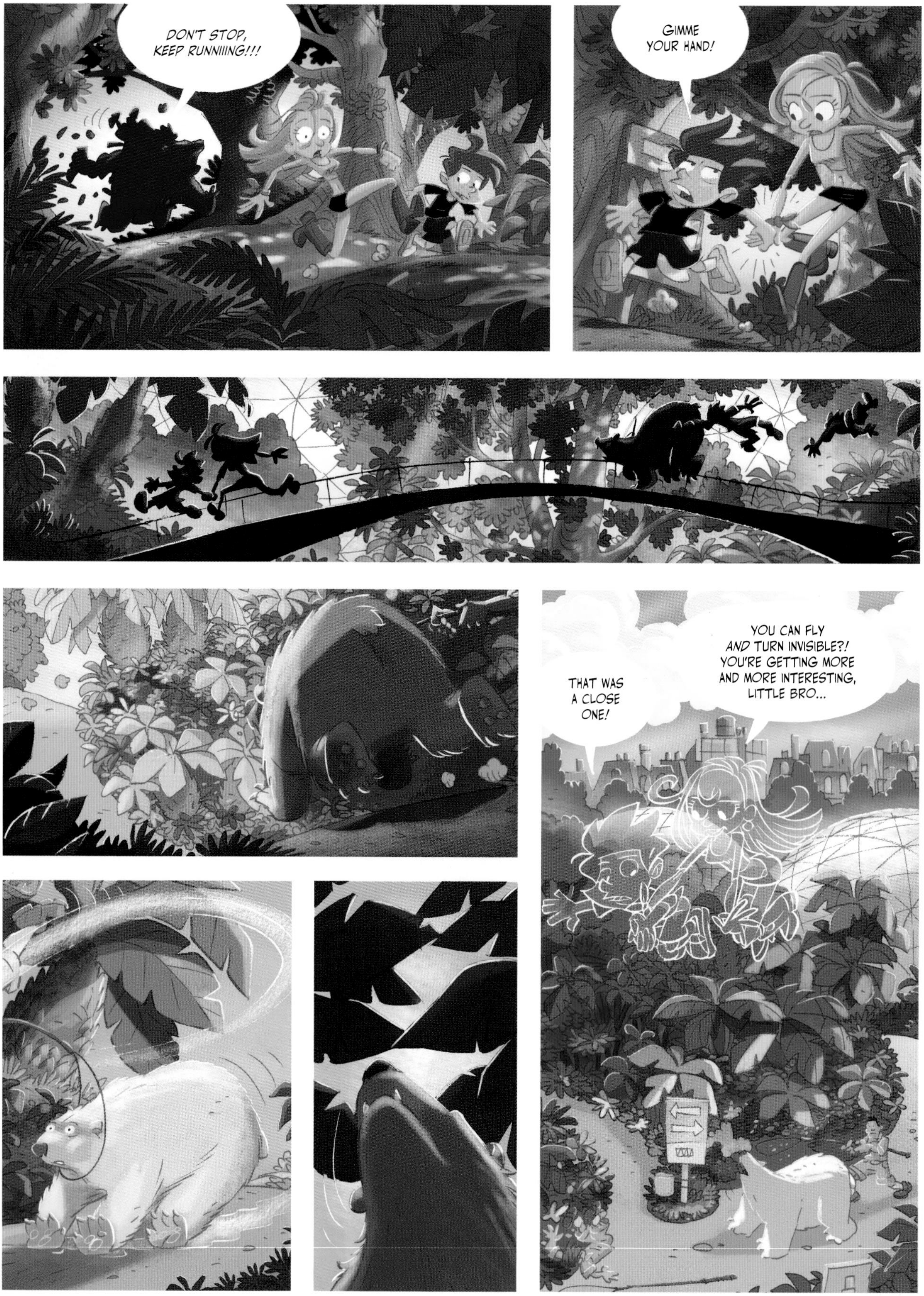
DON'T STOP, KEEP RUNNIIING!!!
GIMME YOUR HAND!
THAT WAS A CLOSE ONE!
YOU CAN FLY AND TURN INVISIBLE?! YOU'RE GETTING MORE AND MORE INTERESTING, LITTLE BRO...

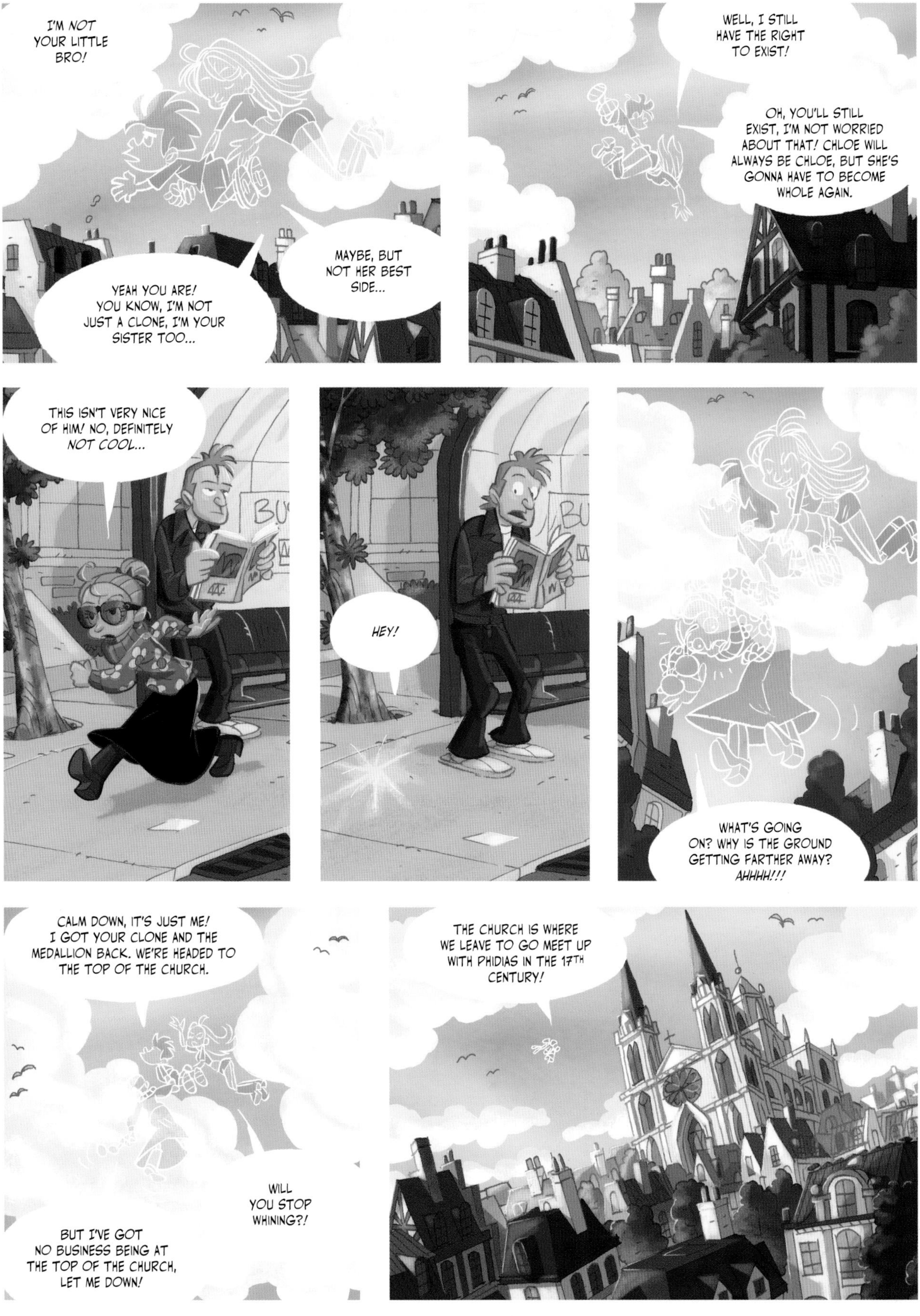
I'M *NOT* YOUR LITTLE BRO!
YEAH YOU ARE! YOU KNOW, I'M NOT JUST A CLONE, I'M YOUR SISTER TOO...
MAYBE, BUT NOT HER BEST SIDE...
WELL, I STILL HAVE THE RIGHT TO EXIST!
OH, YOU'LL STILL EXIST, I'M NOT WORRIED ABOUT THAT! CHLOE WILL ALWAYS BE CHLOE, BUT SHE'S GONNA HAVE TO BECOME WHOLE AGAIN.
THIS ISN'T VERY NICE OF HIM! NO, DEFINITELY *NOT COOL*...
HEY!
WHAT'S GOING ON? WHY IS THE GROUND GETTING FARTHER AWAY? *AHHHH!!!*
CALM DOWN, IT'S JUST ME! I GOT YOUR CLONE AND THE MEDALLION BACK. WE'RE HEADED TO THE TOP OF THE CHURCH.
WILL YOU STOP WHINING?!
BUT I'VE GOT NO BUSINESS BEING AT THE TOP OF THE CHURCH, LET ME DOWN!
THE CHURCH IS WHERE WE LEAVE TO GO MEET UP WITH PHIDIAS IN THE 17TH CENTURY!

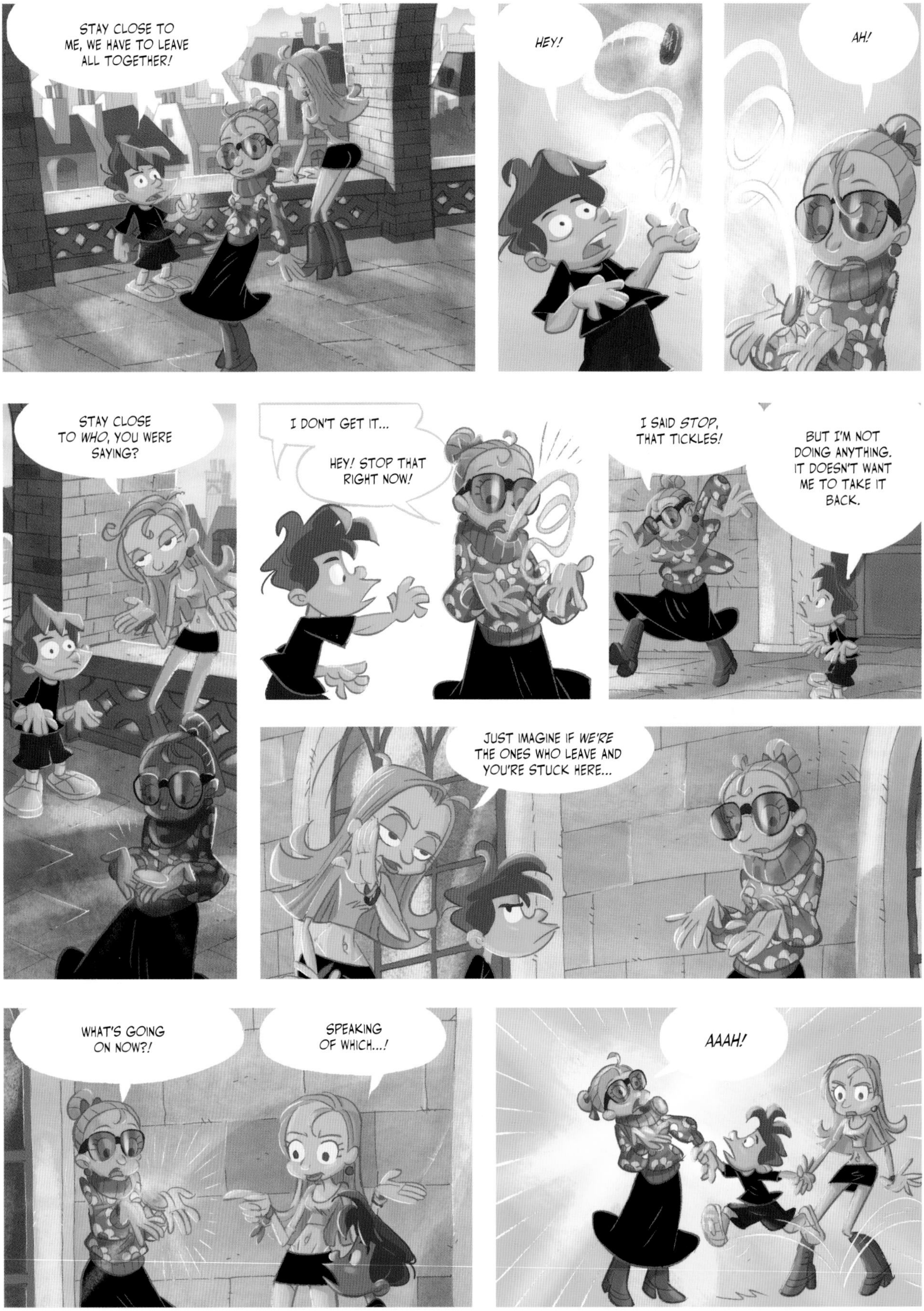
STAY CLOSE TO ME, WE HAVE TO LEAVE ALL TOGETHER!
HEY!
AH!
STAY CLOSE TO *WHO*, YOU WERE SAYING?
I DON'T GET IT...
HEY! STOP THAT RIGHT NOW!
I SAID *STOP*, THAT TICKLES!
BUT I'M NOT DOING ANYTHING. IT DOESN'T WANT ME TO TAKE IT BACK.
JUST IMAGINE IF *WE'RE* THE ONES WHO LEAVE AND YOU'RE STUCK HERE...
WHAT'S GOING ON NOW?!
SPEAKING OF WHICH...!
AAAH!

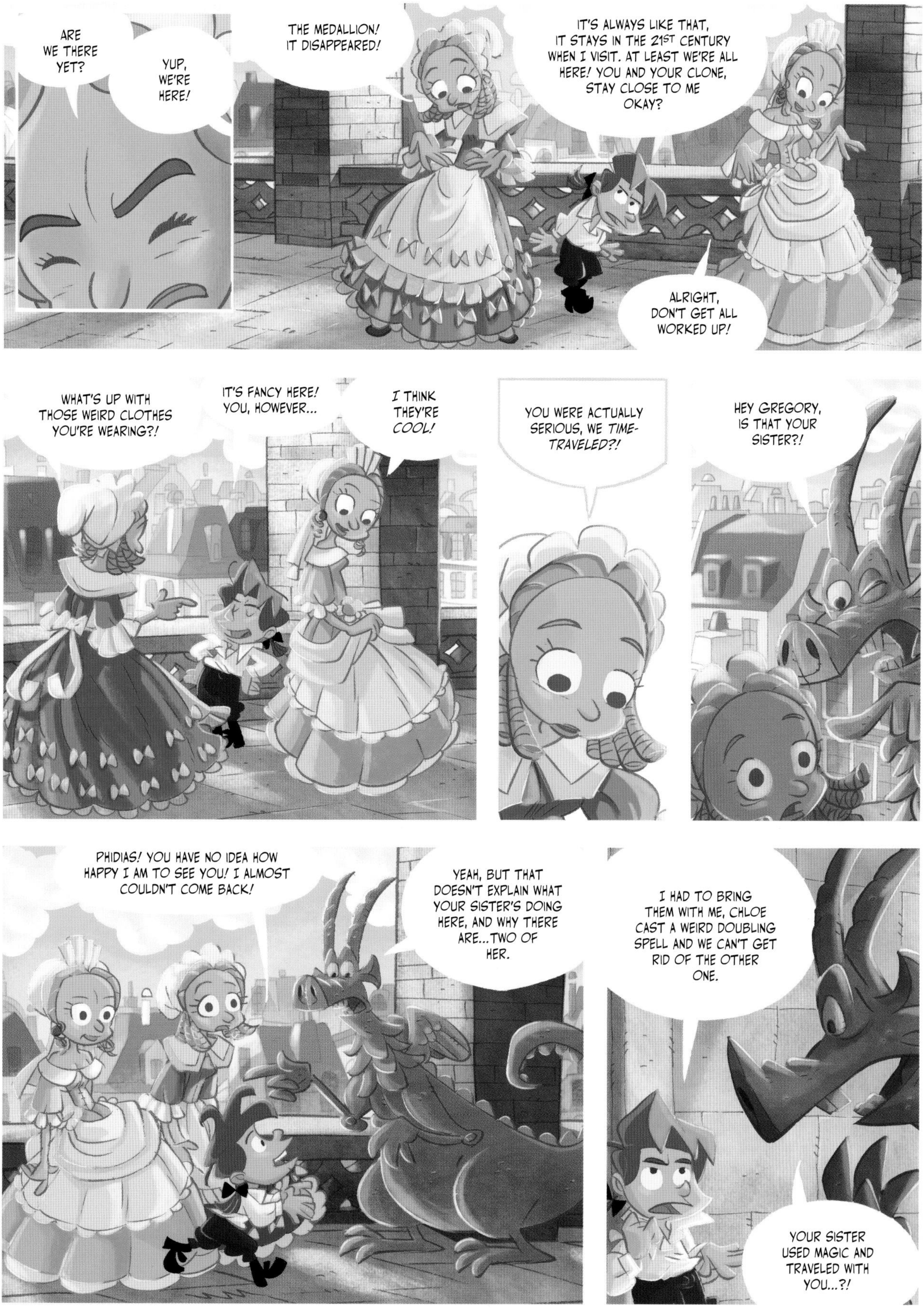

ARE WE THERE YET?
YUP, WE'RE HERE!
THE MEDALLION! IT DISAPPEARED!
IT'S ALWAYS LIKE THAT, IT STAYS IN THE 21ST CENTURY WHEN I VISIT. AT LEAST WE'RE ALL HERE! YOU AND YOUR CLONE, STAY CLOSE TO ME OKAY?
ALRIGHT, DON'T GET ALL WORKED UP!
WHAT'S UP WITH THOSE WEIRD CLOTHES YOU'RE WEARING?!
IT'S FANCY HERE! YOU, HOWEVER...
I THINK THEY'RE COOL!
YOU WERE ACTUALLY SERIOUS, WE TIME-TRAVELED?!
HEY GREGORY, IS THAT YOUR SISTER?!
PHIDIAS! YOU HAVE NO IDEA HOW HAPPY I AM TO SEE YOU! I ALMOST COULDN'T COME BACK!
YEAH, BUT THAT DOESN'T EXPLAIN WHAT YOUR SISTER'S DOING HERE, AND WHY THERE ARE...TWO OF HER.
I HAD TO BRING THEM WITH ME, CHLOE CAST A WEIRD DOUBLING SPELL AND WE CAN'T GET RID OF THE OTHER ONE.
YOUR SISTER USED MAGIC AND TRAVELED WITH YOU...?!

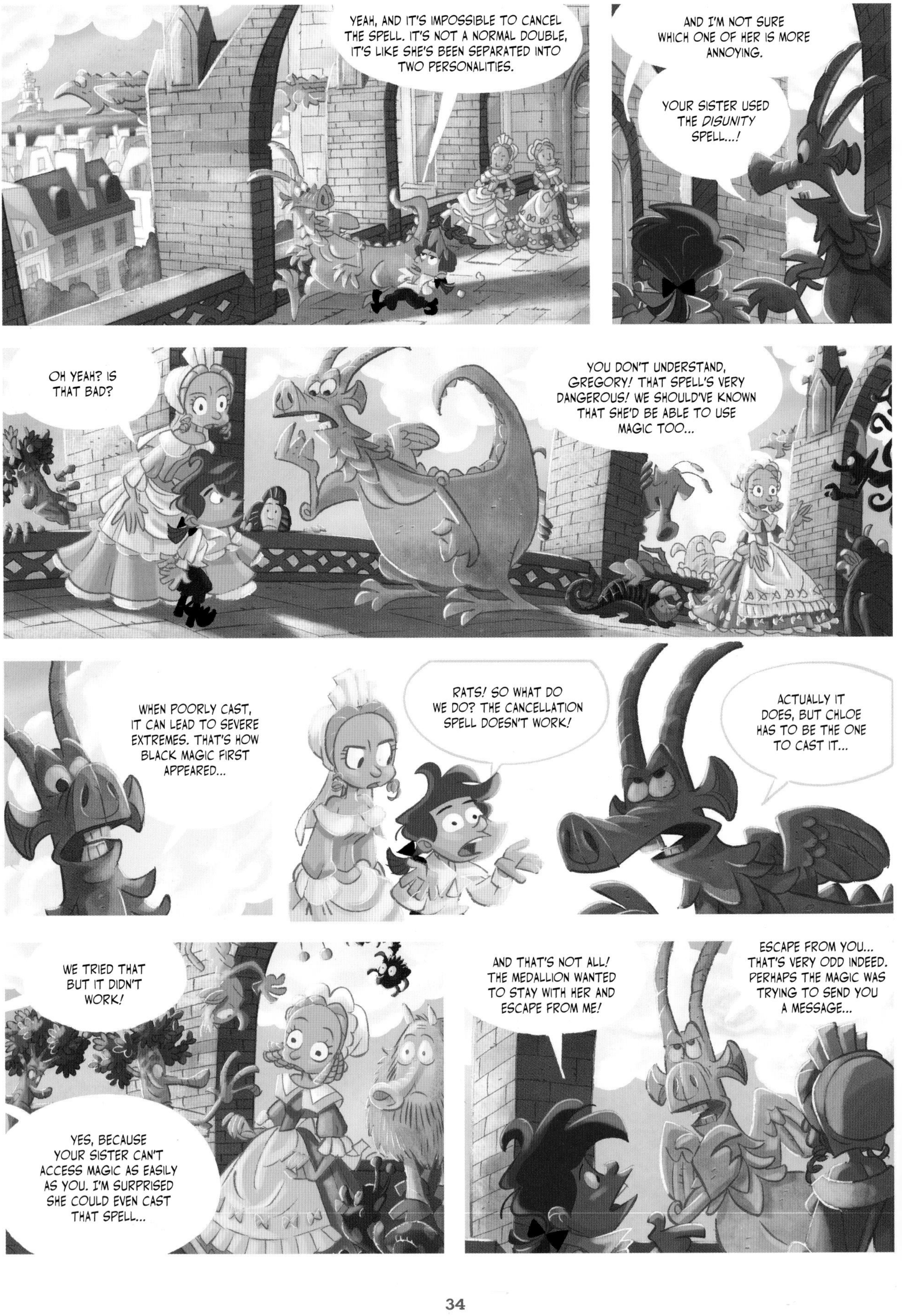
YEAH, AND IT'S IMPOSSIBLE TO CANCEL THE SPELL. IT'S NOT A NORMAL DOUBLE, IT'S LIKE SHE'S BEEN SEPARATED INTO TWO PERSONALITIES.
AND I'M NOT SURE WHICH ONE OF HER IS MORE ANNOYING.
YOUR SISTER USED THE *DISUNITY* SPELL...!
OH YEAH? IS THAT BAD?
YOU DON'T UNDERSTAND, GREGORY! THAT SPELL'S VERY DANGEROUS! WE SHOULD'VE KNOWN THAT SHE'D BE ABLE TO USE MAGIC TOO...
WHEN POORLY CAST, IT CAN LEAD TO SEVERE EXTREMES. THAT'S HOW BLACK MAGIC FIRST APPEARED...
RATS! SO WHAT DO WE DO? THE CANCELLATION SPELL DOESN'T WORK!
ACTUALLY IT DOES, BUT CHLOE HAS TO BE THE ONE TO CAST IT...
WE TRIED THAT BUT IT DIDN'T WORK!
YES, BECAUSE YOUR SISTER CAN'T ACCESS MAGIC AS EASILY AS YOU. I'M SURPRISED SHE COULD EVEN CAST THAT SPELL...
AND THAT'S NOT ALL! THE MEDALLION WANTED TO STAY WITH HER AND ESCAPE FROM ME!
ESCAPE FROM YOU... THAT'S VERY ODD INDEED. PERHAPS THE MAGIC WAS TRYING TO SEND YOU A MESSAGE...

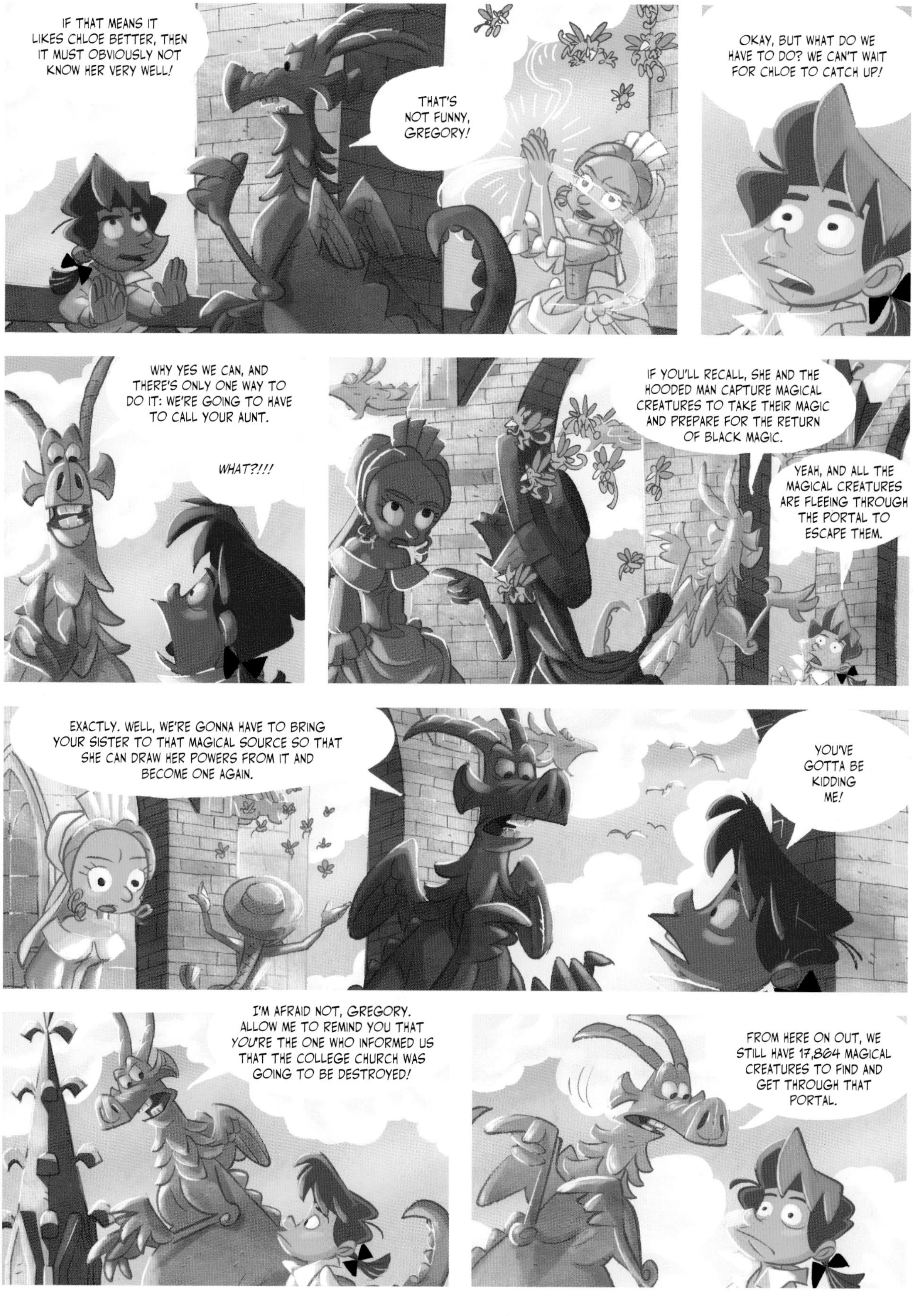

IF THAT MEANS IT LIKES CHLOE BETTER, THEN IT MUST OBVIOUSLY NOT KNOW HER VERY WELL!
THAT'S NOT FUNNY, GREGORY!
OKAY, BUT WHAT DO WE HAVE TO DO? WE CAN'T WAIT FOR CHLOE TO CATCH UP!
WHY YES WE CAN, AND THERE'S ONLY ONE WAY TO DO IT: WE'RE GOING TO HAVE TO CALL YOUR AUNT.
WHAT?!!!
IF YOU'LL RECALL, SHE AND THE HOODED MAN CAPTURE MAGICAL CREATURES TO TAKE THEIR MAGIC AND PREPARE FOR THE RETURN OF BLACK MAGIC.
YEAH, AND ALL THE MAGICAL CREATURES ARE FLEEING THROUGH THE PORTAL TO ESCAPE THEM.
EXACTLY. WELL, WE'RE GONNA HAVE TO BRING YOUR SISTER TO THAT MAGICAL SOURCE SO THAT SHE CAN DRAW HER POWERS FROM IT AND BECOME ONE AGAIN.
YOU'VE GOTTA BE KIDDING ME!
I'M AFRAID NOT, GREGORY. ALLOW ME TO REMIND YOU THAT YOU'RE THE ONE WHO INFORMED US THAT THE COLLEGE CHURCH WAS GOING TO BE DESTROYED!
FROM HERE ON OUT, WE STILL HAVE 17,864 MAGICAL CREATURES TO FIND AND GET THROUGH THAT PORTAL.

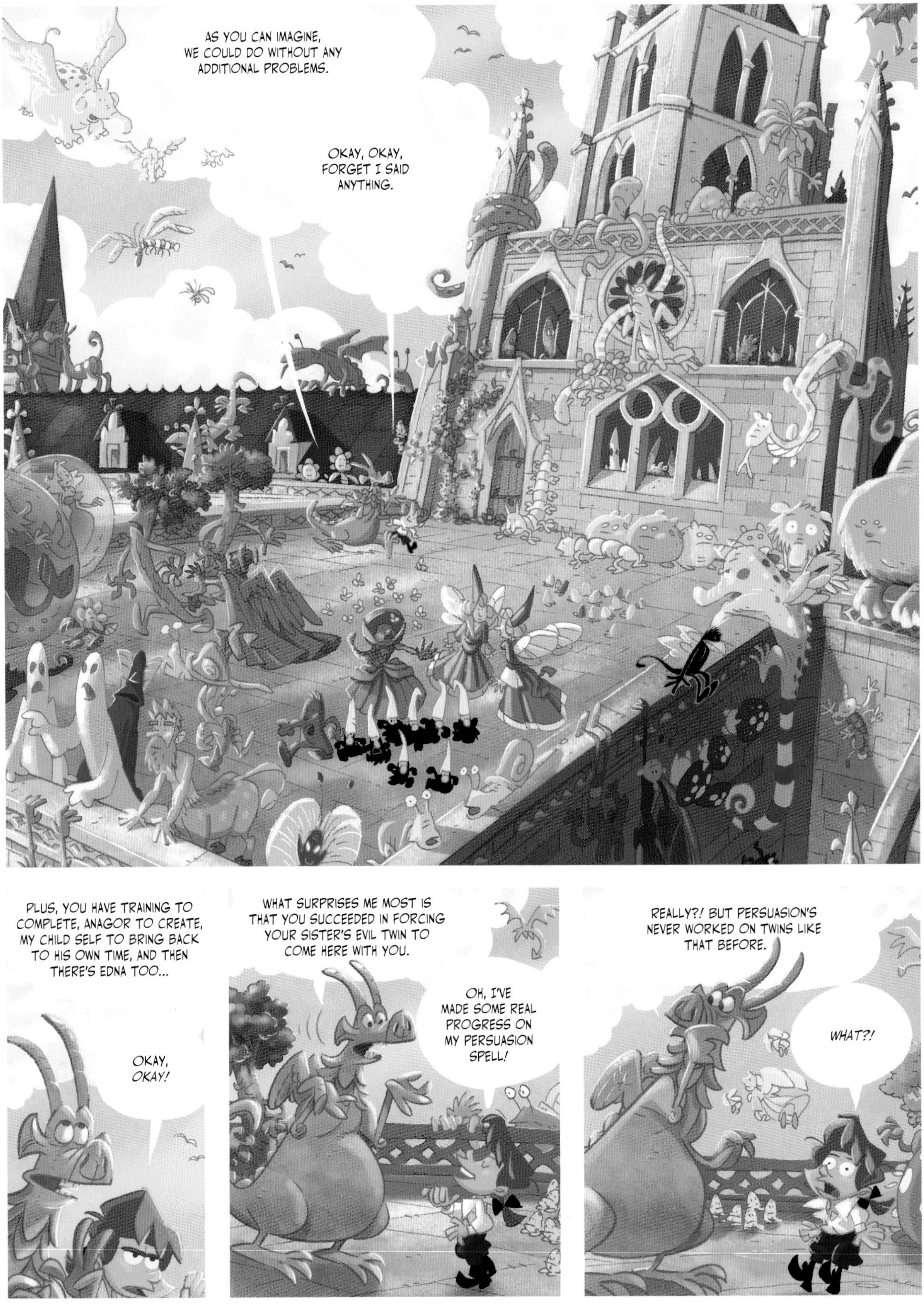
AS YOU CAN IMAGINE, WE COULD DO WITHOUT ANY ADDITIONAL PROBLEMS.
OKAY, OKAY, FORGET I SAID ANYTHING.
PLUS, YOU HAVE TRAINING TO COMPLETE, ANAGOR TO CREATE, MY CHILD SELF TO BRING BACK TO HIS OWN TIME, AND THEN THERE'S EDNA TOO...
OKAY, OKAY!
WHAT SURPRISES ME MOST IS THAT YOU SUCCEEDED IN FORCING YOUR SISTER'S EVIL TWIN TO COME HERE WITH YOU.
OH, I'VE MADE SOME REAL PROGRESS ON MY PERSUASION SPELL!
REALLY?! BUT PERSUASION'S NEVER WORKED ON TWINS LIKE THAT BEFORE.
WHAT?!

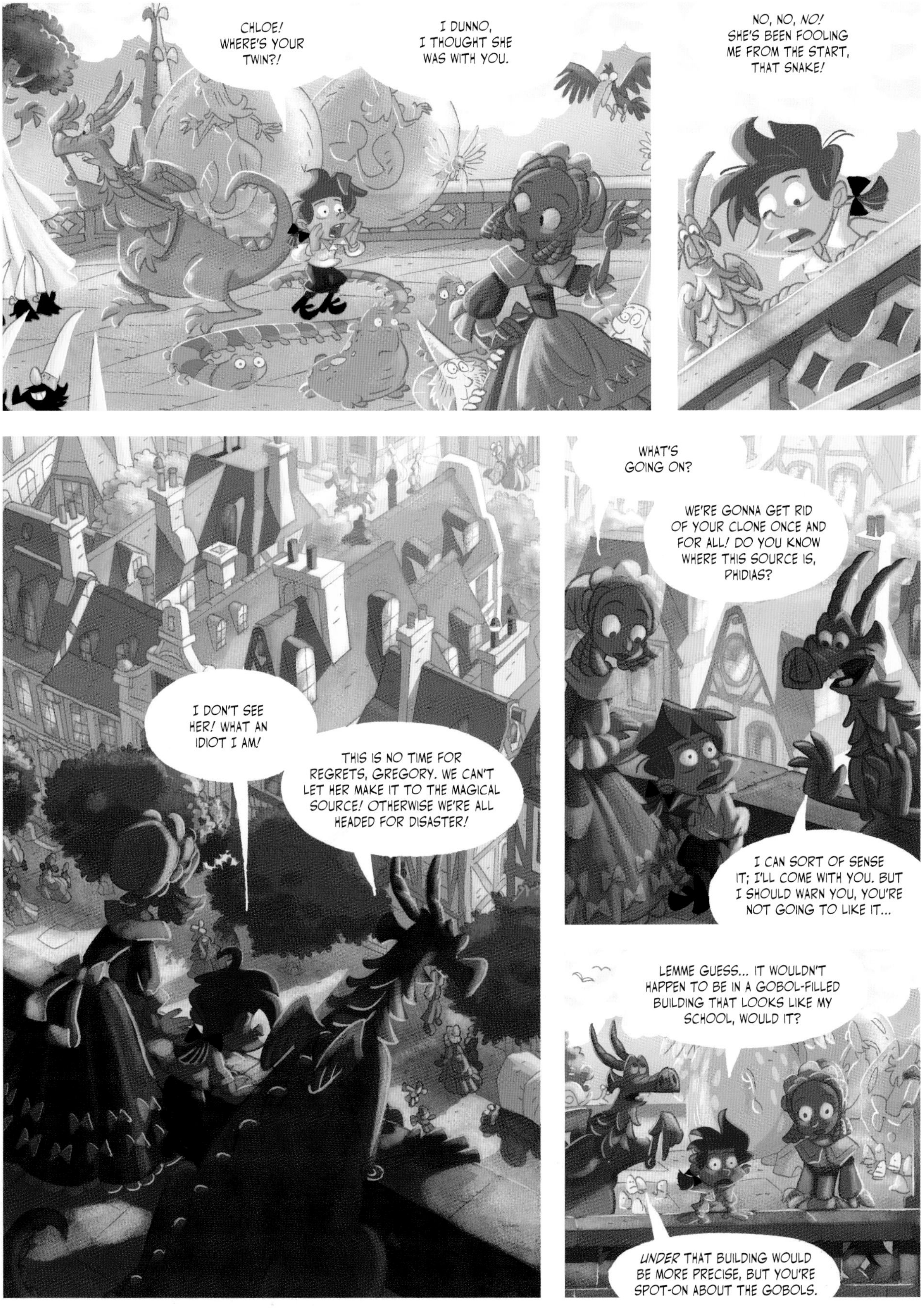
CHLOE! WHERE'S YOUR TWIN?!
I DUNNO, I THOUGHT SHE WAS WITH YOU.
NO, NO, *NO!* SHE'S BEEN FOOLING ME FROM THE START, THAT SNAKE!
I DON'T SEE HER! WHAT AN IDIOT I AM!
THIS IS NO TIME FOR REGRETS, GREGORY. WE CAN'T LET HER MAKE IT TO THE MAGICAL SOURCE! OTHERWISE WE'RE ALL HEADED FOR DISASTER!
WHAT'S GOING ON?
WE'RE GONNA GET RID OF YOUR CLONE ONCE AND FOR ALL! DO YOU KNOW WHERE THIS SOURCE IS, PHIDIAS?
I CAN SORT OF SENSE IT; I'LL COME WITH YOU. BUT I SHOULD WARN YOU, YOU'RE NOT GOING TO LIKE IT...
LEMME GUESS... IT WOULDN'T HAPPEN TO BE IN A GOBOL-FILLED BUILDING THAT LOOKS LIKE MY SCHOOL, WOULD IT?
UNDER THAT BUILDING WOULD BE MORE PRECISE, BUT YOU'RE SPOT-ON ABOUT THE GOBOLS.

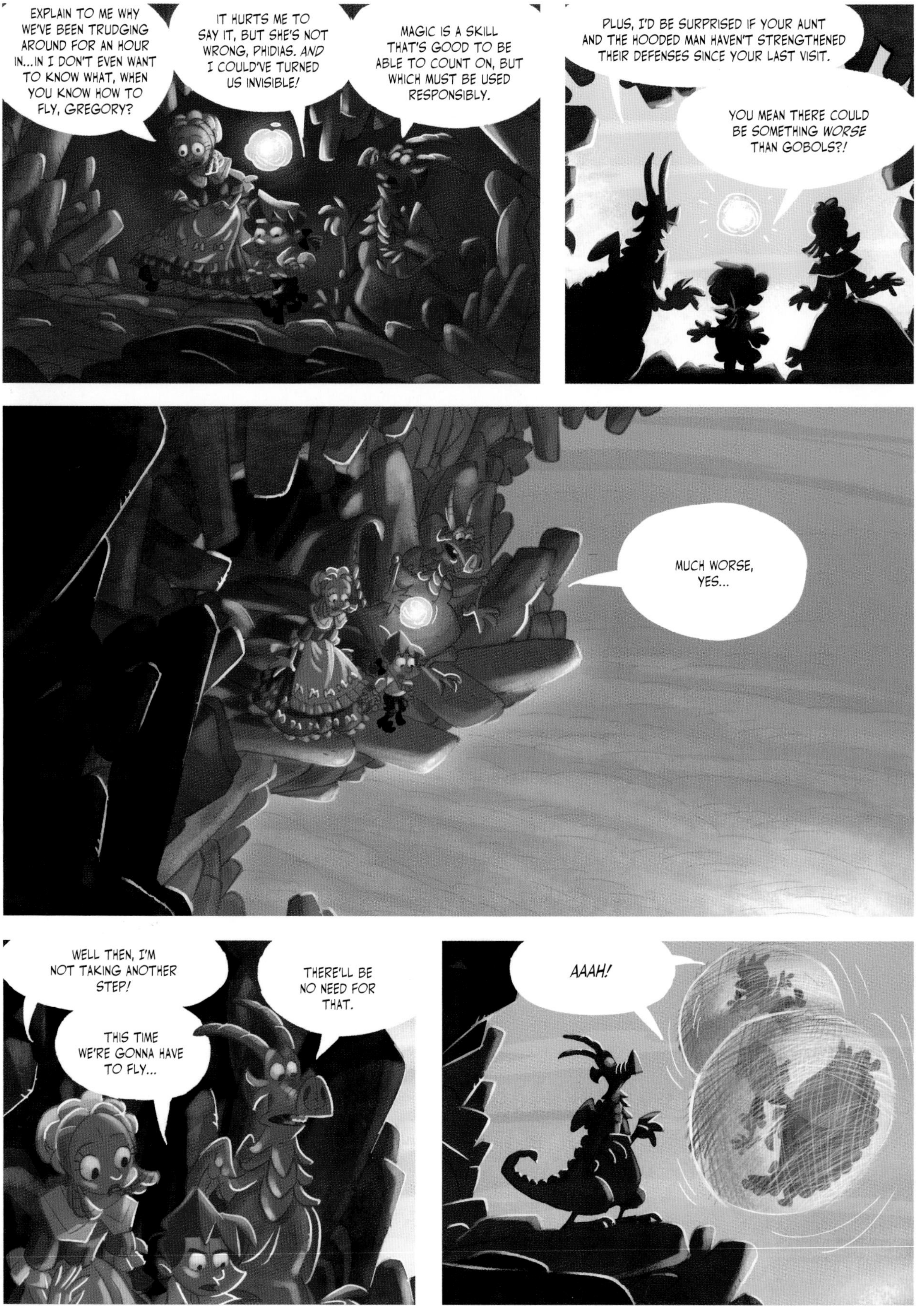
EXPLAIN TO ME WHY WE'VE BEEN TRUDGING AROUND FOR AN HOUR IN... IN I DON'T EVEN WANT TO KNOW WHAT, WHEN YOU KNOW HOW TO FLY, GREGORY?
IT HURTS ME TO SAY IT, BUT SHE'S NOT WRONG, PHIDIAS. AND I COULD'VE TURNED US INVISIBLE!
MAGIC IS A SKILL THAT'S GOOD TO BE ABLE TO COUNT ON, BUT WHICH MUST BE USED RESPONSIBLY.
PLUS, I'D BE SURPRISED IF YOUR AUNT AND THE HOODED MAN HAVEN'T STRENGTHENED THEIR DEFENSES SINCE YOUR LAST VISIT.
YOU MEAN THERE COULD BE SOMETHING WORSE THAN GOBOLS?!
MUCH WORSE, YES...
WELL THEN, I'M NOT TAKING ANOTHER STEP!
THIS TIME WE'RE GONNA HAVE TO FLY...
THERE'LL BE NO NEED FOR THAT.
AAAH!

GREGORY, STOP IT! PUT ME DOWN *RIGHT NOW!*

IT'S NOT ME! WHAT'S GOING ON, PHIDIAS?!

IT'S A MAGICAL CAPTURE SPELL! JUST HOLD STILL AND DON'T DO ANYTHING!

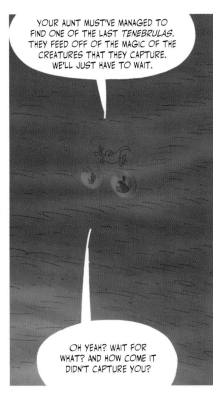

YOUR AUNT MUST'VE MANAGED TO FIND ONE OF THE LAST *TENEBRULAS.* THEY FEED OFF OF THE MAGIC OF THE CREATURES THAT THEY CAPTURE. WE'LL JUST HAVE TO WAIT.

OH YEAH? WAIT FOR WHAT? AND HOW COME IT DIDN'T CAPTURE YOU?

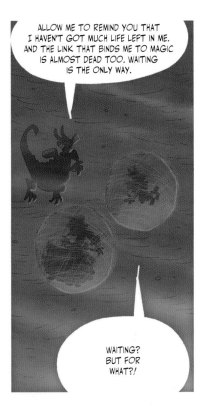

ALLOW ME TO REMIND YOU THAT I HAVEN'T GOT MUCH LIFE LEFT IN ME. AND THE LINK THAT BINDS ME TO MAGIC IS ALMOST DEAD TOO. WAITING IS THE ONLY WAY.

WAITING? BUT FOR WHAT?!

FOR HIM TO SHOW HIMSELF UP.

OH MAN, THAT THING'S UGLY!

GREGORY, I WANNA GO HOME!

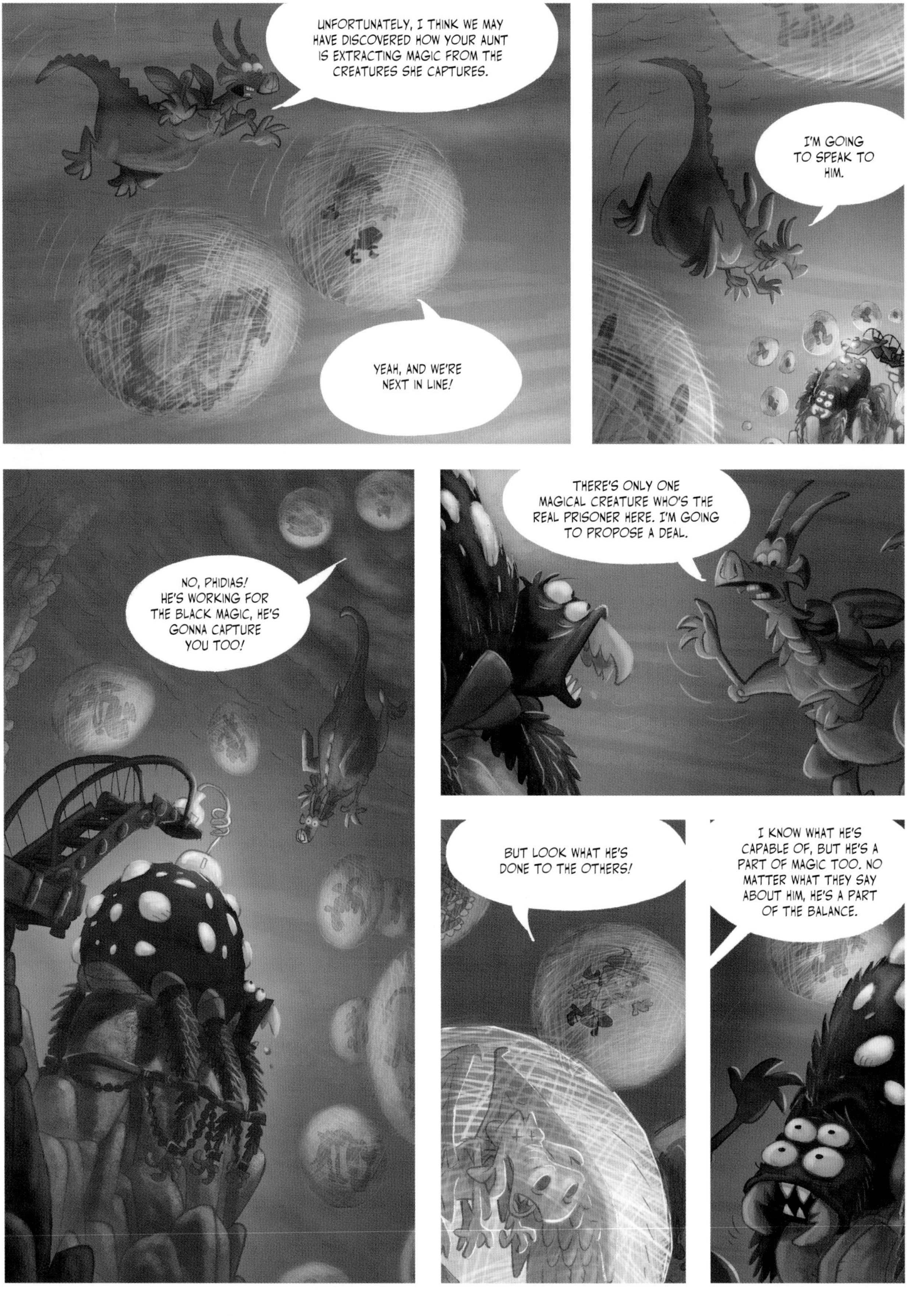
UNFORTUNATELY, I THINK WE MAY HAVE DISCOVERED HOW YOUR AUNT IS EXTRACTING MAGIC FROM THE CREATURES SHE CAPTURES.
YEAH, AND WE'RE NEXT IN LINE!
I'M GOING TO SPEAK TO HIM.
NO, PHIDIAS! HE'S WORKING FOR THE BLACK MAGIC, HE'S GONNA CAPTURE YOU TOO!
THERE'S ONLY ONE MAGICAL CREATURE WHO'S THE REAL PRISONER HERE. I'M GOING TO PROPOSE A DEAL.
BUT LOOK WHAT HE'S DONE TO THE OTHERS!
I KNOW WHAT HE'S CAPABLE OF, BUT HE'S A PART OF MAGIC TOO. NO MATTER WHAT THEY SAY ABOUT HIM, HE'S A PART OF THE BALANCE.

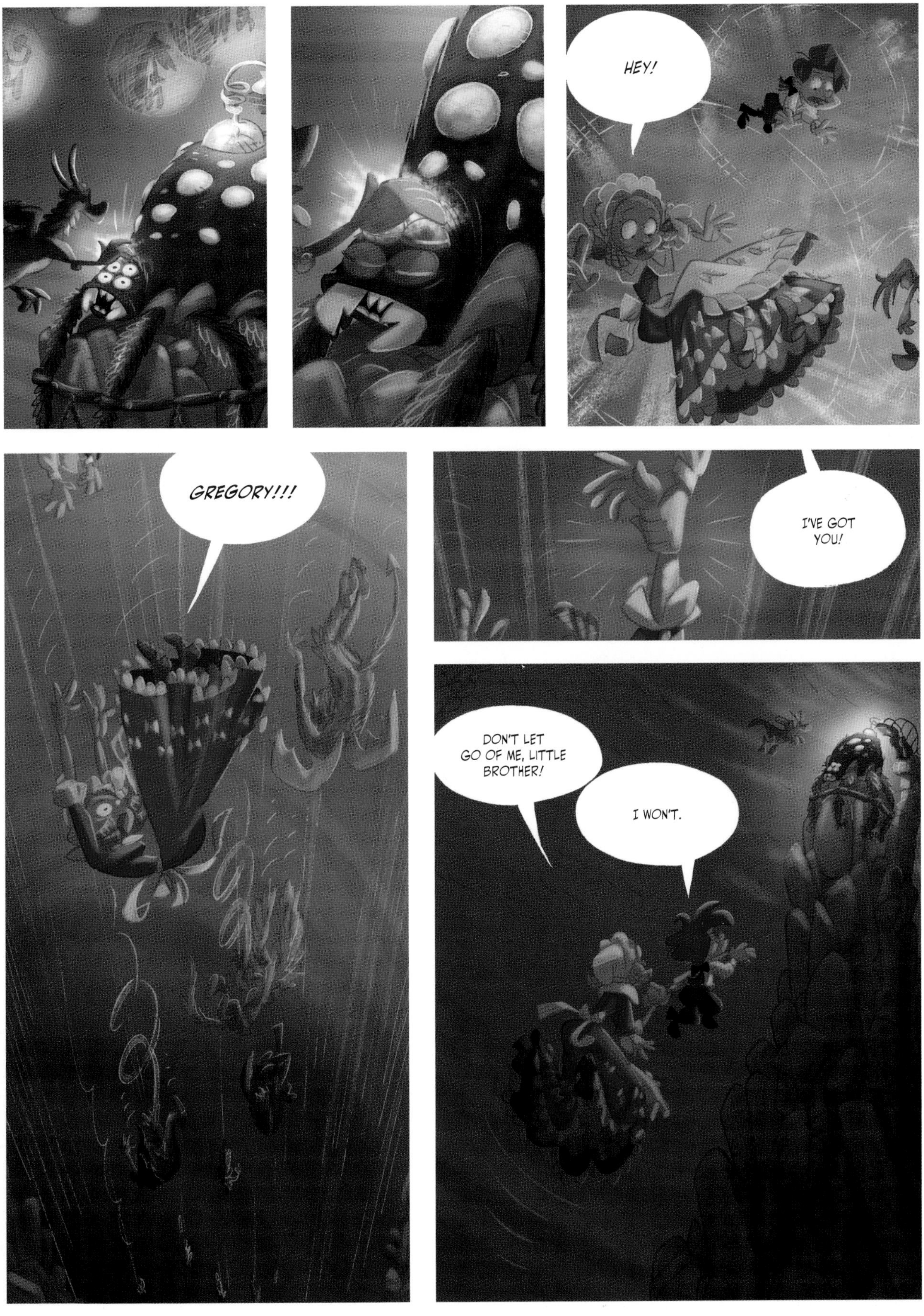
HEY!
GREGORY!!!
I'VE GOT YOU!
DON'T LET GO OF ME, LITTLE BROTHER!
I WON'T.

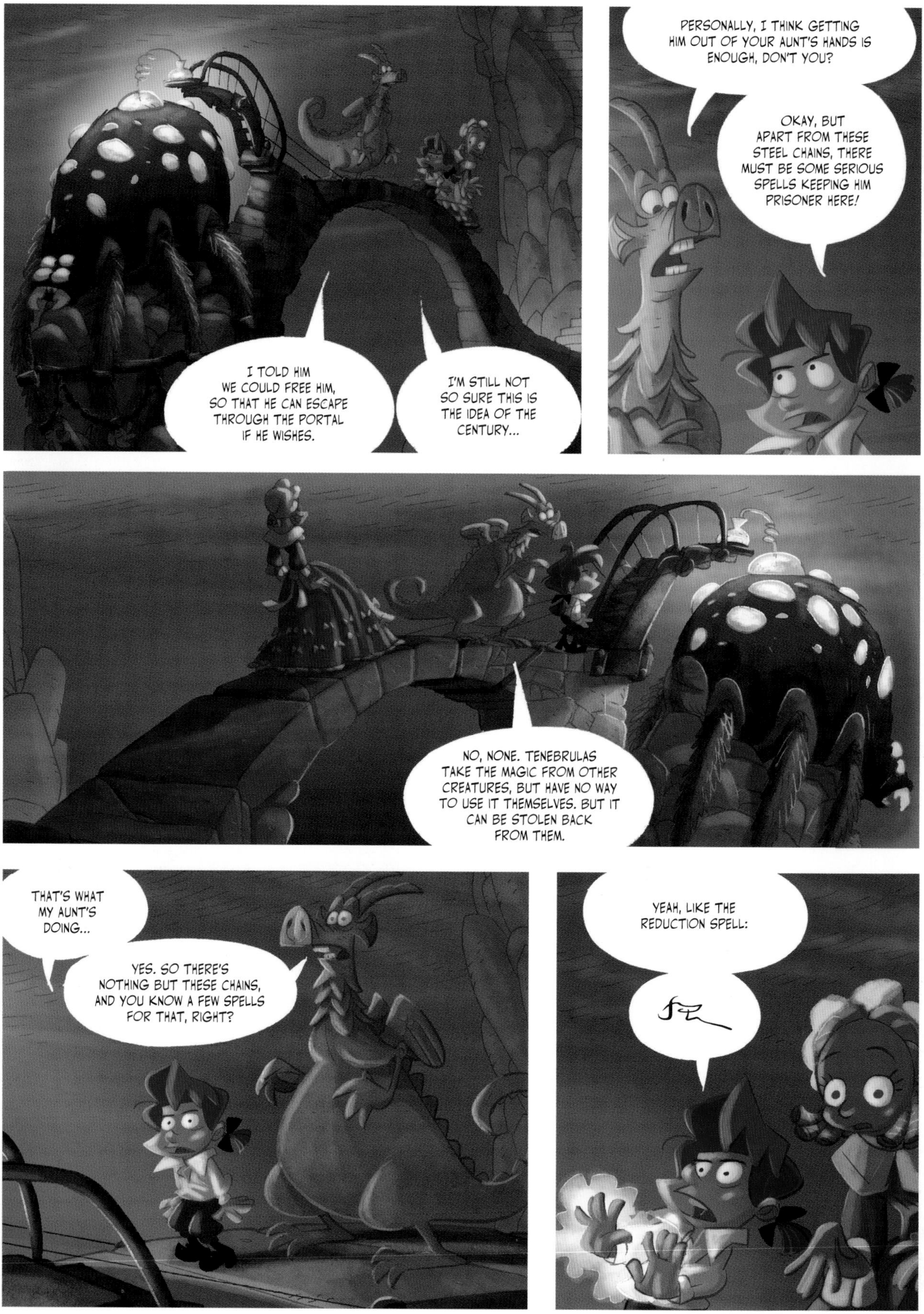
I TOLD HIM WE COULD FREE HIM, SO THAT HE CAN ESCAPE THROUGH THE PORTAL IF HE WISHES.
I'M STILL NOT SO SURE THIS IS THE IDEA OF THE CENTURY...
PERSONALLY, I THINK GETTING HIM OUT OF YOUR AUNT'S HANDS IS ENOUGH, DON'T YOU?
OKAY, BUT APART FROM THESE STEEL CHAINS, THERE MUST BE SOME SERIOUS SPELLS KEEPING HIM PRISONER HERE!
NO, NONE. TENEBRULAS TAKE THE MAGIC FROM OTHER CREATURES, BUT HAVE NO WAY TO USE IT THEMSELVES. BUT IT CAN BE STOLEN BACK FROM THEM.
THAT'S WHAT MY AUNT'S DOING...
YES. SO THERE'S NOTHING BUT THESE CHAINS, AND YOU KNOW A FEW SPELLS FOR THAT, RIGHT?
YEAH, LIKE THE REDUCTION SPELL:

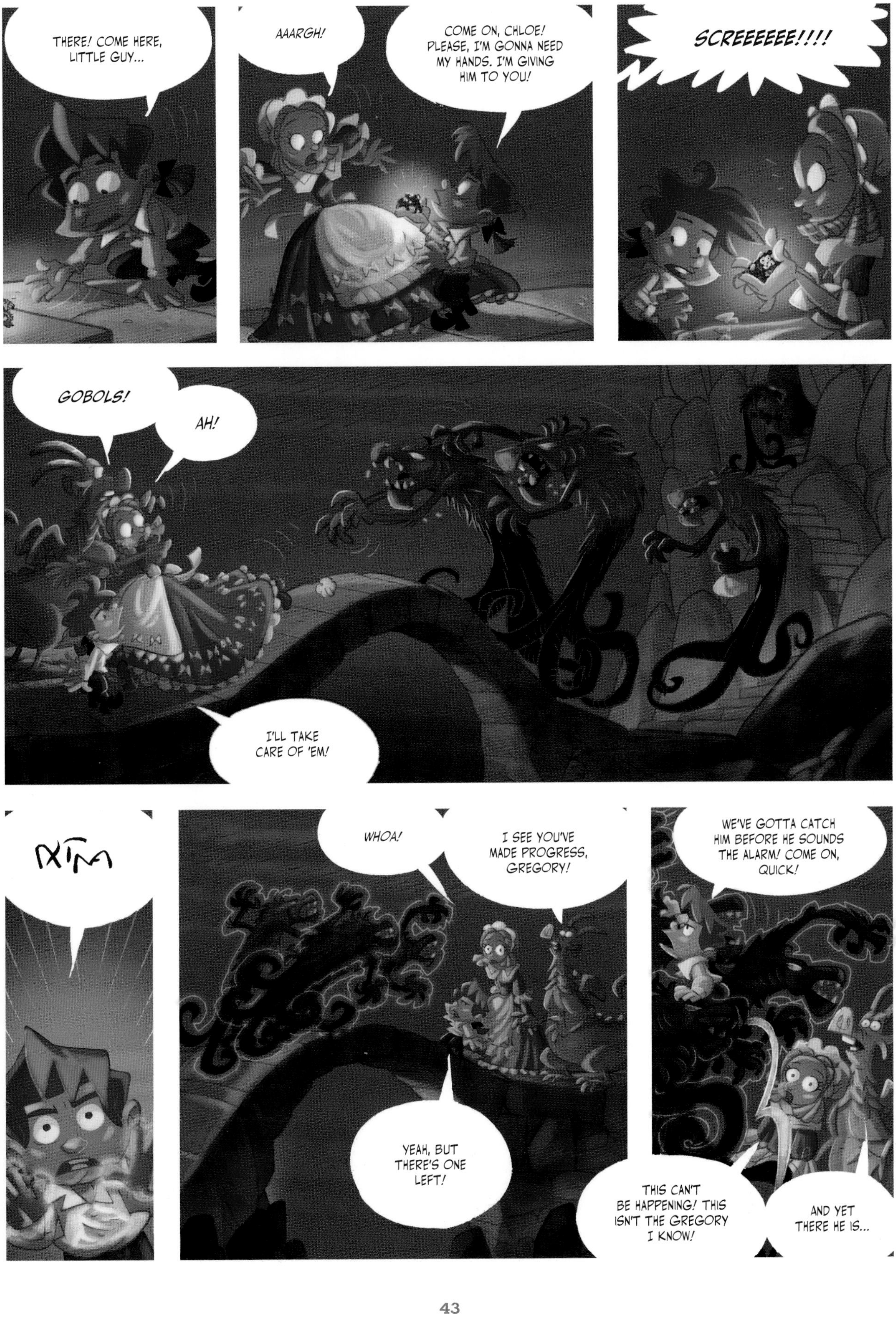

THERE! COME HERE, LITTLE GUY...
AAARGH!
COME ON, CHLOE! PLEASE, I'M GONNA NEED MY HANDS. I'M GIVING HIM TO YOU!
SCREEEEEE!!!!
GOBOLS!
AH!
I'LL TAKE CARE OF 'EM!
WHOA!
I SEE YOU'VE MADE PROGRESS, GREGORY!
YEAH, BUT THERE'S ONE LEFT!
WE'VE GOTTA CATCH HIM BEFORE HE SOUNDS THE ALARM! COME ON, QUICK!
THIS CAN'T BE HAPPENING! THIS ISN'T THE GREGORY I KNOW!
AND YET THERE HE IS...

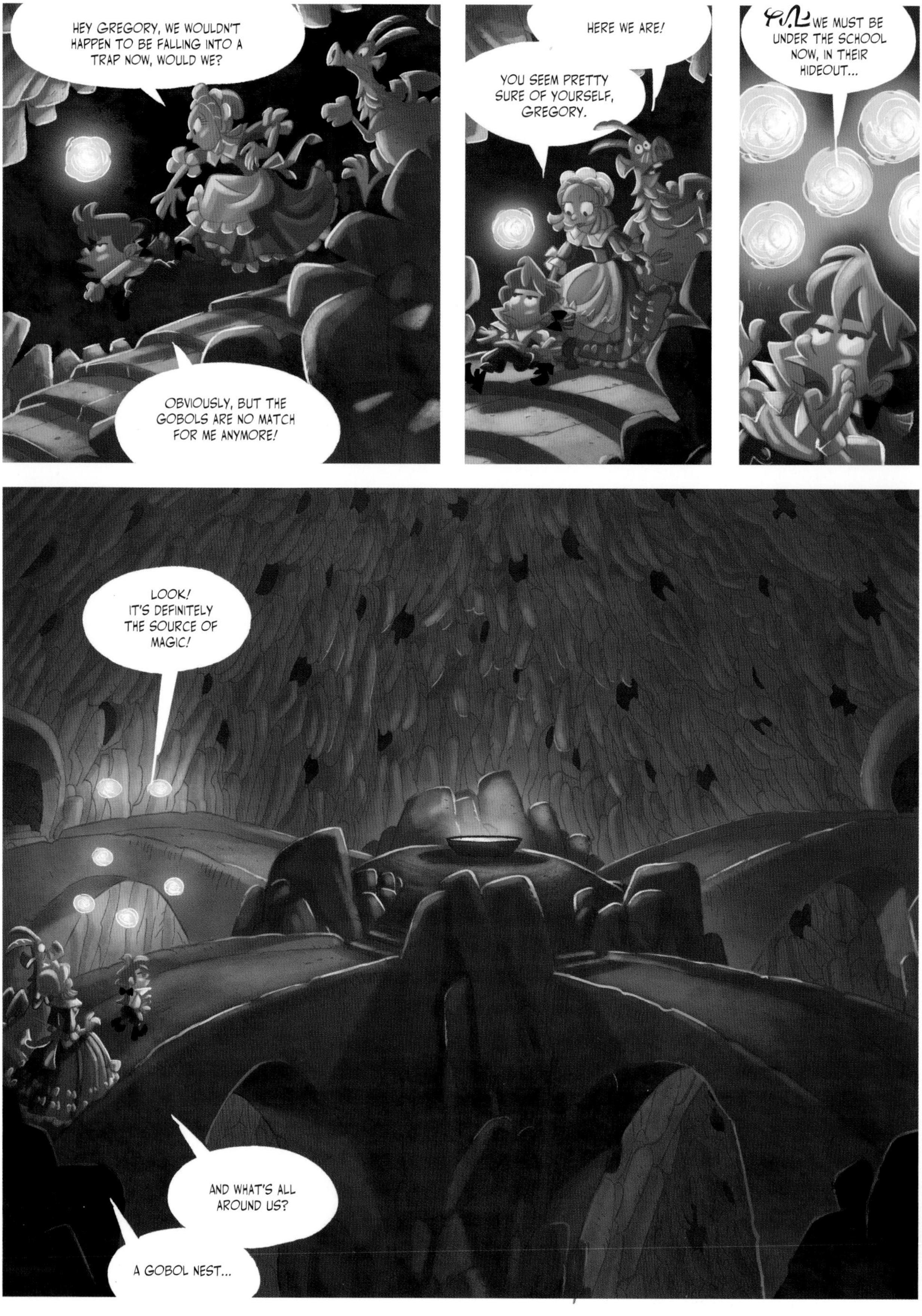
HEY GREGORY, WE WOULDN'T HAPPEN TO BE FALLING INTO A TRAP NOW, WOULD WE?
OBVIOUSLY, BUT THE GOBOLS ARE NO MATCH FOR ME ANYMORE!
HERE WE ARE!
YOU SEEM PRETTY SURE OF YOURSELF, GREGORY.
WE MUST BE UNDER THE SCHOOL NOW, IN THEIR HIDEOUT...
LOOK! IT'S DEFINITELY THE SOURCE OF MAGIC!
AND WHAT'S ALL AROUND US?
A GOBOL NEST...

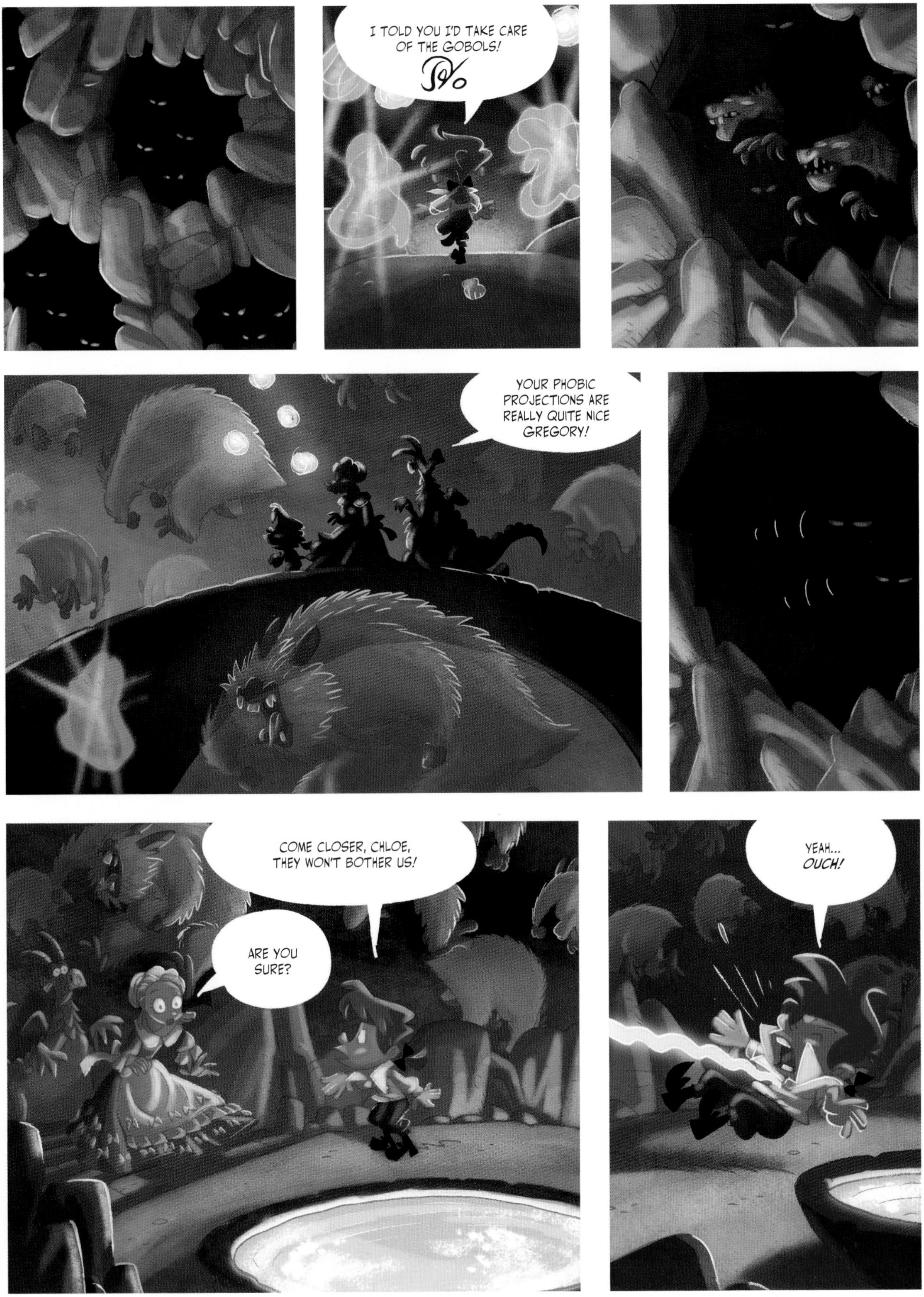
I TOLD YOU I'D TAKE CARE OF THE GOBOLS!
YOUR PHOBIC PROJECTIONS ARE REALLY QUITE NICE GREGORY!
COME CLOSER, CHLOE, THEY WON'T BOTHER US!
ARE YOU SURE?
YEAH... *OUCH!*

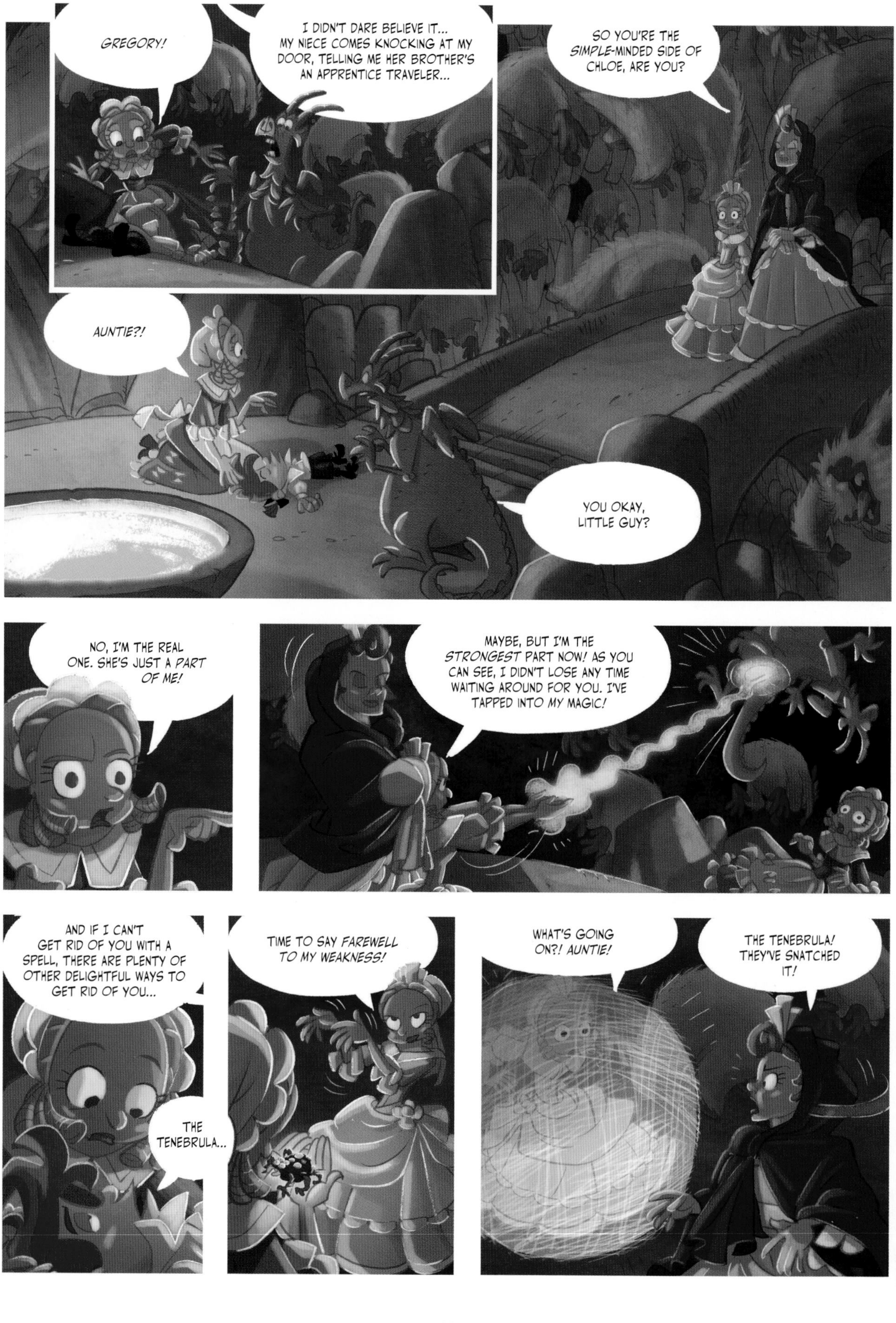
GREGORY!
I DIDN'T DARE BELIEVE IT... MY NIECE COMES KNOCKING AT MY DOOR, TELLING ME HER BROTHER'S AN APPRENTICE TRAVELER...
SO YOU'RE THE SIMPLE-MINDED SIDE OF CHLOE, ARE YOU?
AUNTIE?!
YOU OKAY, LITTLE GUY?
NO, I'M THE REAL ONE. SHE'S JUST A PART OF ME!
MAYBE, BUT I'M THE STRONGEST PART NOW! AS YOU CAN SEE, I DIDN'T LOSE ANY TIME WAITING AROUND FOR YOU. I'VE TAPPED INTO MY MAGIC!
AND IF I CAN'T GET RID OF YOU WITH A SPELL, THERE ARE PLENTY OF OTHER DELIGHTFUL WAYS TO GET RID OF YOU...
THE TENEBRULA...
TIME TO SAY FAREWELL TO MY WEAKNESS!
WHAT'S GOING ON?! AUNTIE!
THE TENEBRULA! THEY'VE SNATCHED IT!

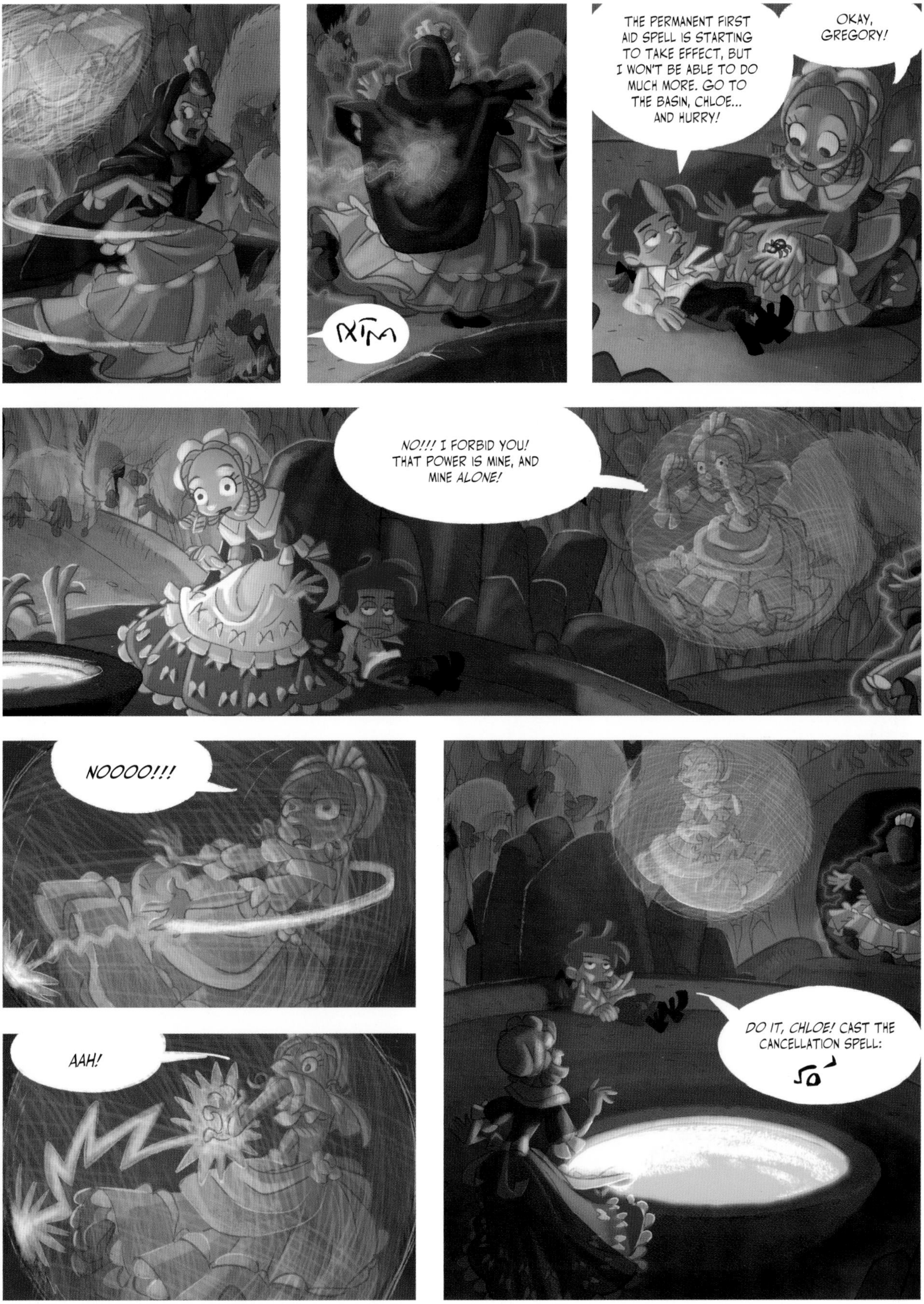

THE PERMANENT FIRST AID SPELL IS STARTING TO TAKE EFFECT, BUT I WON'T BE ABLE TO DO MUCH MORE. GO TO THE BASIN, CHLOE... AND HURRY!
OKAY, GREGORY!
NO!!! I FORBID YOU! THAT POWER IS MINE, AND MINE ALONE!
NOOOO!!!
AAH!
DO IT, CHLOE! CAST THE CANCELLATION SPELL:

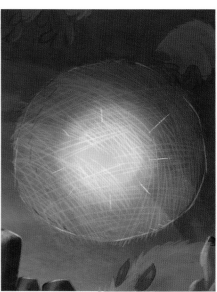

AAAH!

CHLOE!

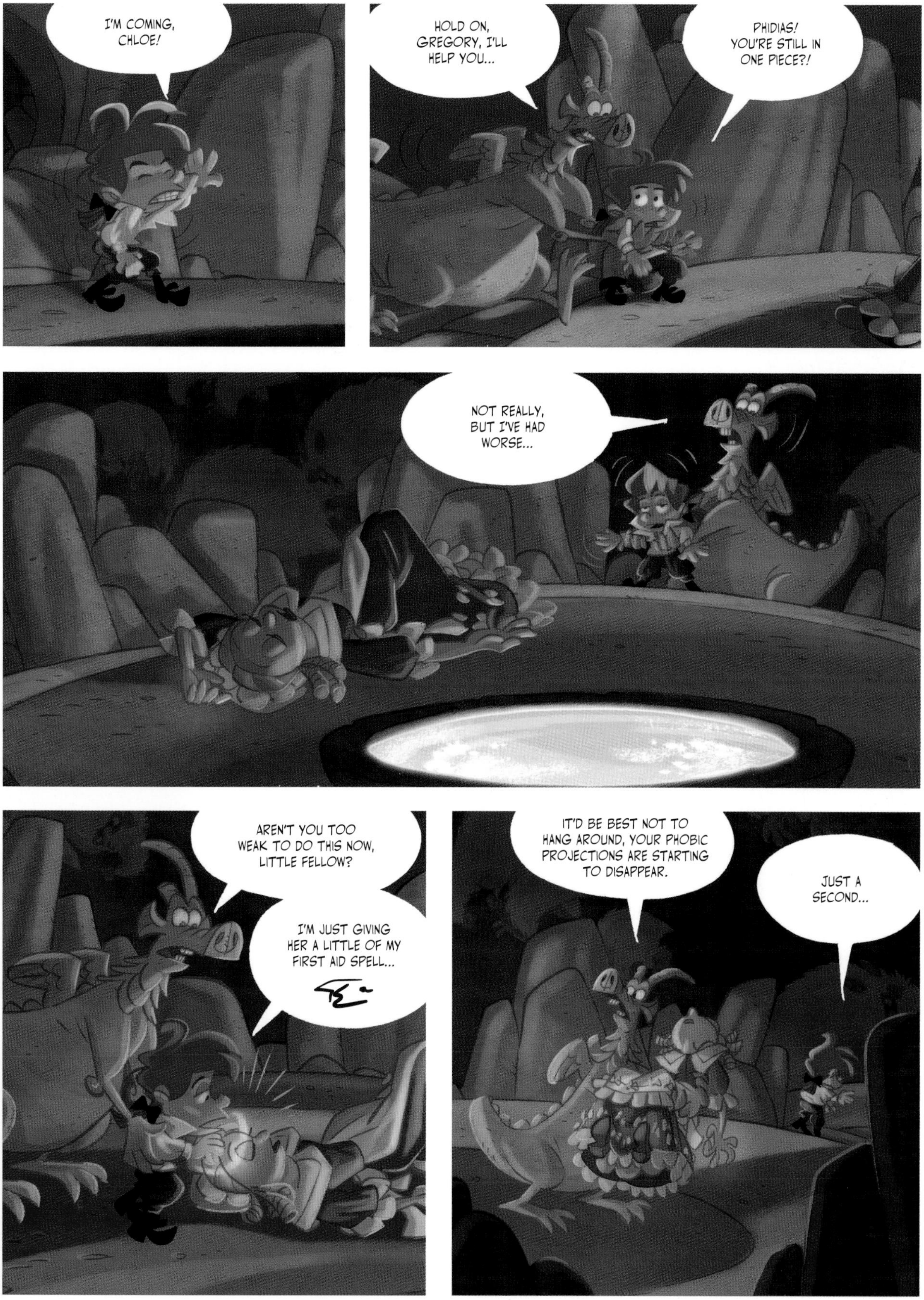
I'M COMING, CHLOE!
HOLD ON, GREGORY, I'LL HELP YOU...
PHIDIAS! YOU'RE STILL IN ONE PIECE?!
NOT REALLY, BUT I'VE HAD WORSE...
AREN'T YOU TOO WEAK TO DO THIS NOW, LITTLE FELLOW?
I'M JUST GIVING HER A LITTLE OF MY FIRST AID SPELL...
IT'D BE BEST NOT TO HANG AROUND, YOUR PHOBIC PROJECTIONS ARE STARTING TO DISAPPEAR.
JUST A SECOND...

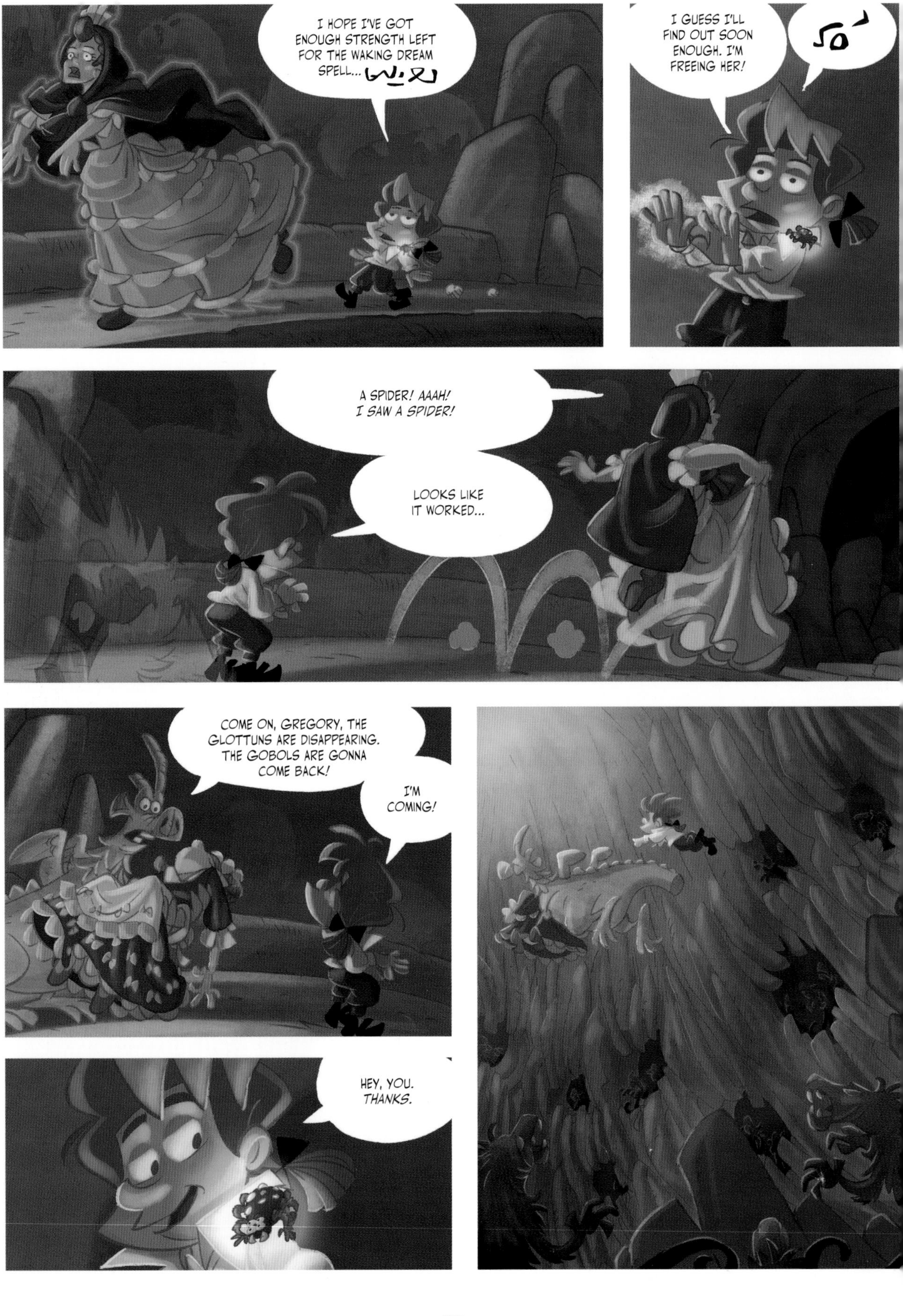
I HOPE I'VE GOT ENOUGH STRENGTH LEFT FOR THE WAKING DREAM SPELL...
I GUESS I'LL FIND OUT SOON ENOUGH. I'M FREEING HER!
A SPIDER! AAAH! I SAW A SPIDER!
LOOKS LIKE IT WORKED...
COME ON, GREGORY, THE GLOTTUNS ARE DISAPPEARING. THE GOBOLS ARE GONNA COME BACK!
I'M COMING!
HEY, YOU. THANKS.

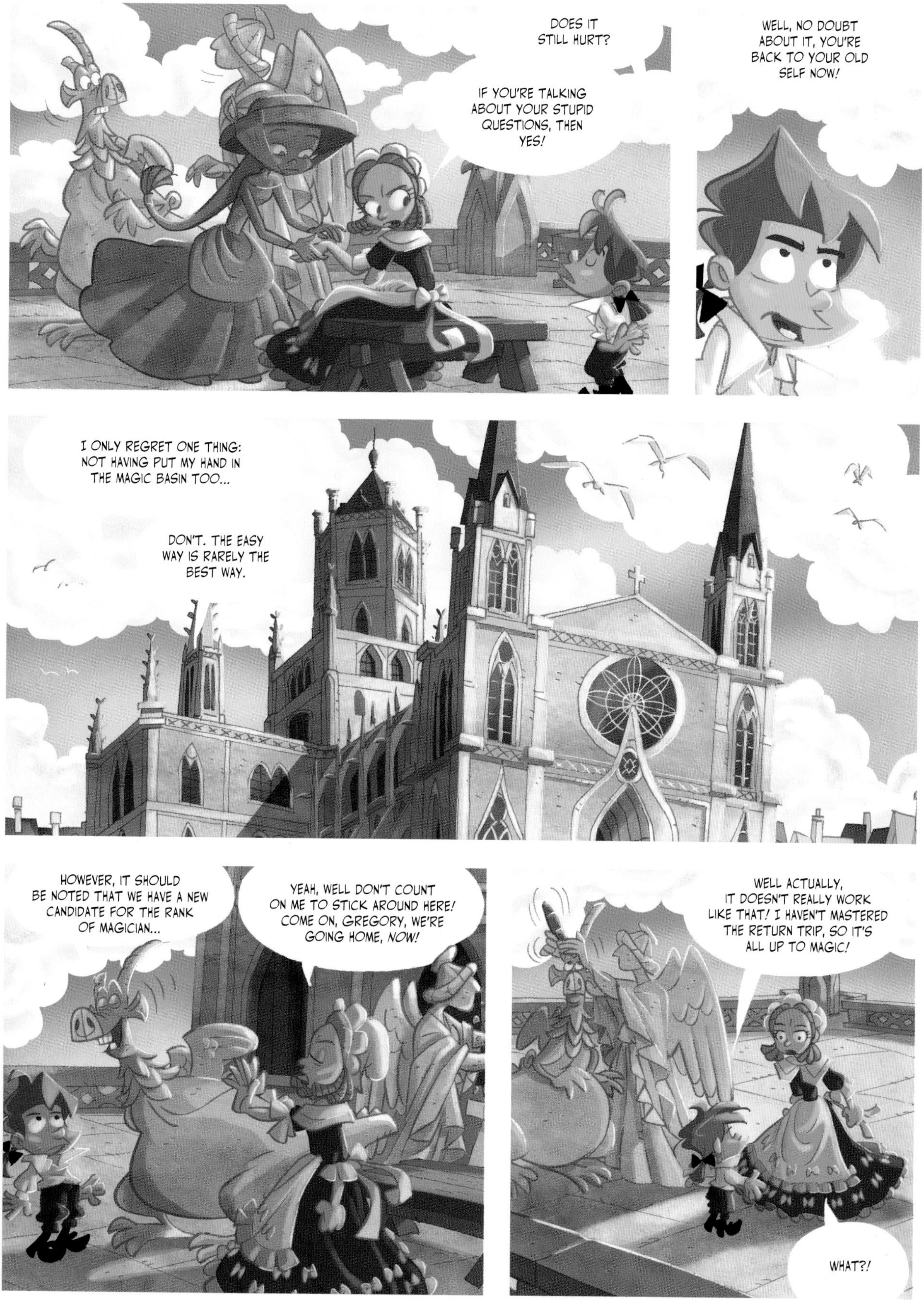
DOES IT STILL HURT?
IF YOU'RE TALKING ABOUT YOUR STUPID QUESTIONS, THEN YES!
WELL, NO DOUBT ABOUT IT, YOU'RE BACK TO YOUR OLD SELF NOW!
I ONLY REGRET ONE THING: NOT HAVING PUT MY HAND IN THE MAGIC BASIN TOO...
DON'T. THE EASY WAY IS RARELY THE BEST WAY.
HOWEVER, IT SHOULD BE NOTED THAT WE HAVE A NEW CANDIDATE FOR THE RANK OF MAGICIAN...
YEAH, WELL DON'T COUNT ON ME TO STICK AROUND HERE! COME ON, GREGORY, WE'RE GOING HOME, *NOW!*
WELL ACTUALLY, IT DOESN'T REALLY WORK LIKE THAT! I HAVEN'T MASTERED THE RETURN TRIP, SO IT'S ALL UP TO MAGIC!
WHAT?!

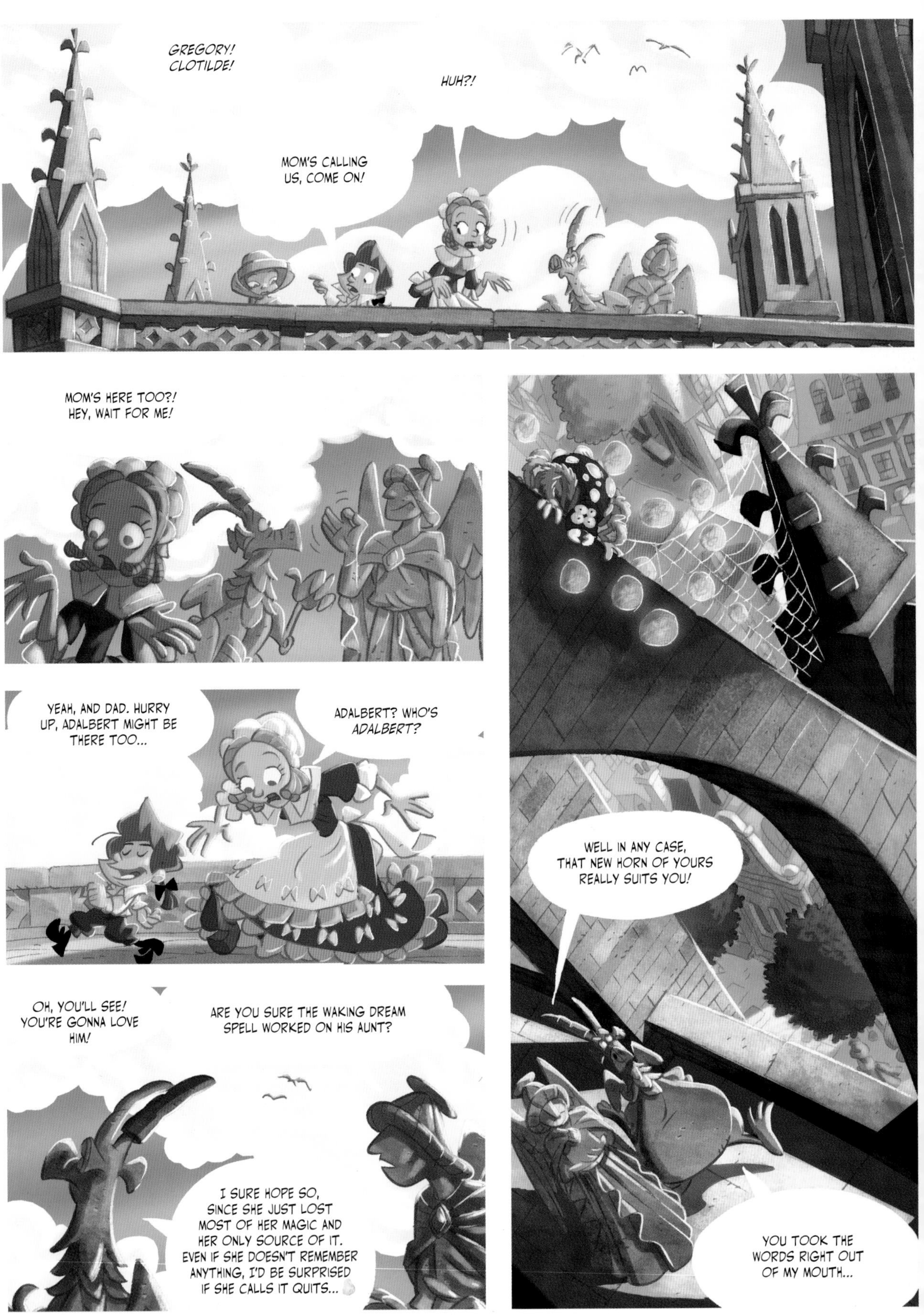
GREGORY!
CLOTILDE!
HUH?!
MOM'S CALLING US, COME ON!
MOM'S HERE TOO?! HEY, WAIT FOR ME!
YEAH, AND DAD. HURRY UP, ADALBERT MIGHT BE THERE TOO...
ADALBERT? WHO'S ADALBERT?
OH, YOU'LL SEE! YOU'RE GONNA LOVE HIM!
ARE YOU SURE THE WAKING DREAM SPELL WORKED ON HIS AUNT?
I SURE HOPE SO, SINCE SHE JUST LOST MOST OF HER MAGIC AND HER ONLY SOURCE OF IT. EVEN IF SHE DOESN'T REMEMBER ANYTHING, I'D BE SURPRISED IF SHE CALLS IT QUITS...
WELL IN ANY CASE, THAT NEW HORN OF YOURS REALLY SUITS YOU!
YOU TOOK THE WORDS RIGHT OUT OF MY MOUTH...

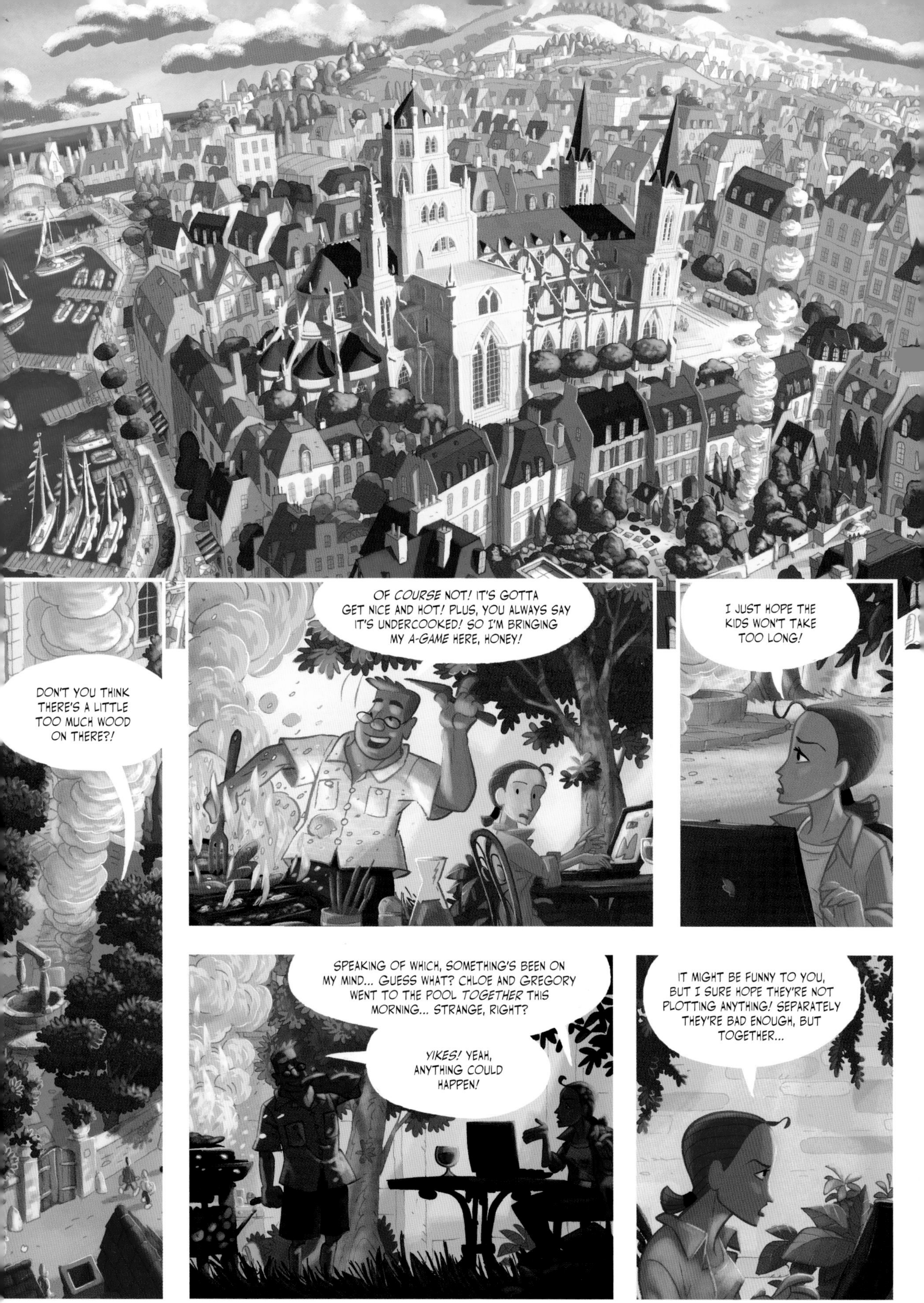
DON'T YOU THINK THERE'S A LITTLE TOO MUCH WOOD ON THERE?!
OF *COURSE* NOT! IT'S GOTTA GET NICE AND HOT! PLUS, YOU ALWAYS SAY IT'S UNDERCOOKED! SO I'M BRINGING MY *A-GAME* HERE, HONEY!
I JUST HOPE THE KIDS WON'T TAKE TOO LONG!
SPEAKING OF WHICH, SOMETHING'S BEEN ON MY MIND... GUESS WHAT? CHLOE AND GREGORY WENT TO THE POOL *TOGETHER* THIS MORNING... STRANGE, RIGHT?
YIKES! YEAH, ANYTHING COULD HAPPEN!
IT MIGHT BE FUNNY TO YOU, BUT I SURE HOPE THEY'RE NOT PLOTTING ANYTHING! SEPARATELY THEY'RE BAD ENOUGH, BUT TOGETHER...

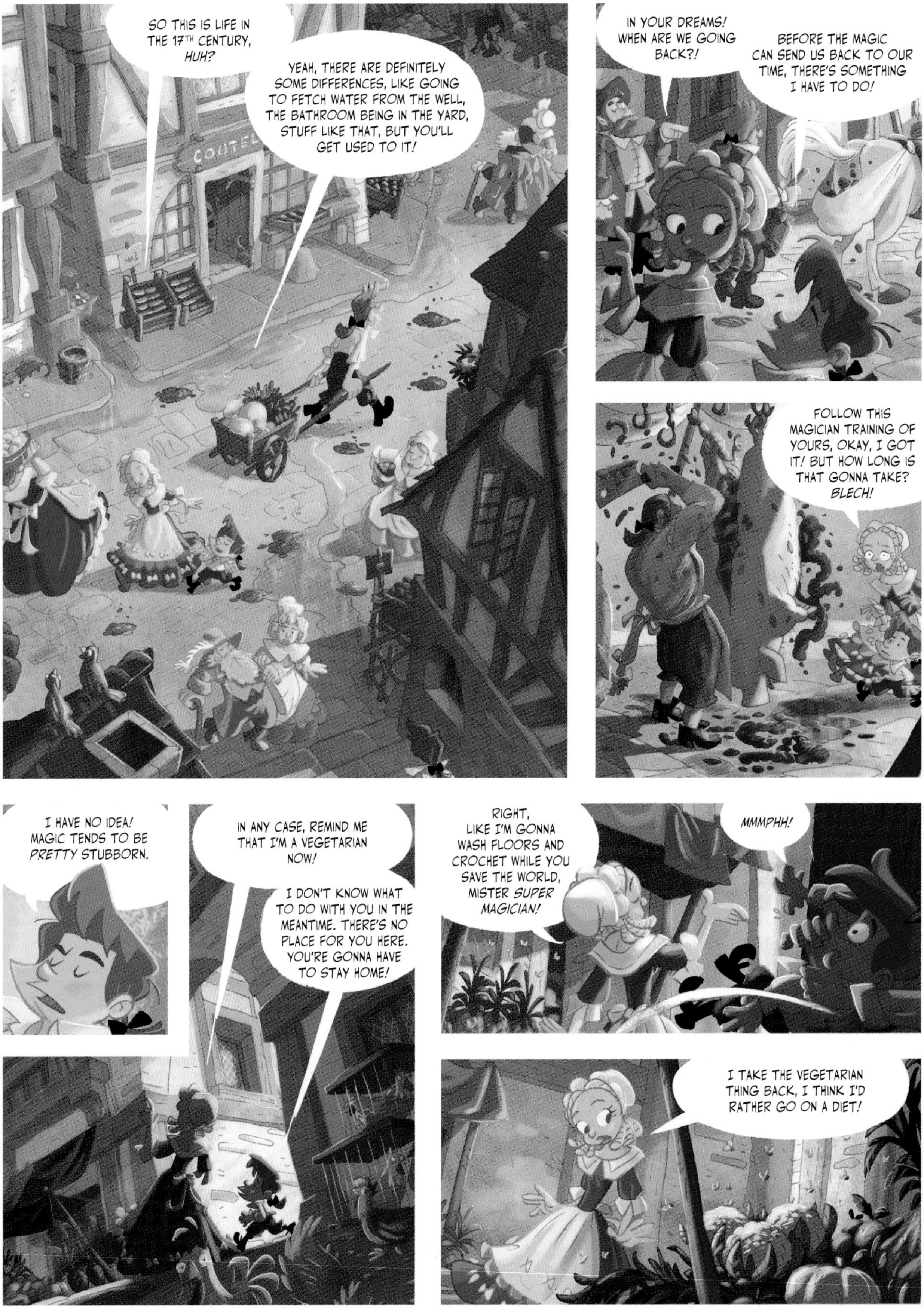
SO THIS IS LIFE IN THE 17TH CENTURY, *HUH?*
YEAH, THERE ARE DEFINITELY SOME DIFFERENCES, LIKE GOING TO FETCH WATER FROM THE WELL, THE BATHROOM BEING IN THE YARD, STUFF LIKE THAT, BUT YOU'LL GET USED TO IT!
COUTEL
IN YOUR DREAMS! WHEN ARE WE GOING BACK?!
BEFORE THE MAGIC CAN SEND US BACK TO OUR TIME, THERE'S SOMETHING I HAVE TO DO!
FOLLOW THIS MAGICIAN TRAINING OF YOURS, OKAY, I GOT IT! BUT HOW LONG IS THAT GONNA TAKE? *BLECH!*
I HAVE NO IDEA! MAGIC TENDS TO BE *PRETTY* STUBBORN.
IN ANY CASE, REMIND ME THAT I'M A VEGETARIAN NOW!
I DON'T KNOW WHAT TO DO WITH YOU IN THE MEANTIME. THERE'S NO PLACE FOR YOU HERE. YOU'RE GONNA HAVE TO STAY HOME!
RIGHT, LIKE I'M GONNA WASH FLOORS AND CROCHET WHILE YOU SAVE THE WORLD, MISTER *SUPER MAGICIAN!*
MMMPHH!
I TAKE THE VEGETARIAN THING BACK, I THINK I'D RATHER GO ON A DIET!

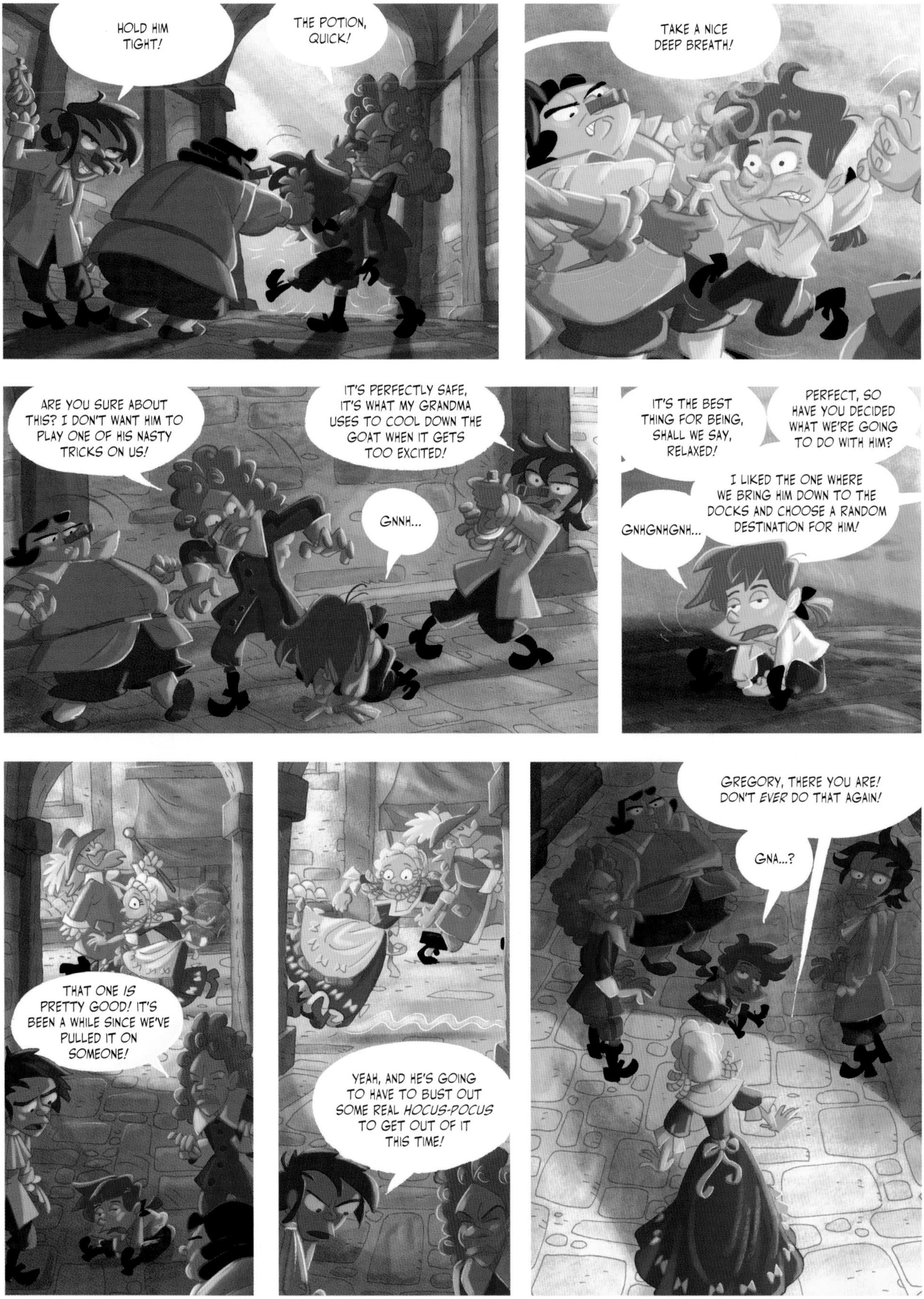
HOLD HIM TIGHT!
THE POTION, QUICK!
TAKE A NICE DEEP BREATH!
ARE YOU SURE ABOUT THIS? I DON'T WANT HIM TO PLAY ONE OF HIS NASTY TRICKS ON US!
IT'S PERFECTLY SAFE, IT'S WHAT MY GRANDMA USES TO COOL DOWN THE GOAT WHEN IT GETS TOO EXCITED!
GNNH...
IT'S THE BEST THING FOR BEING, SHALL WE SAY, RELAXED!
PERFECT, SO HAVE YOU DECIDED WHAT WE'RE GOING TO DO WITH HIM?
I LIKED THE ONE WHERE WE BRING HIM DOWN TO THE DOCKS AND CHOOSE A RANDOM DESTINATION FOR HIM!
GNHGNHGNH...
THAT ONE *IS* PRETTY GOOD! IT'S BEEN A WHILE SINCE WE'VE PULLED IT ON SOMEONE!
YEAH, AND HE'S GOING TO HAVE TO BUST OUT SOME REAL *HOCUS-POCUS* TO GET OUT OF IT THIS TIME!
GREGORY, THERE YOU ARE! DON'T *EVER* DO THAT AGAIN!
GNA...?

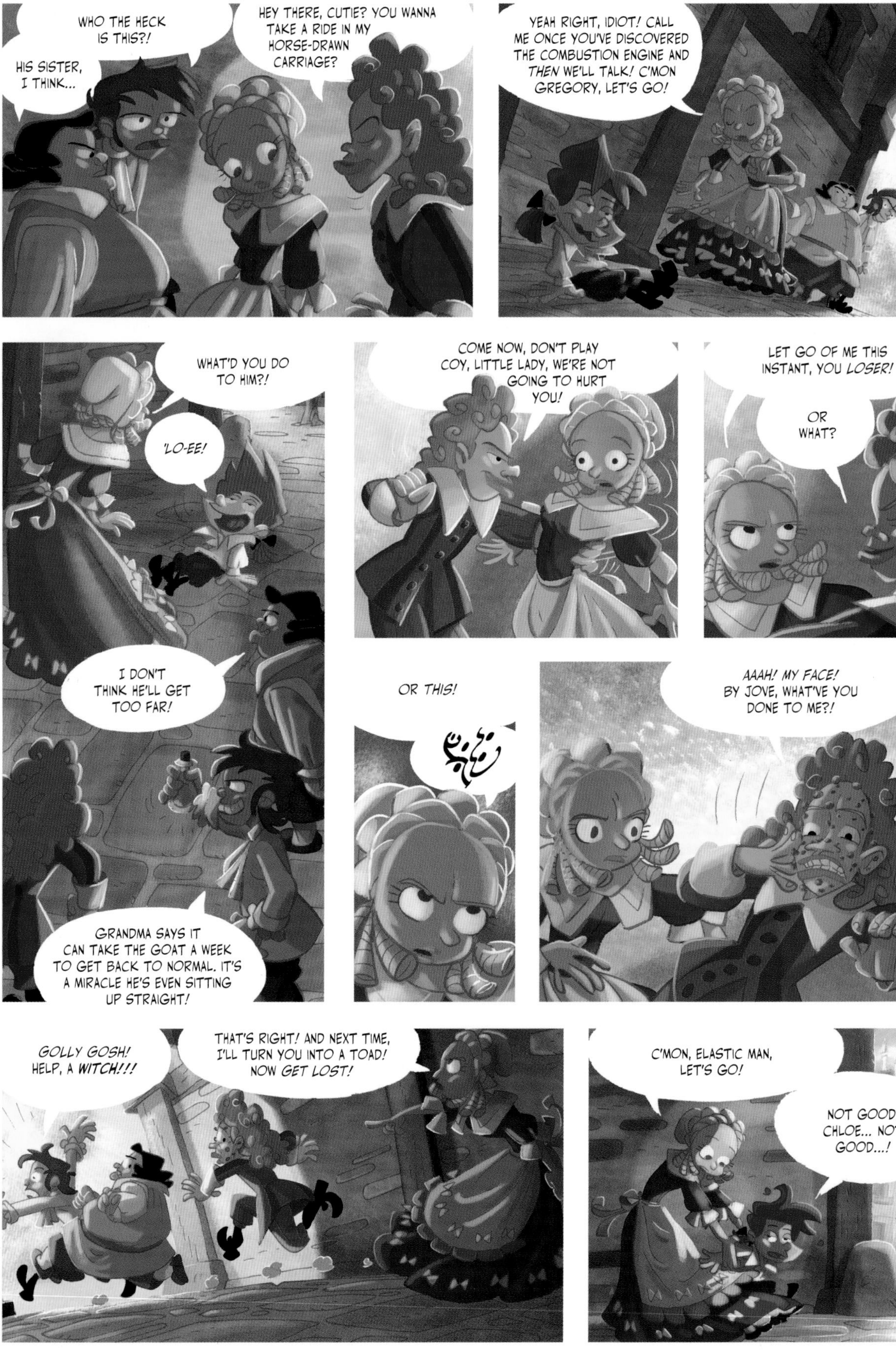

WHO THE HECK IS THIS?!
HIS SISTER, I THINK...
HEY THERE, CUTIE? YOU WANNA TAKE A RIDE IN MY HORSE-DRAWN CARRIAGE?
YEAH RIGHT, IDIOT! CALL ME ONCE YOU'VE DISCOVERED THE COMBUSTION ENGINE AND *THEN* WE'LL TALK! C'MON GREGORY, LET'S GO!
WHAT'D YOU DO TO HIM?!
'LO-EE!
I DON'T THINK HE'LL GET TOO FAR!
GRANDMA SAYS IT CAN TAKE THE GOAT A WEEK TO GET BACK TO NORMAL. IT'S A MIRACLE HE'S EVEN SITTING UP STRAIGHT!
COME NOW, DON'T PLAY COY, LITTLE LADY, WE'RE NOT GOING TO HURT YOU!
LET GO OF ME THIS INSTANT, YOU *LOSER!*
OR WHAT?
OR THIS!
AAAH! MY FACE! BY JOVE, WHAT'VE YOU DONE TO ME?!
GOLLY GOSH! HELP, A *WITCH!!!*
THAT'S RIGHT! AND NEXT TIME, I'LL TURN YOU INTO A TOAD! NOW *GET LOST!*
C'MON, ELASTIC MAN, LET'S GO!
NOT GOOD, CHLOE... NOT GOOD...!

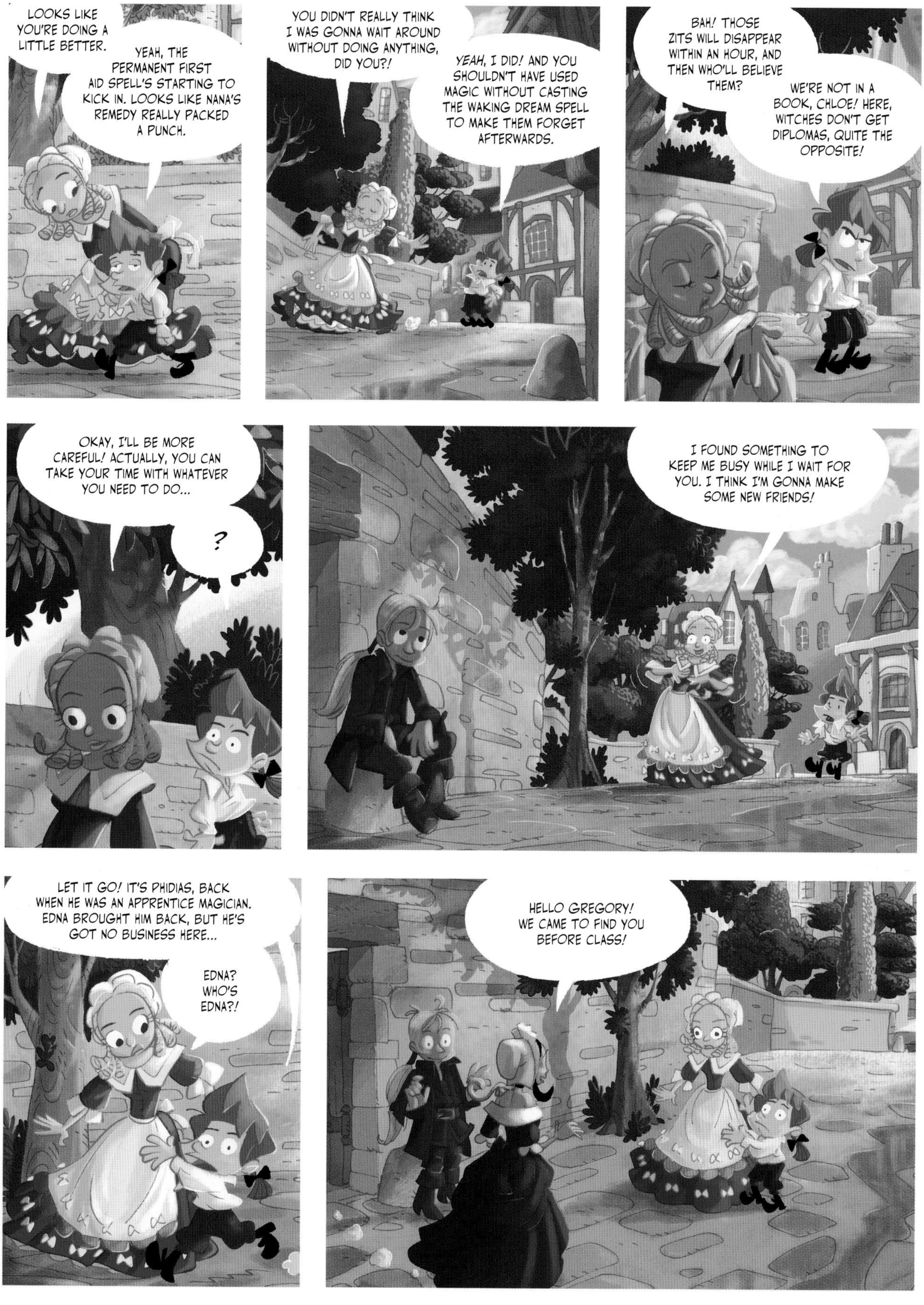
LOOKS LIKE YOU'RE DOING A LITTLE BETTER.
YEAH, THE PERMANENT FIRST AID SPELL'S STARTING TO KICK IN. LOOKS LIKE NANA'S REMEDY REALLY PACKED A PUNCH.
YOU DIDN'T REALLY THINK I WAS GONNA WAIT AROUND WITHOUT DOING ANYTHING, DID YOU?!
YEAH, I DID! AND YOU SHOULDN'T HAVE USED MAGIC WITHOUT CASTING THE WAKING DREAM SPELL TO MAKE THEM FORGET AFTERWARDS.
BAH! THOSE ZITS WILL DISAPPEAR WITHIN AN HOUR, AND THEN WHO'LL BELIEVE THEM?
WE'RE NOT IN A BOOK, CHLOE! HERE, WITCHES DON'T GET DIPLOMAS, QUITE THE OPPOSITE!
OKAY, I'LL BE MORE CAREFUL! ACTUALLY, YOU CAN TAKE YOUR TIME WITH WHATEVER YOU NEED TO DO...
?
I FOUND SOMETHING TO KEEP ME BUSY WHILE I WAIT FOR YOU. I THINK I'M GONNA MAKE SOME NEW FRIENDS!
LET IT GO! IT'S PHIDIAS, BACK WHEN HE WAS AN APPRENTICE MAGICIAN. EDNA BROUGHT HIM BACK, BUT HE'S GOT NO BUSINESS HERE...
EDNA? WHO'S EDNA?!
HELLO GREGORY! WE CAME TO FIND YOU BEFORE CLASS!

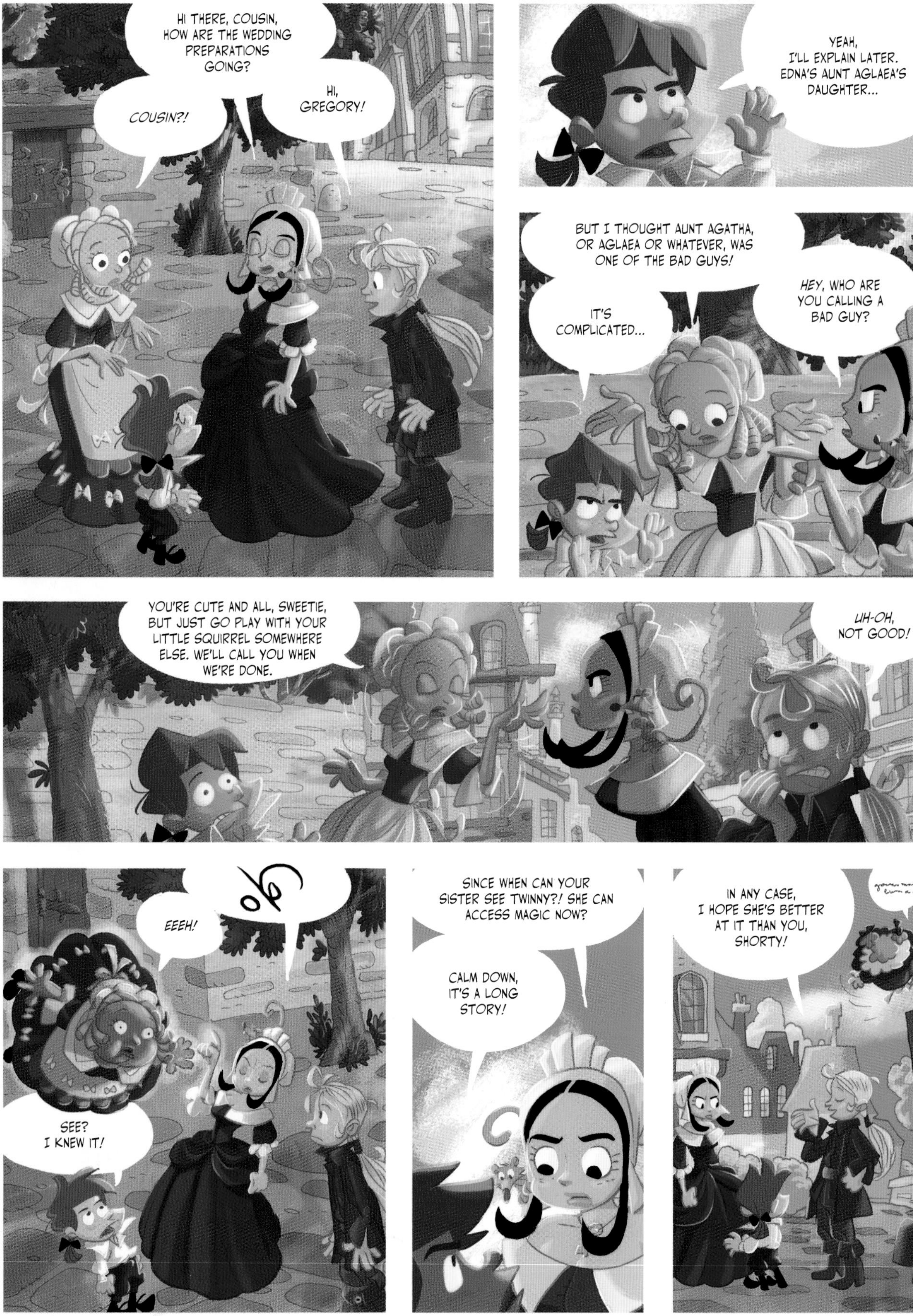
HI THERE, COUSIN, HOW ARE THE WEDDING PREPARATIONS GOING?
COUSIN?!
HI, GREGORY!
YEAH, I'LL EXPLAIN LATER. EDNA'S AUNT AGLAEA'S DAUGHTER...
BUT I THOUGHT AUNT AGATHA, OR AGLAEA OR WHATEVER, WAS ONE OF THE BAD GUYS!
IT'S COMPLICATED...
HEY, WHO ARE YOU CALLING A BAD GUY?
YOU'RE CUTE AND ALL, SWEETIE, BUT JUST GO PLAY WITH YOUR LITTLE SQUIRREL SOMEWHERE ELSE. WE'LL CALL YOU WHEN WE'RE DONE.
UH-OH, NOT GOOD!
EEEH!
SEE? I KNEW IT!
SINCE WHEN CAN YOUR SISTER SEE TWINNY?! SHE CAN ACCESS MAGIC NOW?
CALM DOWN, IT'S A LONG STORY!
IN ANY CASE, I HOPE SHE'S BETTER AT IT THAN YOU, SHORTY!

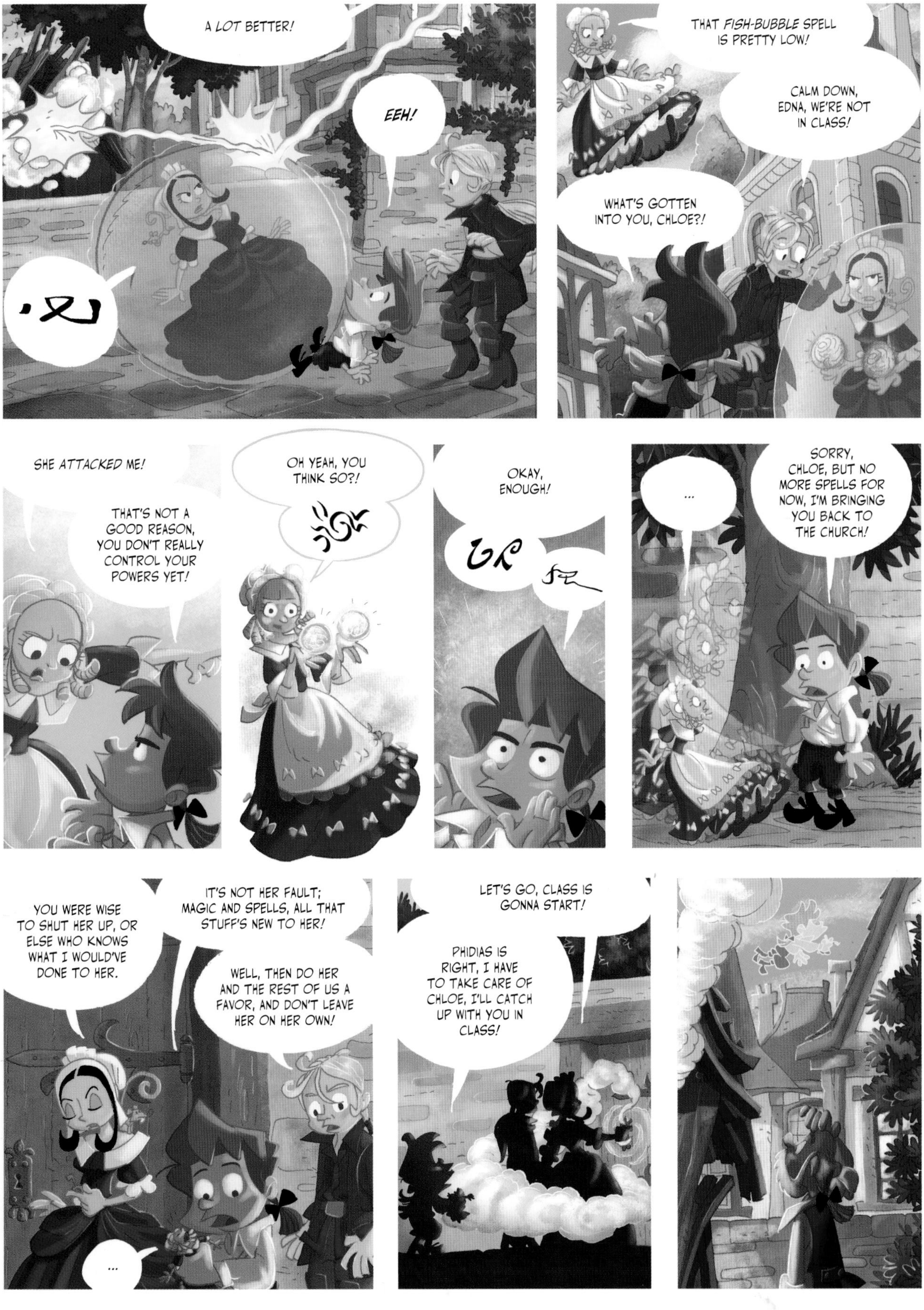
A LOT BETTER!
EEH!
THAT FISH-BUBBLE SPELL IS PRETTY LOW!
CALM DOWN, EDNA, WE'RE NOT IN CLASS!
WHAT'S GOTTEN INTO YOU, CHLOE?!
SHE ATTACKED ME!
THAT'S NOT A GOOD REASON, YOU DON'T REALLY CONTROL YOUR POWERS YET!
OH YEAH, YOU THINK SO?!
OKAY, ENOUGH!
...
SORRY, CHLOE, BUT NO MORE SPELLS FOR NOW, I'M BRINGING YOU BACK TO THE CHURCH!
YOU WERE WISE TO SHUT HER UP, OR ELSE WHO KNOWS WHAT I WOULD'VE DONE TO HER.
IT'S NOT HER FAULT; MAGIC AND SPELLS, ALL THAT STUFF'S NEW TO HER!
WELL, THEN DO HER AND THE REST OF US A FAVOR, AND DON'T LEAVE HER ON HER OWN!
...
LET'S GO, CLASS IS GONNA START!
PHIDIAS IS RIGHT, I HAVE TO TAKE CARE OF CHLOE, I'LL CATCH UP WITH YOU IN CLASS!

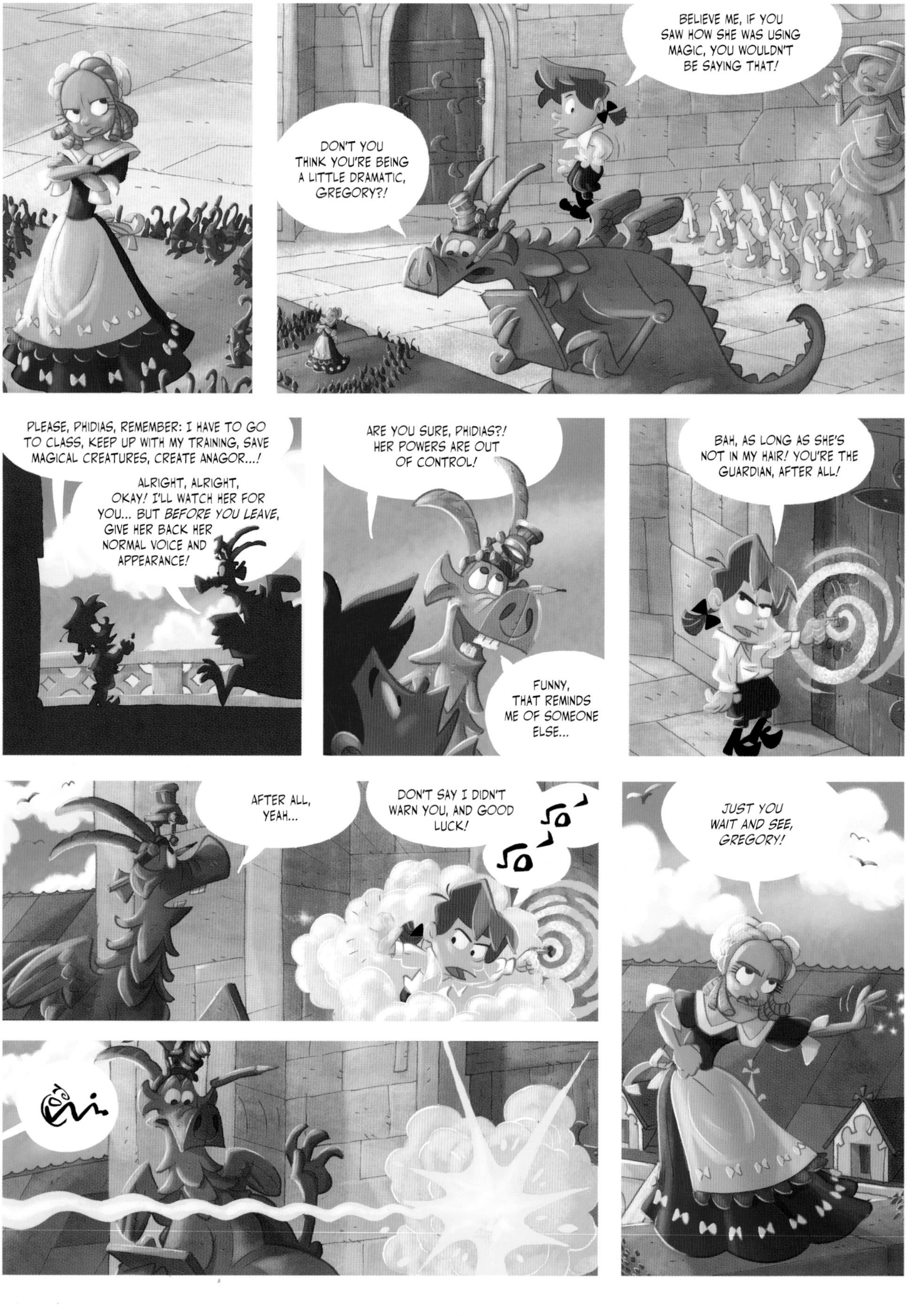

DON'T YOU THINK YOU'RE BEING A LITTLE DRAMATIC, GREGORY?!
BELIEVE ME, IF YOU SAW HOW SHE WAS USING MAGIC, YOU WOULDN'T BE SAYING THAT!
PLEASE, PHIDIAS, REMEMBER: I HAVE TO GO TO CLASS, KEEP UP WITH MY TRAINING, SAVE MAGICAL CREATURES, CREATE ANAGOR...!
ALRIGHT, ALRIGHT, OKAY! I'LL WATCH HER FOR YOU... BUT *BEFORE YOU LEAVE*, GIVE HER BACK HER NORMAL VOICE AND APPEARANCE!
ARE YOU SURE, PHIDIAS?! HER POWERS ARE OUT OF CONTROL!
FUNNY, THAT REMINDS ME OF SOMEONE ELSE...
BAH, AS LONG AS SHE'S NOT IN MY HAIR! YOU'RE THE GUARDIAN, AFTER ALL!
AFTER ALL, YEAH...
DON'T SAY I DIDN'T WARN YOU, AND GOOD LUCK!
JUST YOU WAIT AND SEE, GREGORY!

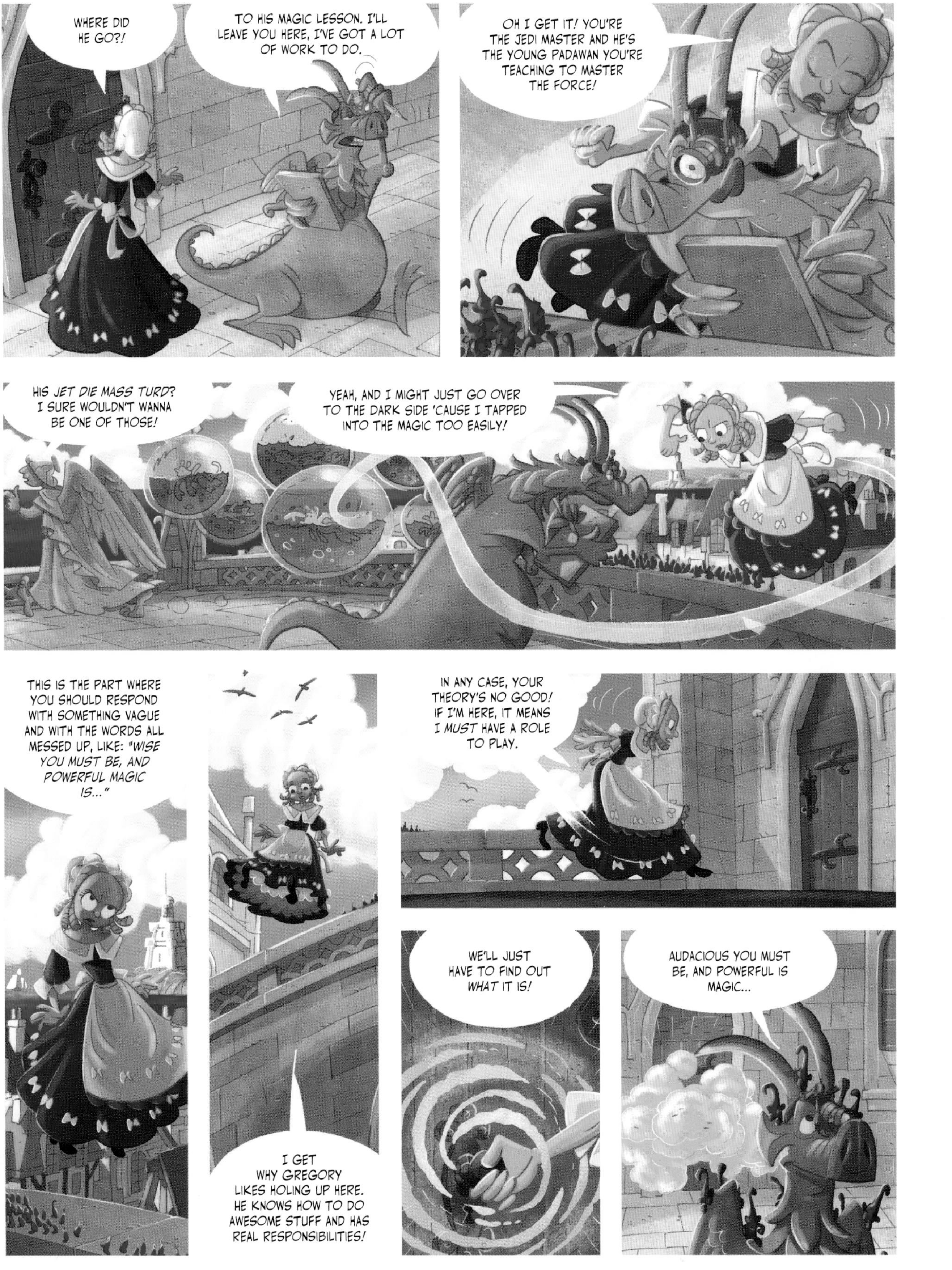
WHERE DID HE GO?!
TO HIS MAGIC LESSON. I'LL LEAVE YOU HERE, I'VE GOT A LOT OF WORK TO DO.
OH I GET IT! YOU'RE THE JEDI MASTER AND HE'S THE YOUNG PADAWAN YOU'RE TEACHING TO MASTER THE FORCE!
HIS JET DIE MASS TURD? I SURE WOULDN'T WANNA BE ONE OF THOSE!
YEAH, AND I MIGHT JUST GO OVER TO THE DARK SIDE 'CAUSE I TAPPED INTO THE MAGIC TOO EASILY!
THIS IS THE PART WHERE YOU SHOULD RESPOND WITH SOMETHING VAGUE AND WITH THE WORDS ALL MESSED UP, LIKE: "WISE YOU MUST BE, AND POWERFUL MAGIC IS..."
I GET WHY GREGORY LIKES HOLING UP HERE. HE KNOWS HOW TO DO AWESOME STUFF AND HAS REAL RESPONSIBILITIES!
IN ANY CASE, YOUR THEORY'S NO GOOD! IF I'M HERE, IT MEANS I MUST HAVE A ROLE TO PLAY.
WE'LL JUST HAVE TO FIND OUT WHAT IT IS!
AUDACIOUS YOU MUST BE, AND POWERFUL IS MAGIC...

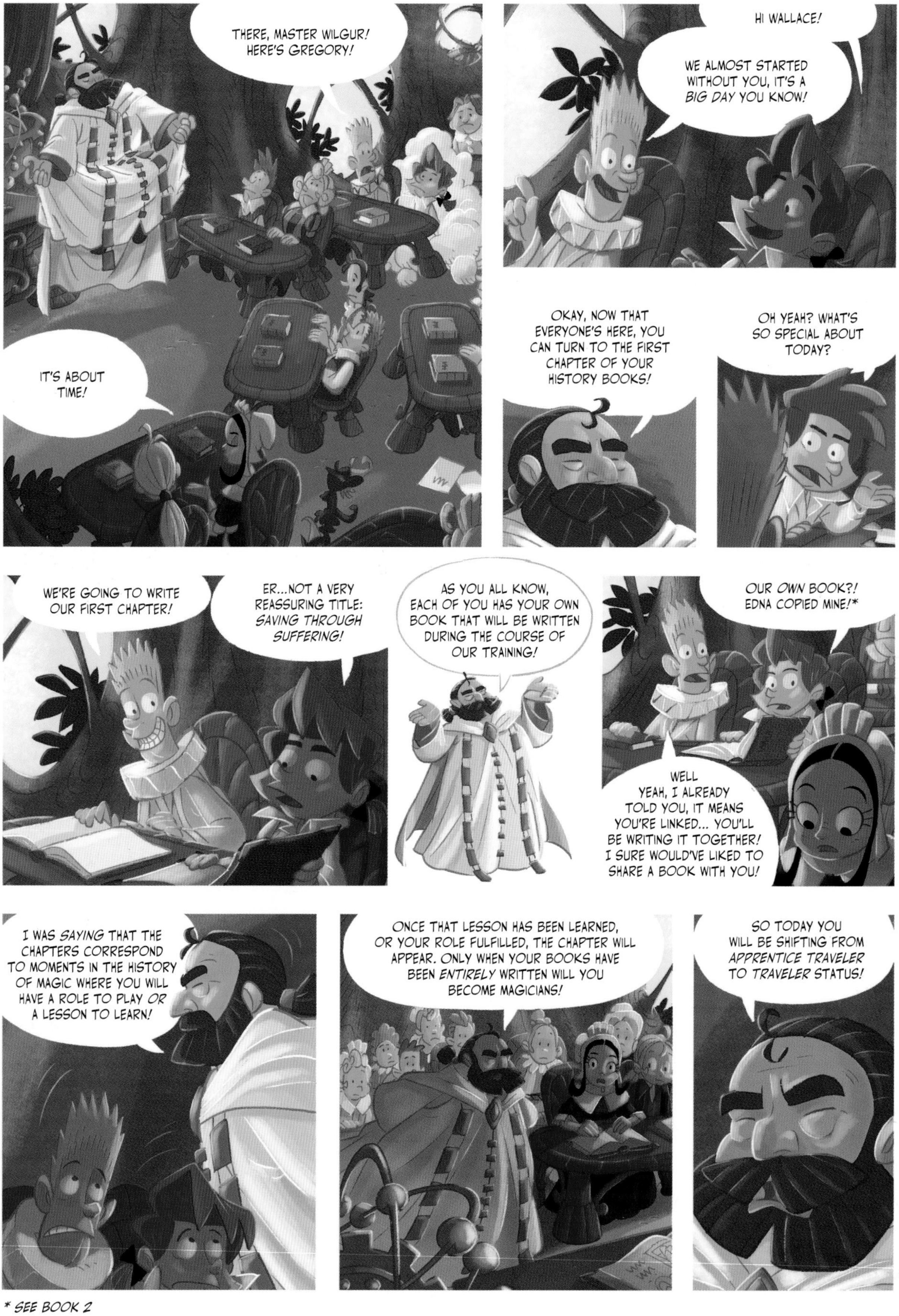
THERE, MASTER WILGUR! HERE'S GREGORY!
IT'S ABOUT TIME!
HI WALLACE!
WE ALMOST STARTED WITHOUT YOU, IT'S A *BIG DAY* YOU KNOW!
OKAY, NOW THAT EVERYONE'S HERE, YOU CAN TURN TO THE FIRST CHAPTER OF YOUR HISTORY BOOKS!
OH YEAH? WHAT'S SO SPECIAL ABOUT TODAY?
WE'RE GOING TO WRITE OUR FIRST CHAPTER!
ER...NOT A VERY REASSURING TITLE: *SAVING THROUGH SUFFERING!*
AS YOU ALL KNOW, EACH OF YOU HAS YOUR OWN BOOK THAT WILL BE WRITTEN DURING THE COURSE OF OUR TRAINING!
OUR *OWN* BOOK?! EDNA COPIED MINE!*
WELL YEAH, I ALREADY TOLD YOU, IT MEANS YOU'RE LINKED... YOU'LL BE WRITING IT TOGETHER! I SURE WOULD'VE LIKED TO SHARE A BOOK WITH YOU!
I WAS *SAYING* THAT THE CHAPTERS CORRESPOND TO MOMENTS IN THE HISTORY OF MAGIC WHERE YOU WILL HAVE A ROLE TO PLAY *OR* A LESSON TO LEARN!
ONCE THAT LESSON HAS BEEN LEARNED, OR YOUR ROLE FULFILLED, THE CHAPTER WILL APPEAR. ONLY WHEN YOUR BOOKS HAVE BEEN *ENTIRELY* WRITTEN WILL YOU BECOME MAGICIANS!
SO TODAY YOU WILL BE SHIFTING FROM *APPRENTICE TRAVELER* TO *TRAVELER* STATUS!

* *SEE BOOK 2*

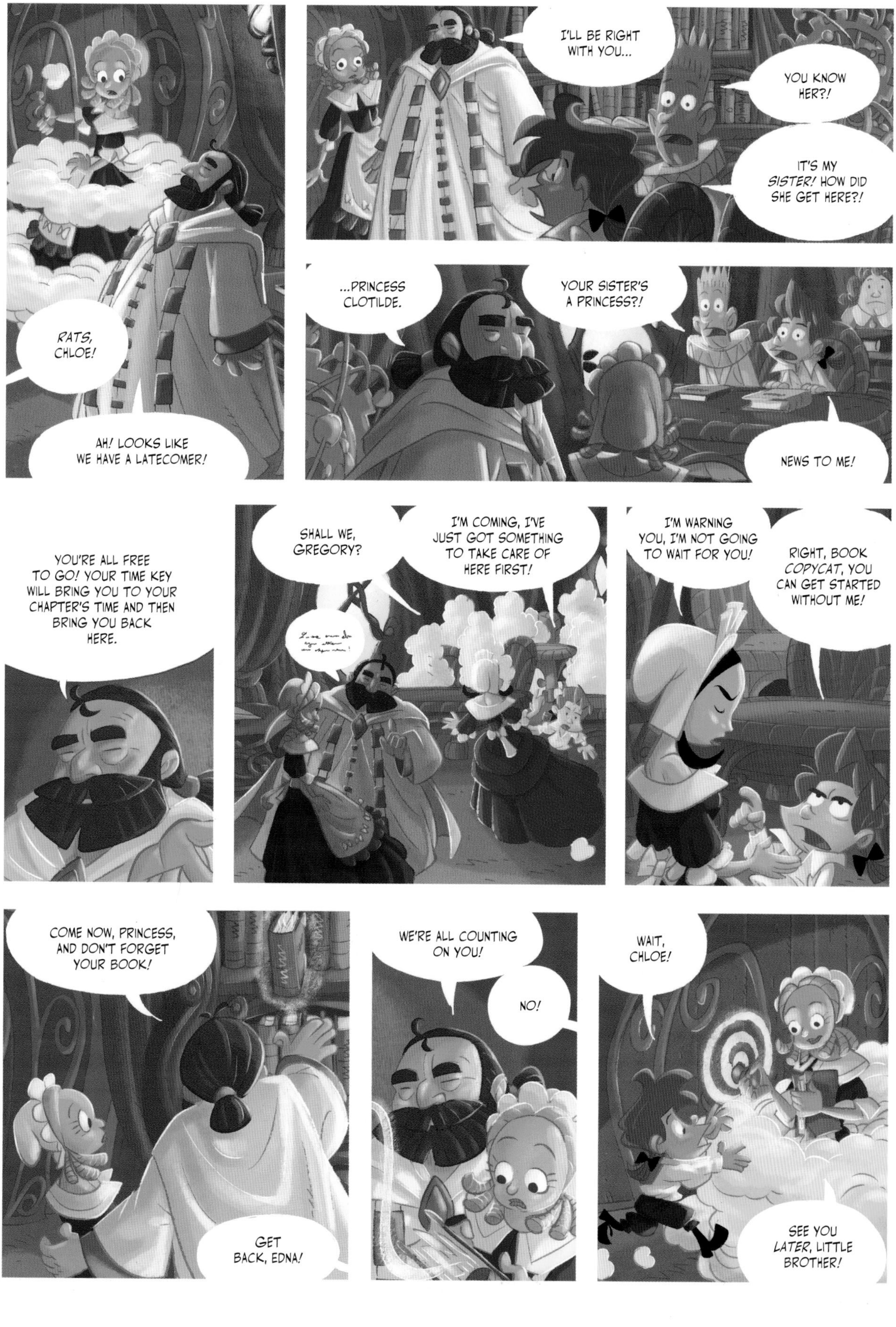
RATS, CHLOE!
AH! LOOKS LIKE WE HAVE A LATECOMER!
I'LL BE RIGHT WITH YOU...
YOU KNOW HER?!
IT'S MY SISTER! HOW DID SHE GET HERE?!
...PRINCESS CLOTILDE.
YOUR SISTER'S A PRINCESS?!
NEWS TO ME!
YOU'RE ALL FREE TO GO! YOUR TIME KEY WILL BRING YOU TO YOUR CHAPTER'S TIME AND THEN BRING YOU BACK HERE.
SHALL WE, GREGORY?
I'M COMING, I'VE JUST GOT SOMETHING TO TAKE CARE OF HERE FIRST!
I'M WARNING YOU, I'M NOT GOING TO WAIT FOR YOU!
RIGHT, BOOK COPYCAT, YOU CAN GET STARTED WITHOUT ME!
COME NOW, PRINCESS, AND DON'T FORGET YOUR BOOK!
GET BACK, EDNA!
WE'RE ALL COUNTING ON YOU!
NO!
WAIT, CHLOE!
SEE YOU LATER, LITTLE BROTHER!

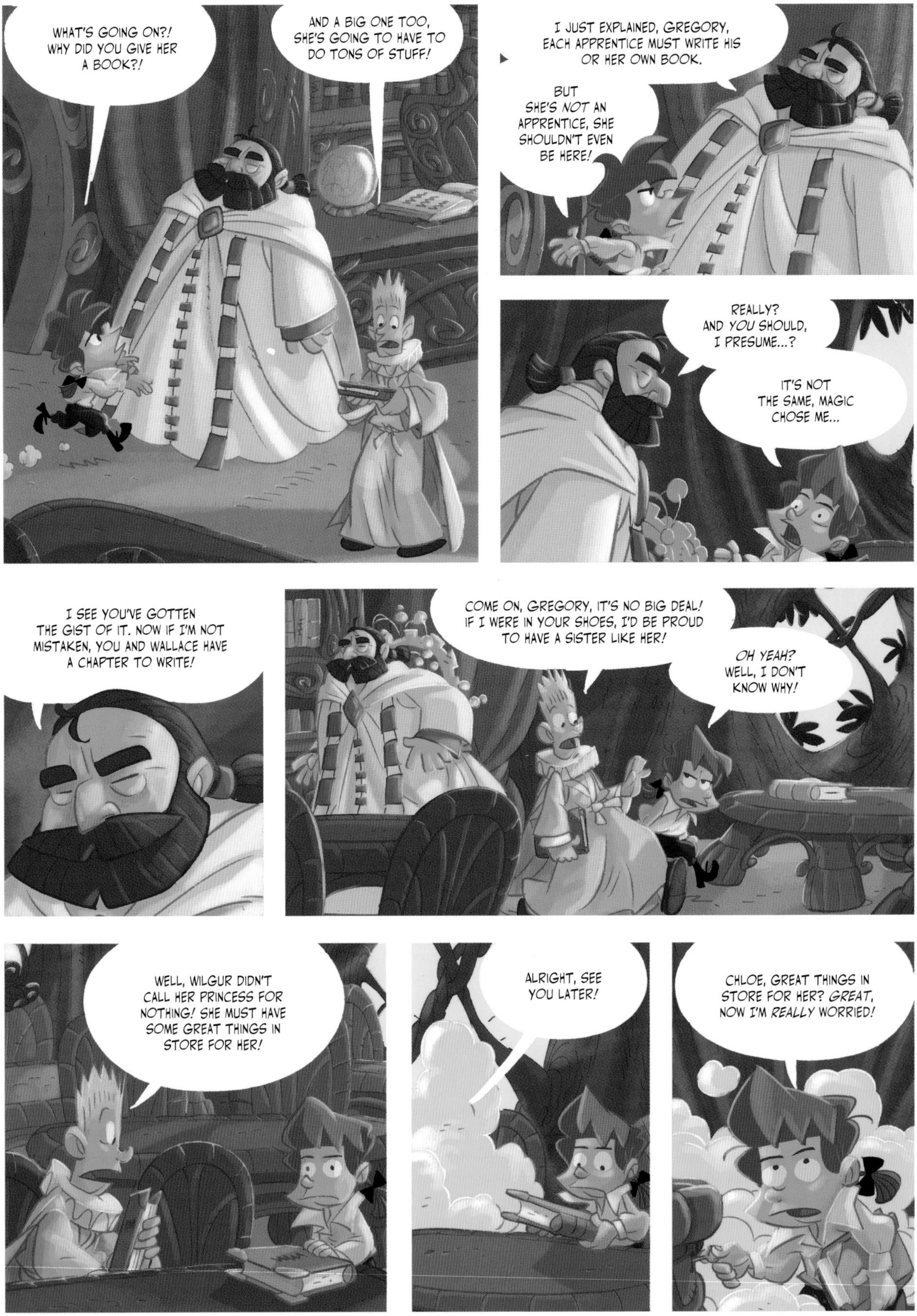
WHAT'S GOING ON?! WHY DID YOU GIVE HER A BOOK?!
AND A BIG ONE TOO, SHE'S GOING TO HAVE TO DO TONS OF STUFF!
I JUST EXPLAINED, GREGORY, EACH APPRENTICE MUST WRITE HIS OR HER OWN BOOK.
BUT SHE'S *NOT* AN APPRENTICE, SHE SHOULDN'T EVEN BE HERE!
REALLY? AND *YOU* SHOULD, I PRESUME...?
IT'S NOT THE SAME, MAGIC CHOSE ME...
I SEE YOU'VE GOTTEN THE GIST OF IT. NOW IF I'M NOT MISTAKEN, YOU AND WALLACE HAVE A CHAPTER TO WRITE!
COME ON, GREGORY, IT'S NO BIG DEAL! IF I WERE IN YOUR SHOES, I'D BE PROUD TO HAVE A SISTER LIKE HER!
OH YEAH? WELL, I DON'T KNOW WHY!
WELL, WILGUR DIDN'T CALL HER PRINCESS FOR NOTHING! SHE MUST HAVE SOME GREAT THINGS IN STORE FOR HER!
ALRIGHT, SEE YOU LATER!
CHLOE, GREAT THINGS IN STORE FOR HER? *GREAT*, NOW I'M *REALLY* WORRIED!

HEY!

OKAY, BUT DON'T STRAY TOO FAR! WHERE DID SHE GO? EDNA?! EDNA...!

EEERK! EEERK! EEERK!

NOW SHE'S REALLY DONE IT, AND SHE DIDN'T EVEN WAIT FOR ME! *MMH...?*

AAAH!

EEERK! EEERK! EEERK!

THOSE ARE FULIGINOUS GRIFFINS! I FEEL SORRY FOR THEIR CAPTIVES...

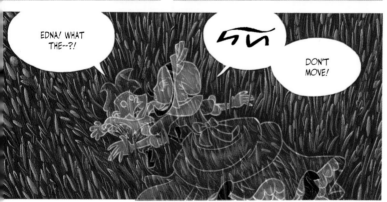

EDNA! WHAT THE--?!

DON'T MOVE!

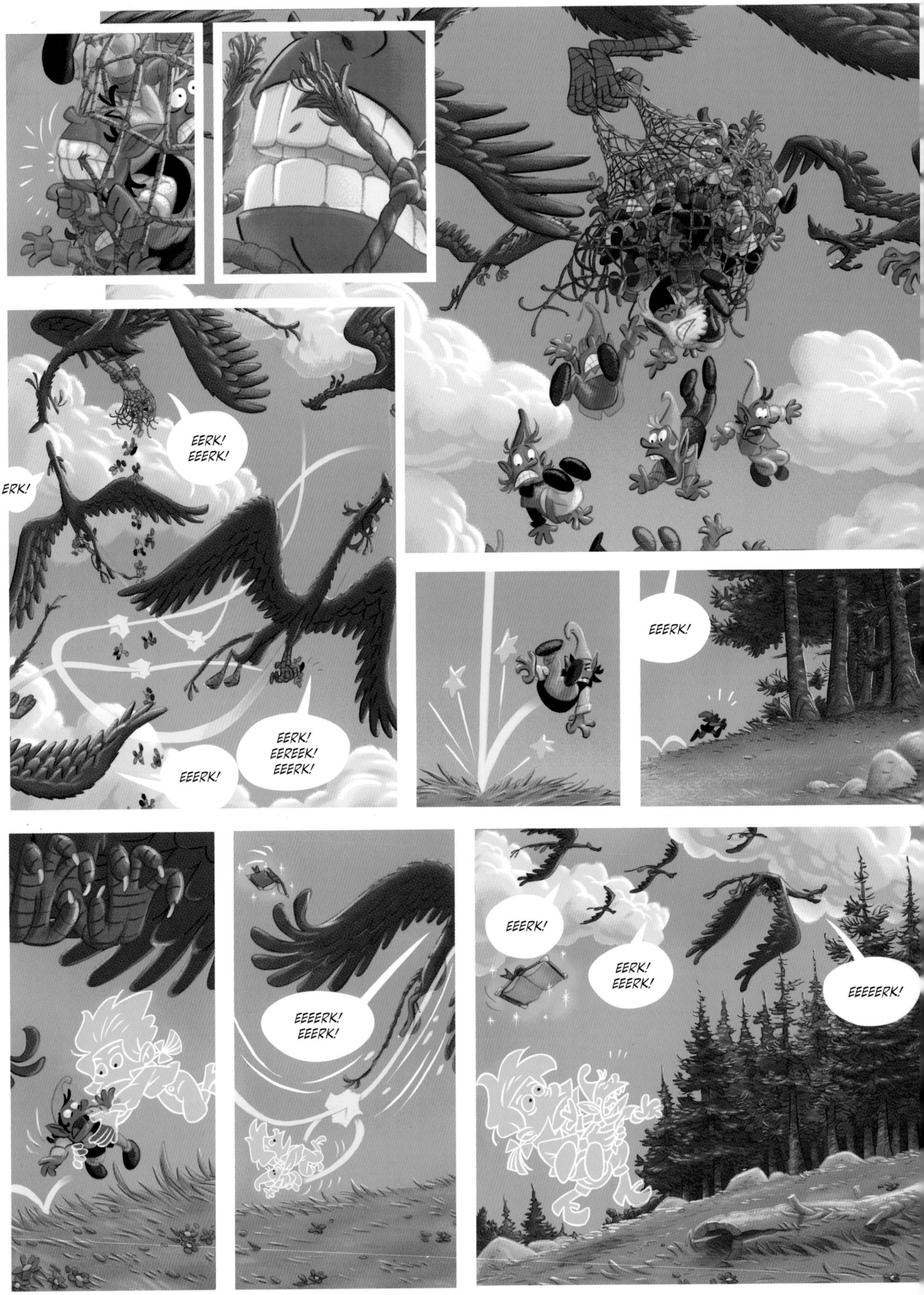

EERK!
EEERK!
ERK!
EERK!
EEREEK!
EEERK!
EEERK!
EEERK!
EEEERK!
EEERK!
EEERK!
EERK!
EEERK!
EEEEERK!

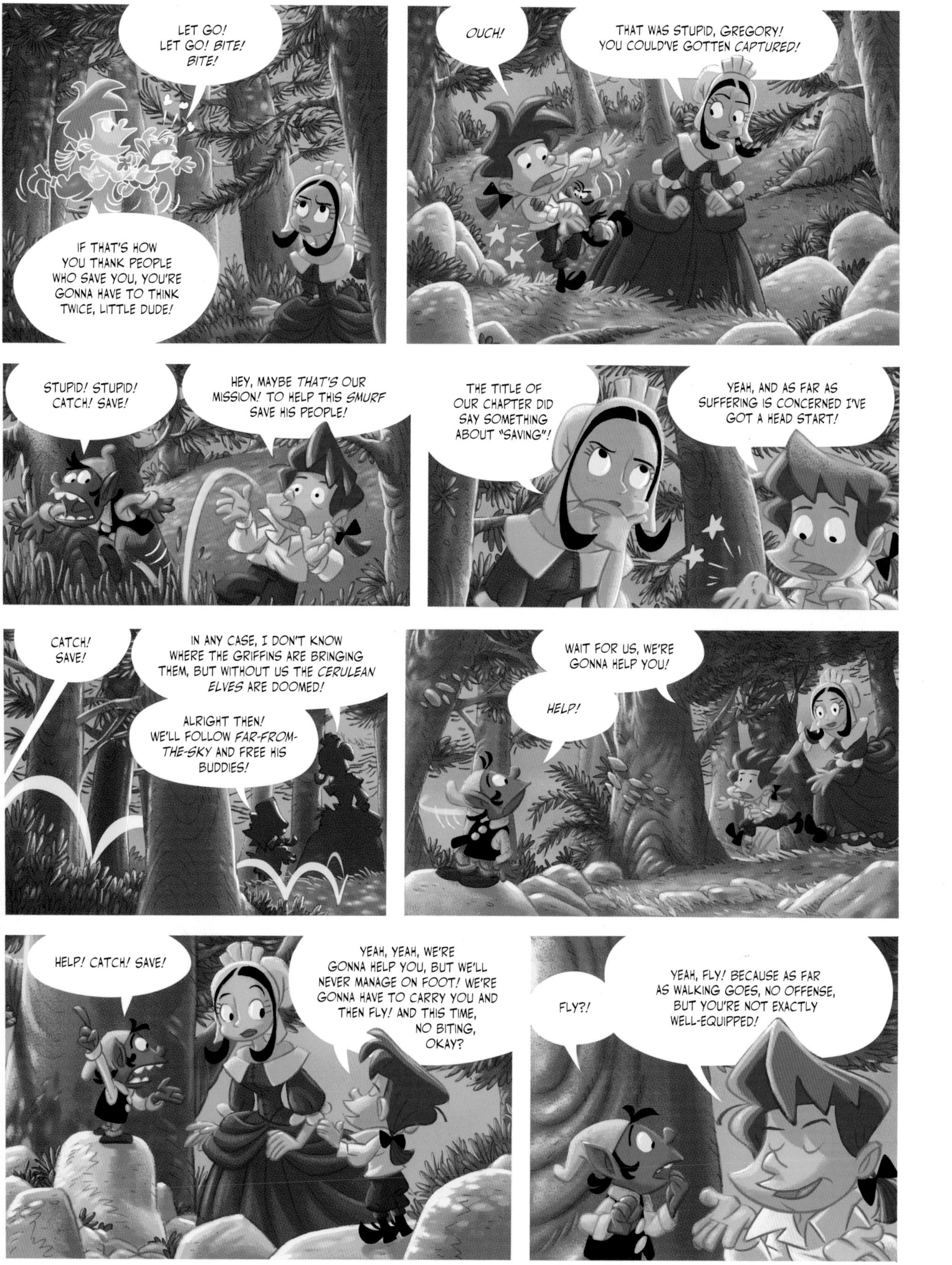

LET GO! LET GO! BITE! BITE!
IF THAT'S HOW YOU THANK PEOPLE WHO SAVE YOU, YOU'RE GONNA HAVE TO THINK TWICE, LITTLE DUDE!
OUCH!
THAT WAS STUPID, GREGORY! YOU COULD'VE GOTTEN CAPTURED!
STUPID! STUPID! CATCH! SAVE!
HEY, MAYBE THAT'S OUR MISSION! TO HELP THIS SMURF SAVE HIS PEOPLE!
THE TITLE OF OUR CHAPTER DID SAY SOMETHING ABOUT "SAVING"!
YEAH, AND AS FAR AS SUFFERING IS CONCERNED I'VE GOT A HEAD START!
CATCH! SAVE!
IN ANY CASE, I DON'T KNOW WHERE THE GRIFFINS ARE BRINGING THEM, BUT WITHOUT US THE CERULEAN ELVES ARE DOOMED!
ALRIGHT THEN! WE'LL FOLLOW FAR-FROM-THE-SKY AND FREE HIS BUDDIES!
WAIT FOR US, WE'RE GONNA HELP YOU!
HELP!
HELP! CATCH! SAVE!
YEAH, YEAH, WE'RE GONNA HELP YOU, BUT WE'LL NEVER MANAGE ON FOOT! WE'RE GONNA HAVE TO CARRY YOU AND THEN FLY! AND THIS TIME, NO BITING, OKAY?
FLY?!
YEAH, FLY! BECAUSE AS FAR AS WALKING GOES, NO OFFENSE, BUT YOU'RE NOT EXACTLY WELL-EQUIPPED!

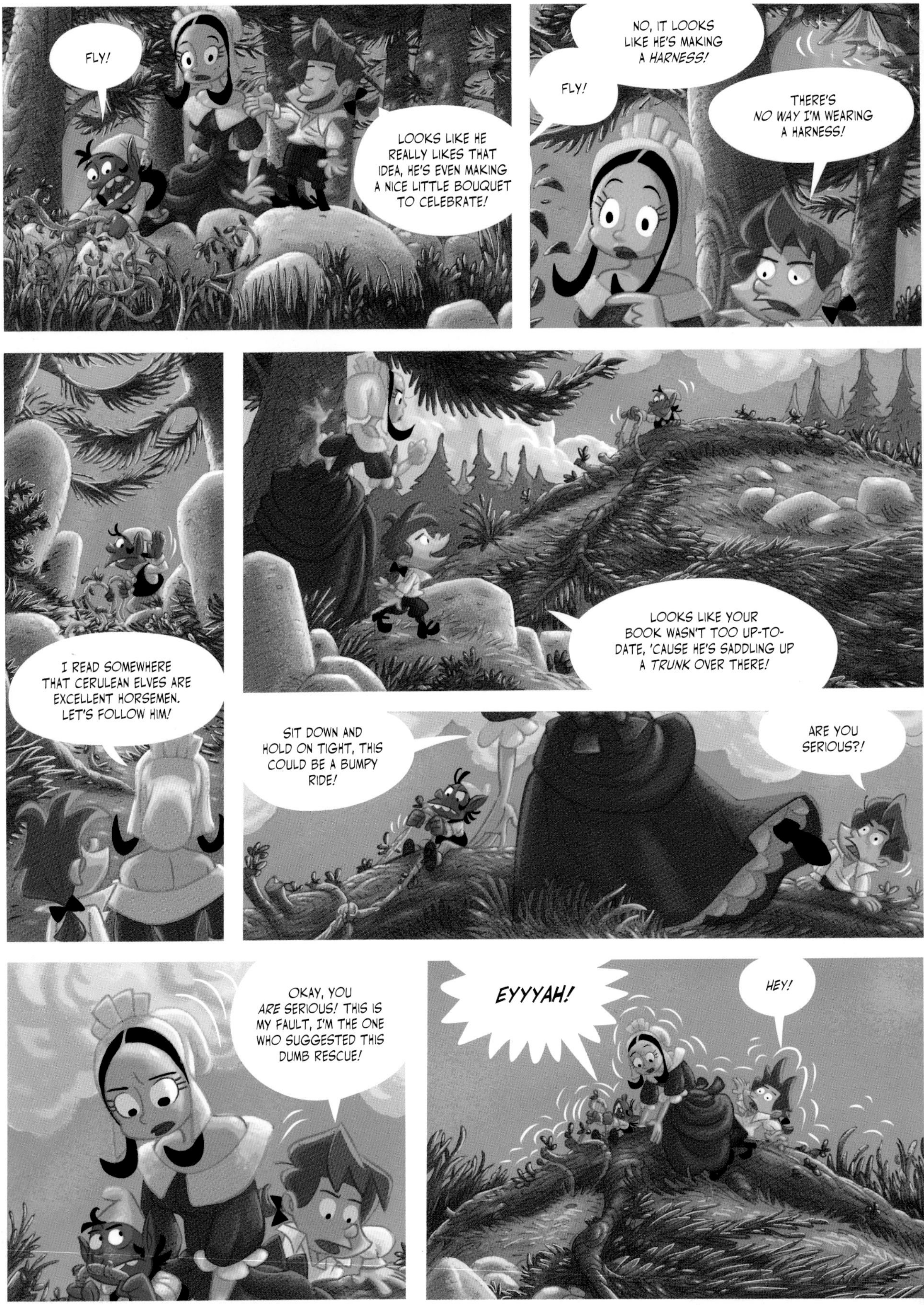
FLY!
LOOKS LIKE HE REALLY LIKES THAT IDEA, HE'S EVEN MAKING A NICE LITTLE BOUQUET TO CELEBRATE!
FLY!
NO, IT LOOKS LIKE HE'S MAKING A *HARNESS!*
THERE'S *NO WAY* I'M WEARING A HARNESS!
I READ SOMEWHERE THAT CERULEAN ELVES ARE EXCELLENT HORSEMEN. LET'S FOLLOW HIM!
LOOKS LIKE YOUR BOOK WASN'T TOO UP-TO-DATE, 'CAUSE HE'S SADDLING UP A *TRUNK* OVER THERE!
SIT DOWN AND HOLD ON TIGHT, THIS COULD BE A BUMPY RIDE!
ARE YOU SERIOUS?!
OKAY, YOU *ARE SERIOUS!* THIS IS MY FAULT, I'M THE ONE WHO SUGGESTED THIS DUMB RESCUE!
EYYYAH!
HEY!

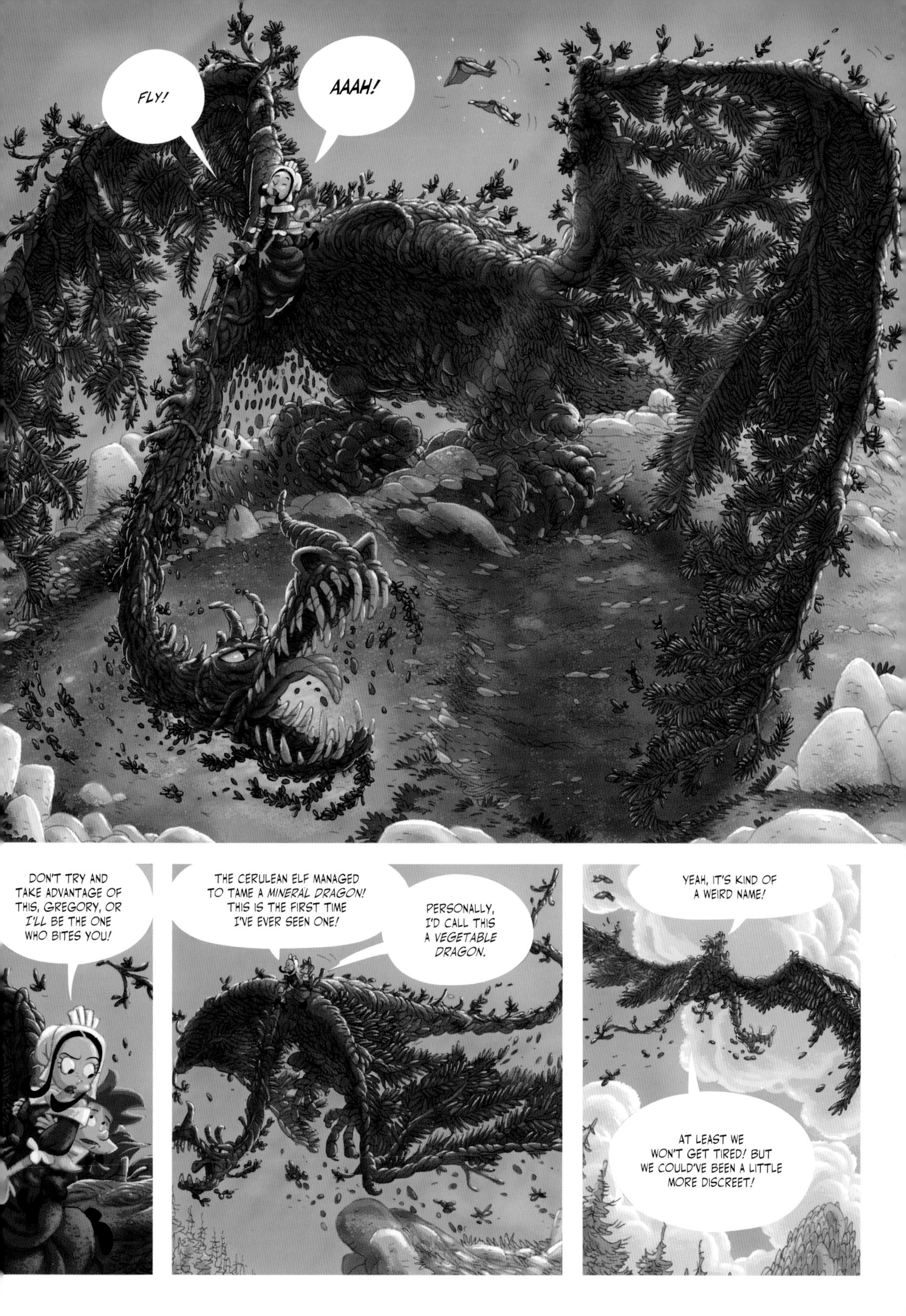
FLY!
AAAH!
DON'T TRY AND TAKE ADVANTAGE OF THIS, GREGORY, OR *I'LL* BE THE ONE WHO BITES YOU!
THE CERULEAN ELF MANAGED TO TAME A *MINERAL DRAGON!* THIS IS THE FIRST TIME I'VE EVER SEEN ONE!
PERSONALLY, I'D CALL THIS A *VEGETABLE DRAGON.*
YEAH, IT'S KIND OF A WEIRD NAME!
AT LEAST WE WON'T GET TIRED! BUT WE COULD'VE BEEN A LITTLE MORE DISCREET!

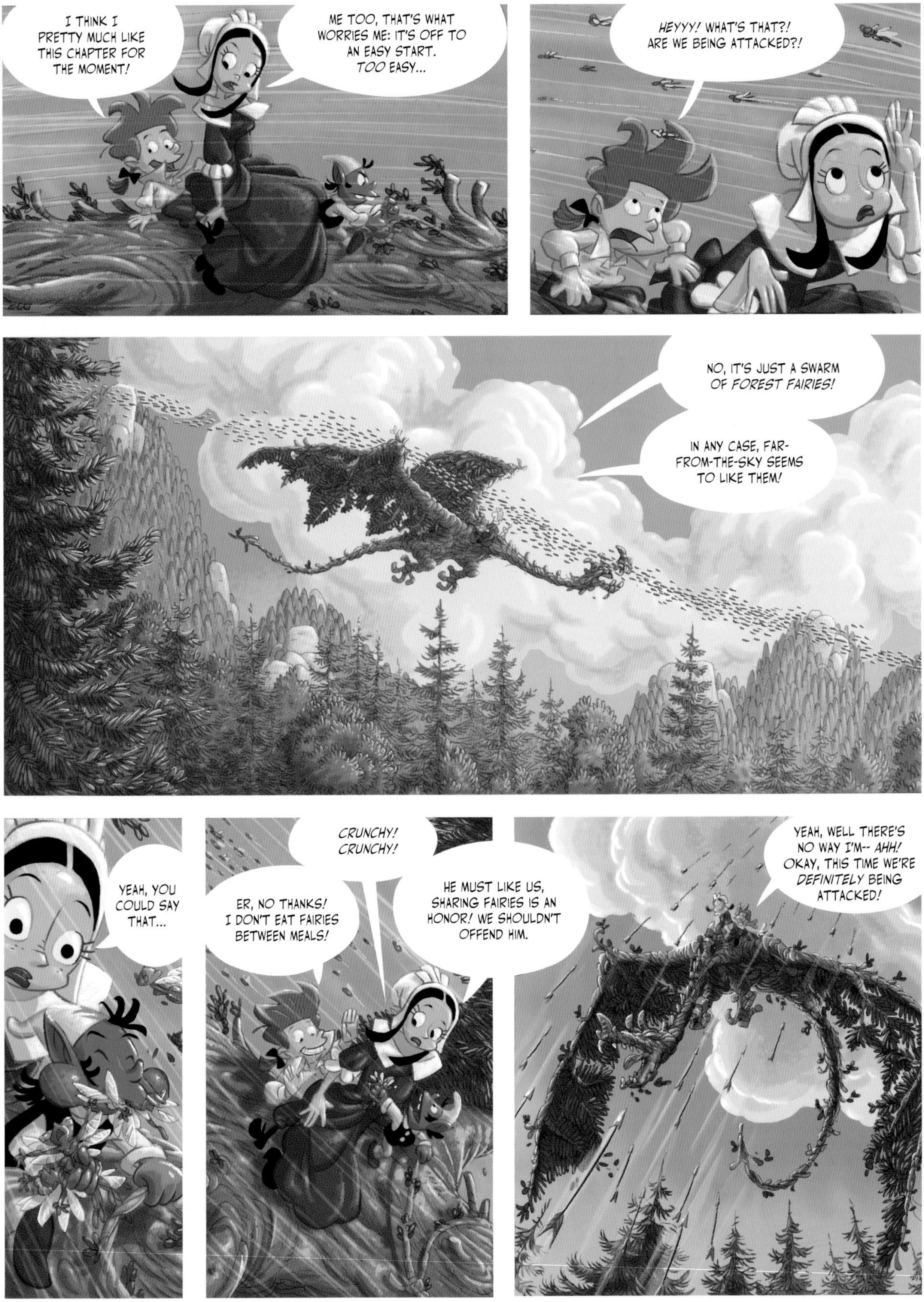
I THINK I PRETTY MUCH LIKE THIS CHAPTER FOR THE MOMENT!
ME TOO, THAT'S WHAT WORRIES ME: IT'S OFF TO AN EASY START. TOO EASY...
HEYYY! WHAT'S THAT?! ARE WE BEING ATTACKED?!
NO, IT'S JUST A SWARM OF FOREST FAIRIES!
IN ANY CASE, FAR-FROM-THE-SKY SEEMS TO LIKE THEM!
YEAH, YOU COULD SAY THAT...
CRUNCHY! CRUNCHY!
ER, NO THANKS! I DON'T EAT FAIRIES BETWEEN MEALS!
HE MUST LIKE US, SHARING FAIRIES IS AN HONOR! WE SHOULDN'T OFFEND HIM.
YEAH, WELL THERE'S NO WAY I'M-- AHH! OKAY, THIS TIME WE'RE DEFINITELY BEING ATTACKED!

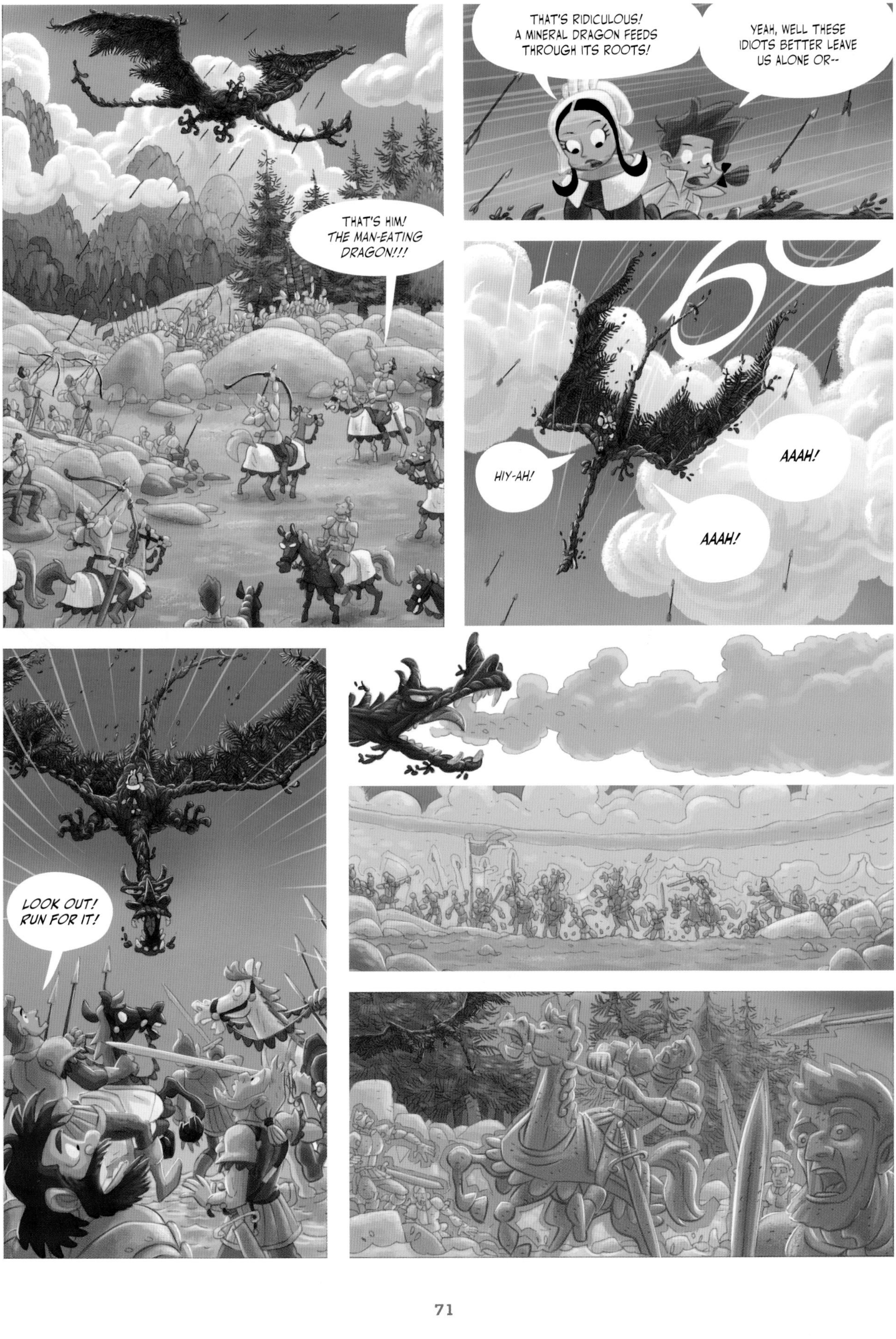
THAT'S HIM! THE MAN-EATING DRAGON!!!
THAT'S RIDICULOUS! A MINERAL DRAGON FEEDS THROUGH ITS ROOTS!
YEAH, WELL THESE IDIOTS BETTER LEAVE US ALONE OR--
HIY-AH!
AAAH!
AAAH!
LOOK OUT! RUN FOR IT!

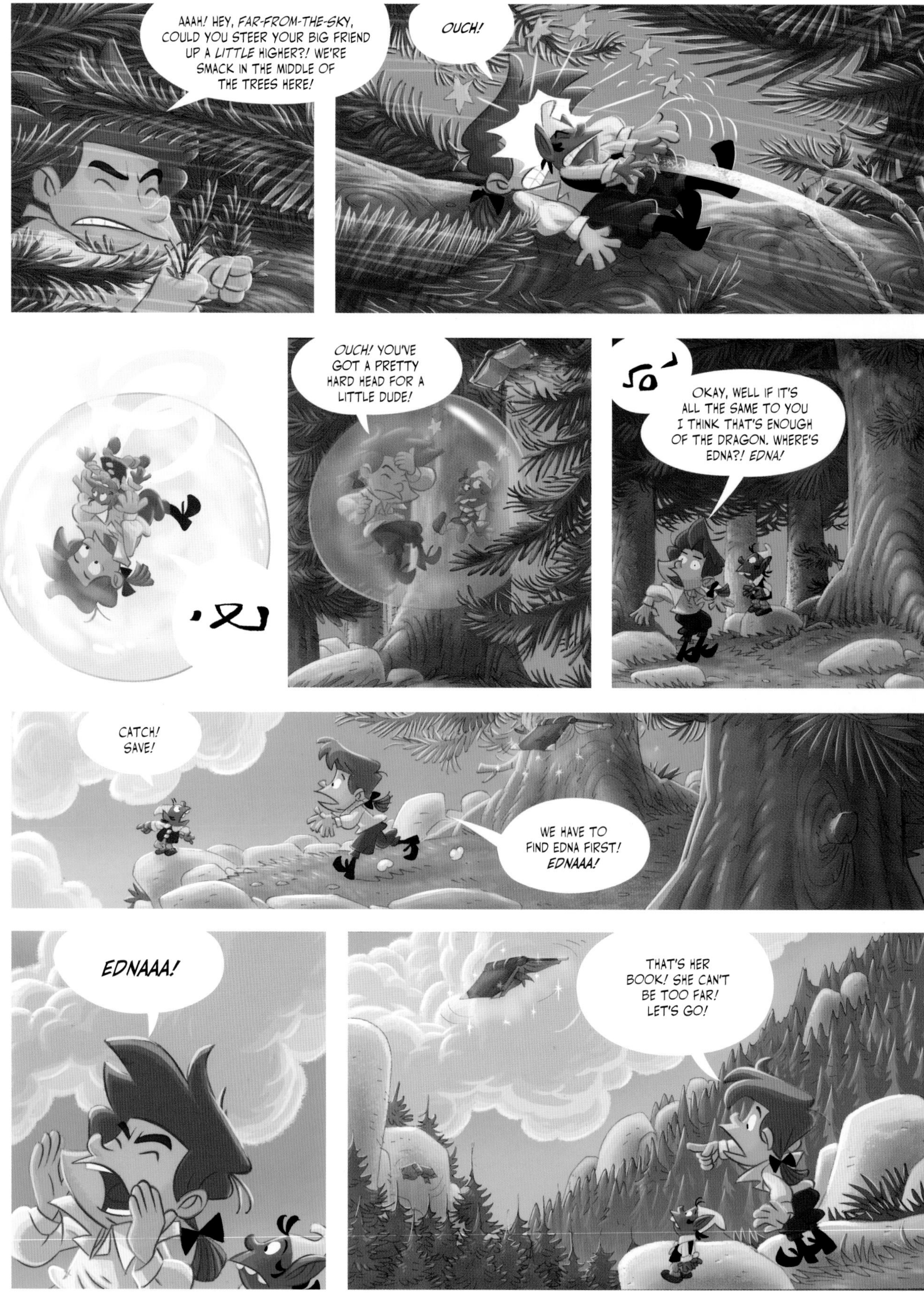
AAAH! HEY, *FAR-FROM-THE-SKY*, COULD YOU STEER YOUR BIG FRIEND UP A *LITTLE* HIGHER?! WE'RE SMACK IN THE MIDDLE OF THE TREES HERE!
OUCH!
OUCH! YOU'VE GOT A PRETTY HARD HEAD FOR A LITTLE DUDE!
OKAY, WELL IF IT'S ALL THE SAME TO YOU I THINK THAT'S ENOUGH OF THE DRAGON. WHERE'S EDNA?! *EDNA!*
CATCH! SAVE!
WE HAVE TO FIND EDNA FIRST! *EDNAAA!*
EDNAAA!
THAT'S HER BOOK! SHE CAN'T BE TOO FAR! LET'S GO!

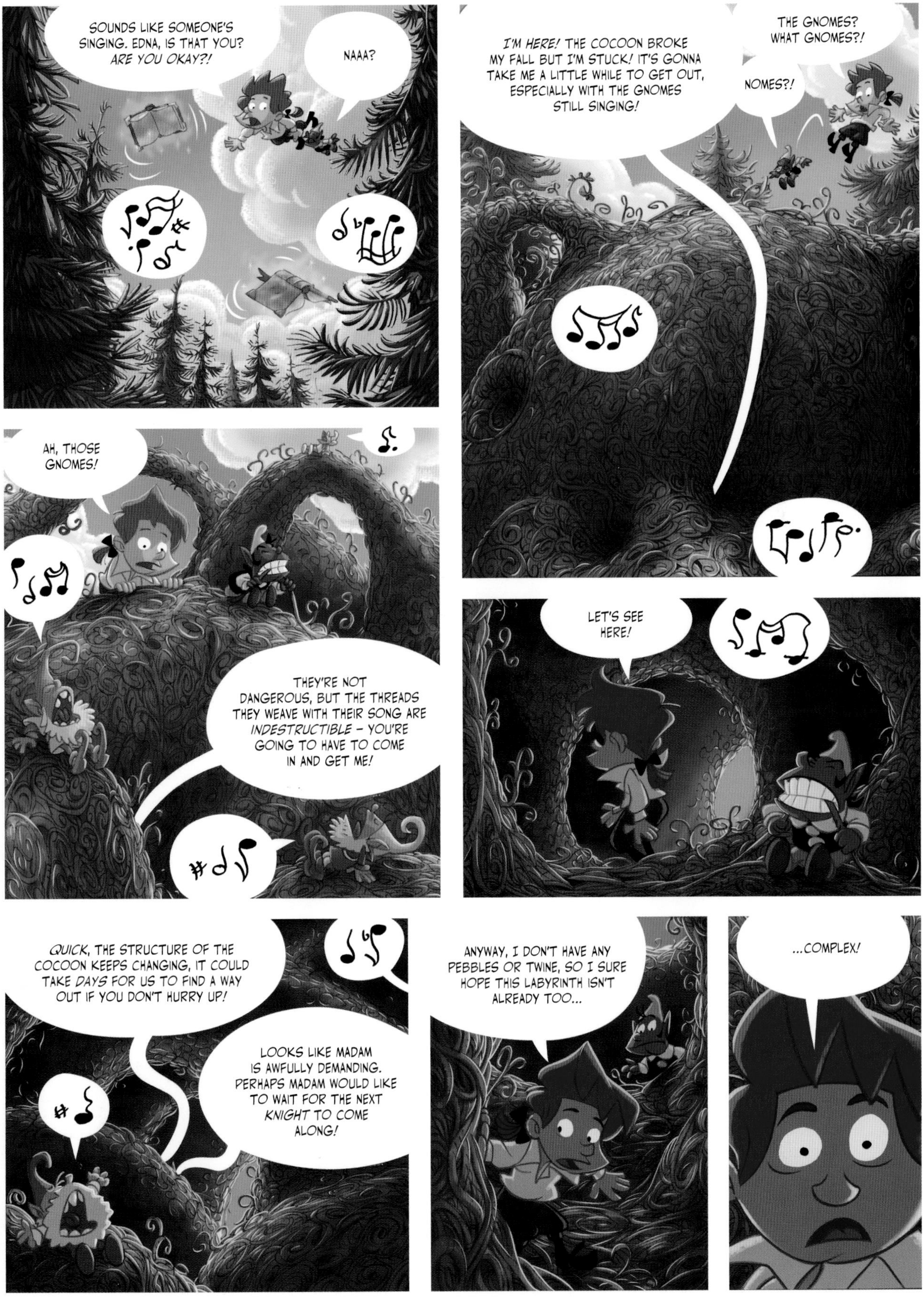
SOUNDS LIKE SOMEONE'S SINGING. EDNA, IS THAT YOU? *ARE YOU OKAY?!*
NAAA?
I'M HERE! THE COCOON BROKE MY FALL BUT I'M STUCK! IT'S GONNA TAKE ME A LITTLE WHILE TO GET OUT, ESPECIALLY WITH THE GNOMES STILL SINGING!
THE GNOMES? WHAT GNOMES?!
NOMES?!
AH, THOSE GNOMES!
THEY'RE NOT DANGEROUS, BUT THE THREADS THEY WEAVE WITH THEIR SONG ARE *INDESTRUCTIBLE* – YOU'RE GOING TO HAVE TO COME IN AND GET ME!
LET'S SEE HERE!
QUICK, THE STRUCTURE OF THE COCOON KEEPS CHANGING, IT COULD TAKE *DAYS* FOR US TO FIND A WAY OUT IF YOU DON'T HURRY UP!
LOOKS LIKE MADAM IS AWFULLY DEMANDING. PERHAPS MADAM WOULD LIKE TO WAIT FOR THE NEXT *KNIGHT* TO COME ALONG!
ANYWAY, I DON'T HAVE ANY PEBBLES OR TWINE, SO I SURE HOPE THIS LABYRINTH ISN'T ALREADY TOO...
...COMPLEX!

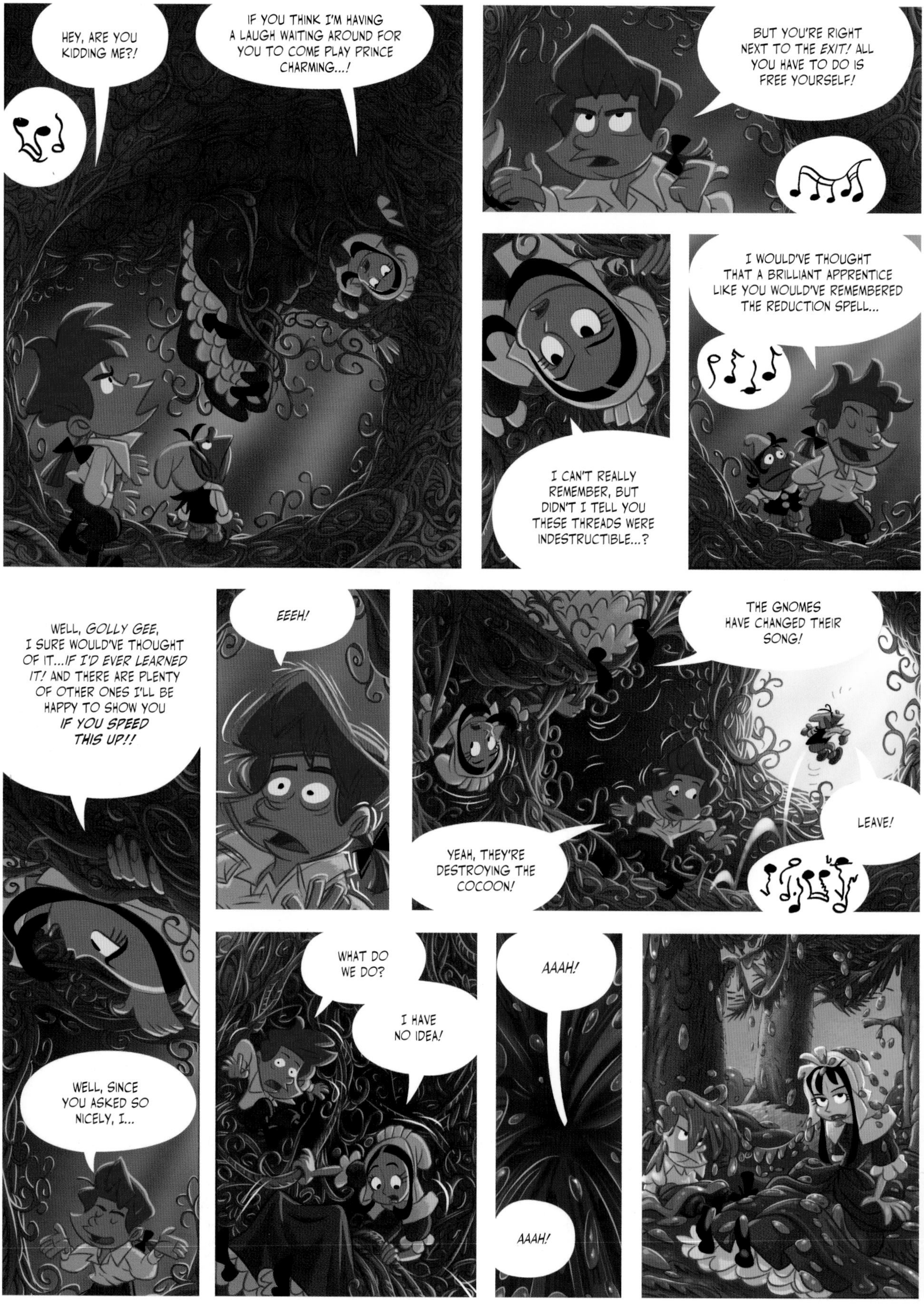
HEY, ARE YOU KIDDING ME?!
IF YOU THINK I'M HAVING A LAUGH WAITING AROUND FOR YOU TO COME PLAY PRINCE CHARMING...!
BUT YOU'RE RIGHT NEXT TO THE *EXIT!* ALL YOU HAVE TO DO IS FREE YOURSELF!
I CAN'T REALLY REMEMBER, BUT DIDN'T I TELL YOU THESE THREADS WERE INDESTRUCTIBLE...?
I WOULD'VE THOUGHT THAT A BRILLIANT APPRENTICE LIKE YOU WOULD'VE REMEMBERED THE REDUCTION SPELL...
WELL, *GOLLY GEE*, I SURE WOULD'VE THOUGHT OF IT...*IF I'D EVER LEARNED IT!* AND THERE ARE PLENTY OF OTHER ONES I'LL BE HAPPY TO SHOW YOU ***IF YOU SPEED THIS UP!!***
WELL, SINCE YOU ASKED SO NICELY, I...
EEEH!
THE GNOMES HAVE CHANGED THEIR SONG!
YEAH, THEY'RE DESTROYING THE COCOON!
LEAVE!
WHAT DO WE DO?
I HAVE NO IDEA!
AAAH!
AAAH!

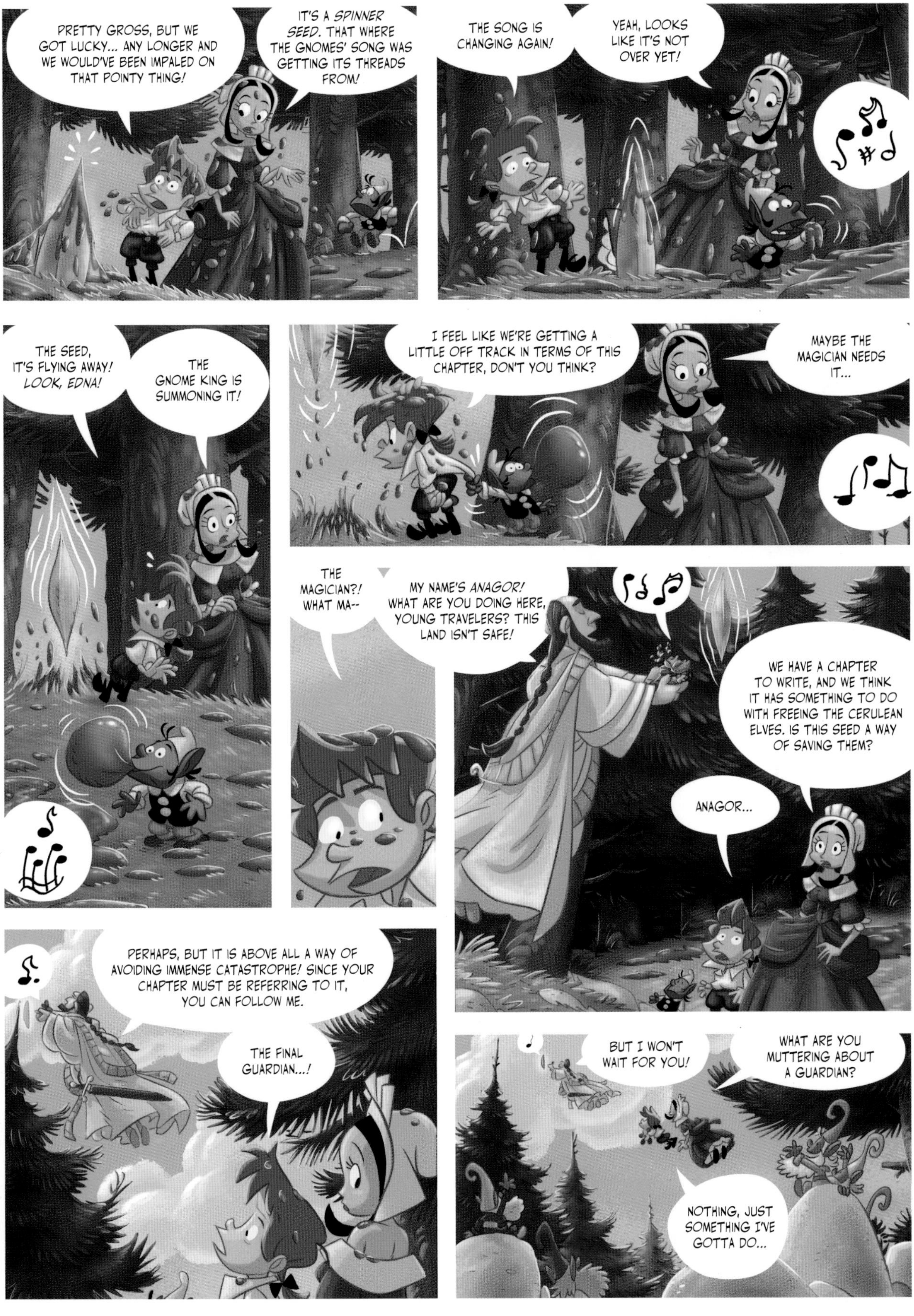

PRETTY GROSS, BUT WE GOT LUCKY... ANY LONGER AND WE WOULD'VE BEEN IMPALED ON THAT POINTY THING!
IT'S A *SPINNER SEED*. THAT WHERE THE GNOMES' SONG WAS GETTING ITS THREADS FROM!
THE SONG IS CHANGING AGAIN!
YEAH, LOOKS LIKE IT'S NOT OVER YET!
THE SEED, IT'S FLYING AWAY! *LOOK, EDNA!*
THE GNOME KING IS SUMMONING IT!
I FEEL LIKE WE'RE GETTING A LITTLE OFF TRACK IN TERMS OF THIS CHAPTER, DON'T YOU THINK?
MAYBE THE MAGICIAN NEEDS IT...
THE MAGICIAN?! WHAT MA--
MY NAME'S *ANAGOR!* WHAT ARE YOU DOING HERE, YOUNG TRAVELERS? THIS LAND ISN'T SAFE!
WE HAVE A CHAPTER TO WRITE, AND WE THINK IT HAS SOMETHING TO DO WITH FREEING THE CERULEAN ELVES. IS THIS SEED A WAY OF SAVING THEM?
ANAGOR...
PERHAPS, BUT IT IS ABOVE ALL A WAY OF AVOIDING IMMENSE CATASTROPHE! SINCE YOUR CHAPTER MUST BE REFERRING TO IT, YOU CAN FOLLOW ME.
THE FINAL GUARDIAN...!
BUT I WON'T WAIT FOR YOU!
WHAT ARE YOU MUTTERING ABOUT A GUARDIAN?
NOTHING, JUST SOMETHING I'VE GOTTA DO...

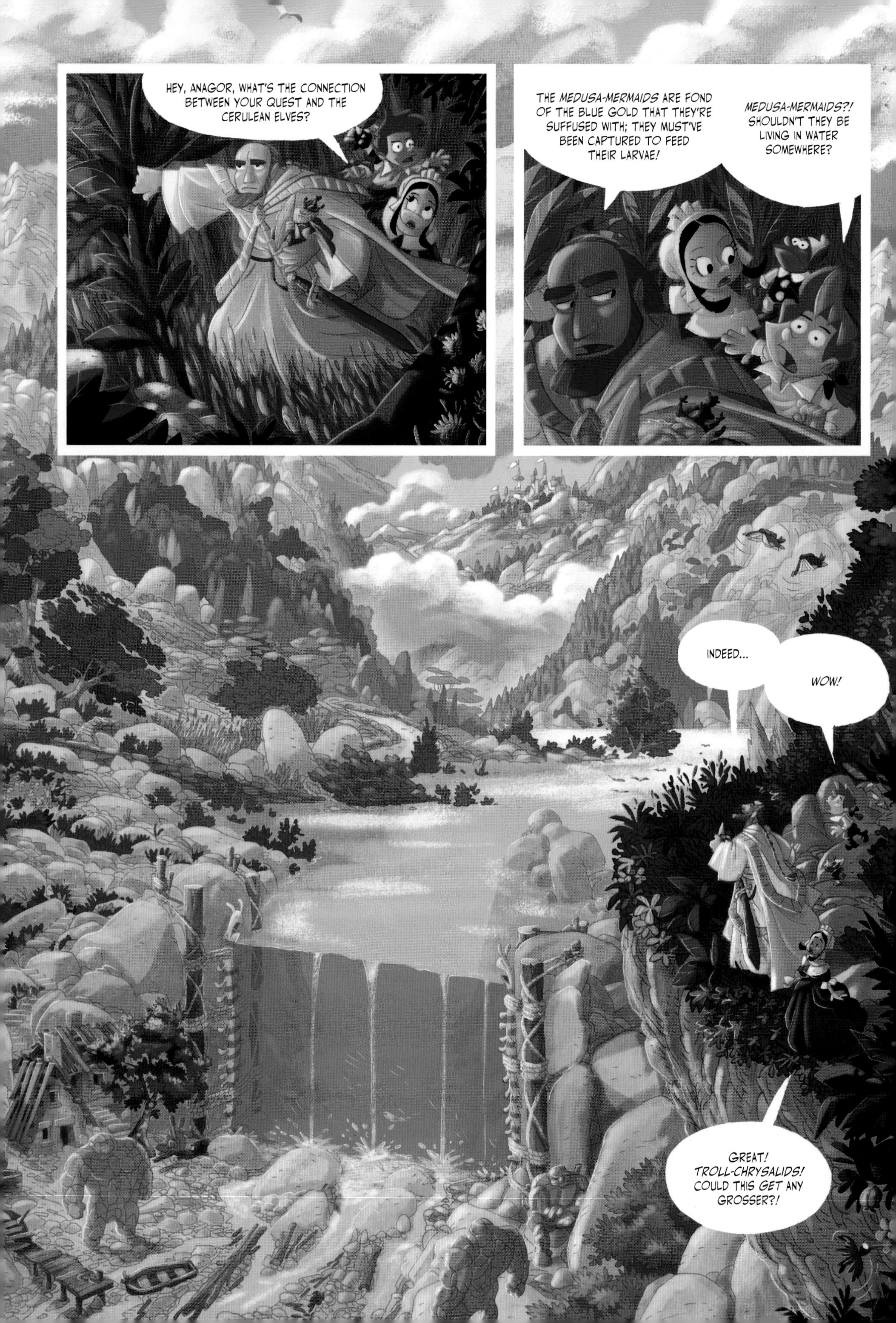
HEY, ANAGOR, WHAT'S THE CONNECTION BETWEEN YOUR QUEST AND THE CERULEAN ELVES?
THE *MEDUSA-MERMAIDS* ARE FOND OF THE BLUE GOLD THAT THEY'RE SUFFUSED WITH; THEY MUST'VE BEEN CAPTURED TO FEED THEIR LARVAE!
MEDUSA-MERMAIDS?! SHOULDN'T THEY BE LIVING IN WATER SOMEWHERE?
INDEED...
WOW!
GREAT! *TROLL-CHRYSALIDS!* COULD THIS *GET* ANY GROSSER?!

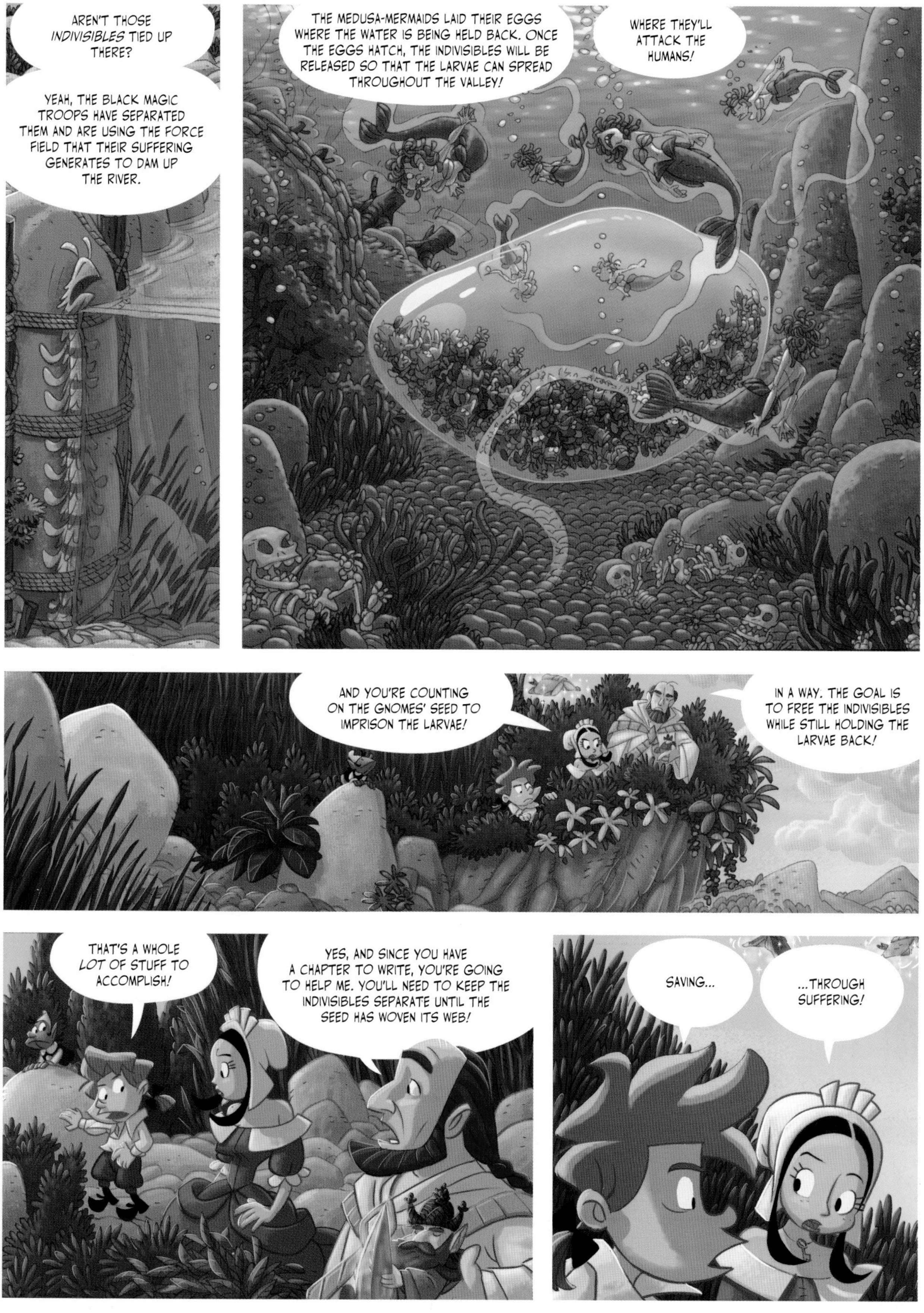
AREN'T THOSE *INDIVISIBLES* TIED UP THERE?
YEAH, THE BLACK MAGIC TROOPS HAVE SEPARATED THEM AND ARE USING THE FORCE FIELD THAT THEIR SUFFERING GENERATES TO DAM UP THE RIVER.
THE MEDUSA-MERMAIDS LAID THEIR EGGS WHERE THE WATER IS BEING HELD BACK. ONCE THE EGGS HATCH, THE INDIVISIBLES WILL BE RELEASED SO THAT THE LARVAE CAN SPREAD THROUGHOUT THE VALLEY!
WHERE THEY'LL ATTACK THE HUMANS!
AND YOU'RE COUNTING ON THE GNOMES' SEED TO IMPRISON THE LARVAE!
IN A WAY. THE GOAL IS TO FREE THE INDIVISIBLES WHILE STILL HOLDING THE LARVAE BACK!
THAT'S A WHOLE *LOT* OF STUFF TO ACCOMPLISH!
YES, AND SINCE YOU HAVE A CHAPTER TO WRITE, YOU'RE GOING TO HELP ME. YOU'LL NEED TO KEEP THE INDIVISIBLES SEPARATE UNTIL THE SEED HAS WOVEN ITS WEB!
SAVING...
...THROUGH SUFFERING!

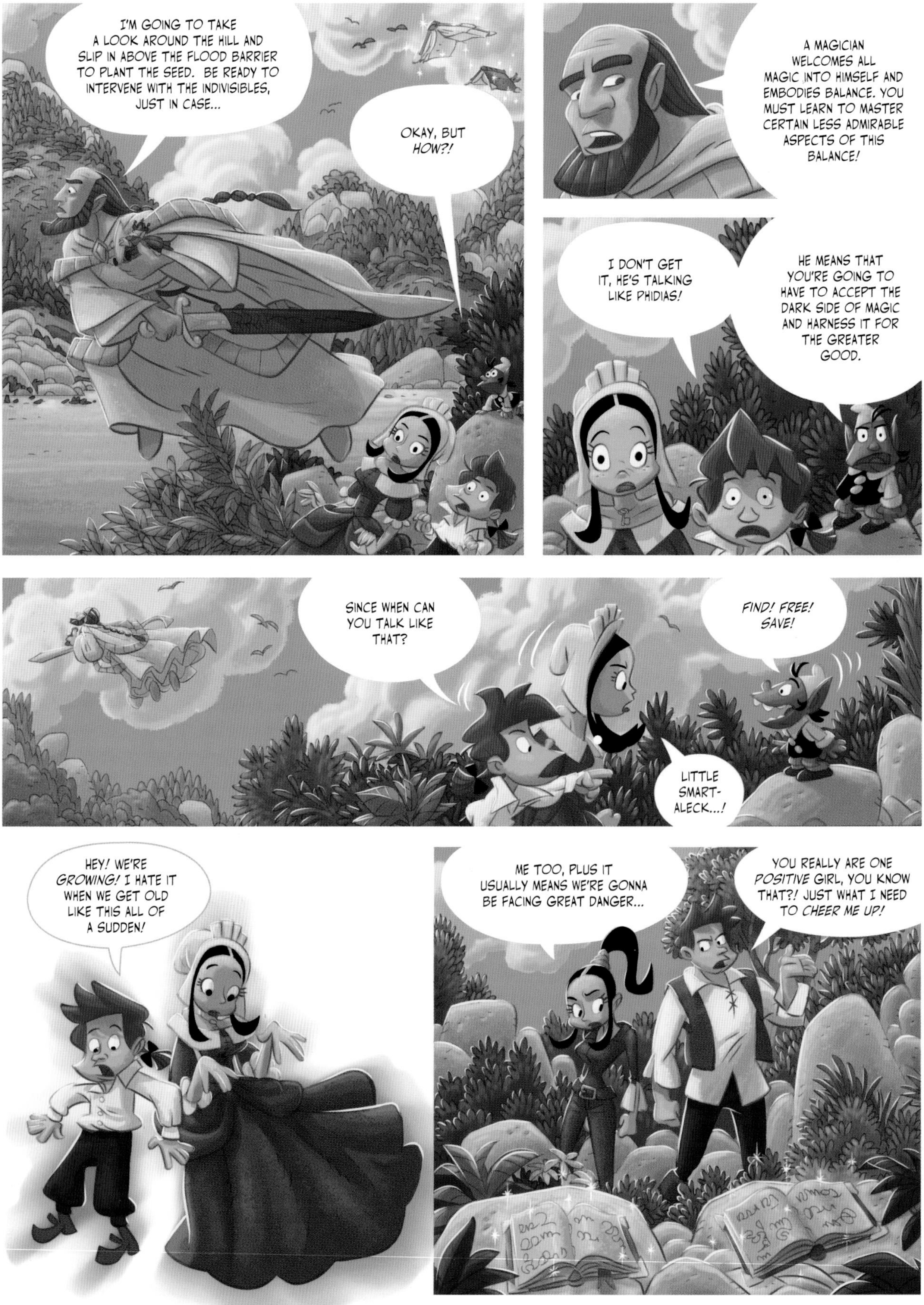

I'M GOING TO TAKE A LOOK AROUND THE HILL AND SLIP IN ABOVE THE FLOOD BARRIER TO PLANT THE SEED. BE READY TO INTERVENE WITH THE INDIVISIBLES, JUST IN CASE...
OKAY, BUT *HOW?!*
A MAGICIAN WELCOMES ALL MAGIC INTO HIMSELF AND EMBODIES BALANCE. YOU MUST LEARN TO MASTER CERTAIN LESS ADMIRABLE ASPECTS OF THIS BALANCE!
I DON'T GET IT, HE'S TALKING LIKE PHIDIAS!
HE MEANS THAT YOU'RE GOING TO HAVE TO ACCEPT THE DARK SIDE OF MAGIC AND HARNESS IT FOR THE GREATER GOOD.
SINCE WHEN CAN YOU TALK LIKE THAT?
FIND! FREE! SAVE!
LITTLE SMART-ALECK...!
HEY! WE'RE *GROWING!* I HATE IT WHEN WE GET OLD LIKE THIS ALL OF A SUDDEN!
ME TOO, PLUS IT USUALLY MEANS WE'RE GONNA BE FACING GREAT DANGER...
YOU REALLY ARE ONE *POSITIVE* GIRL, YOU KNOW THAT?! JUST WHAT I NEED TO *CHEER ME UP!*

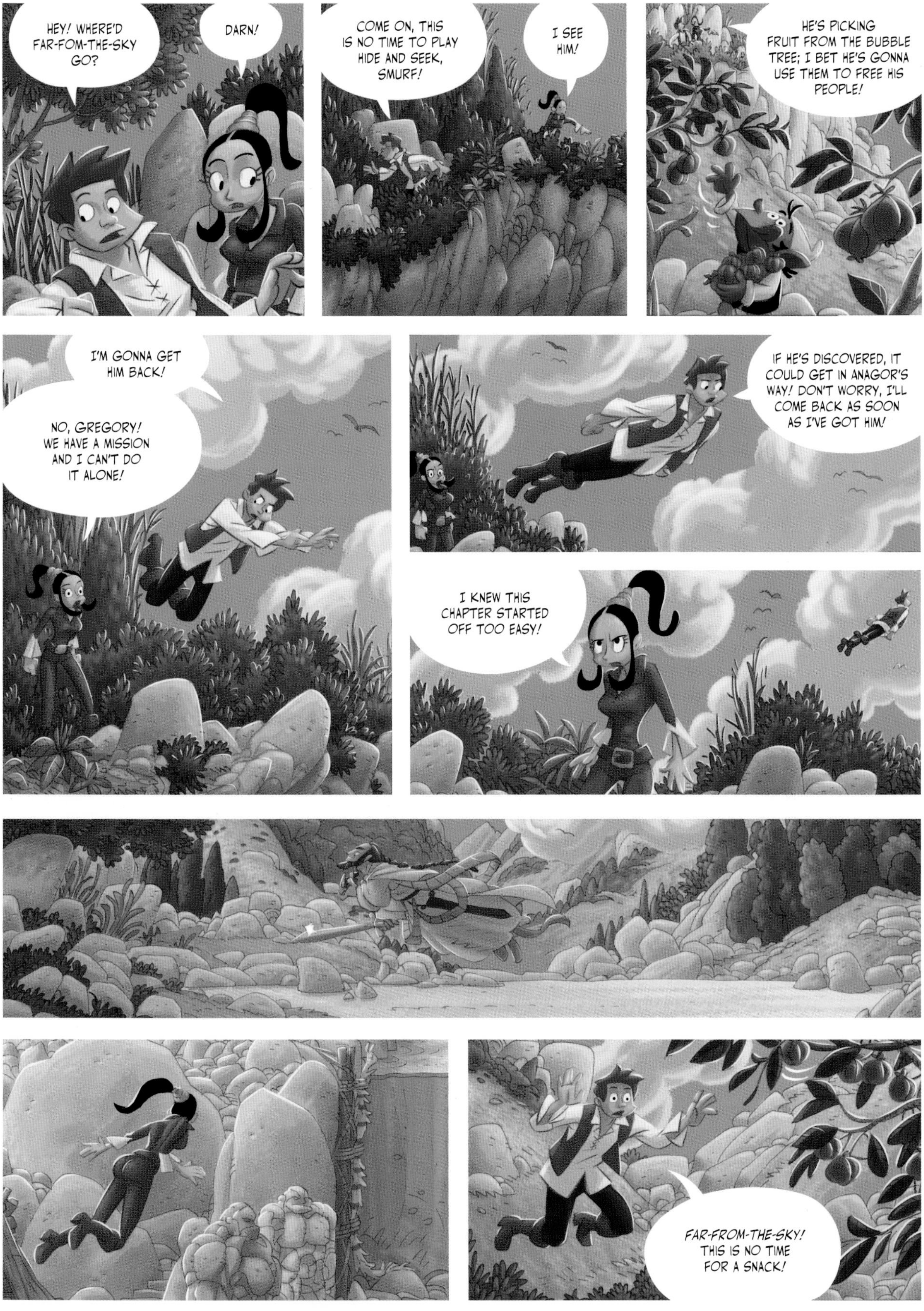
HEY! WHERE'D FAR-FOM-THE-SKY GO?
DARN!
COME ON, THIS IS NO TIME TO PLAY HIDE AND SEEK, SMURF!
I SEE HIM!
HE'S PICKING FRUIT FROM THE BUBBLE TREE; I BET HE'S GONNA USE THEM TO FREE HIS PEOPLE!
I'M GONNA GET HIM BACK!
NO, GREGORY! WE HAVE A MISSION AND I CAN'T DO IT ALONE!
IF HE'S DISCOVERED, IT COULD GET IN ANAGOR'S WAY! DON'T WORRY, I'LL COME BACK AS SOON AS I'VE GOT HIM!
I KNEW THIS CHAPTER STARTED OFF TOO EASY!
FAR-FROM-THE-SKY! THIS IS NO TIME FOR A SNACK!

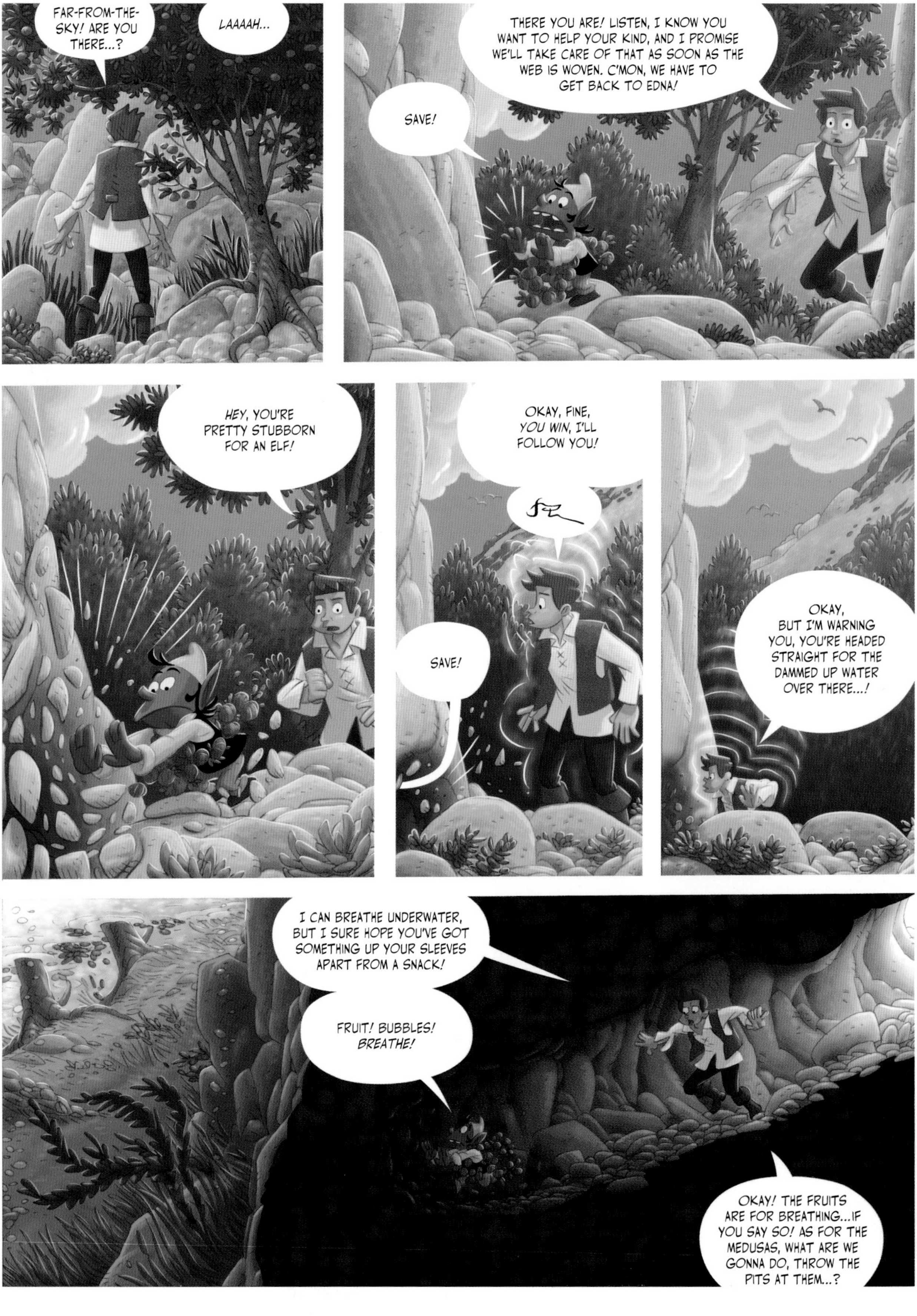
FAR-FROM-THE-SKY! ARE YOU THERE...?
LAAAAH...
THERE YOU ARE! LISTEN, I KNOW YOU WANT TO HELP YOUR KIND, AND I PROMISE WE'LL TAKE CARE OF THAT AS SOON AS THE WEB IS WOVEN. C'MON, WE HAVE TO GET BACK TO EDNA!
SAVE!
HEY, YOU'RE PRETTY STUBBORN FOR AN ELF!
OKAY, FINE, YOU WIN, I'LL FOLLOW YOU!
SAVE!
OKAY, BUT I'M WARNING YOU, YOU'RE HEADED STRAIGHT FOR THE DAMMED UP WATER OVER THERE...!
I CAN BREATHE UNDERWATER, BUT I SURE HOPE YOU'VE GOT SOMETHING UP YOUR SLEEVES APART FROM A SNACK!
FRUIT! BUBBLES! BREATHE!
OKAY! THE FRUITS ARE FOR BREATHING...IF YOU SAY SO! AS FOR THE MEDUSAS, WHAT ARE WE GONNA DO, THROW THE PITS AT THEM...?

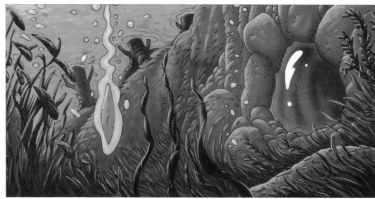
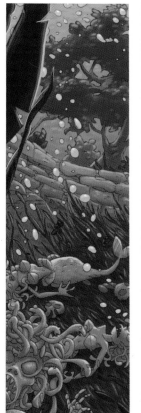

COME ON, COME ON, LITTLE DUDES! I WAS ABLE TO FREEZE THOSE ONES, BUT THE NOVELTY'S GONNA WEAR OFF PRETTY SOON!

I HOPE EDNA IS OKAY WITHOUT ME...

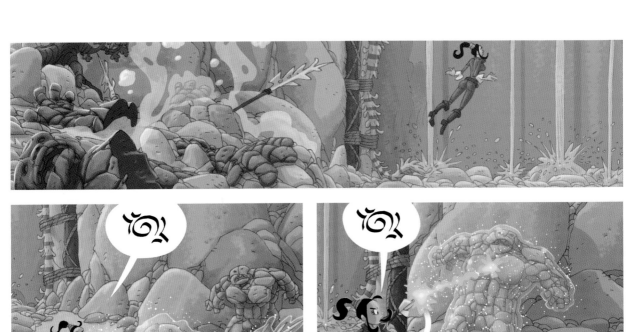

NOW HURRY UP, GREGORY!

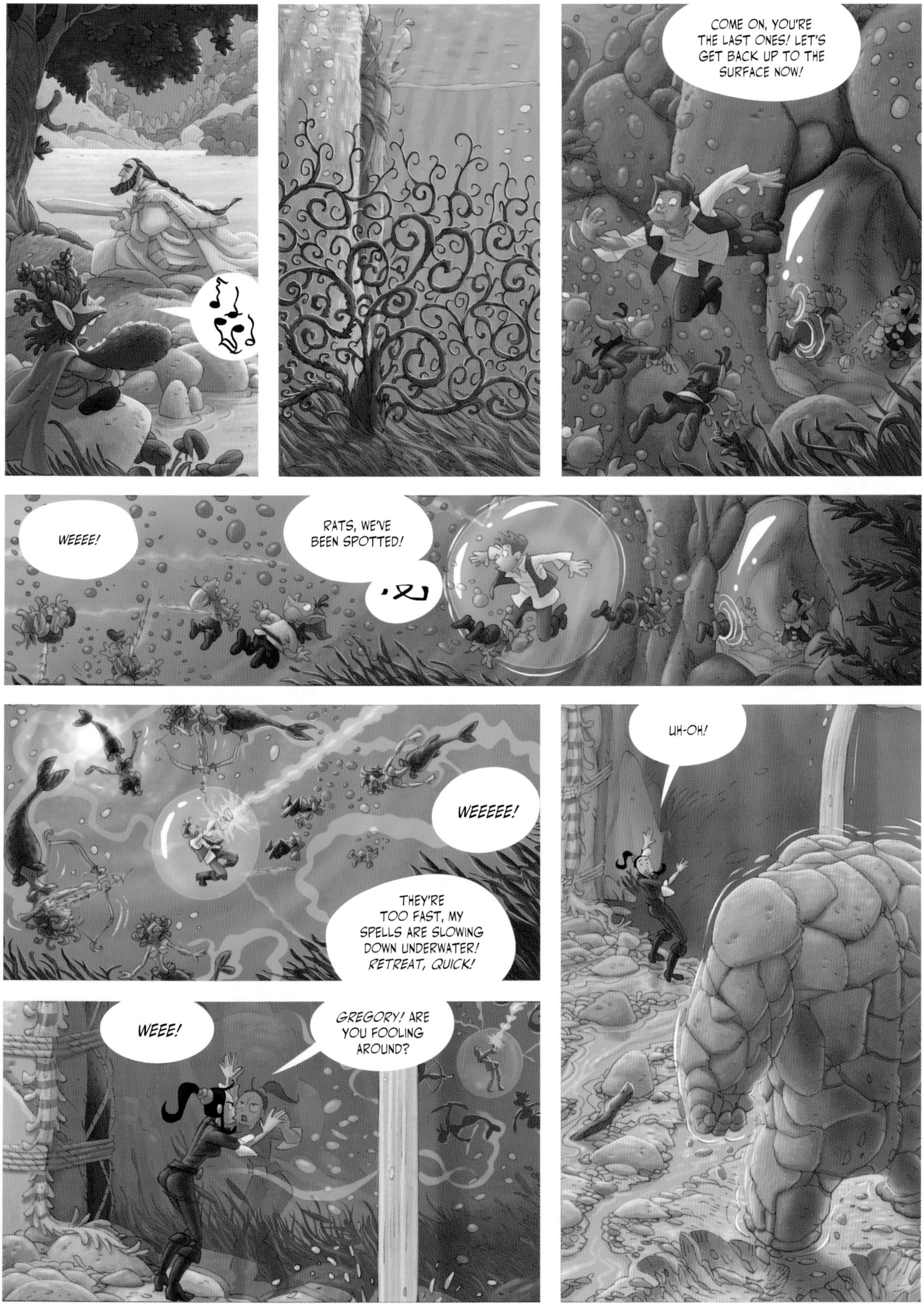
COME ON, YOU'RE THE LAST ONES! LET'S GET BACK UP TO THE SURFACE NOW!
WEEEE!
RATS, WE'VE BEEN SPOTTED!
WEEEEE!
THEY'RE TOO FAST, MY SPELLS ARE SLOWING DOWN UNDERWATER! RETREAT, QUICK!
WEEE!
GREGORY! ARE YOU FOOLING AROUND?
UH-OH!

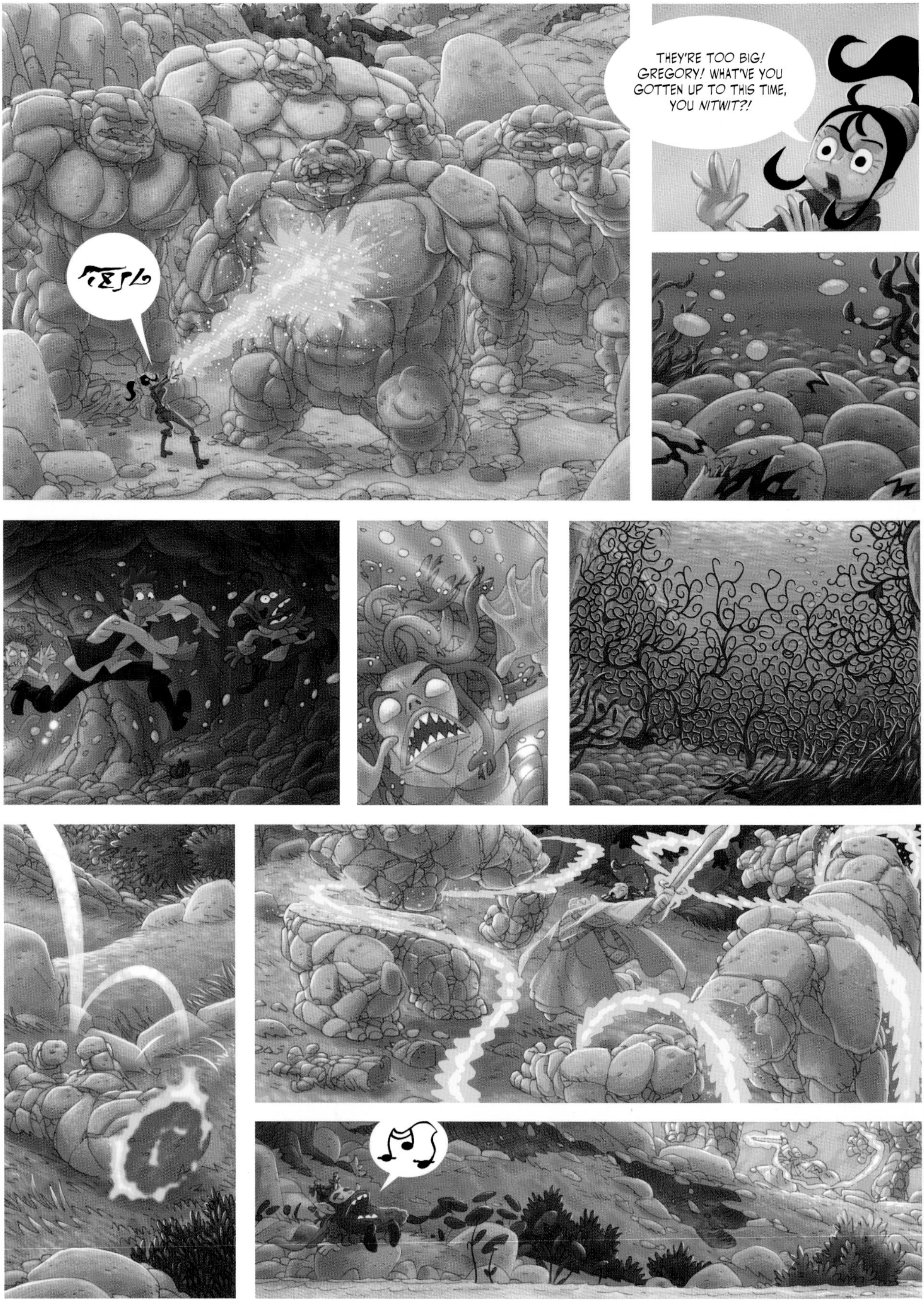
THEY'RE TOO BIG! GREGORY! WHAT'VE YOU GOTTEN UP TO THIS TIME, YOU NITWIT?!

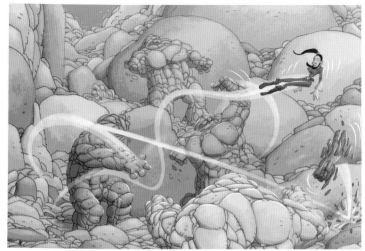

NO WAY, BIG GUY!

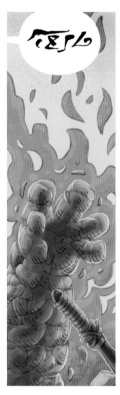

NOOOO!

NO!

I'M...SO... SORRY...

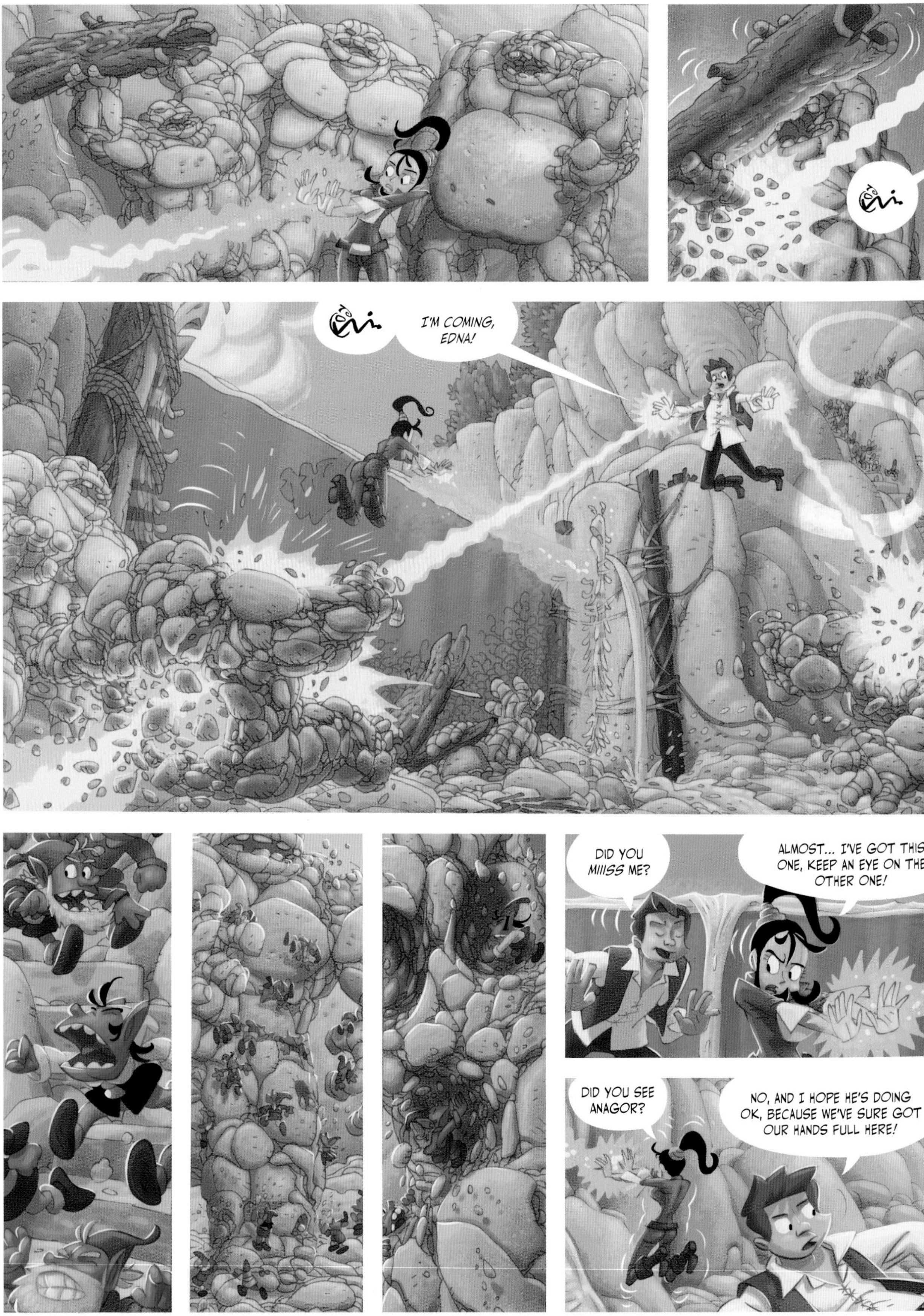
I'M COMING, EDNA!
DID YOU MIIISS ME?
ALMOST... I'VE GOT THIS ONE, KEEP AN EYE ON THE OTHER ONE!
DID YOU SEE ANAGOR?
NO, AND I HOPE HE'S DOING OK, BECAUSE WE'VE SURE GOT OUR HANDS FULL HERE!

THIS TIME, YOUR HIGHNESS, I WON'T BE ABLE TO HOLD ON MUCH LONGER...

WE'RE GOING TO NEED SOME HELP!

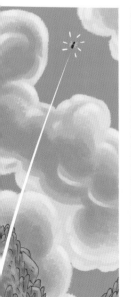

THAT LIGHT... IS THAT A LANTERN-CREATURE?!

YES! IT MUST NOT BE GOING WELL... ANAGOR'S CALLING ON THE OTHER MAGICIANS TO HELP HIM!

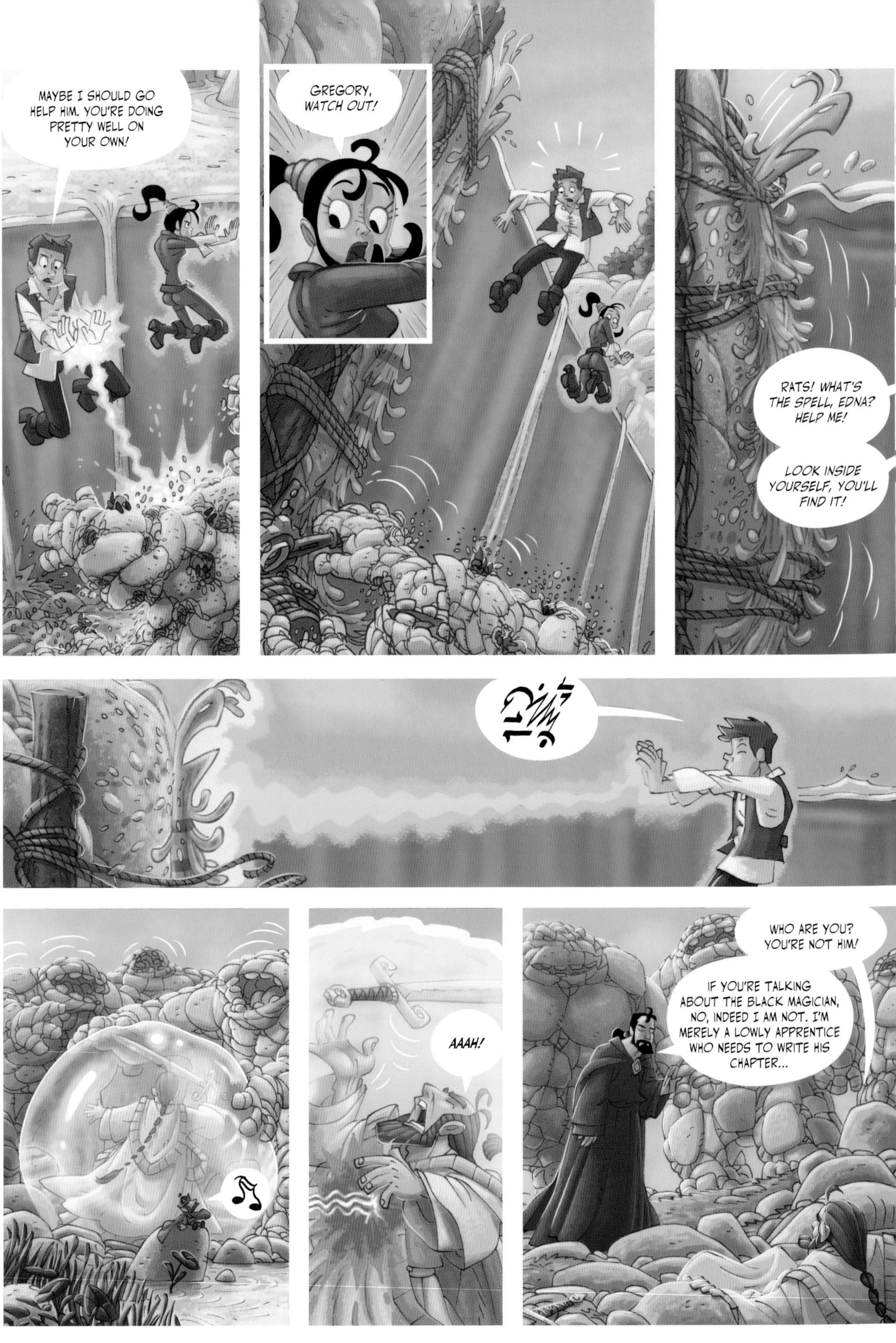

MAYBE I SHOULD GO HELP HIM. YOU'RE DOING PRETTY WELL ON YOUR OWN!
GREGORY, WATCH OUT!
RATS! WHAT'S THE SPELL, EDNA? HELP ME!
LOOK INSIDE YOURSELF, YOU'LL FIND IT!
AAAH!
WHO ARE YOU? YOU'RE NOT HIM!
IF YOU'RE TALKING ABOUT THE BLACK MAGICIAN, NO, INDEED I AM NOT. I'M MERELY A LOWLY APPRENTICE WHO NEEDS TO WRITE HIS CHAPTER...

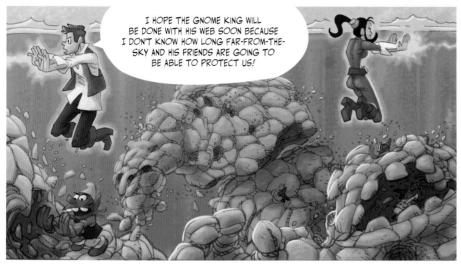

I HOPE THE GNOME KING WILL BE DONE WITH HIS WEB SOON BECAUSE I DON'T KNOW HOW LONG FAR-FROM-THE-SKY AND HIS FRIENDS ARE GOING TO BE ABLE TO PROTECT US!

UH, I DON'T KNOW... BUT I'M NOT...GOING TO BE ABLE TO...HOLD ON MUCH... LONGER...

RESISTANCE IS FUTILE, YOU'RE EXHAUSTED! MIGHT AS WELL GET IT OVER WITH RIGHT NOW!

OUCH!

LOOKS LIKE YOU'VE GOT SOME BACK-UP!

DO YOU REALLY THINK YOU'RE A MATCH FOR ME?!

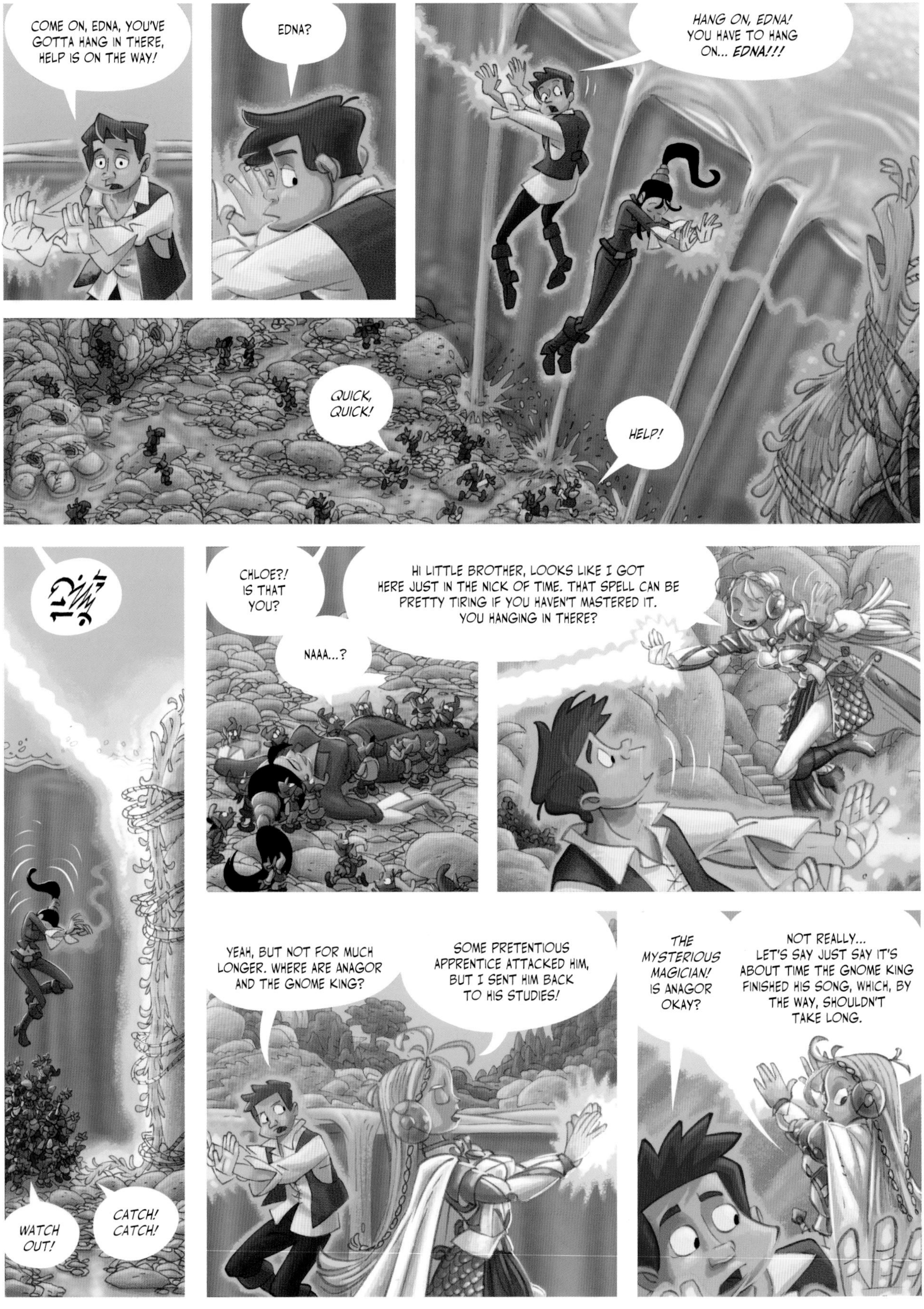
COME ON, EDNA, YOU'VE GOTTA HANG IN THERE, HELP IS ON THE WAY!
EDNA?
HANG ON, EDNA! YOU HAVE TO HANG ON... EDNA!!!
QUICK, QUICK!
HELP!
CHLOE?! IS THAT YOU?
HI LITTLE BROTHER, LOOKS LIKE I GOT HERE JUST IN THE NICK OF TIME. THAT SPELL CAN BE PRETTY TIRING IF YOU HAVEN'T MASTERED IT. YOU HANGING IN THERE?
NAAA...?
WATCH OUT!
CATCH! CATCH!
YEAH, BUT NOT FOR MUCH LONGER. WHERE ARE ANAGOR AND THE GNOME KING?
SOME PRETENTIOUS APPRENTICE ATTACKED HIM, BUT I SENT HIM BACK TO HIS STUDIES!
THE MYSTERIOUS MAGICIAN! IS ANAGOR OKAY?
NOT REALLY... LET'S SAY JUST SAY IT'S ABOUT TIME THE GNOME KING FINISHED HIS SONG, WHICH, BY THE WAY, SHOULDN'T TAKE LONG.

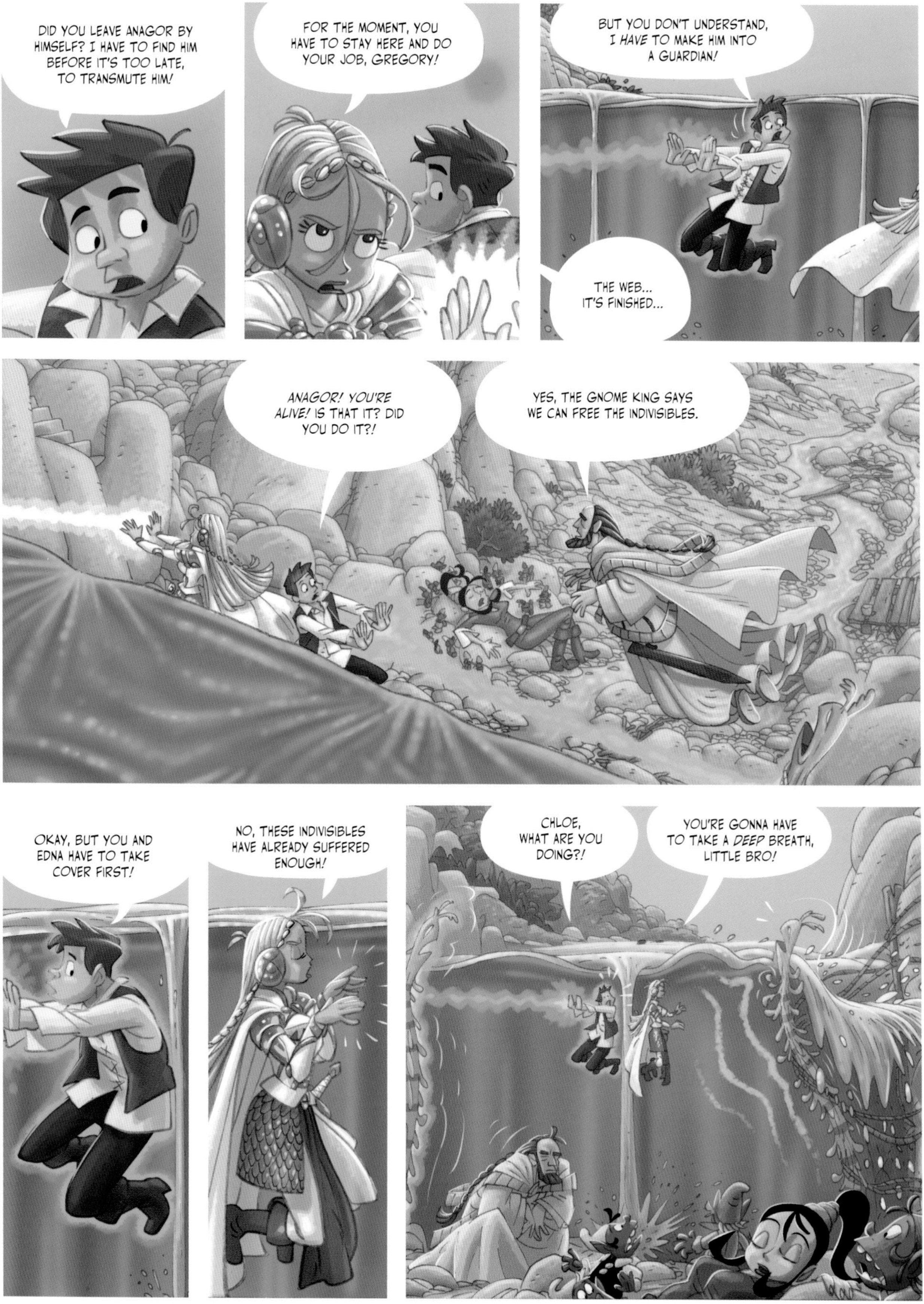
DID YOU LEAVE ANAGOR BY HIMSELF? I HAVE TO FIND HIM BEFORE IT'S TOO LATE, TO TRANSMUTE HIM!
FOR THE MOMENT, YOU HAVE TO STAY HERE AND DO YOUR JOB, GREGORY!
BUT YOU DON'T UNDERSTAND, I HAVE TO MAKE HIM INTO A GUARDIAN!
THE WEB... IT'S FINISHED...
ANAGOR! YOU'RE ALIVE! IS THAT IT? DID YOU DO IT?!
YES, THE GNOME KING SAYS WE CAN FREE THE INDIVISIBLES.
OKAY, BUT YOU AND EDNA HAVE TO TAKE COVER FIRST!
NO, THESE INDIVISIBLES HAVE ALREADY SUFFERED ENOUGH!
CHLOE, WHAT ARE YOU DOING?!
YOU'RE GONNA HAVE TO TAKE A DEEP BREATH, LITTLE BRO!

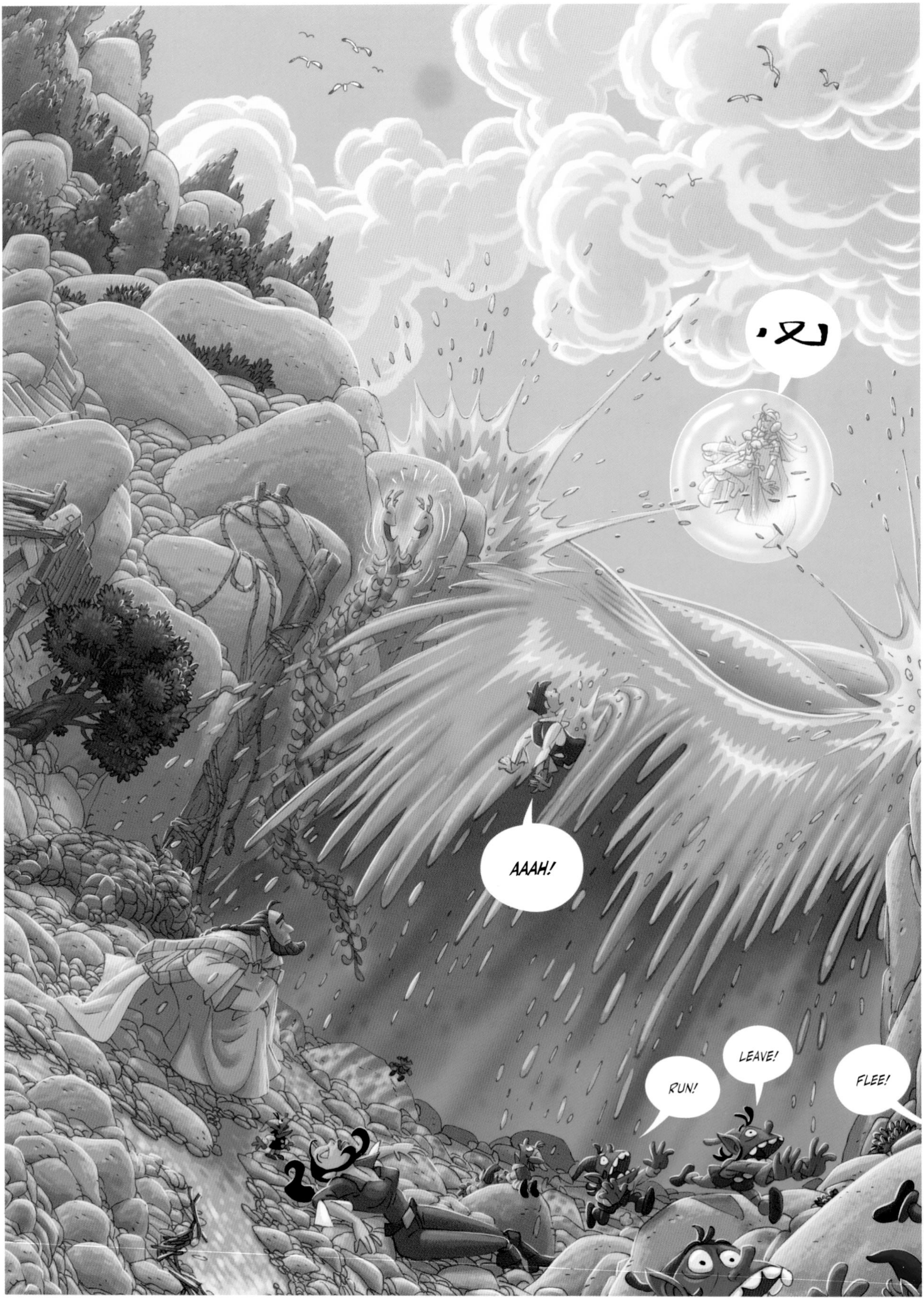
AAAH!
RUN!
LEAVE!
FLEE!

CHLOE! EDNA!
ANAGOR!

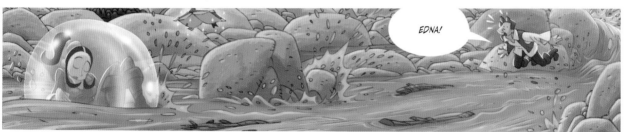

EDNA!

EDNA...

IT'S GONNA BE
OKAY, EDNA, I'LL TAKE
CARE OF YOU!

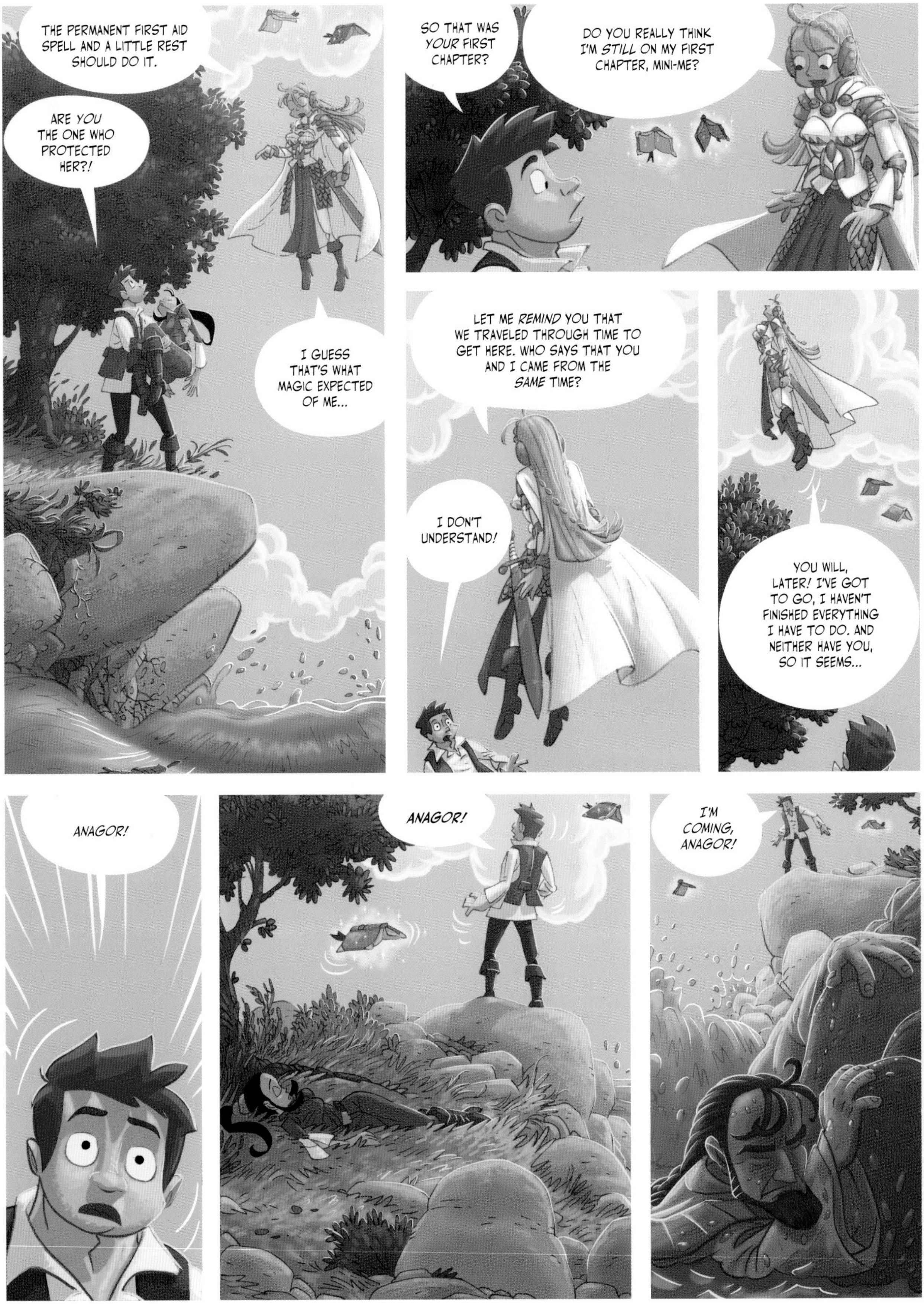
THE PERMANENT FIRST AID SPELL AND A LITTLE REST SHOULD DO IT.
ARE *YOU* THE ONE WHO PROTECTED HER?!
I GUESS THAT'S WHAT MAGIC EXPECTED OF ME...
SO THAT WAS *YOUR* FIRST CHAPTER?
DO YOU REALLY THINK I'M *STILL* ON MY FIRST CHAPTER, MINI-ME?
LET ME *REMIND* YOU THAT WE TRAVELED THROUGH TIME TO GET HERE. WHO SAYS THAT YOU AND I CAME FROM THE *SAME* TIME?
I DON'T UNDERSTAND!
YOU WILL, LATER! I'VE GOT TO GO, I HAVEN'T FINISHED EVERYTHING I HAVE TO DO. AND NEITHER HAVE YOU, SO IT SEEMS...
ANAGOR!
ANAGOR!
I'M COMING, ANAGOR!

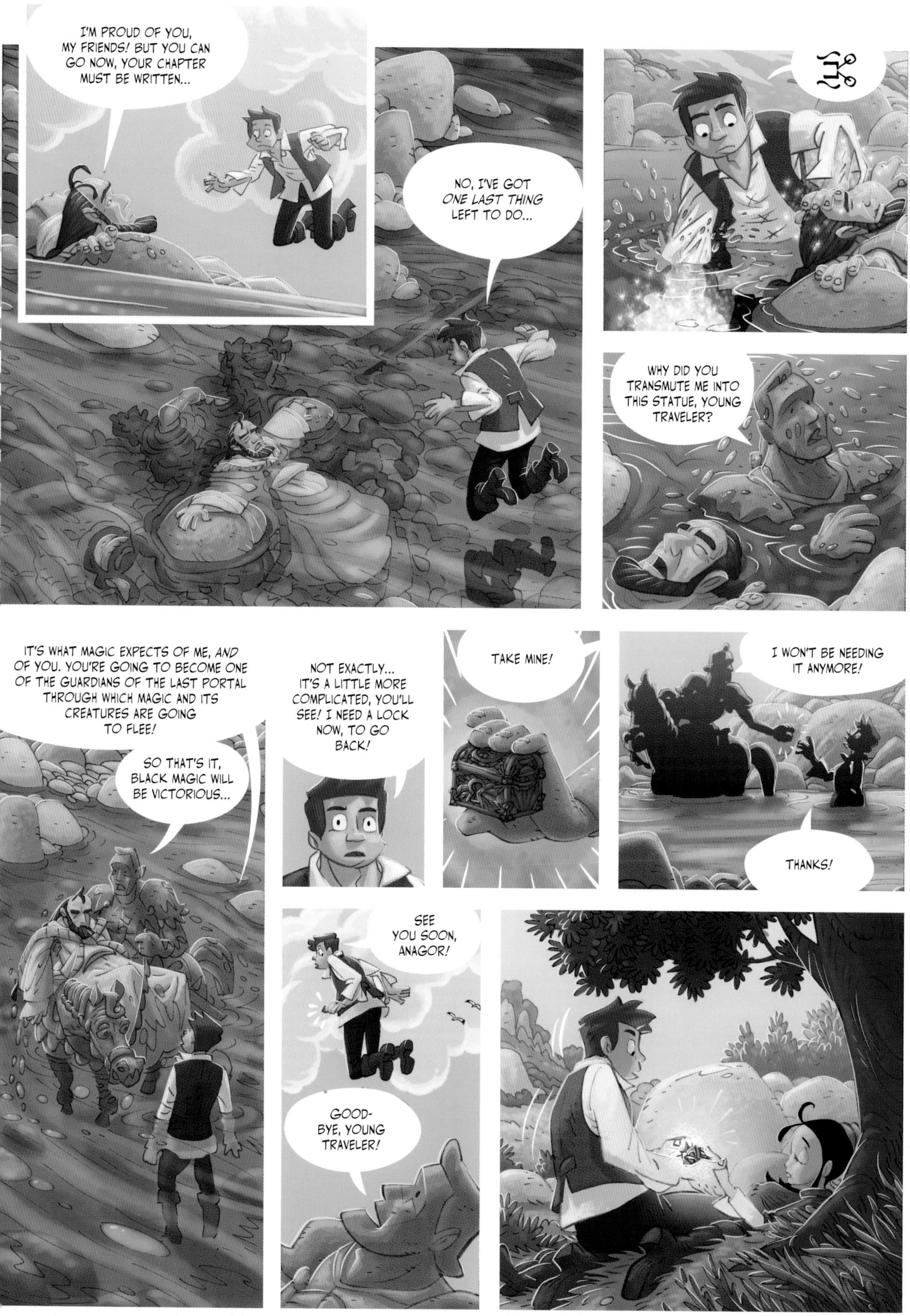
I'M PROUD OF YOU, MY FRIENDS! BUT YOU CAN GO NOW, YOUR CHAPTER MUST BE WRITTEN...
NO, I'VE GOT ONE LAST THING LEFT TO DO...
WHY DID YOU TRANSMUTE ME INTO THIS STATUE, YOUNG TRAVELER?
IT'S WHAT MAGIC EXPECTS OF ME, AND OF YOU. YOU'RE GOING TO BECOME ONE OF THE GUARDIANS OF THE LAST PORTAL THROUGH WHICH MAGIC AND ITS CREATURES ARE GOING TO FLEE!
SO THAT'S IT, BLACK MAGIC WILL BE VICTORIOUS...
NOT EXACTLY... IT'S A LITTLE MORE COMPLICATED, YOU'LL SEE! I NEED A LOCK NOW, TO GO BACK!
TAKE MINE!
I WON'T BE NEEDING IT ANYMORE!
THANKS!
SEE YOU SOON, ANAGOR!
GOOD-BYE, YOUNG TRAVELER!

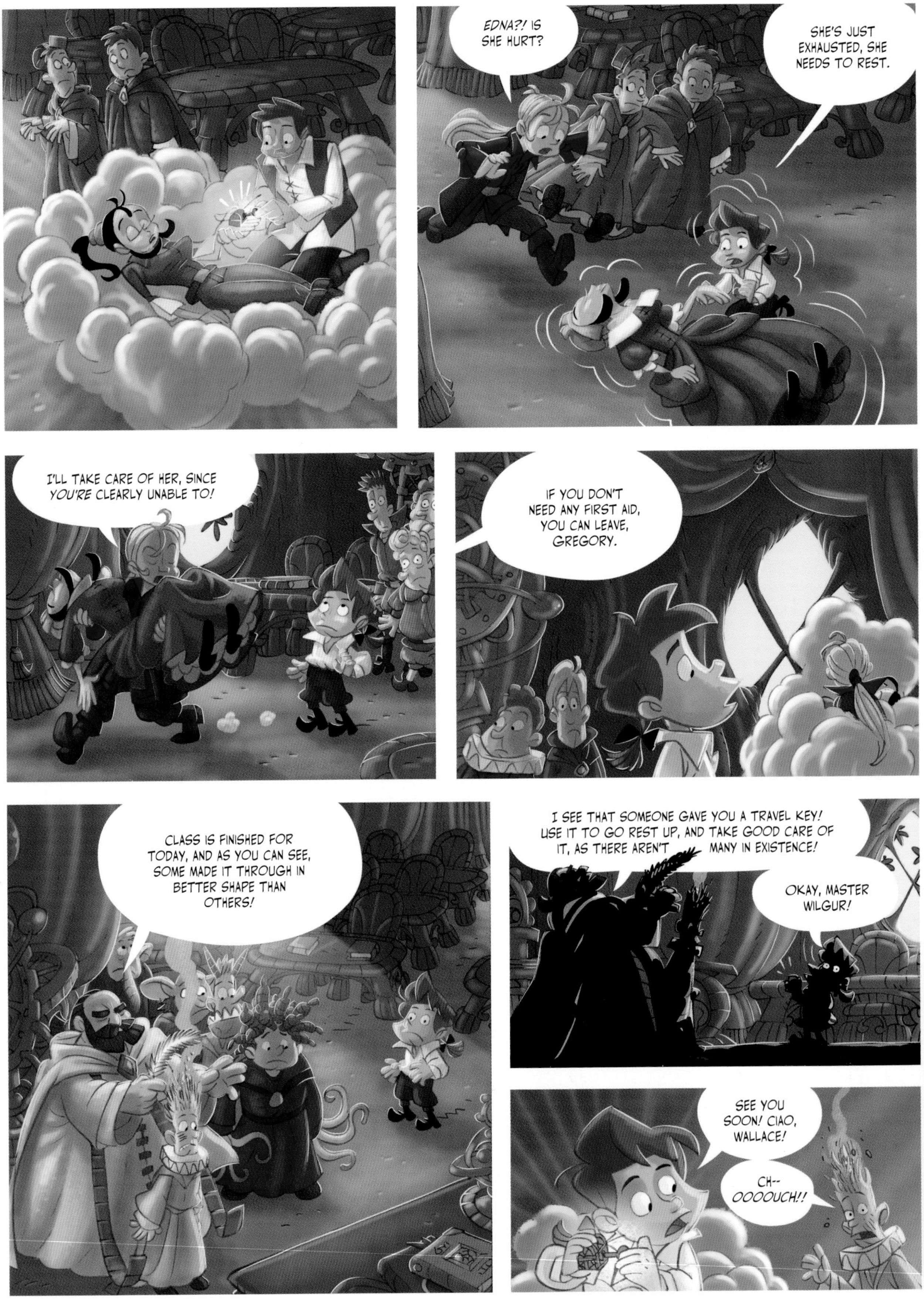
EDNA?! IS SHE HURT?
SHE'S JUST EXHAUSTED, SHE NEEDS TO REST.
I'LL TAKE CARE OF HER, SINCE YOU'RE CLEARLY UNABLE TO!
IF YOU DON'T NEED ANY FIRST AID, YOU CAN LEAVE, GREGORY.
CLASS IS FINISHED FOR TODAY, AND AS YOU CAN SEE, SOME MADE IT THROUGH IN BETTER SHAPE THAN OTHERS!
I SEE THAT SOMEONE GAVE YOU A TRAVEL KEY! USE IT TO GO REST UP, AND TAKE GOOD CARE OF IT, AS THERE AREN'T MANY IN EXISTENCE!
OKAY, MASTER WILGUR!
SEE YOU SOON! CIAO, WALLACE!
CH-- OOOOUCH!!

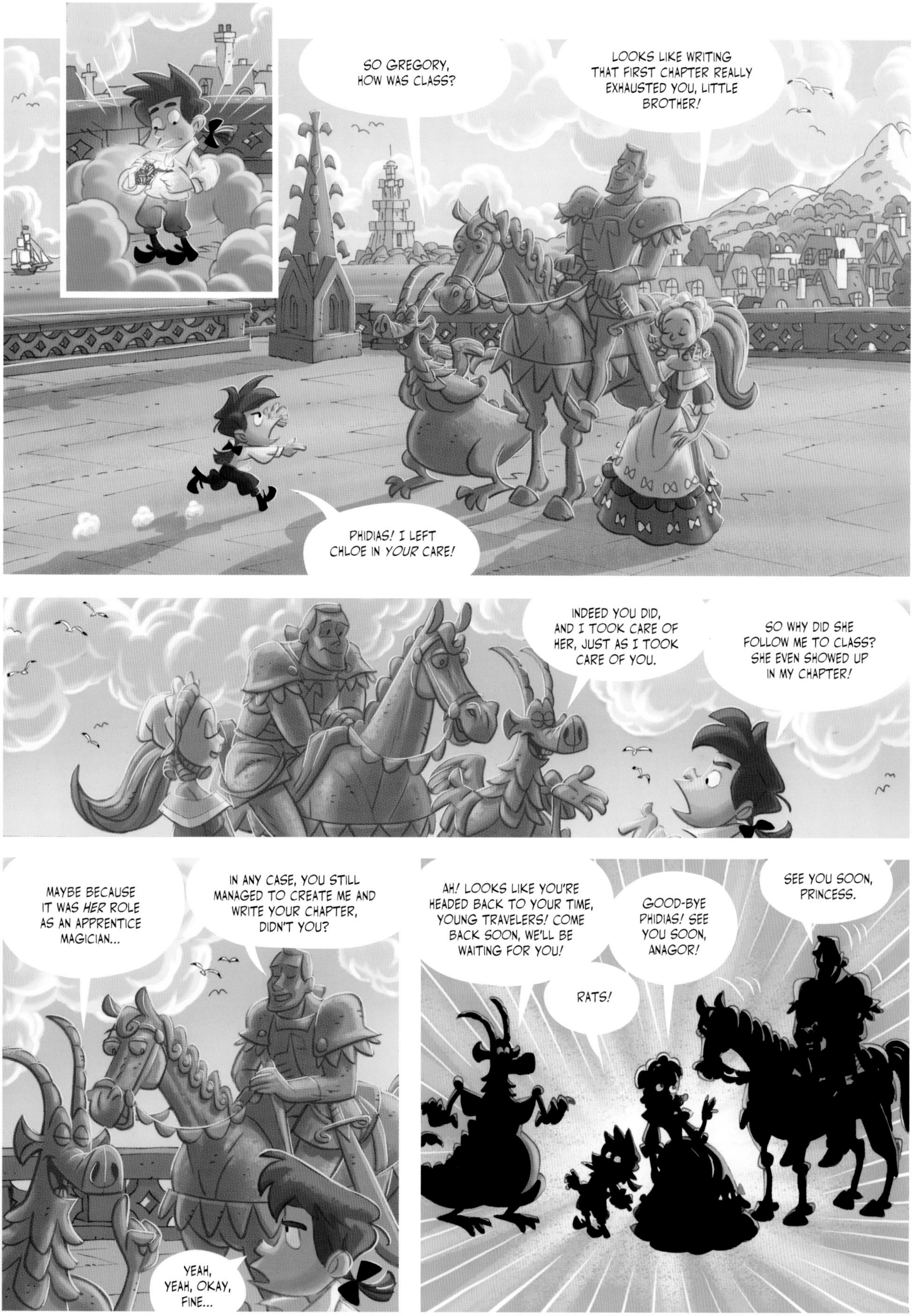
SO GREGORY, HOW WAS CLASS?
LOOKS LIKE WRITING THAT FIRST CHAPTER REALLY EXHAUSTED YOU, LITTLE BROTHER!
PHIDIAS! I LEFT CHLOE IN *YOUR* CARE!
INDEED YOU DID, AND I TOOK CARE OF HER, JUST AS I TOOK CARE OF YOU.
SO WHY DID SHE FOLLOW ME TO CLASS? SHE EVEN SHOWED UP IN MY CHAPTER!
MAYBE BECAUSE IT WAS *HER* ROLE AS AN APPRENTICE MAGICIAN...
IN ANY CASE, YOU STILL MANAGED TO CREATE ME AND WRITE YOUR CHAPTER, DIDN'T YOU?
YEAH, YEAH, OKAY, FINE...
AH! LOOKS LIKE YOU'RE HEADED BACK TO YOUR TIME, YOUNG TRAVELERS! COME BACK SOON, WE'LL BE WAITING FOR YOU!
RATS!
GOOD-BYE PHIDIAS! SEE YOU SOON, ANAGOR!
SEE YOU SOON, PRINCESS.

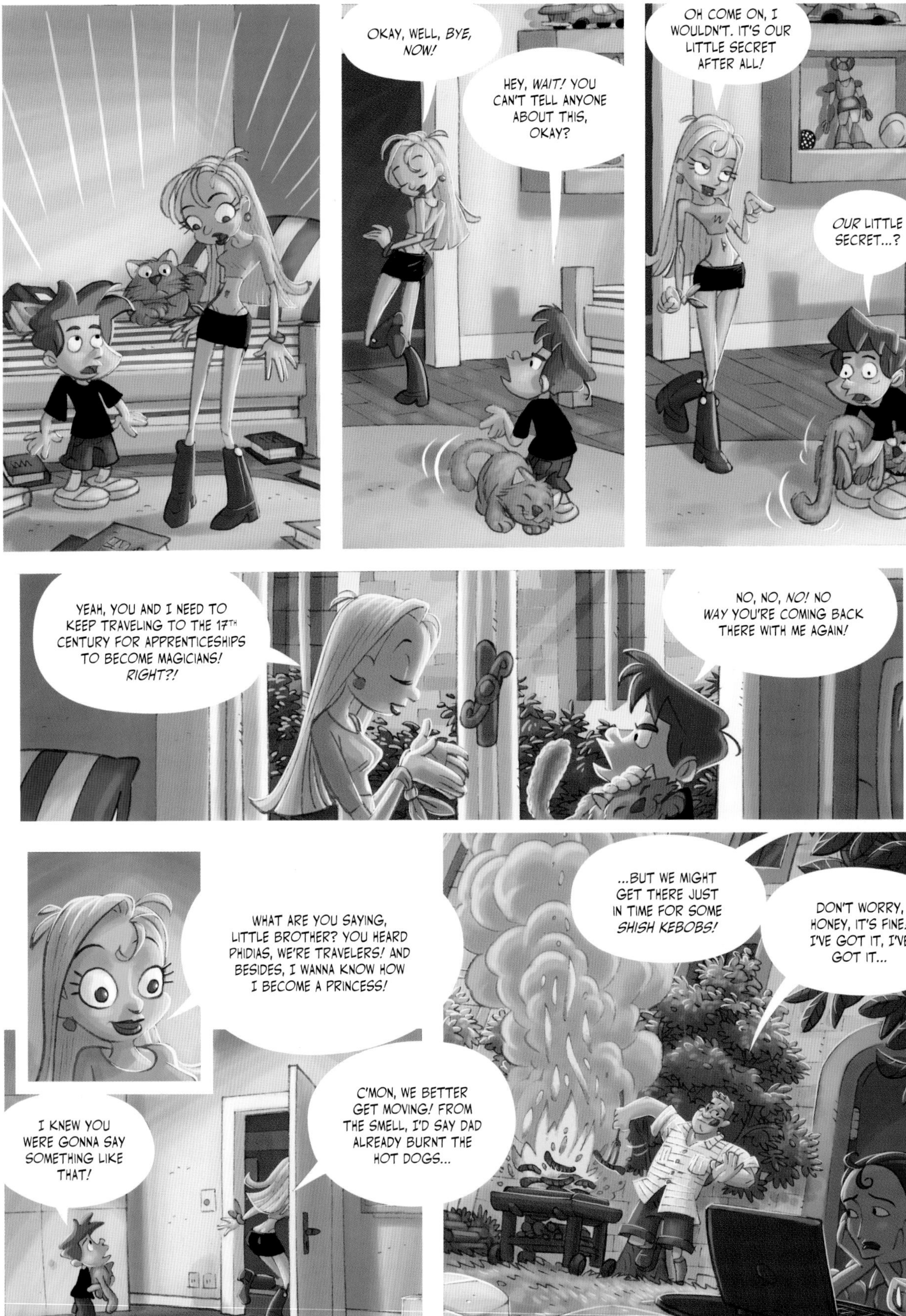
OKAY, WELL, BYE, NOW!
HEY, WAIT! YOU CAN'T TELL ANYONE ABOUT THIS, OKAY?
OH COME ON, I WOULDN'T. IT'S OUR LITTLE SECRET AFTER ALL!
OUR LITTLE SECRET...?
YEAH, YOU AND I NEED TO KEEP TRAVELING TO THE 17TH CENTURY FOR APPRENTICESHIPS TO BECOME MAGICIANS! RIGHT?!
NO, NO, NO! NO WAY YOU'RE COMING BACK THERE WITH ME AGAIN!
WHAT ARE YOU SAYING, LITTLE BROTHER? YOU HEARD PHIDIAS, WE'RE TRAVELERS! AND BESIDES, I WANNA KNOW HOW I BECOME A PRINCESS!
I KNEW YOU WERE GONNA SAY SOMETHING LIKE THAT!
C'MON, WE BETTER GET MOVING! FROM THE SMELL, I'D SAY DAD ALREADY BURNT THE HOT DOGS...
...BUT WE MIGHT GET THERE JUST IN TIME FOR SOME SHISH KEBOBS!
DON'T WORRY, HONEY, IT'S FINE! I'VE GOT IT, I'VE GOT IT...

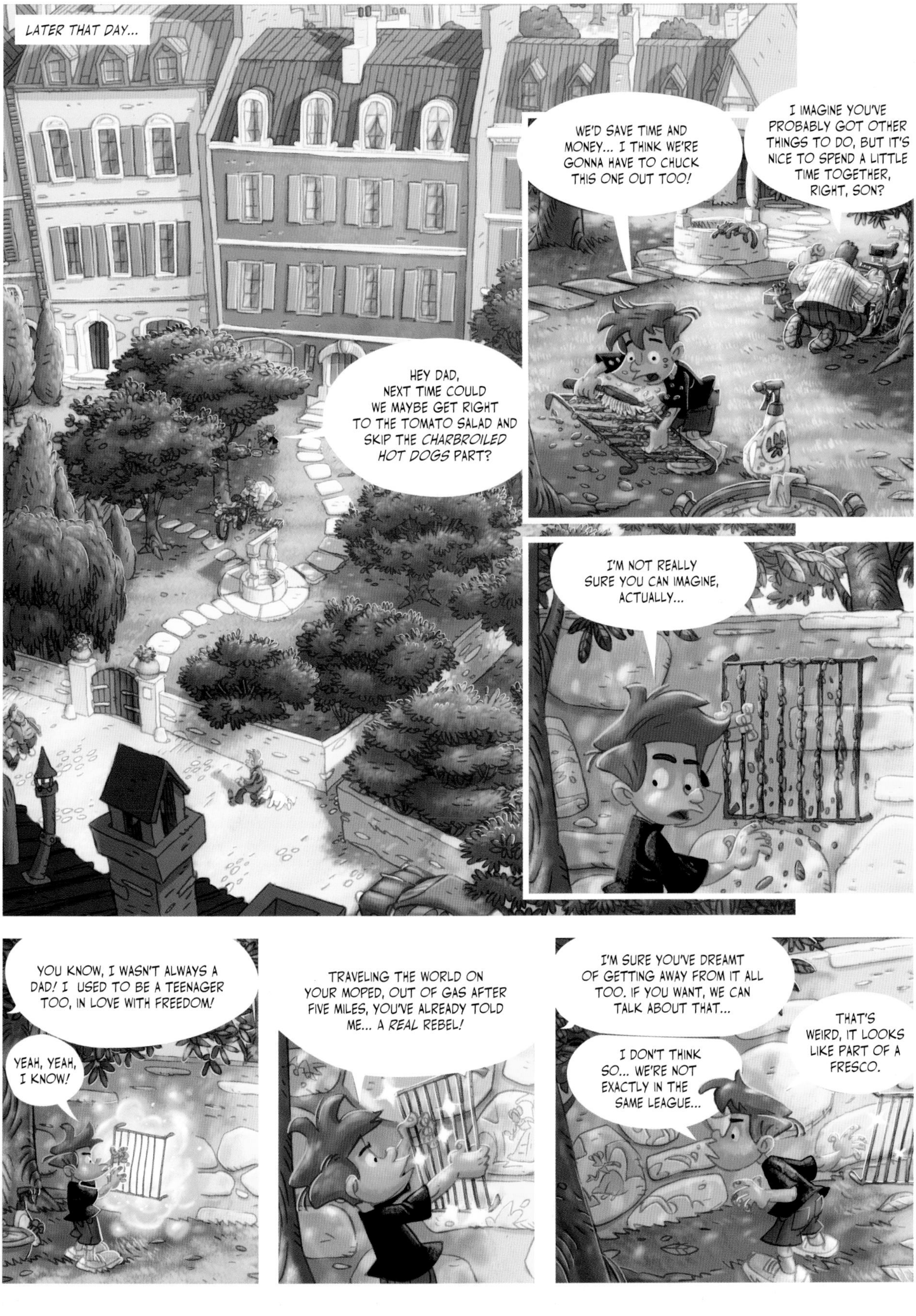
LATER THAT DAY...
HEY DAD, NEXT TIME COULD WE MAYBE GET RIGHT TO THE TOMATO SALAD AND SKIP THE *CHARBROILED HOT DOGS* PART?
WE'D SAVE TIME AND MONEY... I THINK WE'RE GONNA HAVE TO CHUCK THIS ONE OUT TOO!
I IMAGINE YOU'VE PROBABLY GOT OTHER THINGS TO DO, BUT IT'S NICE TO SPEND A LITTLE TIME TOGETHER, RIGHT, SON?
I'M NOT REALLY SURE YOU CAN IMAGINE, ACTUALLY...
YOU KNOW, I WASN'T ALWAYS A DAD! I USED TO BE A TEENAGER TOO, IN LOVE WITH FREEDOM!
YEAH, YEAH, I KNOW!
TRAVELING THE WORLD ON YOUR MOPED, OUT OF GAS AFTER FIVE MILES, YOU'VE ALREADY TOLD ME... A *REAL* REBEL!
I'M SURE YOU'VE DREAMT OF GETTING AWAY FROM IT ALL TOO. IF YOU WANT, WE CAN TALK ABOUT THAT...
I DON'T THINK SO... WE'RE NOT EXACTLY IN THE SAME LEAGUE...
THAT'S WEIRD, IT LOOKS LIKE PART OF A FRESCO.

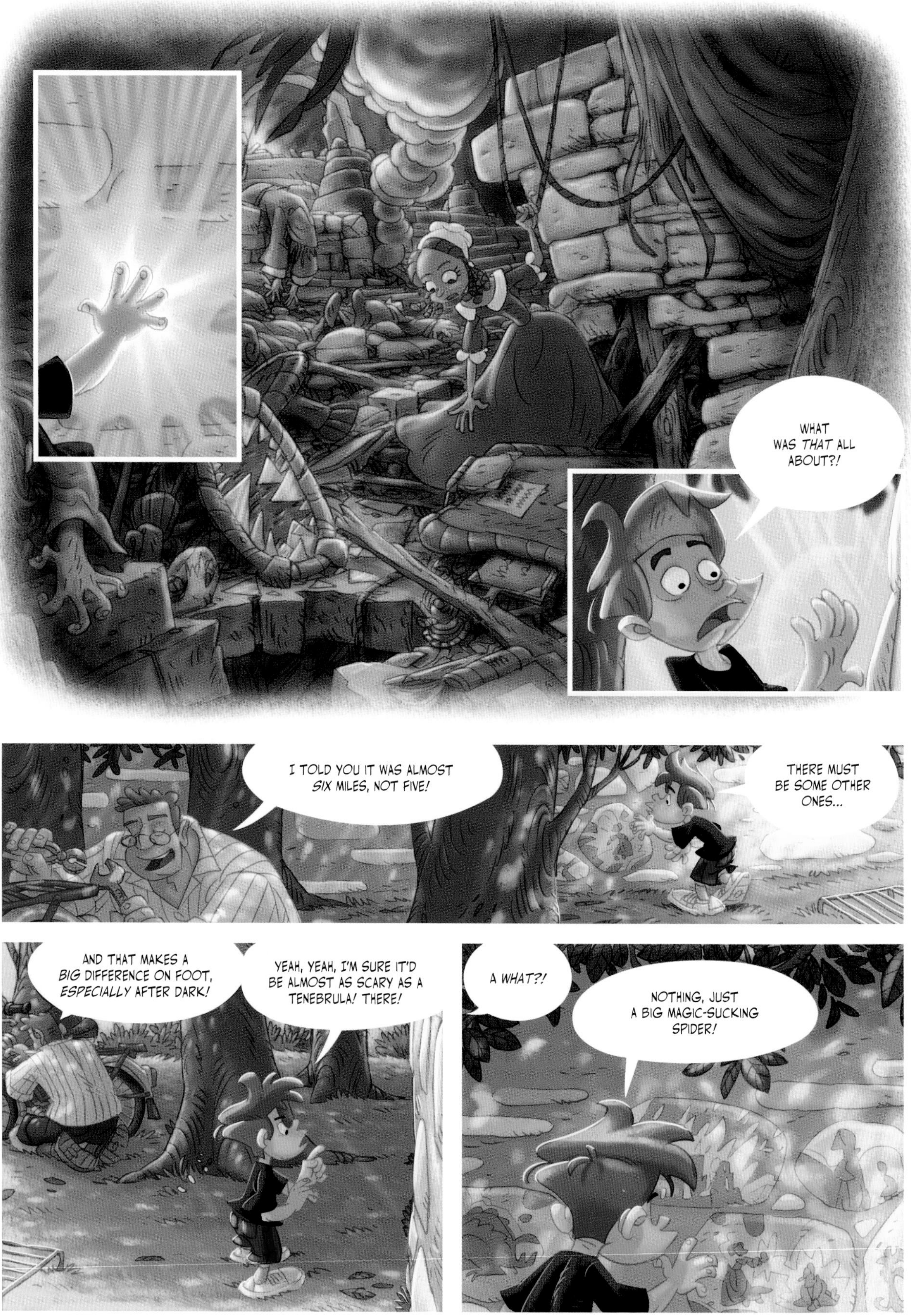
WHAT WAS THAT ALL ABOUT?!
I TOLD YOU IT WAS ALMOST SIX MILES, NOT FIVE!
THERE MUST BE SOME OTHER ONES...
AND THAT MAKES A BIG DIFFERENCE ON FOOT, ESPECIALLY AFTER DARK!
YEAH, YEAH, I'M SURE IT'D BE ALMOST AS SCARY AS A TENEBRULA! THERE!
A WHAT?!
NOTHING, JUST A BIG MAGIC-SUCKING SPIDER!

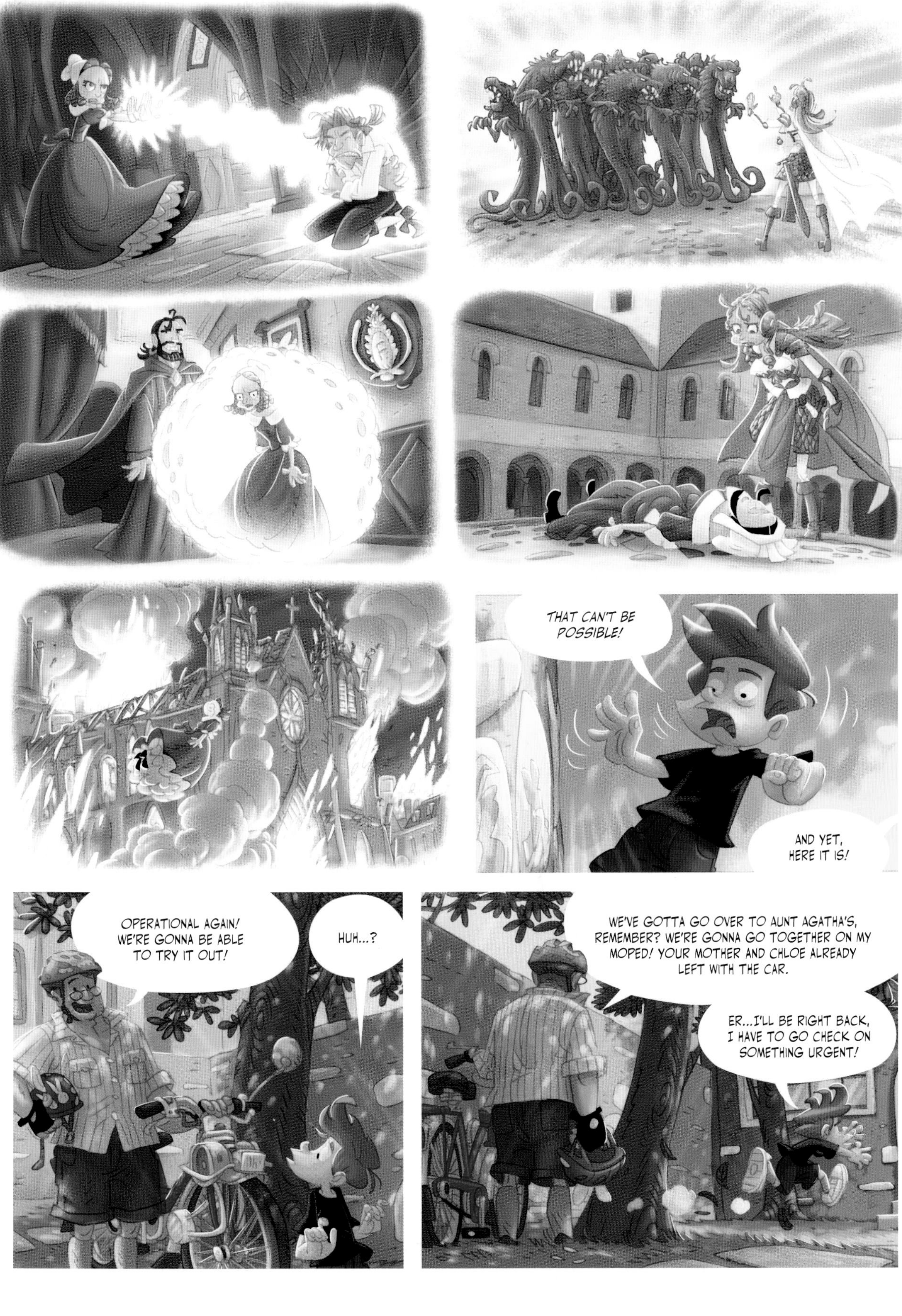
THAT CAN'T BE POSSIBLE!
AND YET, HERE IT IS!
OPERATIONAL AGAIN! WE'RE GONNA BE ABLE TO TRY IT OUT!
HUH...?
WE'VE GOTTA GO OVER TO AUNT AGATHA'S, REMEMBER? WE'RE GONNA GO TOGETHER ON MY MOPED! YOUR MOTHER AND CHLOE ALREADY LEFT WITH THE CAR.
ER...I'LL BE RIGHT BACK, I HAVE TO GO CHECK ON SOMETHING URGENT!

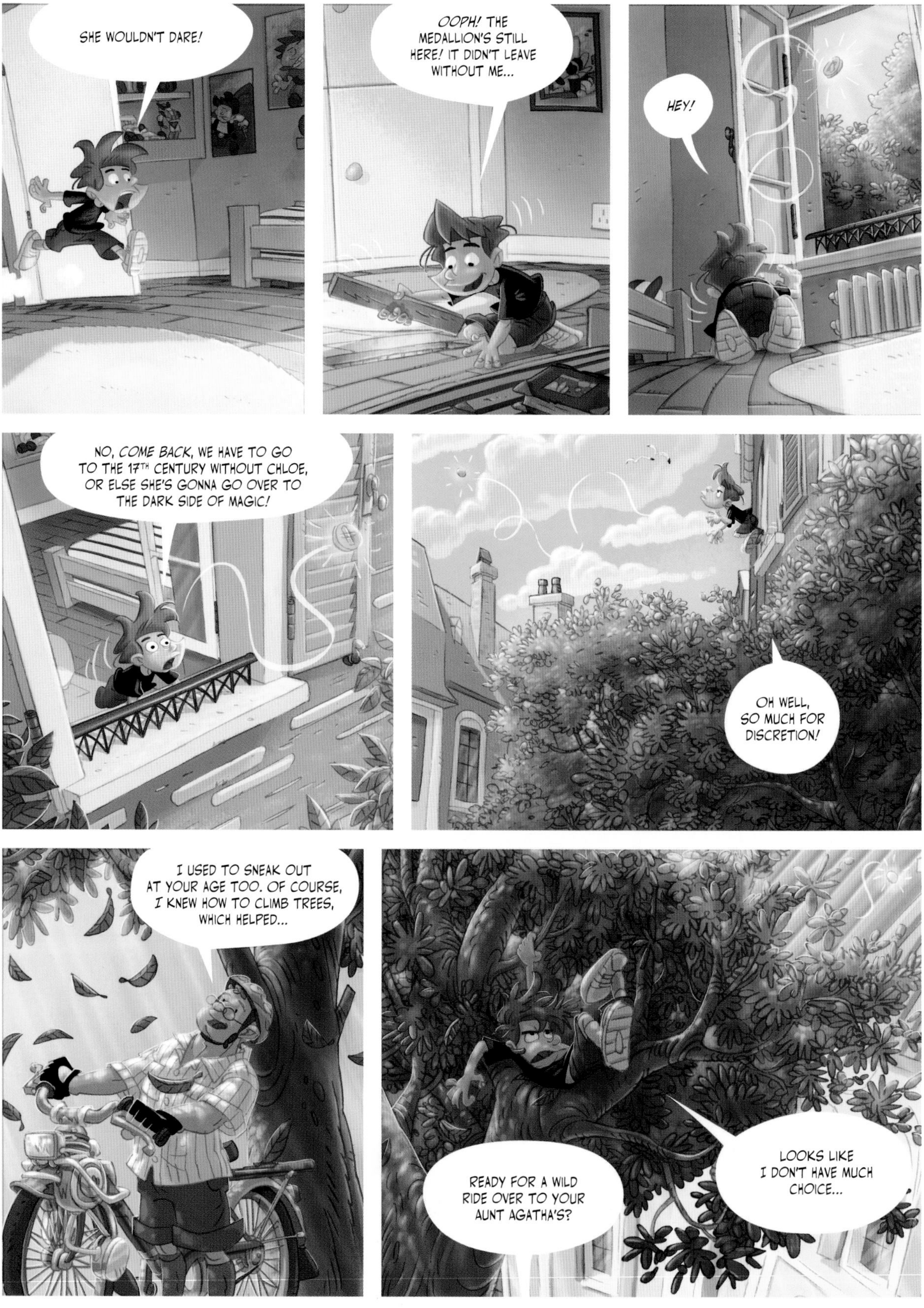
SHE WOULDN'T DARE!
OOPH! THE MEDALLION'S STILL HERE! IT DIDN'T LEAVE WITHOUT ME...
HEY!
NO, *COME BACK*, WE HAVE TO GO TO THE 17TH CENTURY WITHOUT CHLOE, OR ELSE SHE'S GONNA GO OVER TO THE DARK SIDE OF MAGIC!
OH WELL, SO MUCH FOR DISCRETION!
I USED TO SNEAK OUT AT YOUR AGE TOO. OF COURSE, I KNEW HOW TO CLIMB TREES, WHICH HELPED...
READY FOR A WILD RIDE OVER TO YOUR AUNT AGATHA'S?
LOOKS LIKE I DON'T HAVE MUCH CHOICE...

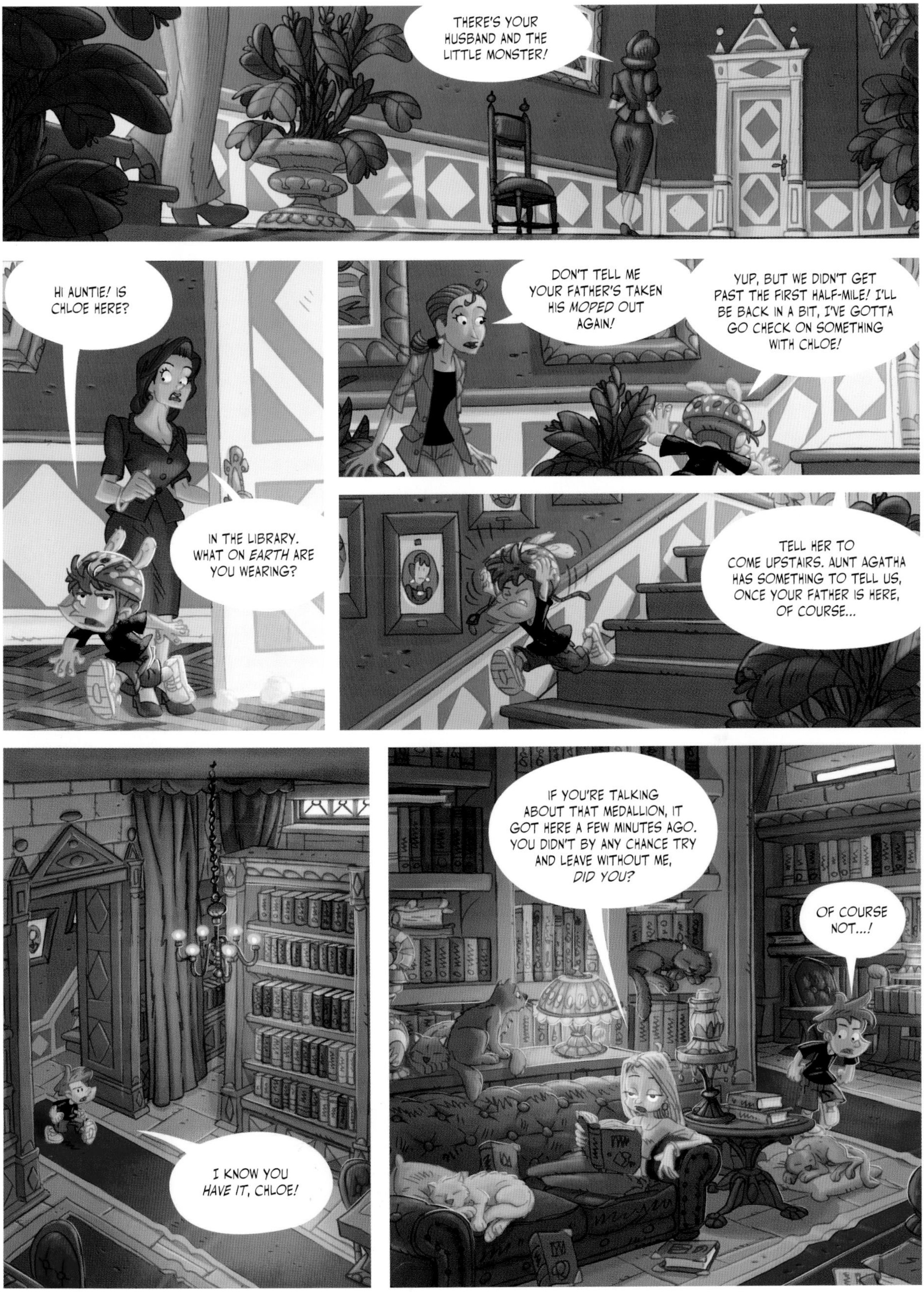
THERE'S YOUR HUSBAND AND THE LITTLE MONSTER!
HI AUNTIE! IS CHLOE HERE?
IN THE LIBRARY. WHAT ON *EARTH* ARE YOU WEARING?
DON'T TELL ME YOUR FATHER'S TAKEN HIS *MOPED* OUT AGAIN!
YUP, BUT WE DIDN'T GET PAST THE FIRST HALF-MILE! I'LL BE BACK IN A BIT, I'VE GOTTA GO CHECK ON SOMETHING WITH CHLOE!
TELL HER TO COME UPSTAIRS. AUNT AGATHA HAS SOMETHING TO TELL US, ONCE YOUR FATHER IS HERE, OF COURSE...
I KNOW YOU *HAVE IT*, CHLOE!
IF YOU'RE TALKING ABOUT THAT MEDALLION, IT GOT HERE A FEW MINUTES AGO. YOU DIDN'T BY ANY CHANCE TRY AND LEAVE WITHOUT ME, *DID YOU?*
OF COURSE NOT...!

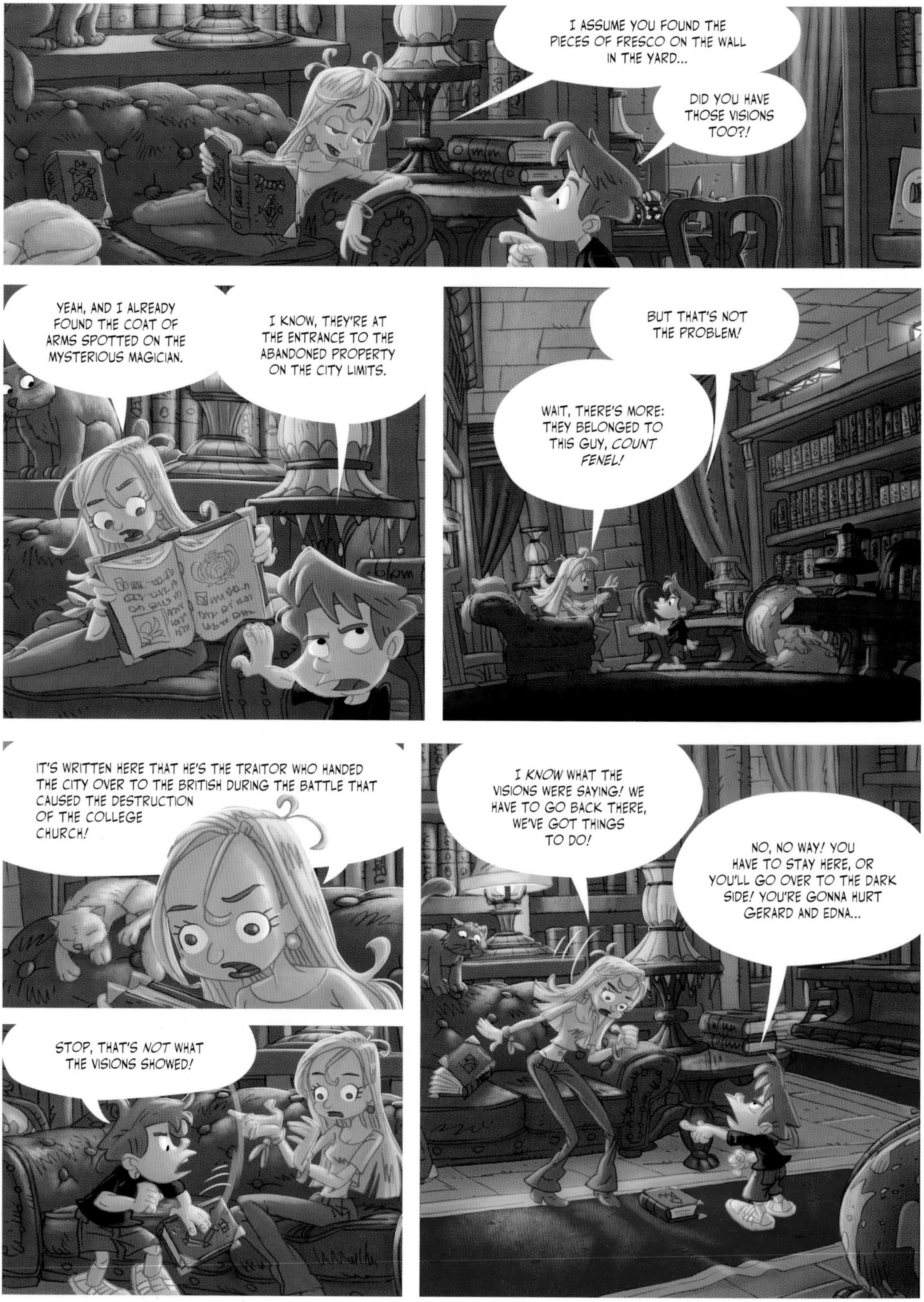
I ASSUME YOU FOUND THE PIECES OF FRESCO ON THE WALL IN THE YARD...
DID YOU HAVE THOSE VISIONS TOO?!
YEAH, AND I ALREADY FOUND THE COAT OF ARMS SPOTTED ON THE MYSTERIOUS MAGICIAN.
I KNOW, THEY'RE AT THE ENTRANCE TO THE ABANDONED PROPERTY ON THE CITY LIMITS.
BUT THAT'S NOT THE PROBLEM!
WAIT, THERE'S MORE: THEY BELONGED TO THIS GUY, *COUNT FENEL!*
IT'S WRITTEN HERE THAT HE'S THE TRAITOR WHO HANDED THE CITY OVER TO THE BRITISH DURING THE BATTLE THAT CAUSED THE DESTRUCTION OF THE COLLEGE CHURCH!
STOP, THAT'S *NOT* WHAT THE VISIONS SHOWED!
I *KNOW* WHAT THE VISIONS WERE SAYING! WE HAVE TO GO BACK THERE, WE'VE GOT THINGS TO DO!
NO, NO WAY! YOU HAVE TO STAY HERE, OR YOU'LL GO OVER TO THE DARK SIDE! YOU'RE GONNA HURT GERARD AND EDNA...

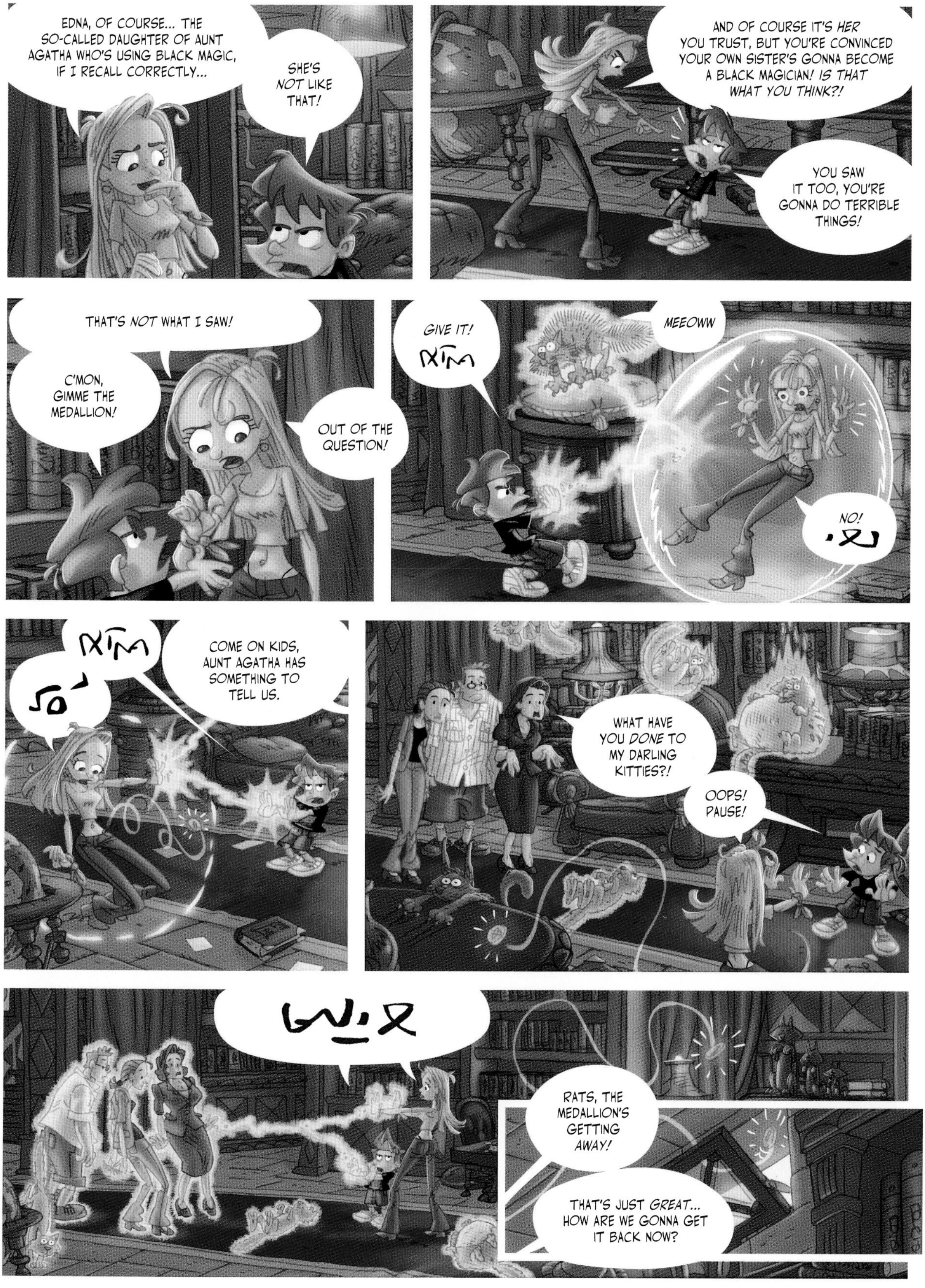
EDNA, OF COURSE... THE SO-CALLED DAUGHTER OF AUNT AGATHA WHO'S USING BLACK MAGIC, IF I RECALL CORRECTLY...
SHE'S *NOT* LIKE THAT!
AND OF COURSE IT'S *HER* YOU TRUST, BUT YOU'RE CONVINCED YOUR OWN SISTER'S GONNA BECOME A BLACK MAGICIAN! *IS THAT WHAT YOU THINK?!*
YOU SAW IT TOO, YOU'RE GONNA DO TERRIBLE THINGS!
THAT'S *NOT* WHAT I SAW!
C'MON, GIMME THE MEDALLION!
OUT OF THE QUESTION!
GIVE IT!
MEEOWW
NO!
COME ON KIDS, AUNT AGATHA HAS SOMETHING TO TELL US.
WHAT HAVE YOU *DONE* TO MY DARLING KITTIES?!
OOPS! PAUSE!
RATS, THE MEDALLION'S GETTING *AWAY!*
THAT'S JUST *GREAT*... HOW ARE WE GONNA GET IT BACK NOW?

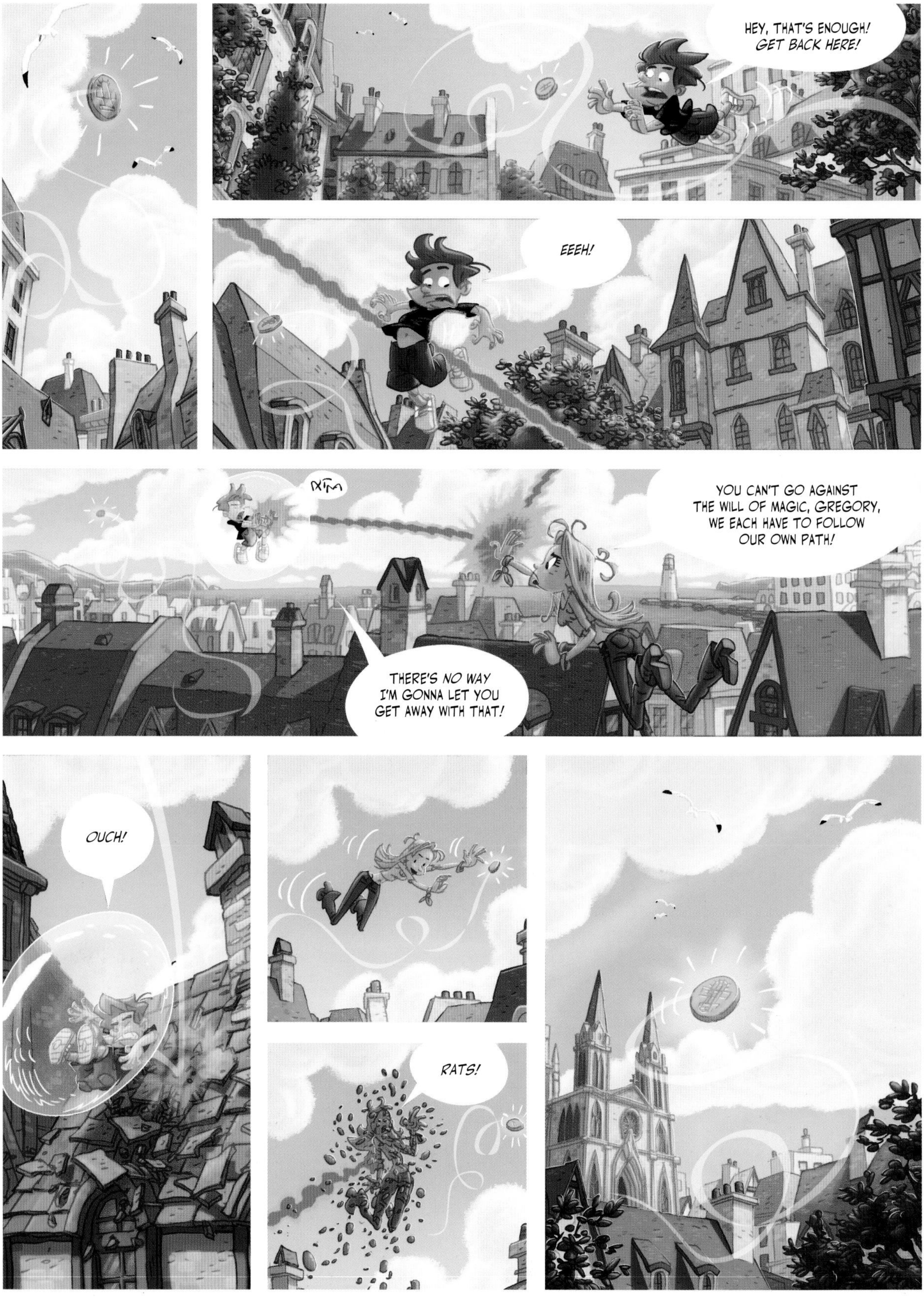
HEY, THAT'S ENOUGH! GET BACK HERE!
EEEH!
YOU CAN'T GO AGAINST THE WILL OF MAGIC, GREGORY, WE EACH HAVE TO FOLLOW OUR OWN PATH!
THERE'S NO WAY I'M GONNA LET YOU GET AWAY WITH THAT!
OUCH!
RATS!

IT'S USELESS TO KEEP FIGHTING, YOU CAN SEE AS WELL AS I DO THAT IT'S HEADED FOR THE CHURCH. IT WANTS US *BOTH* TO GO!

WE'LL SEE ABOUT THAT...

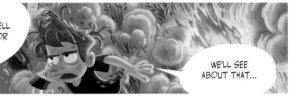

PFEW, JUST IN TIME!

WELL? GO ON, SHOO!

WERE YOU WAITING FOR ME?

MMMPH!

THAT MOUTH-SEWN-SHUT SPELL SURE COMES IN HANDY!

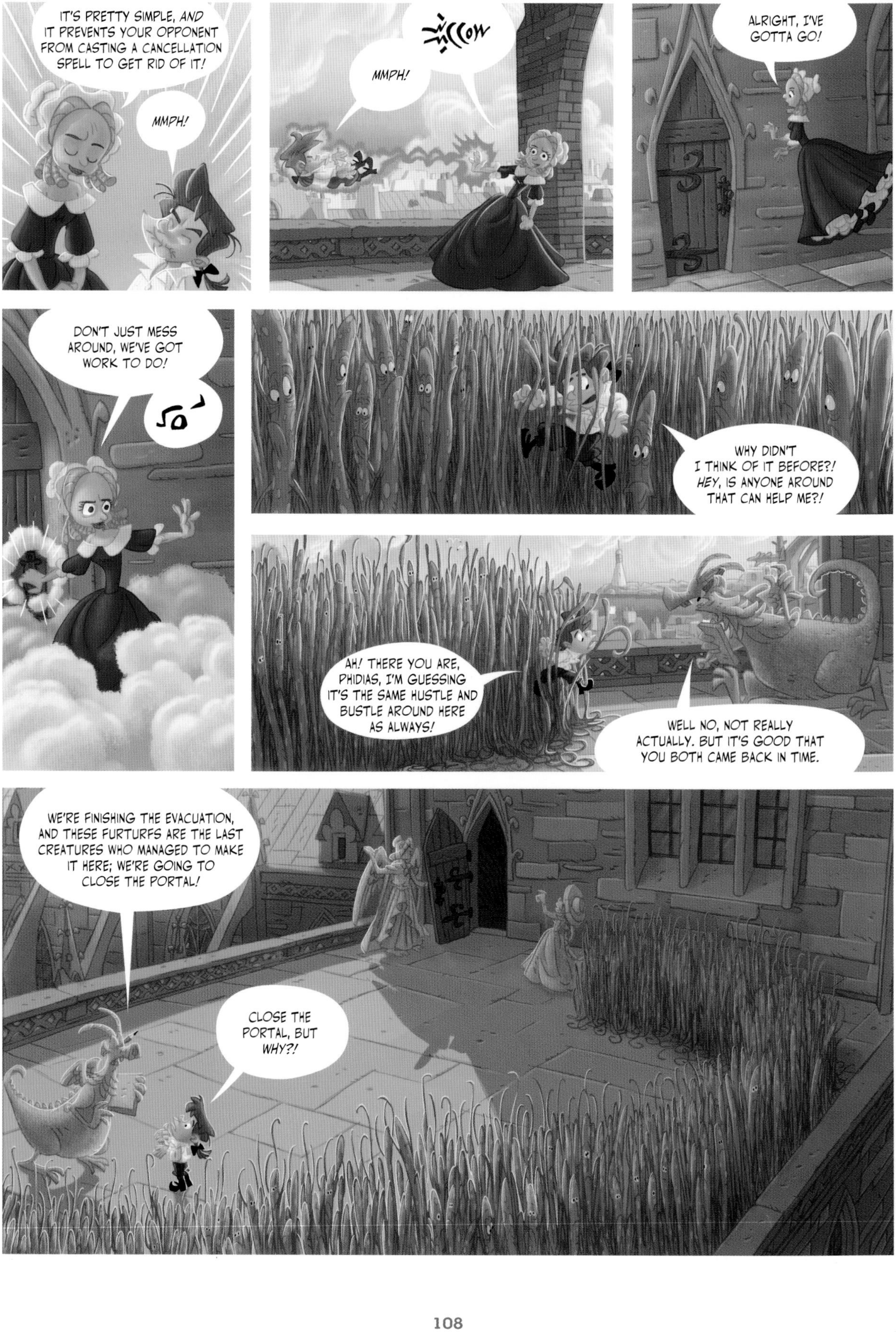
IT'S PRETTY SIMPLE, *AND* IT PREVENTS YOUR OPPONENT FROM CASTING A CANCELLATION SPELL TO GET RID OF IT!
MMPH!
MMPH!
ALRIGHT, I'VE GOTTA GO!
DON'T JUST MESS AROUND, WE'VE GOT WORK TO DO!
WHY DIDN'T I THINK OF IT BEFORE?! *HEY*, IS ANYONE AROUND THAT CAN HELP ME?!
AH! THERE YOU ARE, PHIDIAS, I'M GUESSING IT'S THE SAME HUSTLE AND BUSTLE AROUND HERE AS ALWAYS!
WELL NO, NOT REALLY ACTUALLY. BUT IT'S GOOD THAT YOU BOTH CAME BACK IN TIME.
WE'RE FINISHING THE EVACUATION, AND THESE FURTURFS ARE THE LAST CREATURES WHO MANAGED TO MAKE IT HERE; WE'RE GOING TO CLOSE THE PORTAL!
CLOSE THE PORTAL, BUT *WHY*?!

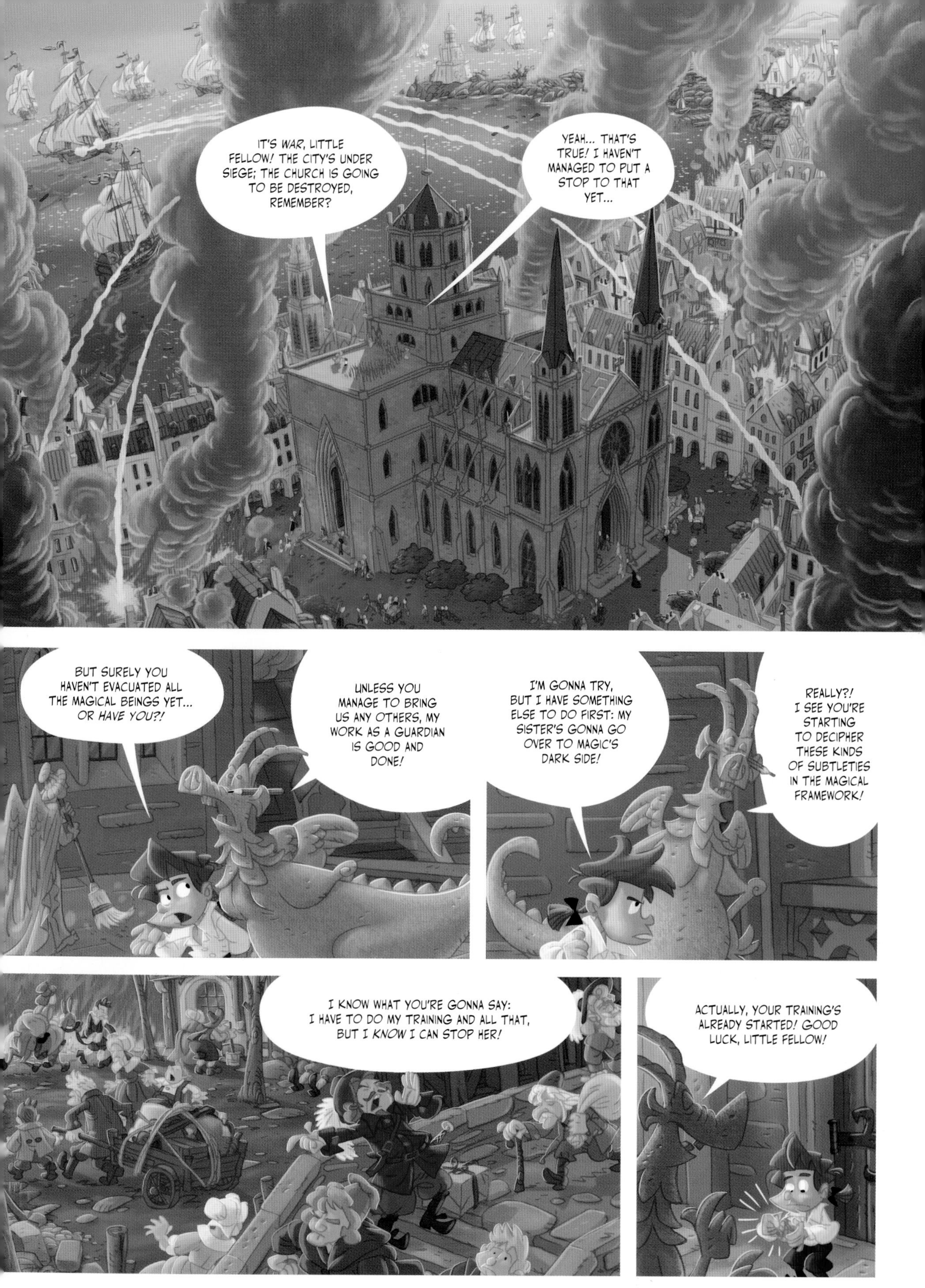
IT'S *WAR*, LITTLE FELLOW! THE CITY'S UNDER SIEGE; THE CHURCH IS GOING TO BE DESTROYED, REMEMBER?
YEAH... THAT'S TRUE! I HAVEN'T MANAGED TO PUT A STOP TO THAT YET...
BUT SURELY YOU HAVEN'T EVACUATED ALL THE MAGICAL BEINGS YET... OR *HAVE YOU?!*
UNLESS YOU MANAGE TO BRING US ANY OTHERS, MY WORK AS A GUARDIAN IS GOOD AND DONE!
I'M GONNA TRY, BUT I HAVE SOMETHING ELSE TO DO FIRST: MY SISTER'S GONNA GO OVER TO MAGIC'S DARK SIDE!
REALLY?! I SEE YOU'RE STARTING TO DECIPHER THESE KINDS OF SUBTLETIES IN THE MAGICAL FRAMEWORK!
I KNOW WHAT YOU'RE GONNA SAY: I HAVE TO DO MY TRAINING AND ALL THAT, BUT I *KNOW* I CAN STOP HER!
ACTUALLY, YOUR TRAINING'S ALREADY STARTED! GOOD LUCK, LITTLE FELLOW!

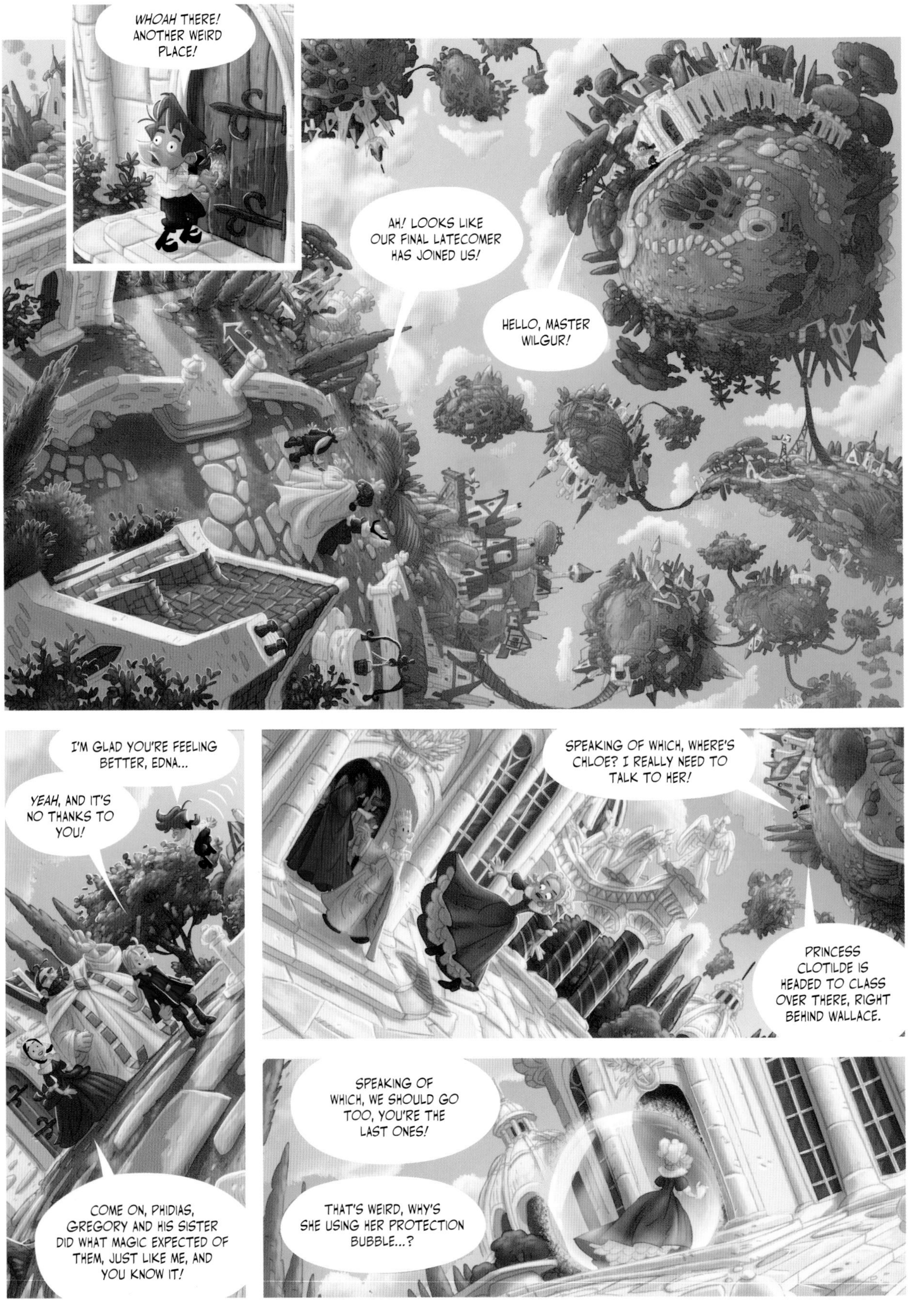
WHOAH THERE! ANOTHER WEIRD PLACE!
AH! LOOKS LIKE OUR FINAL LATECOMER HAS JOINED US!
HELLO, MASTER WILGUR!
I'M GLAD YOU'RE FEELING BETTER, EDNA...
YEAH, AND IT'S NO THANKS TO YOU!
COME ON, PHIDIAS, GREGORY AND HIS SISTER DID WHAT MAGIC EXPECTED OF THEM, JUST LIKE ME, AND YOU KNOW IT!
SPEAKING OF WHICH, WHERE'S CHLOE? I REALLY NEED TO TALK TO HER!
PRINCESS CLOTILDE IS HEADED TO CLASS OVER THERE, RIGHT BEHIND WALLACE.
SPEAKING OF WHICH, WE SHOULD GO TOO, YOU'RE THE LAST ONES!
THAT'S WEIRD, WHY'S SHE USING HER PROTECTION BUBBLE...?

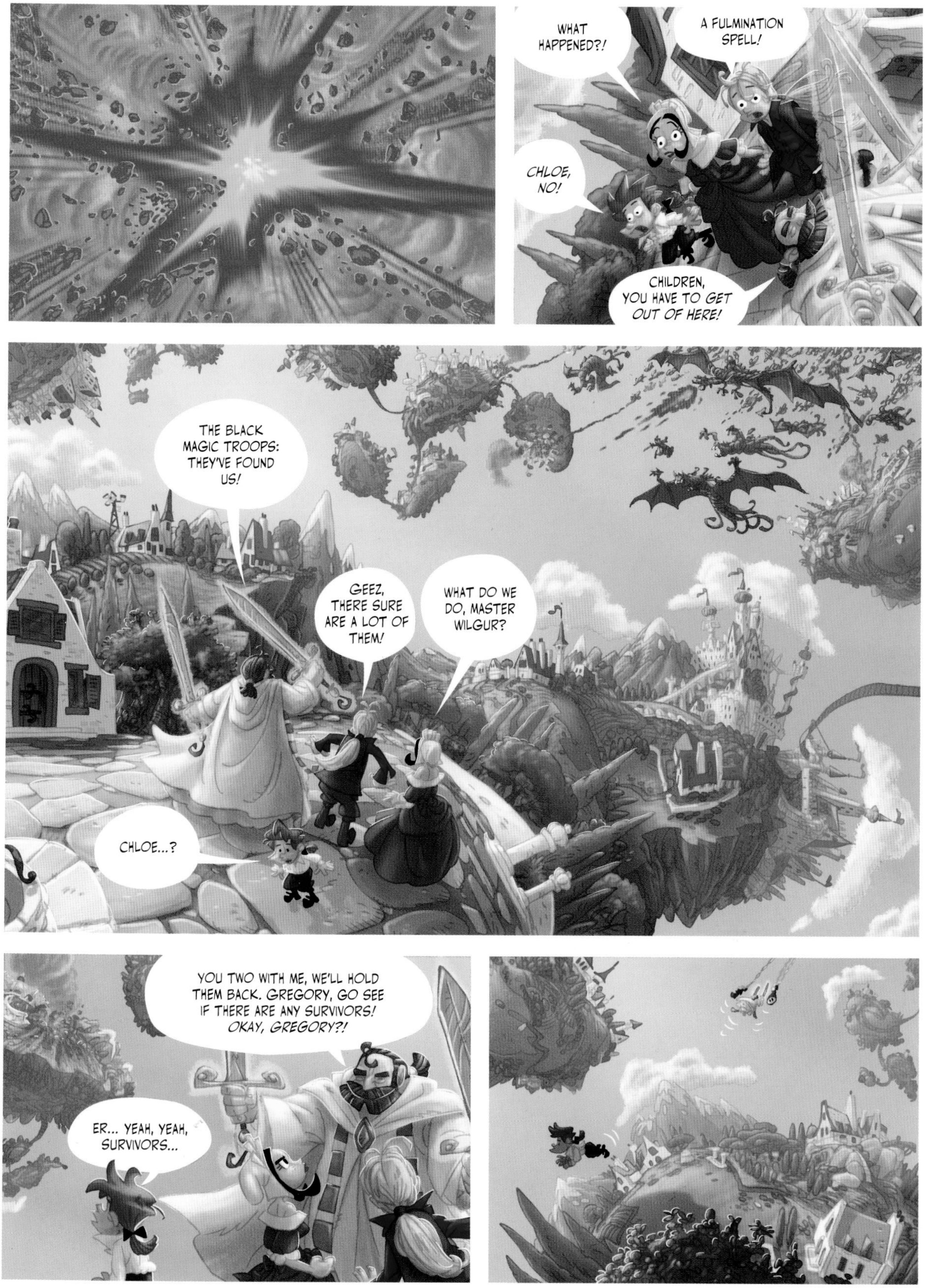
WHAT HAPPENED?!
A FULMINATION SPELL!
CHLOE, NO!
CHILDREN, YOU HAVE TO GET OUT OF HERE!
THE BLACK MAGIC TROOPS: THEY'VE FOUND US!
GEEZ, THERE SURE ARE A LOT OF THEM!
WHAT DO WE DO, MASTER WILGUR?
CHLOE...?
YOU TWO WITH ME, WE'LL HOLD THEM BACK. GREGORY, GO SEE IF THERE ARE ANY SURVIVORS! OKAY, GREGORY?!
ER... YEAH, YEAH, SURVIVORS...

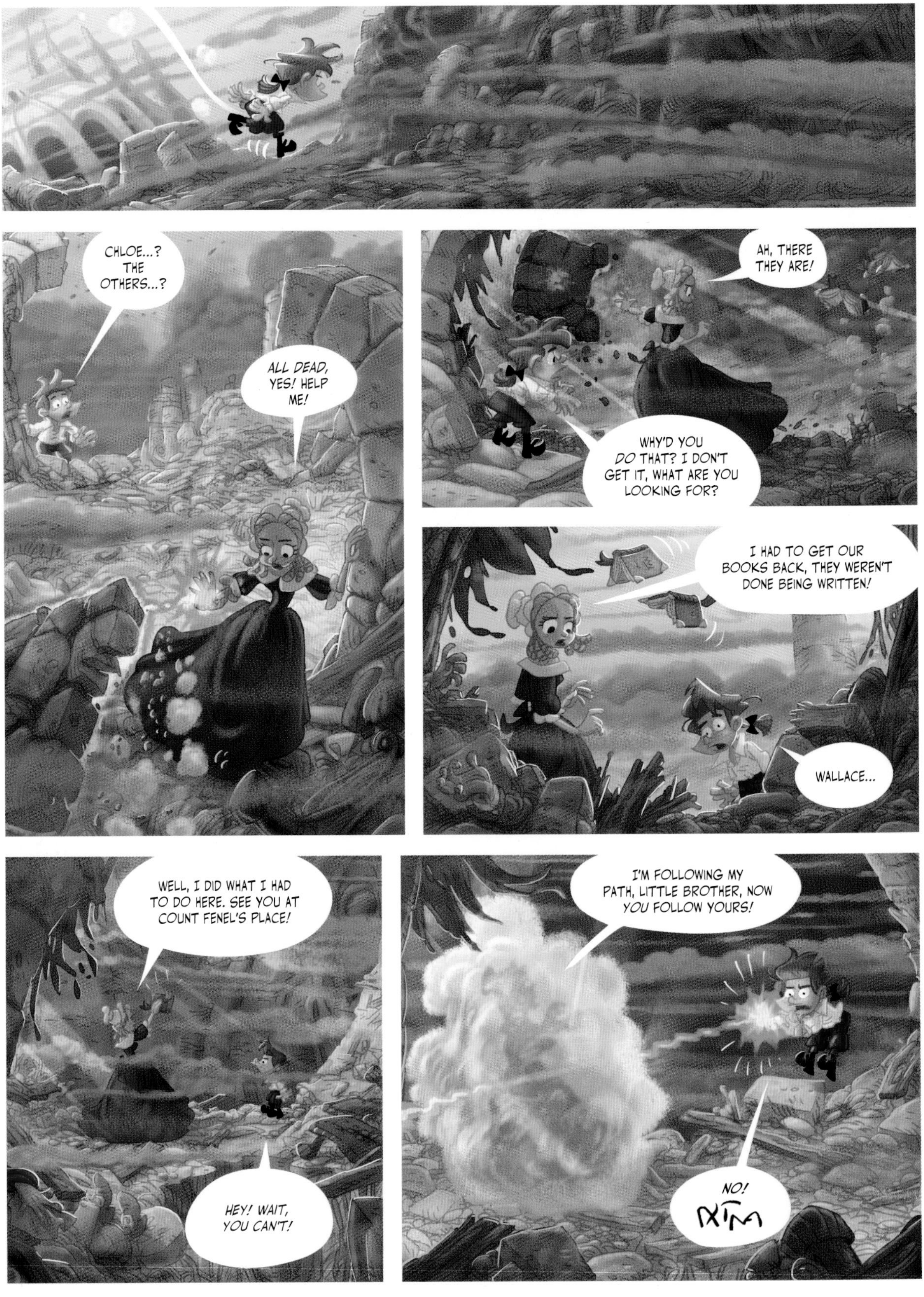
CHLOE...? THE OTHERS...?
ALL DEAD, YES! HELP ME!
AH, THERE THEY ARE!
WHY'D YOU DO THAT? I DON'T GET IT, WHAT ARE YOU LOOKING FOR?
I HAD TO GET OUR BOOKS BACK, THEY WEREN'T DONE BEING WRITTEN!
WALLACE...
WELL, I DID WHAT I HAD TO DO HERE. SEE YOU AT COUNT FENEL'S PLACE!
HEY! WAIT, YOU CAN'T!
I'M FOLLOWING MY PATH, LITTLE BROTHER, NOW YOU FOLLOW YOURS!
NO!

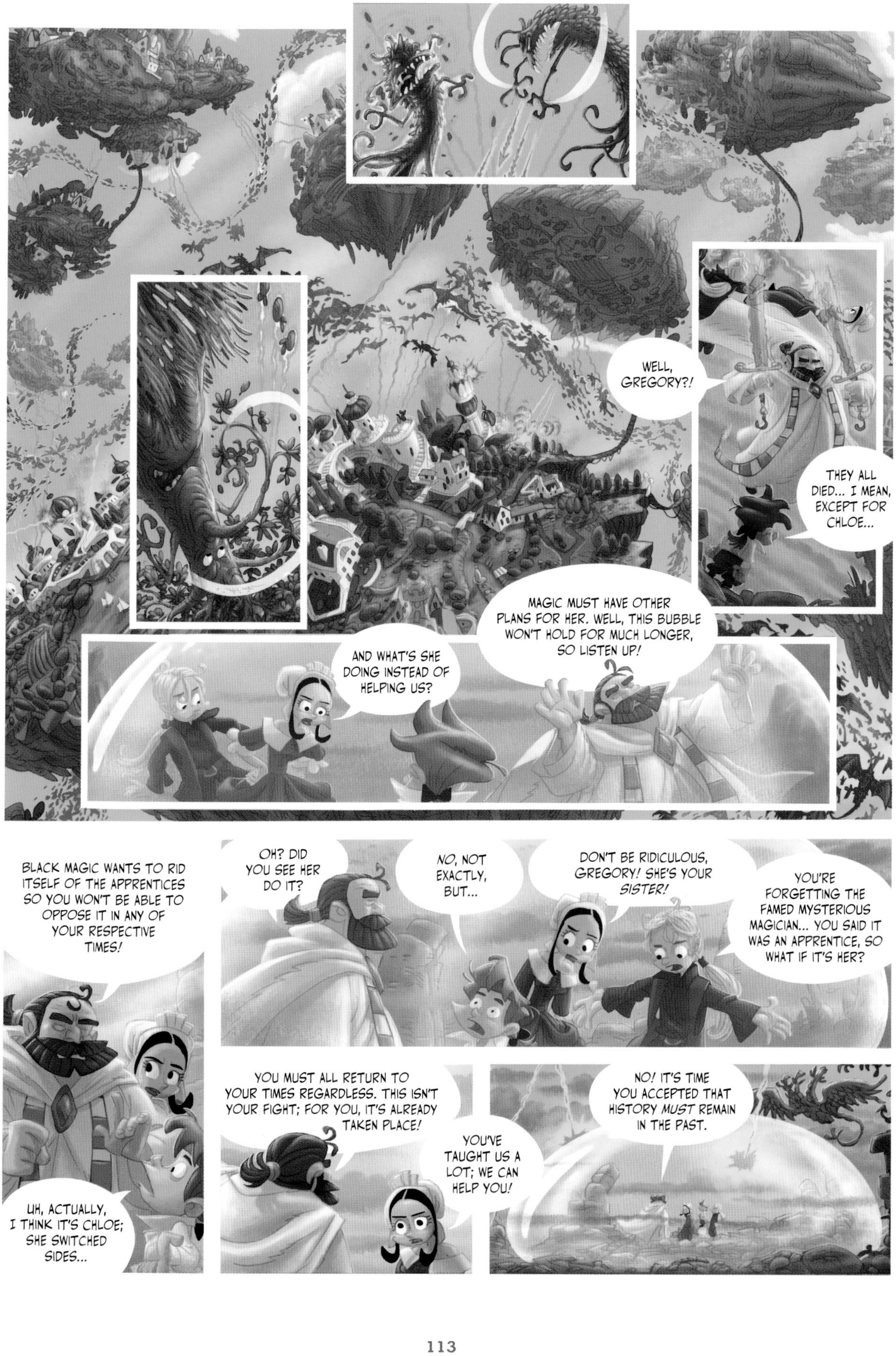
WELL, GREGORY?!
THEY ALL DIED... I MEAN, EXCEPT FOR CHLOE...
MAGIC MUST HAVE OTHER PLANS FOR HER. WELL, THIS BUBBLE WON'T HOLD FOR MUCH LONGER, SO LISTEN UP!
AND WHAT'S SHE DOING INSTEAD OF HELPING US?
BLACK MAGIC WANTS TO RID ITSELF OF THE APPRENTICES SO YOU WON'T BE ABLE TO OPPOSE IT IN ANY OF YOUR RESPECTIVE TIMES!
UH, ACTUALLY, I THINK IT'S CHLOE; SHE SWITCHED SIDES...
OH? DID YOU SEE HER DO IT?
NO, NOT EXACTLY, BUT...
DON'T BE RIDICULOUS, GREGORY! SHE'S YOUR *SISTER!*
YOU'RE FORGETTING THE FAMED MYSTERIOUS MAGICIAN... YOU SAID IT WAS AN APPRENTICE, SO WHAT IF IT'S HER?
YOU MUST ALL RETURN TO YOUR TIMES REGARDLESS. THIS ISN'T YOUR FIGHT; FOR YOU, IT'S ALREADY TAKEN PLACE!
YOU'VE TAUGHT US A LOT; WE CAN HELP YOU!
NO! IT'S TIME YOU ACCEPTED THAT HISTORY *MUST* REMAIN IN THE PAST.

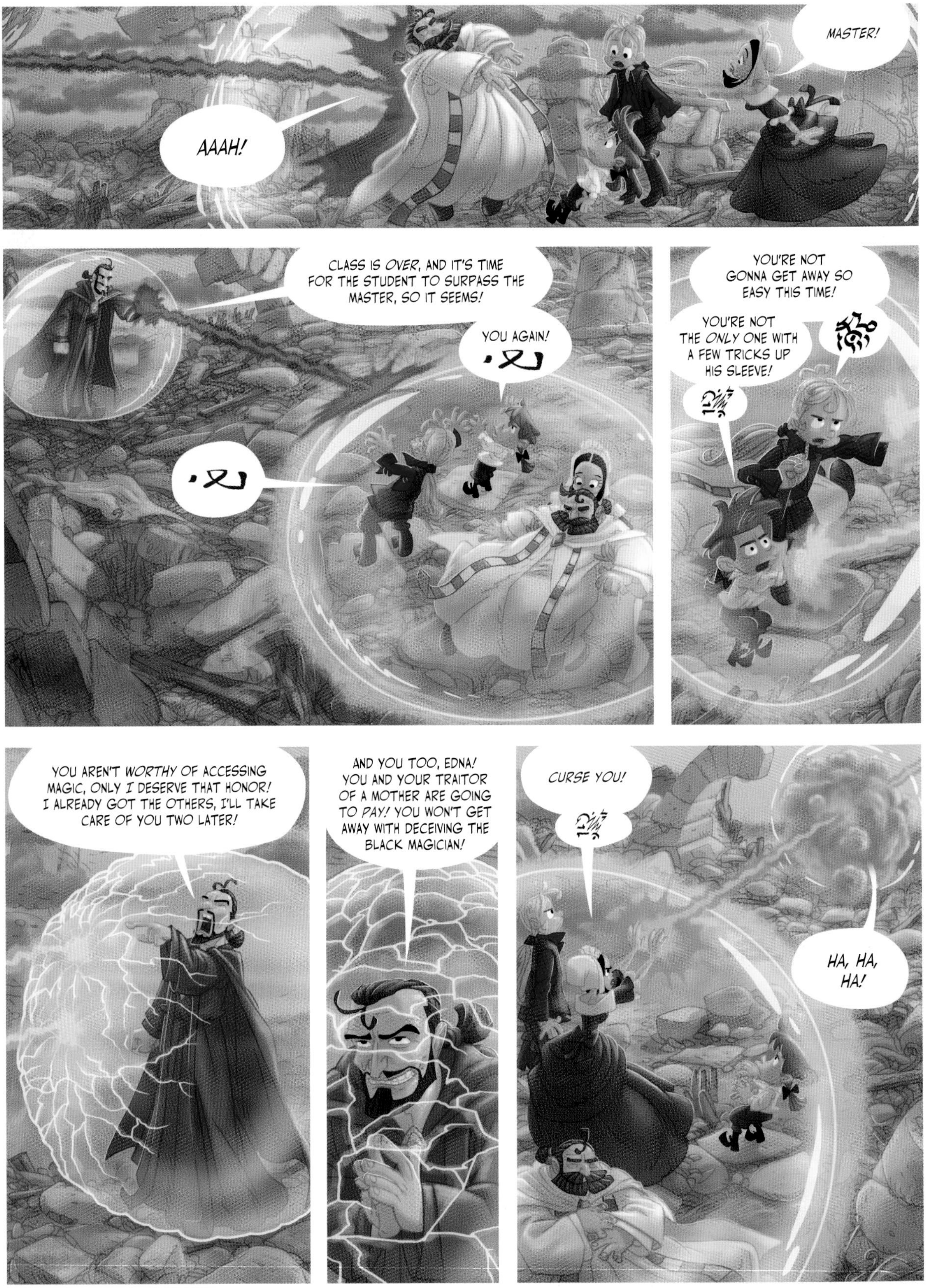

MASTER!
AAAH!
CLASS IS *OVER*, AND IT'S TIME FOR THE STUDENT TO SURPASS THE MASTER, SO IT SEEMS!
YOU AGAIN!
YOU'RE NOT GONNA GET AWAY SO EASY THIS TIME!
YOU'RE NOT THE *ONLY* ONE WITH A FEW TRICKS UP HIS SLEEVE!
YOU AREN'T *WORTHY* OF ACCESSING MAGIC, ONLY *I* DESERVE THAT HONOR! I ALREADY GOT THE OTHERS, I'LL TAKE CARE OF YOU TWO LATER!
AND YOU TOO, EDNA! YOU AND YOUR TRAITOR OF A MOTHER ARE GOING TO *PAY!* YOU WON'T GET AWAY WITH DECEIVING THE BLACK MAGICIAN!
CURSE YOU!
HA, HA, HA!

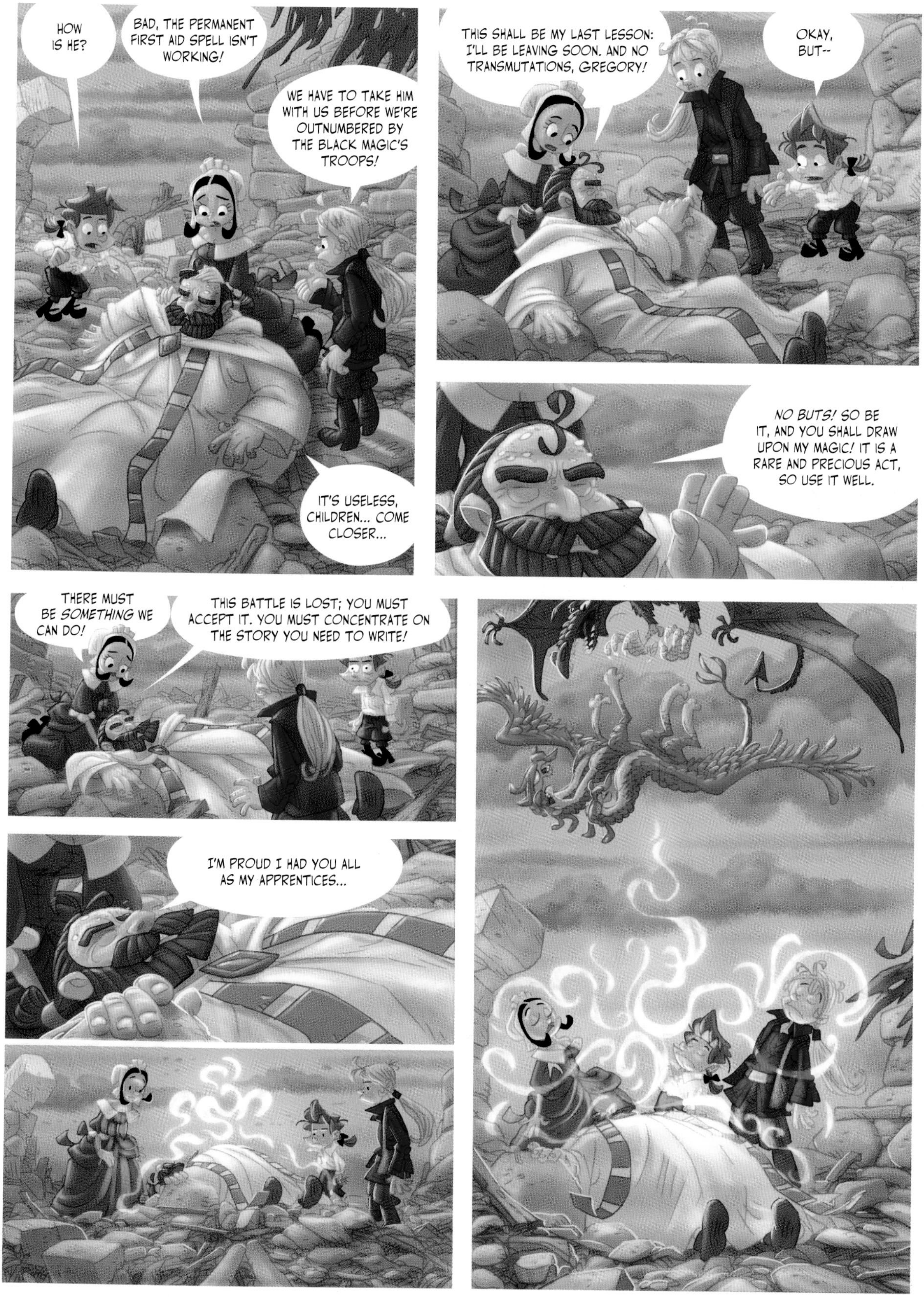
HOW IS HE?
BAD, THE PERMANENT FIRST AID SPELL ISN'T WORKING!
WE HAVE TO TAKE HIM WITH US BEFORE WE'RE OUTNUMBERED BY THE BLACK MAGIC'S TROOPS!
IT'S USELESS, CHILDREN... COME CLOSER...
THIS SHALL BE MY LAST LESSON: I'LL BE LEAVING SOON. AND NO TRANSMUTATIONS, GREGORY!
OKAY, BUT--
NO BUTS! SO BE IT, AND YOU SHALL DRAW UPON MY MAGIC! IT IS A RARE AND PRECIOUS ACT, SO USE IT WELL.
THERE MUST BE SOMETHING WE CAN DO!
THIS BATTLE IS LOST; YOU MUST ACCEPT IT. YOU MUST CONCENTRATE ON THE STORY YOU NEED TO WRITE!
I'M PROUD I HAD YOU ALL AS MY APPRENTICES...

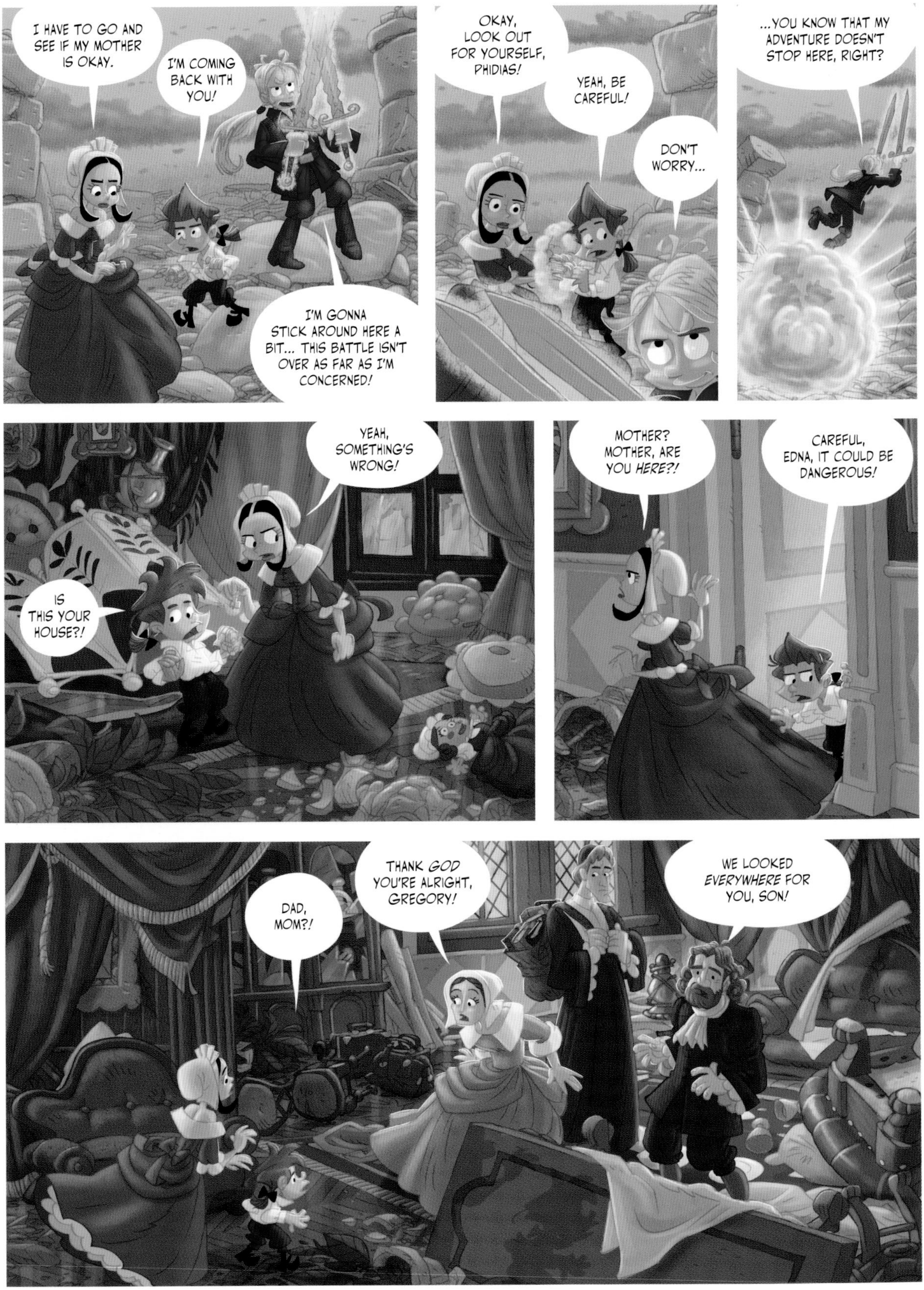
I HAVE TO GO AND SEE IF MY MOTHER IS OKAY.
I'M COMING BACK WITH YOU!
I'M GONNA STICK AROUND HERE A BIT... THIS BATTLE ISN'T OVER AS FAR AS I'M CONCERNED!
OKAY, LOOK OUT FOR YOURSELF, PHIDIAS!
YEAH, BE CAREFUL!
DON'T WORRY...
...YOU KNOW THAT MY ADVENTURE DOESN'T STOP HERE, RIGHT?
YEAH, SOMETHING'S WRONG!
IS THIS YOUR HOUSE?!
MOTHER? MOTHER, ARE YOU HERE?!
CAREFUL, EDNA, IT COULD BE DANGEROUS!
DAD, MOM?!
THANK GOD YOU'RE ALRIGHT, GREGORY!
WE LOOKED EVERYWHERE FOR YOU, SON!

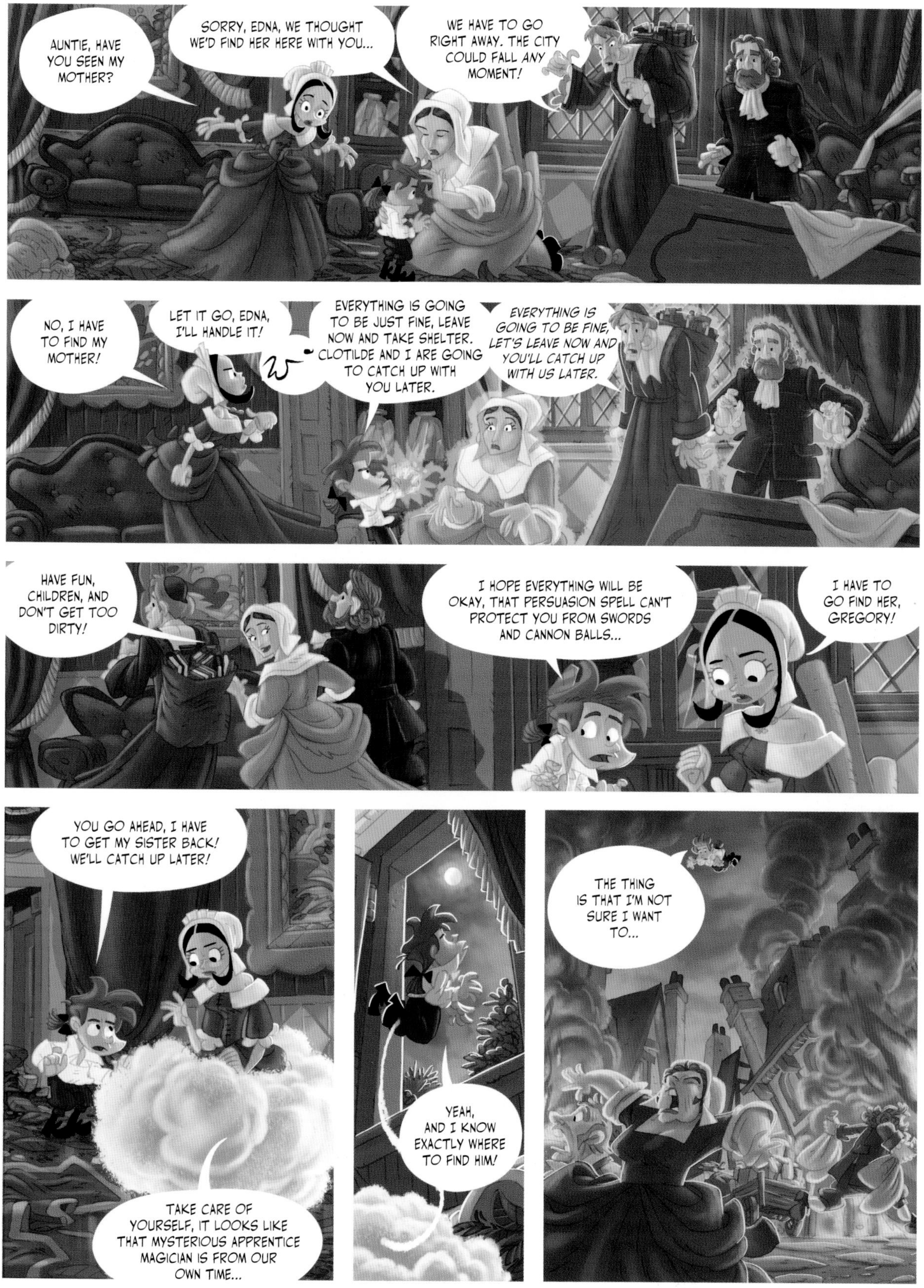
AUNTIE, HAVE YOU SEEN MY MOTHER?
SORRY, EDNA, WE THOUGHT WE'D FIND HER HERE WITH YOU...
WE HAVE TO GO RIGHT AWAY. THE CITY COULD FALL ANY MOMENT!
NO, I HAVE TO FIND MY MOTHER!
LET IT GO, EDNA, I'LL HANDLE IT!
EVERYTHING IS GOING TO BE JUST FINE, LEAVE NOW AND TAKE SHELTER. CLOTILDE AND I ARE GOING TO CATCH UP WITH YOU LATER.
EVERYTHING IS GOING TO BE FINE, LET'S LEAVE NOW AND YOU'LL CATCH UP WITH US LATER.
HAVE FUN, CHILDREN, AND DON'T GET TOO DIRTY!
I HOPE EVERYTHING WILL BE OKAY, THAT PERSUASION SPELL CAN'T PROTECT YOU FROM SWORDS AND CANNON BALLS...
I HAVE TO GO FIND HER, GREGORY!
YOU GO AHEAD, I HAVE TO GET MY SISTER BACK! WE'LL CATCH UP LATER!
TAKE CARE OF YOURSELF, IT LOOKS LIKE THAT MYSTERIOUS APPRENTICE MAGICIAN IS FROM OUR OWN TIME...
YEAH, AND I KNOW EXACTLY WHERE TO FIND HIM!
THE THING IS THAT I'M NOT SURE I WANT TO...

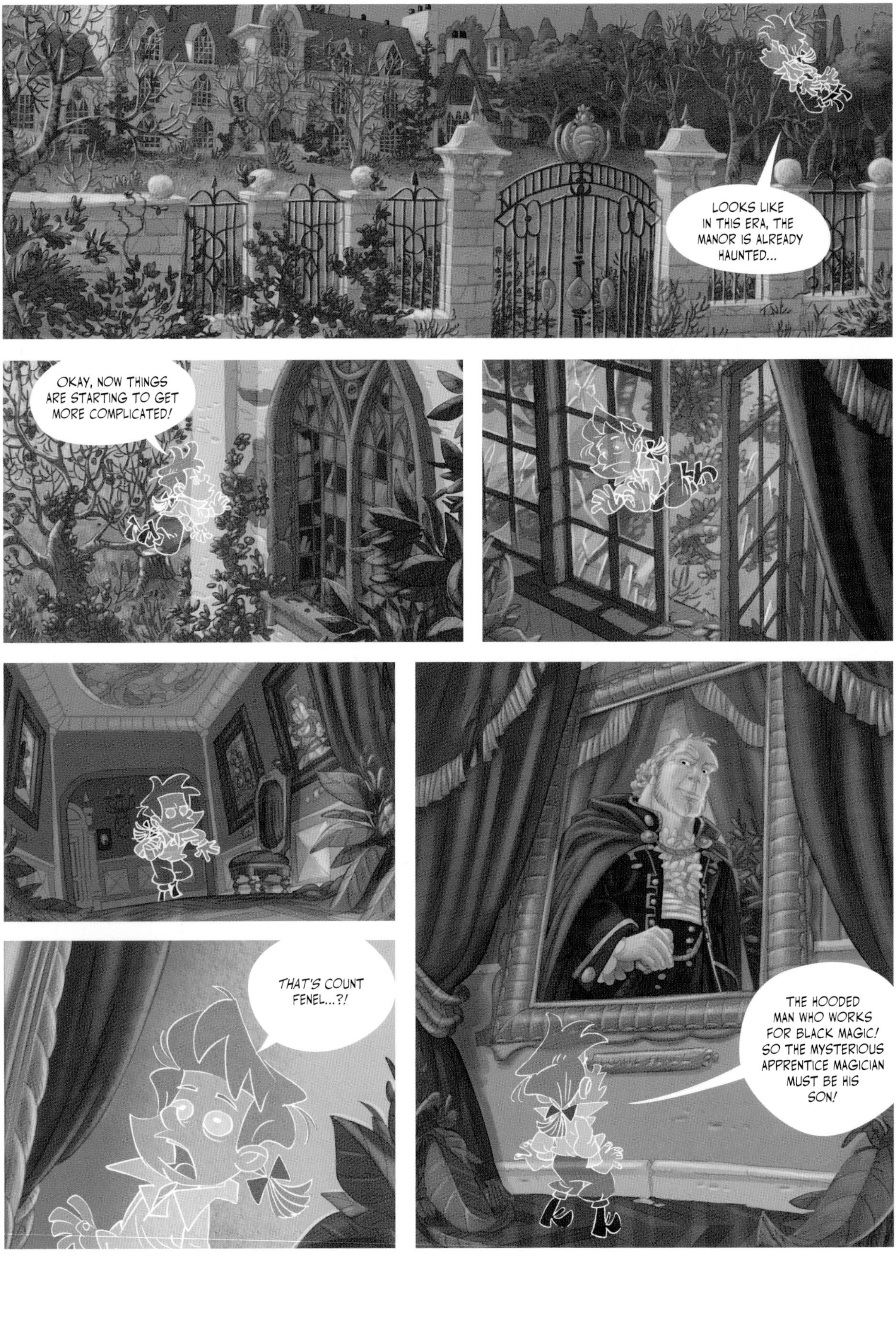
LOOKS LIKE IN THIS ERA, THE MANOR IS ALREADY HAUNTED...
OKAY, NOW THINGS ARE STARTING TO GET MORE COMPLICATED!
THAT'S COUNT FENEL...?!
THE HOODED MAN WHO WORKS FOR BLACK MAGIC! SO THE MYSTERIOUS APPRENTICE MAGICIAN MUST BE HIS SON!

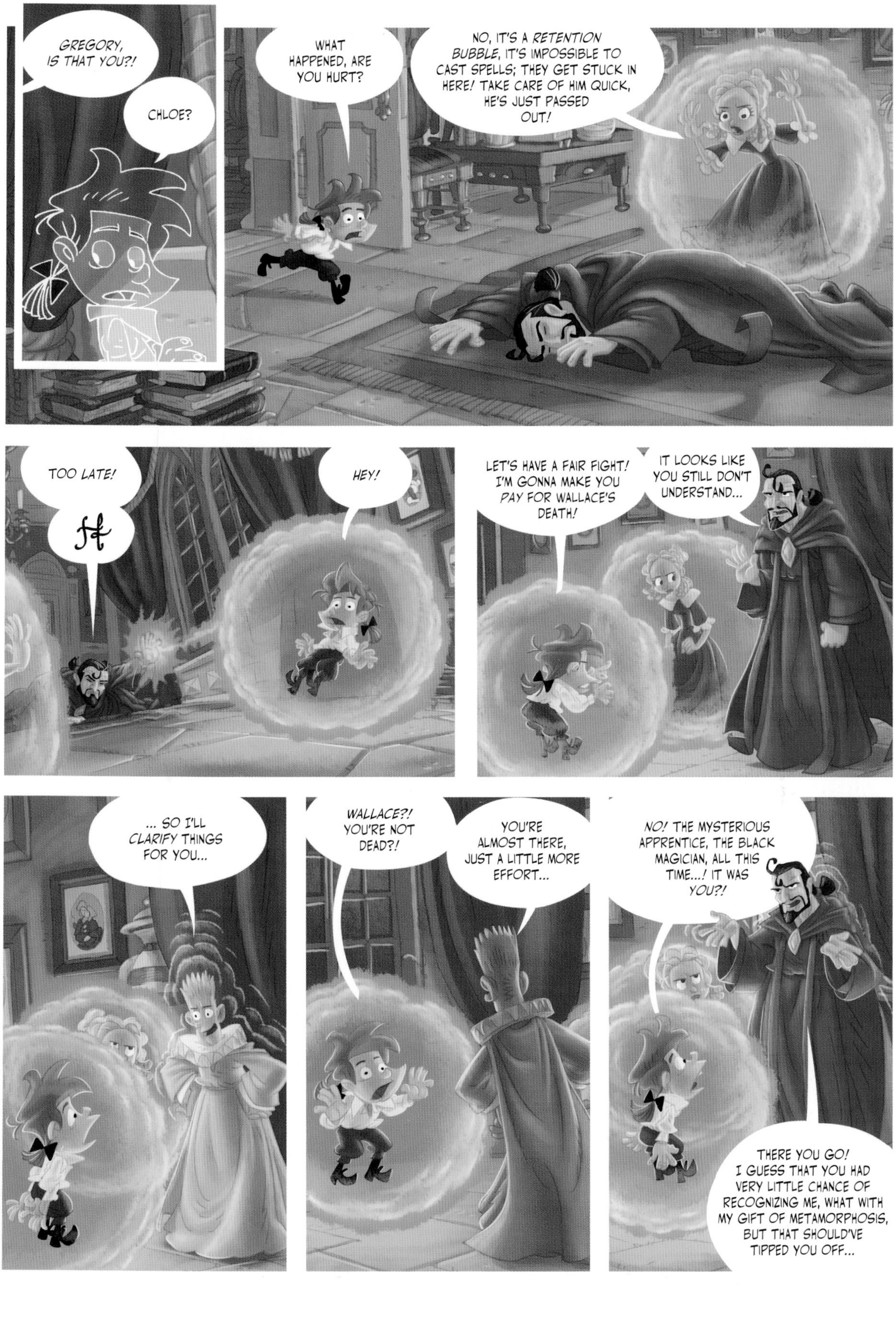
GREGORY, IS THAT YOU?!
CHLOE?
WHAT HAPPENED, ARE YOU HURT?
NO, IT'S A RETENTION BUBBLE, IT'S IMPOSSIBLE TO CAST SPELLS; THEY GET STUCK IN HERE! TAKE CARE OF HIM QUICK, HE'S JUST PASSED OUT!
TOO LATE!
HEY!
LET'S HAVE A FAIR FIGHT! I'M GONNA MAKE YOU PAY FOR WALLACE'S DEATH!
IT LOOKS LIKE YOU STILL DON'T UNDERSTAND...
... SO I'LL CLARIFY THINGS FOR YOU...
WALLACE?! YOU'RE NOT DEAD?!
YOU'RE ALMOST THERE, JUST A LITTLE MORE EFFORT...
NO! THE MYSTERIOUS APPRENTICE, THE BLACK MAGICIAN, ALL THIS TIME...! IT WAS YOU?!
THERE YOU GO! I GUESS THAT YOU HAD VERY LITTLE CHANCE OF RECOGNIZING ME, WHAT WITH MY GIFT OF METAMORPHOSIS, BUT THAT SHOULD'VE TIPPED YOU OFF...

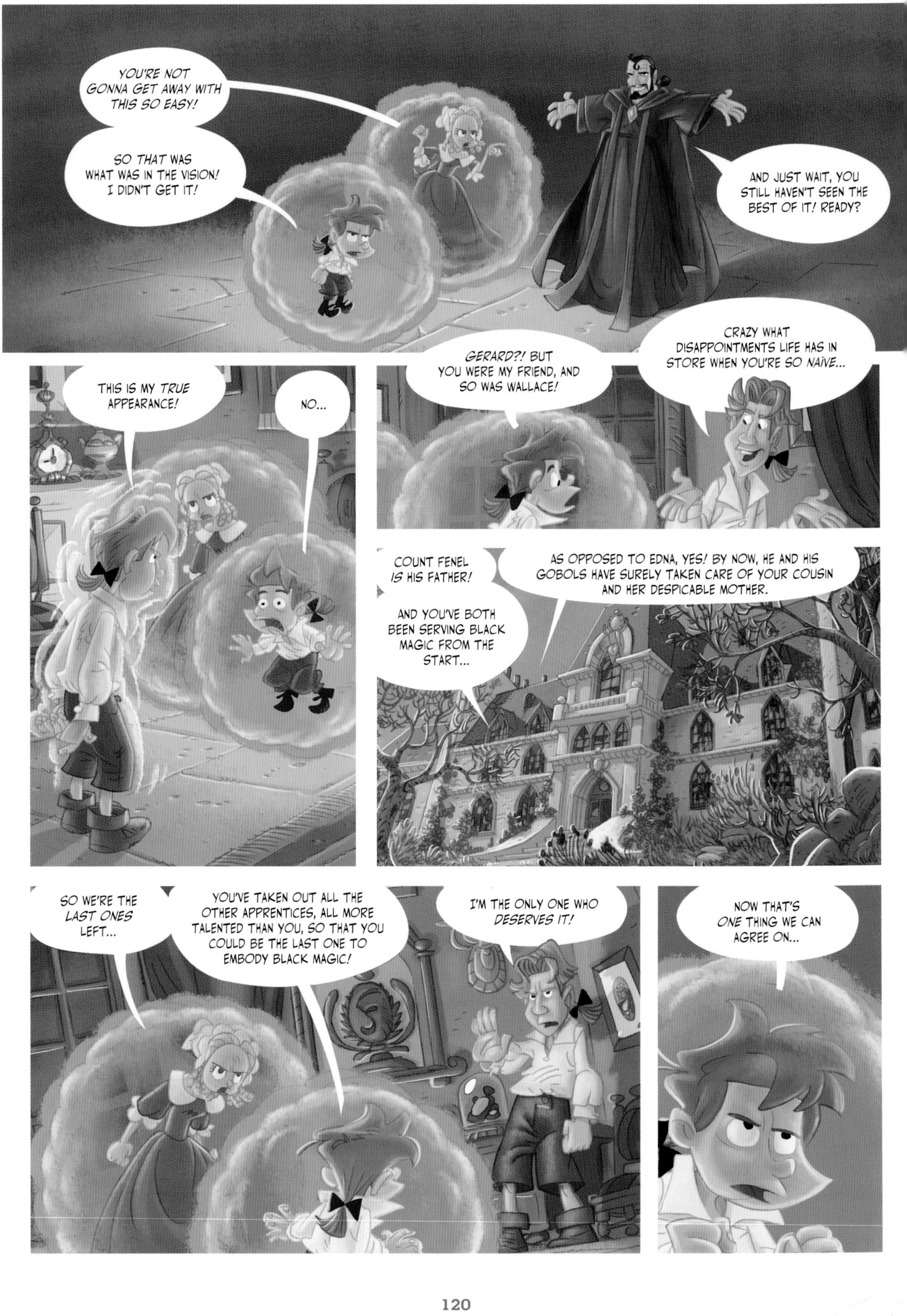
YOU'RE NOT GONNA GET AWAY WITH THIS SO EASY!
SO THAT WAS WHAT WAS IN THE VISION! I DIDN'T GET IT!
AND JUST WAIT, YOU STILL HAVEN'T SEEN THE BEST OF IT! READY?
THIS IS MY TRUE APPEARANCE!
NO...
GERARD?! BUT YOU WERE MY FRIEND, AND SO WAS WALLACE!
CRAZY WHAT DISAPPOINTMENTS LIFE HAS IN STORE WHEN YOU'RE SO NAÏVE...
COUNT FENEL IS HIS FATHER!
AND YOU'VE BOTH BEEN SERVING BLACK MAGIC FROM THE START...
AS OPPOSED TO EDNA, YES! BY NOW, HE AND HIS GOBOLS HAVE SURELY TAKEN CARE OF YOUR COUSIN AND HER DESPICABLE MOTHER.
SO WE'RE THE LAST ONES LEFT...
YOU'VE TAKEN OUT ALL THE OTHER APPRENTICES, ALL MORE TALENTED THAN YOU, SO THAT YOU COULD BE THE LAST ONE TO EMBODY BLACK MAGIC!
I'M THE ONLY ONE WHO DESERVES IT!
NOW THAT'S ONE THING WE CAN AGREE ON...

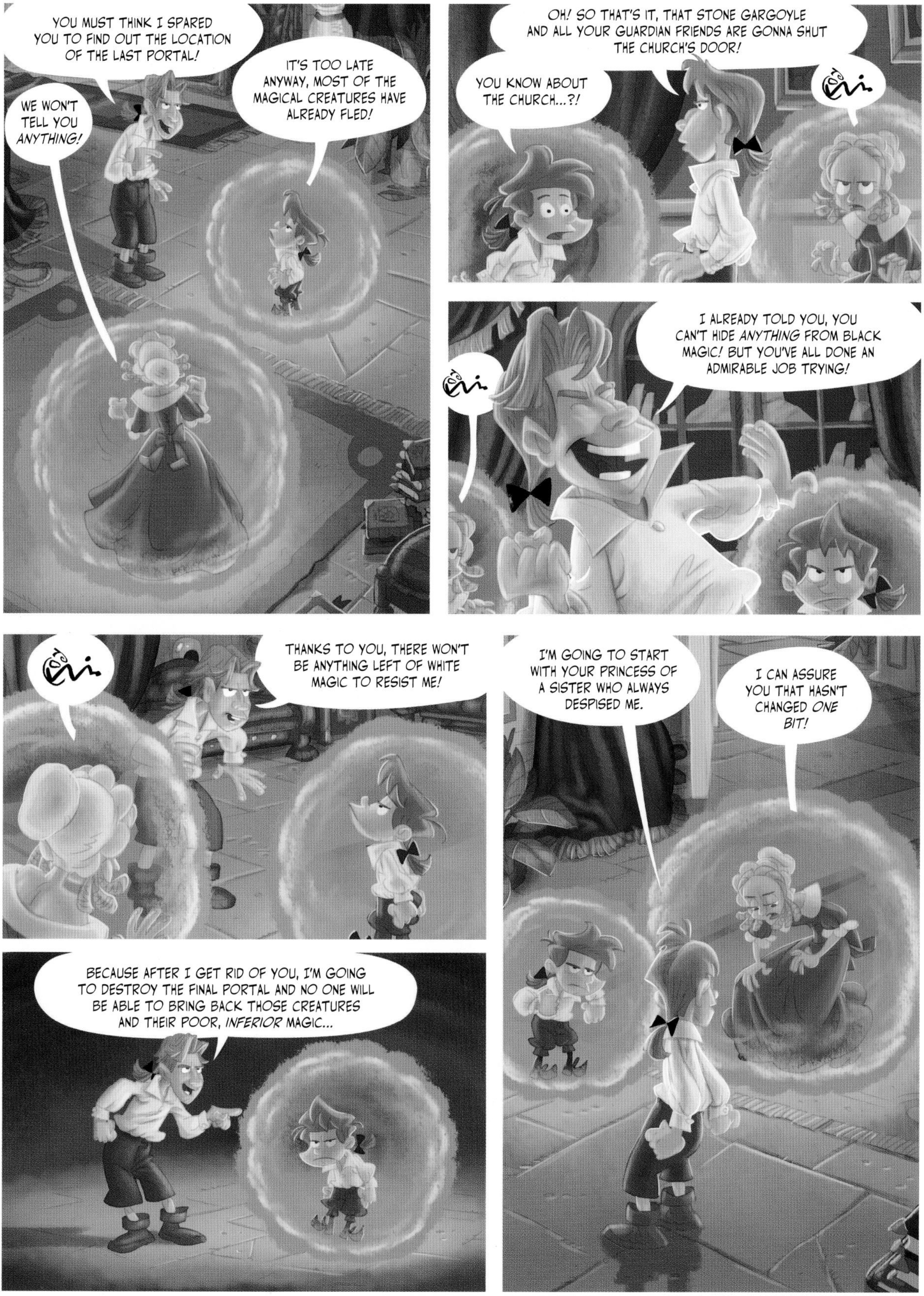
YOU MUST THINK I SPARED YOU TO FIND OUT THE LOCATION OF THE LAST PORTAL!
WE WON'T TELL YOU *ANYTHING!*
IT'S TOO LATE ANYWAY, MOST OF THE MAGICAL CREATURES HAVE ALREADY FLED!
OH! SO THAT'S IT, THAT STONE GARGOYLE AND ALL YOUR GUARDIAN FRIENDS ARE GONNA SHUT THE CHURCH'S DOOR!
YOU KNOW ABOUT THE CHURCH...?!
I ALREADY TOLD YOU, YOU CAN'T HIDE *ANYTHING* FROM BLACK MAGIC! BUT YOU'VE ALL DONE AN ADMIRABLE JOB TRYING!
THANKS TO YOU, THERE WON'T BE ANYTHING LEFT OF WHITE MAGIC TO RESIST ME!
BECAUSE AFTER I GET RID OF YOU, I'M GOING TO DESTROY THE FINAL PORTAL AND NO ONE WILL BE ABLE TO BRING BACK THOSE CREATURES AND THEIR POOR, *INFERIOR* MAGIC...
I'M GOING TO START WITH YOUR PRINCESS OF A SISTER WHO ALWAYS DESPISED ME.
I CAN ASSURE YOU THAT HASN'T CHANGED *ONE* BIT!

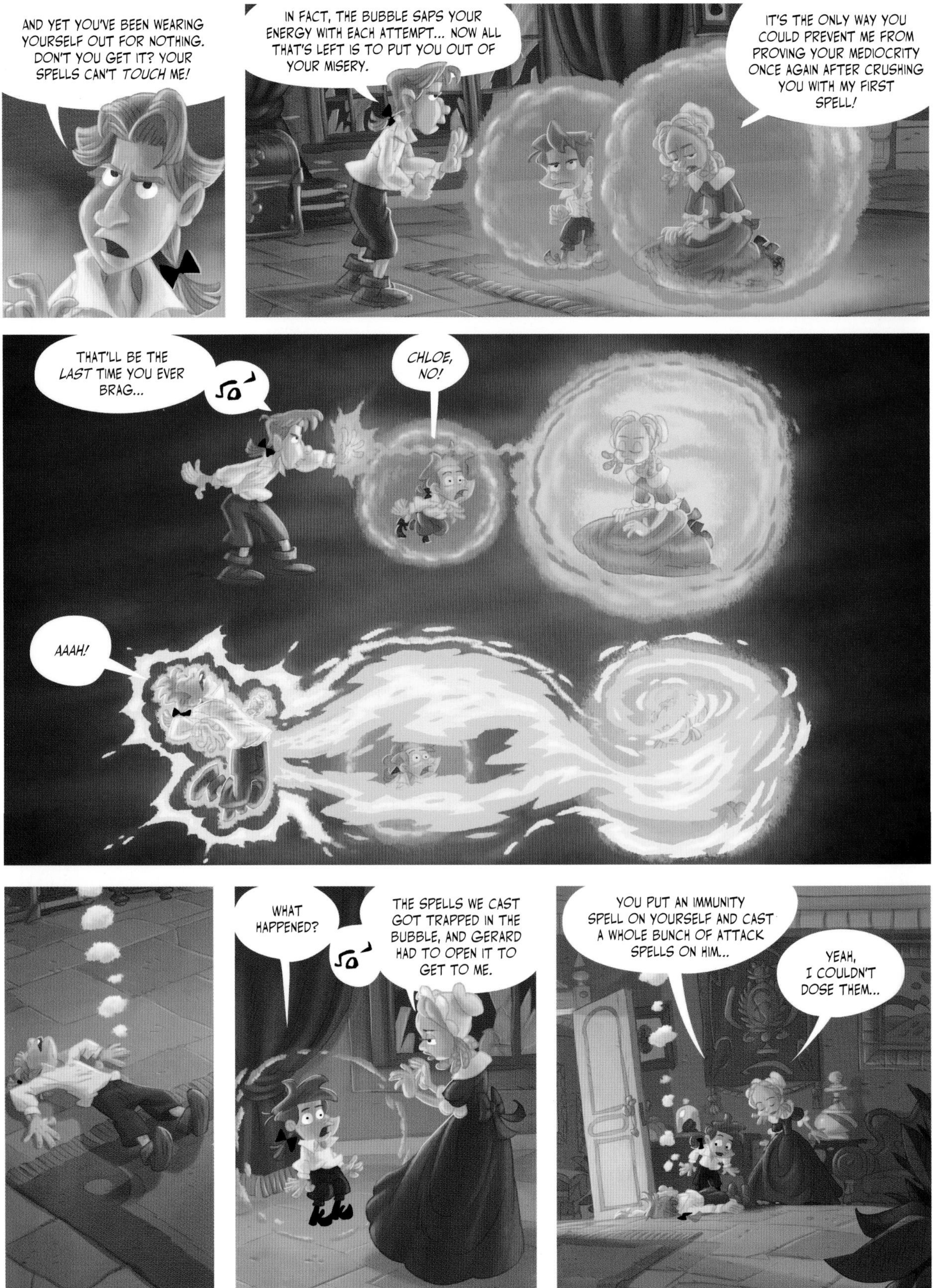
AND YET YOU'VE BEEN WEARING YOURSELF OUT FOR NOTHING. DON'T YOU GET IT? YOUR SPELLS CAN'T *TOUCH* ME!
IN FACT, THE BUBBLE SAPS YOUR ENERGY WITH EACH ATTEMPT... NOW ALL THAT'S LEFT IS TO PUT YOU OUT OF YOUR MISERY.
IT'S THE ONLY WAY YOU COULD PREVENT ME FROM PROVING YOUR MEDIOCRITY ONCE AGAIN AFTER CRUSHING YOU WITH MY FIRST SPELL!
THAT'LL BE THE *LAST* TIME YOU EVER BRAG...
CHLOE, NO!
AAAH!
WHAT HAPPENED?
THE SPELLS WE CAST GOT TRAPPED IN THE BUBBLE, AND GERARD HAD TO OPEN IT TO GET TO ME.
YOU PUT AN IMMUNITY SPELL ON YOURSELF AND CAST A WHOLE BUNCH OF ATTACK SPELLS ON HIM...
YEAH, I COULDN'T DOSE THEM...

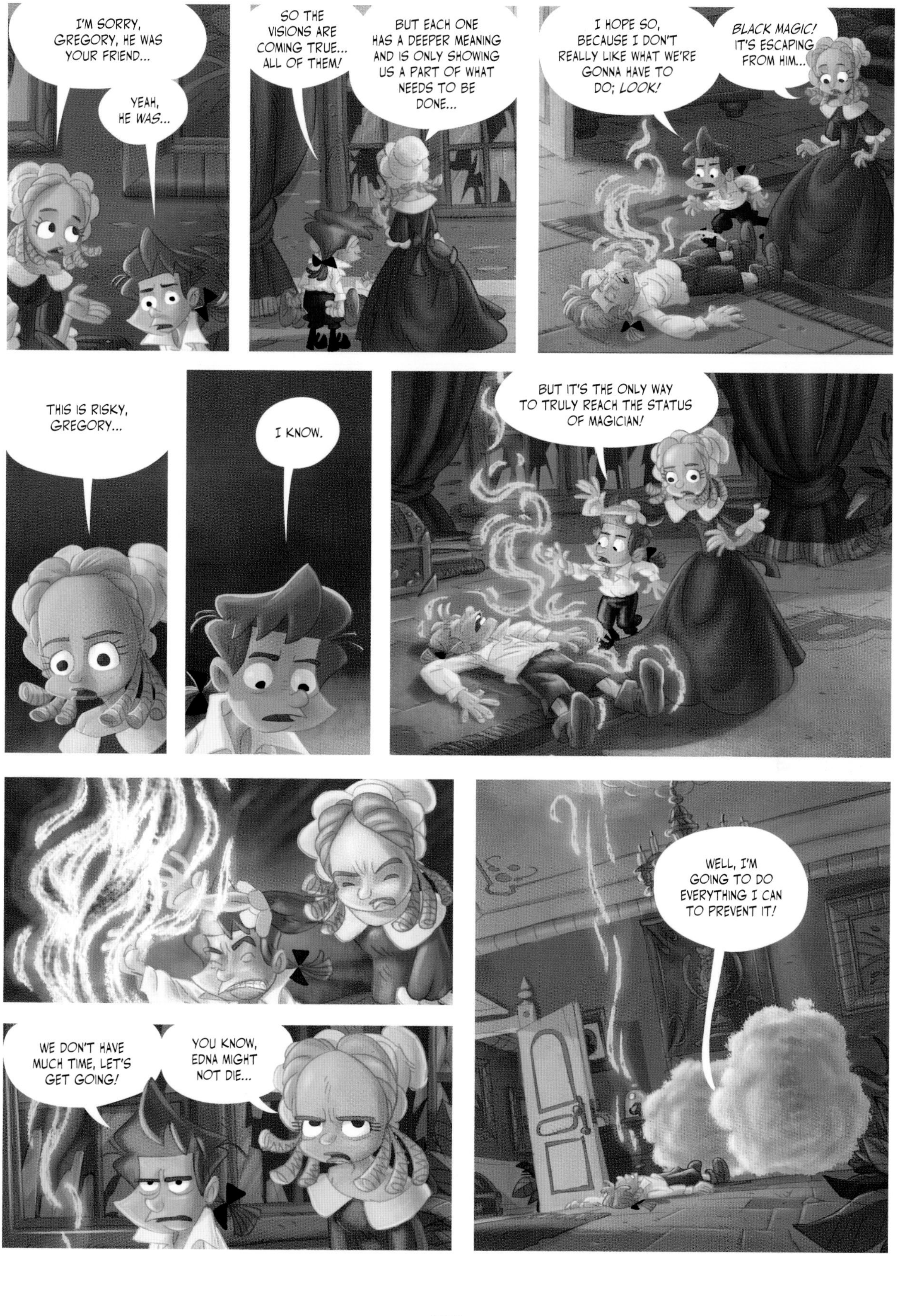
I'M SORRY, GREGORY, HE WAS YOUR FRIEND...
YEAH, HE WAS...
SO THE VISIONS ARE COMING TRUE... ALL OF THEM!
BUT EACH ONE HAS A DEEPER MEANING AND IS ONLY SHOWING US A PART OF WHAT NEEDS TO BE DONE...
I HOPE SO, BECAUSE I DON'T REALLY LIKE WHAT WE'RE GONNA HAVE TO DO; *LOOK!*
BLACK MAGIC! IT'S ESCAPING FROM HIM...
THIS IS RISKY, GREGORY...
I KNOW.
BUT IT'S THE ONLY WAY TO TRULY REACH THE STATUS OF MAGICIAN!
WE DON'T HAVE MUCH TIME, LET'S GET GOING!
YOU KNOW, EDNA MIGHT NOT DIE...
WELL, I'M GOING TO DO EVERYTHING I CAN TO PREVENT IT!

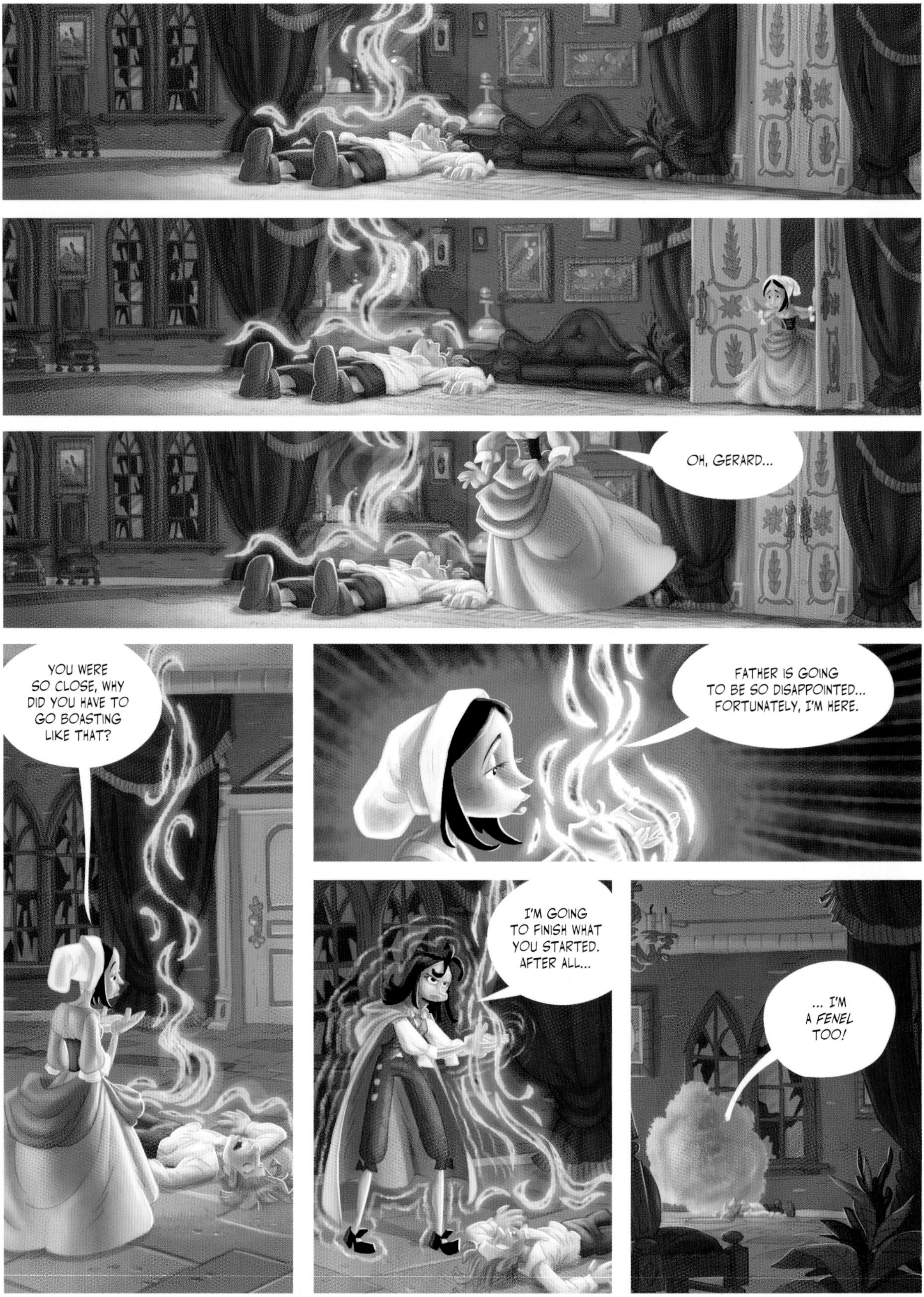
OH, GERARD...
YOU WERE SO CLOSE, WHY DID YOU HAVE TO GO BOASTING LIKE THAT?
FATHER IS GOING TO BE SO DISAPPOINTED... FORTUNATELY, I'M HERE.
I'M GOING TO FINISH WHAT YOU STARTED. AFTER ALL...
... I'M A *FENEL* TOO!

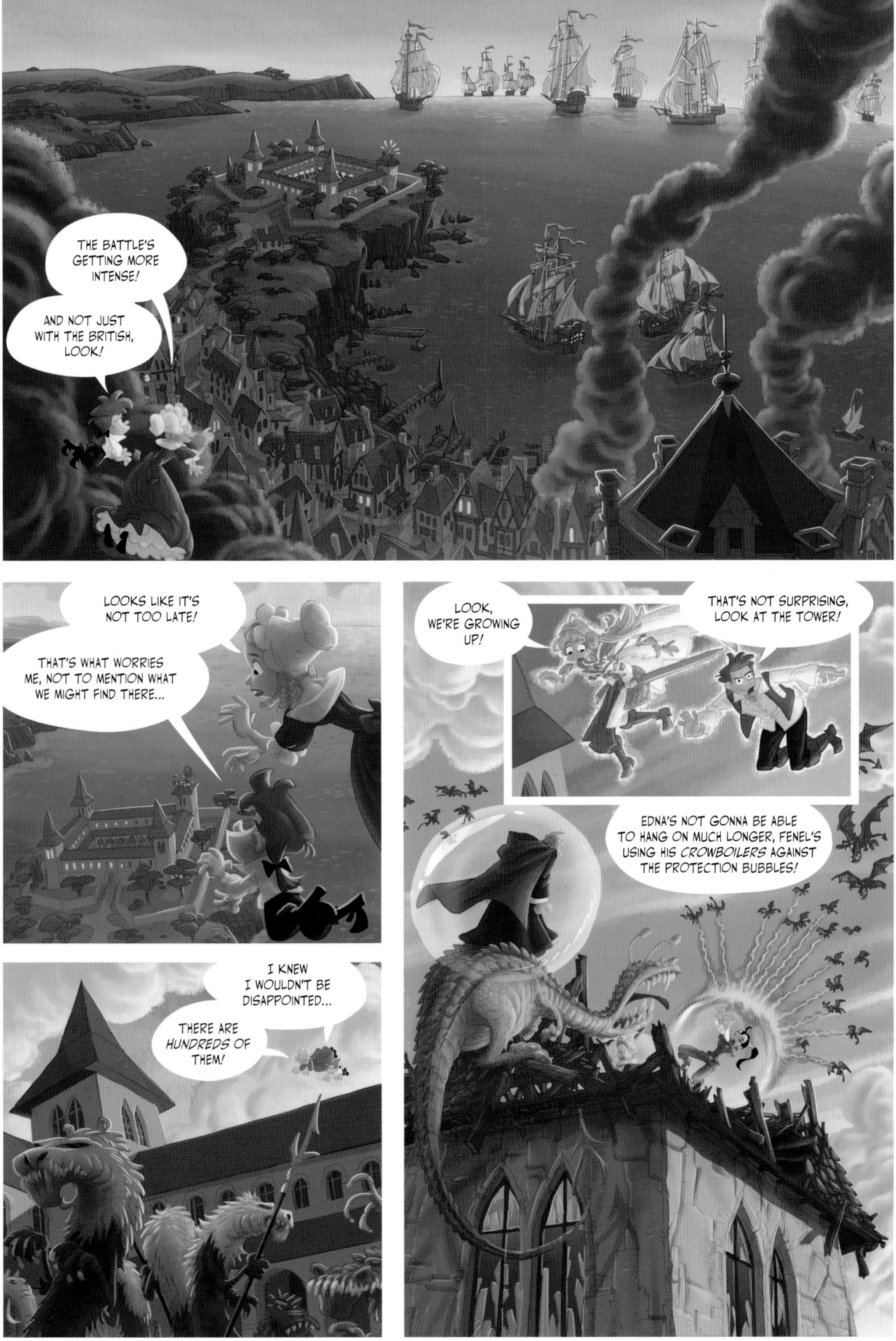
THE BATTLE'S GETTING MORE INTENSE!
AND NOT JUST WITH THE BRITISH, LOOK!
LOOKS LIKE IT'S NOT TOO LATE!
THAT'S WHAT WORRIES ME, NOT TO MENTION WHAT WE MIGHT FIND THERE...
I KNEW I WOULDN'T BE DISAPPOINTED...
THERE ARE *HUNDREDS* OF THEM!
LOOK, WE'RE GROWING UP!
THAT'S NOT SURPRISING, LOOK AT THE TOWER!
EDNA'S NOT GONNA BE ABLE TO HANG ON MUCH LONGER, FENEL'S USING HIS *CROWBOILERS* AGAINST THE PROTECTION BUBBLES!

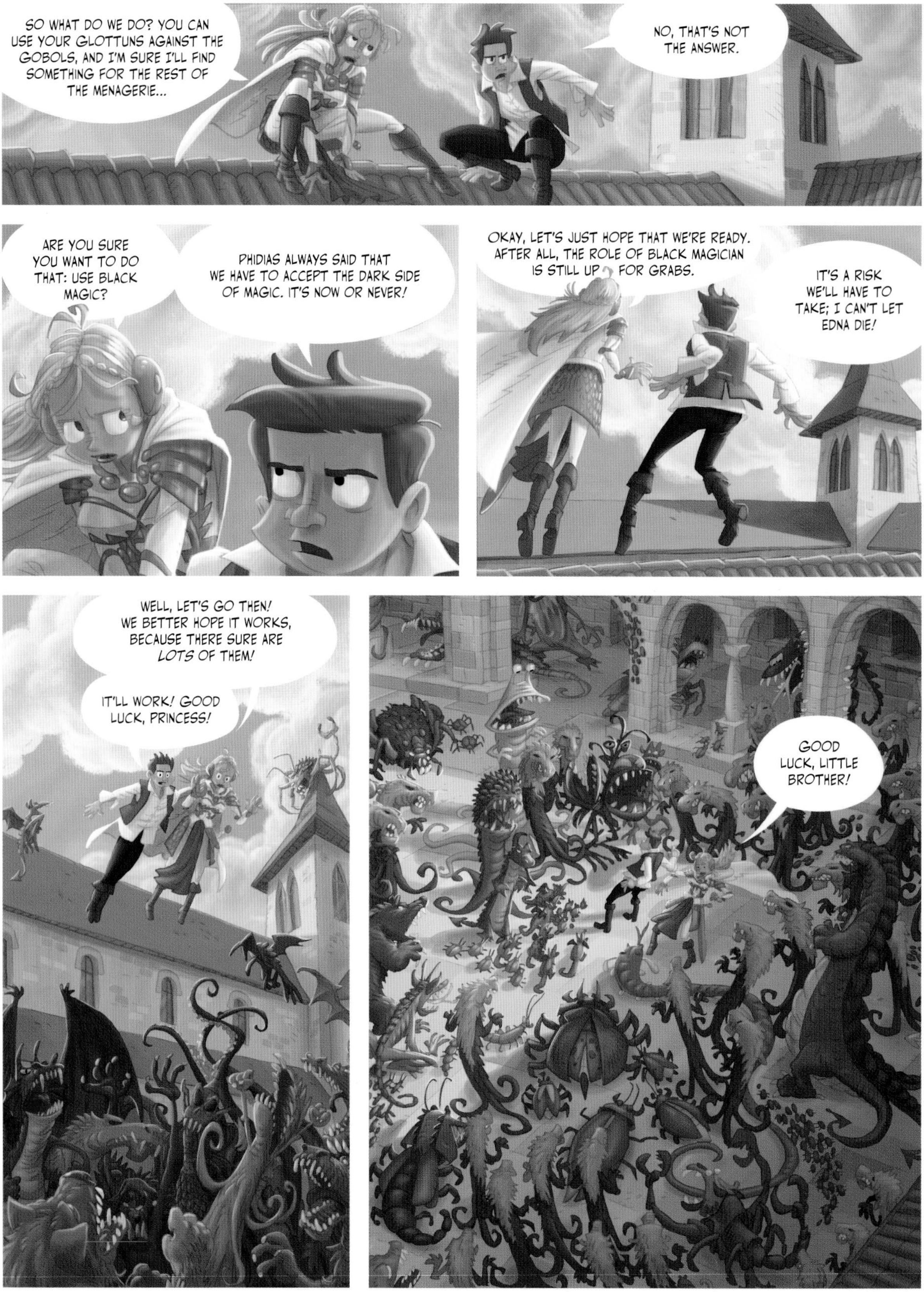
SO WHAT DO WE DO? YOU CAN USE YOUR GLOTTUNS AGAINST THE GOBOLS, AND I'M SURE I'LL FIND SOMETHING FOR THE REST OF THE MENAGERIE...
NO, THAT'S NOT THE ANSWER.
ARE YOU SURE YOU WANT TO DO THAT: USE BLACK MAGIC?
PHIDIAS ALWAYS SAID THAT WE HAVE TO ACCEPT THE DARK SIDE OF MAGIC. IT'S NOW OR NEVER!
OKAY, LET'S JUST HOPE THAT WE'RE READY. AFTER ALL, THE ROLE OF BLACK MAGICIAN IS STILL UP FOR GRABS.
IT'S A RISK WE'LL HAVE TO TAKE; I CAN'T LET EDNA DIE!
WELL, LET'S GO THEN! WE BETTER HOPE IT WORKS, BECAUSE THERE SURE ARE *LOTS* OF THEM!
IT'LL WORK! GOOD LUCK, PRINCESS!
GOOD LUCK, LITTLE BROTHER!

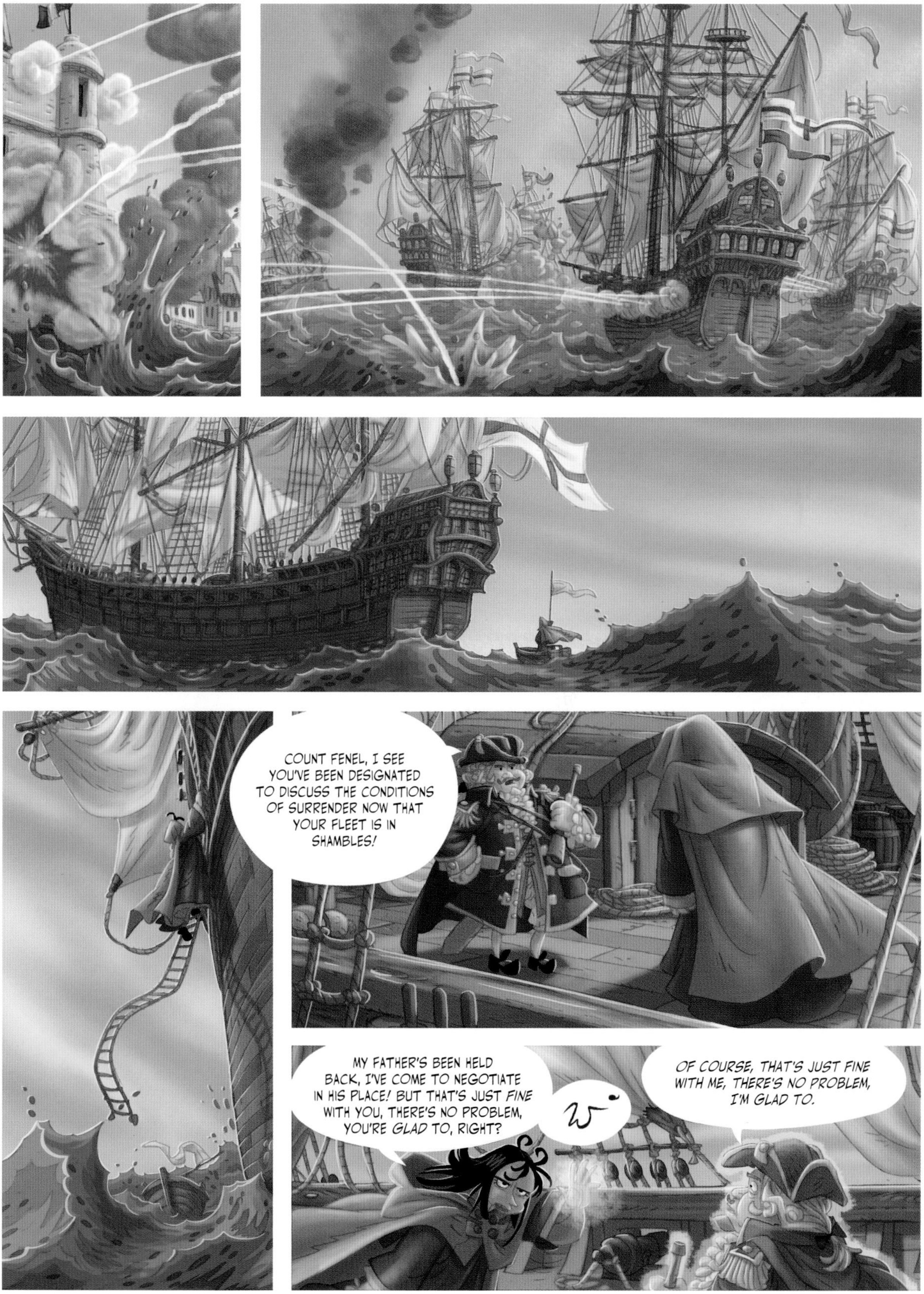
COUNT FENEL, I SEE YOU'VE BEEN DESIGNATED TO DISCUSS THE CONDITIONS OF SURRENDER NOW THAT YOUR FLEET IS IN SHAMBLES!
MY FATHER'S BEEN HELD BACK, I'VE COME TO NEGOTIATE IN HIS PLACE! BUT THAT'S JUST *FINE* WITH YOU, THERE'S NO PROBLEM, YOU'RE *GLAD* TO, RIGHT?
OF COURSE, THAT'S JUST FINE WITH ME, THERE'S NO PROBLEM, I'M GLAD TO.

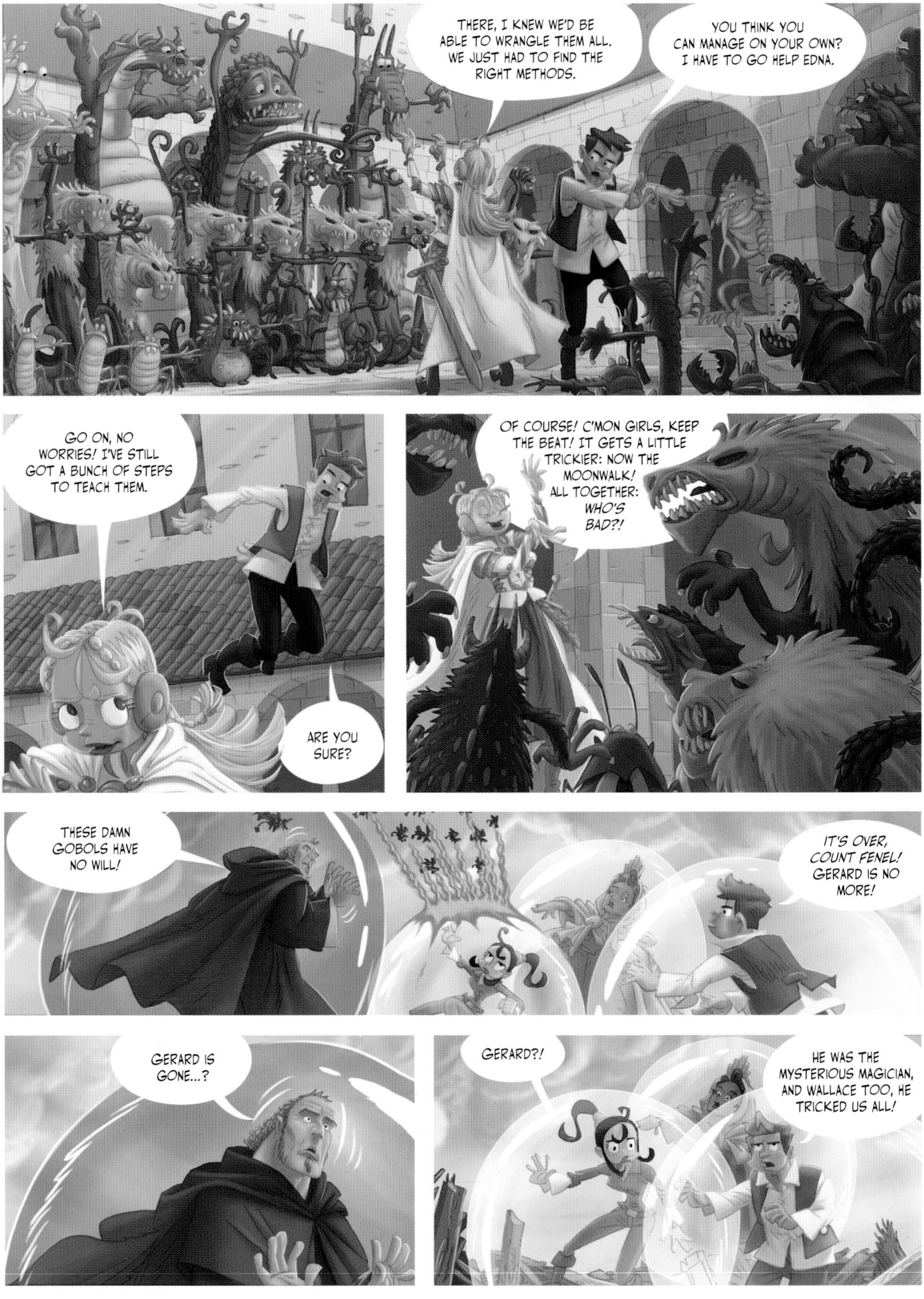

THERE, I KNEW WE'D BE ABLE TO WRANGLE THEM ALL. WE JUST HAD TO FIND THE RIGHT METHODS.
YOU THINK YOU CAN MANAGE ON YOUR OWN? I HAVE TO GO HELP EDNA.
GO ON, NO WORRIES! I'VE STILL GOT A BUNCH OF STEPS TO TEACH THEM.
ARE YOU SURE?
OF COURSE! C'MON GIRLS, KEEP THE BEAT! IT GETS A LITTLE TRICKIER: NOW THE MOONWALK! ALL TOGETHER: WHO'S BAD?!
THESE DAMN GOBOLS HAVE NO WILL!
IT'S OVER, COUNT FENEL! GERARD IS NO MORE!
GERARD IS GONE...?
GERARD?!
HE WAS THE MYSTERIOUS MAGICIAN, AND WALLACE TOO, HE TRICKED US ALL!

BUT IT'S OVER, YOU CAN FORGET YOUR DREAMS OF BLACK MAGIC, YOU'VE FAILED!

NO, IT'S FAR FROM OVER!

WATCH OUT, GREGORY!

I TOLD YOU, IT'S OVER! CHLOE AND I HAVE WELCOMED MAGIC WITHIN US, ALL MAGIC!

YES! YOU'RE NO LONGER DEALING WITH APPRENTICES, BUT MAGICIANS!

THEN THE GREAT MAGICIANS THAT YOU ARE MUST SURELY KNOW WHAT HAPPENS WHEN TWO PROTECTION BUBBLES CHARGED WITH ENERGY COLLIDE...

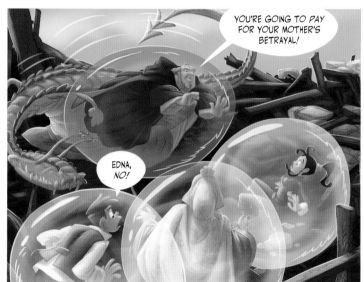

YOU'RE GOING TO PAY FOR YOUR MOTHER'S BETRAYAL!

EDNA, NO!

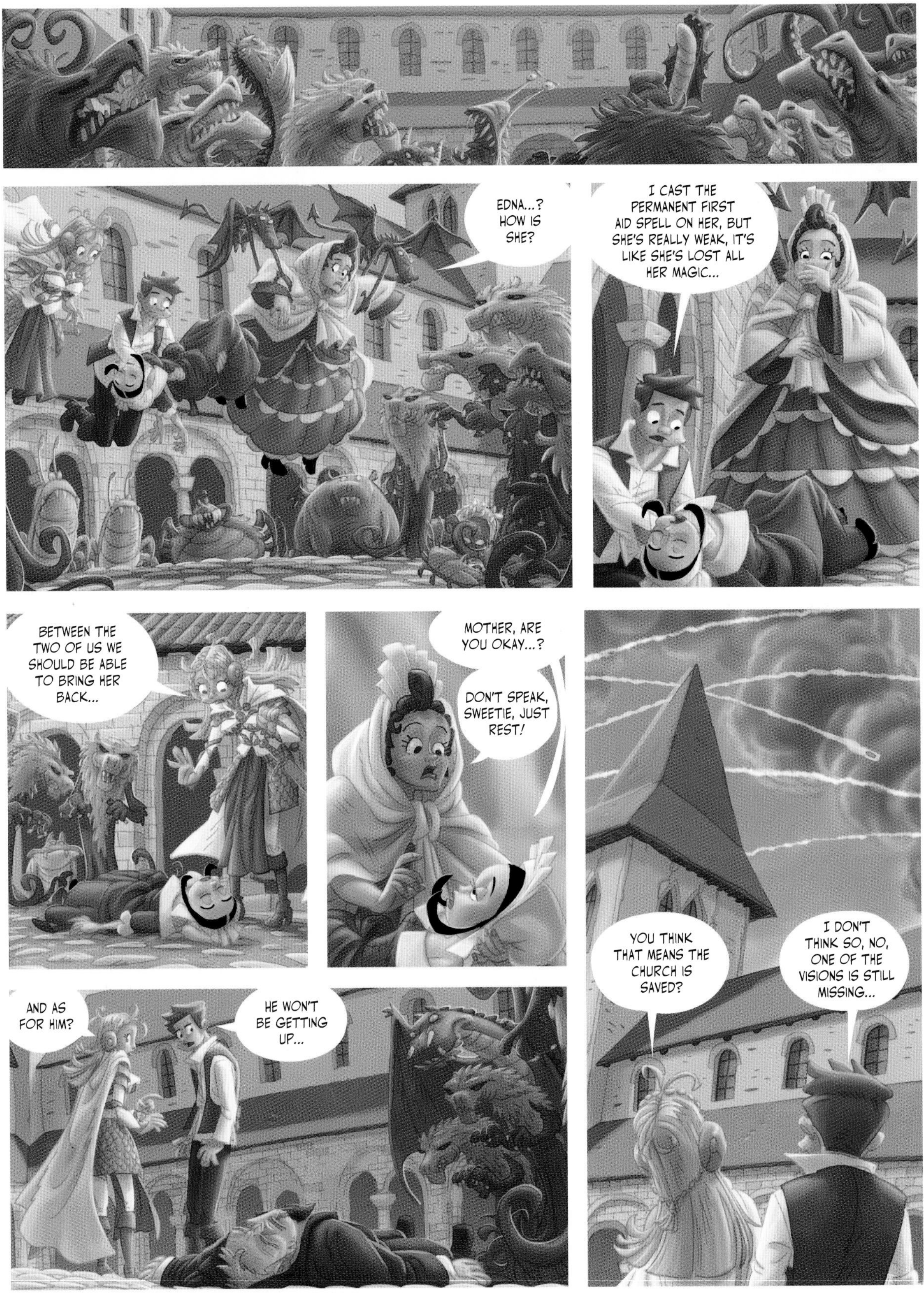
EDNA...? HOW IS SHE?
I CAST THE PERMANENT FIRST AID SPELL ON HER, BUT SHE'S REALLY WEAK, IT'S LIKE SHE'S LOST ALL HER MAGIC...
BETWEEN THE TWO OF US WE SHOULD BE ABLE TO BRING HER BACK...
MOTHER, ARE YOU OKAY...?
DON'T SPEAK, SWEETIE, JUST REST!
AND AS FOR HIM?
HE WON'T BE GETTING UP...
YOU THINK THAT MEANS THE CHURCH IS SAVED?
I DON'T THINK SO, NO, ONE OF THE VISIONS IS STILL MISSING...

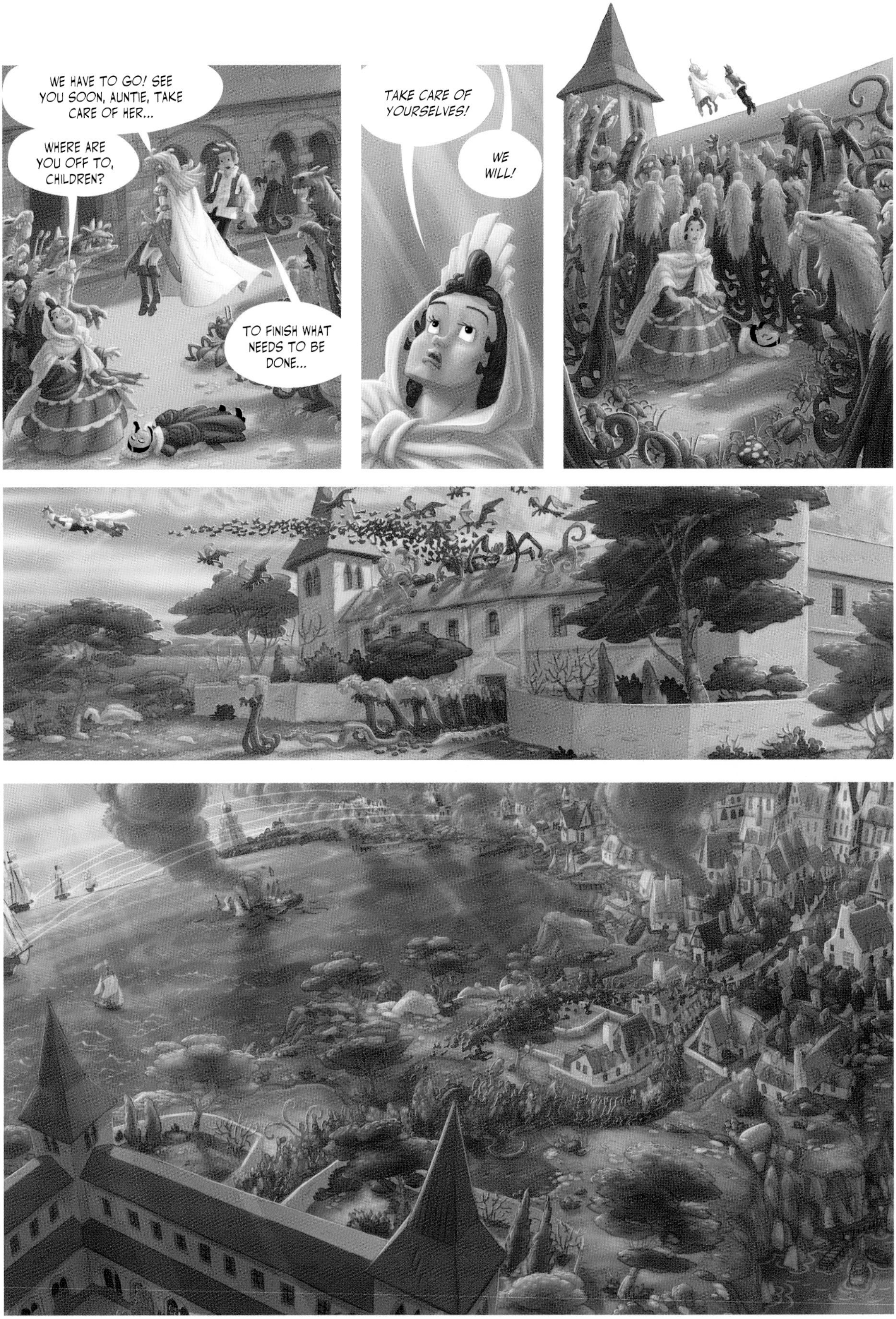
WE HAVE TO GO! SEE YOU SOON, AUNTIE, TAKE CARE OF HER...
WHERE ARE YOU OFF TO, CHILDREN?
TO FINISH WHAT NEEDS TO BE DONE...
TAKE CARE OF YOURSELVES!
WE WILL!

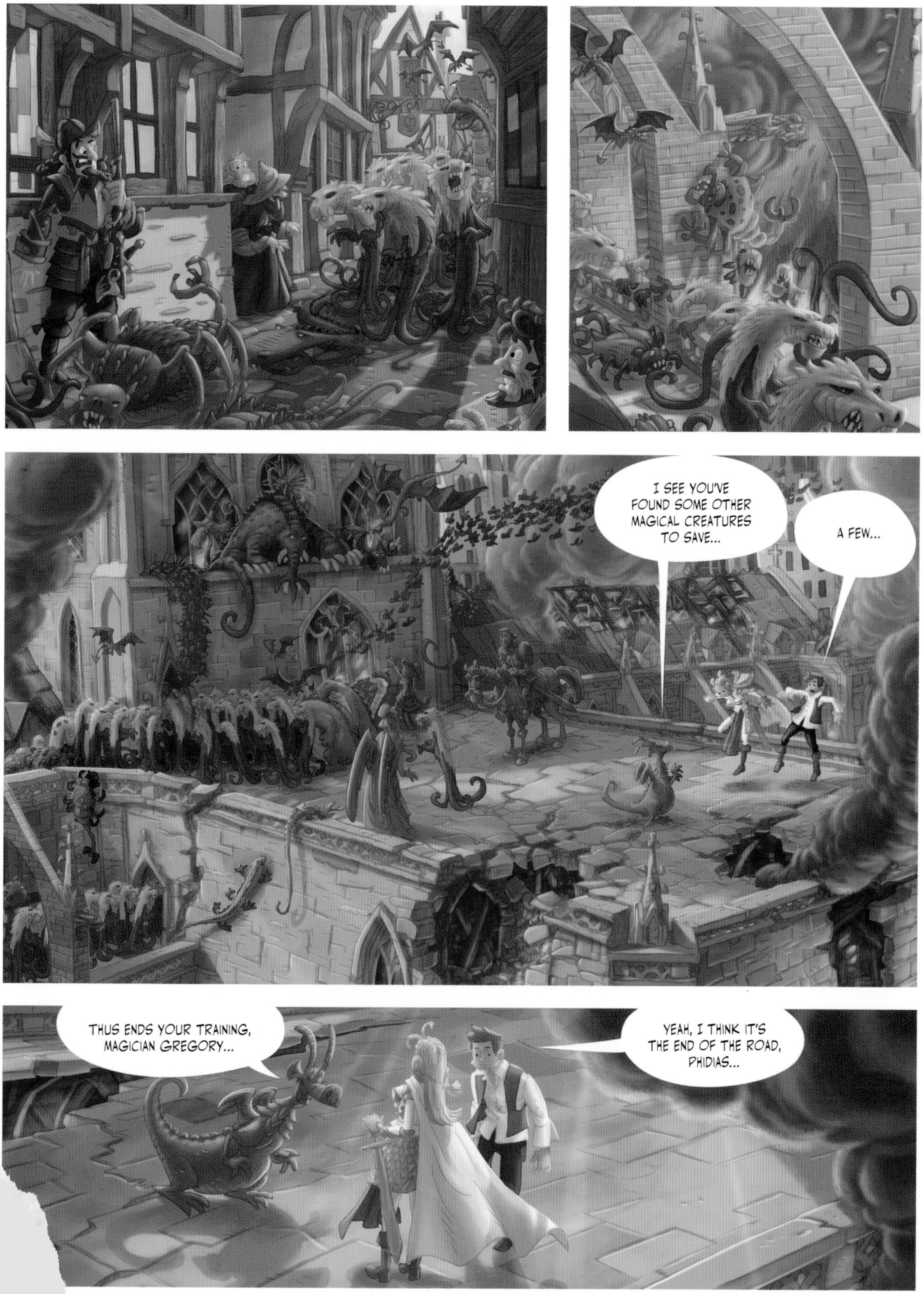
I SEE YOU'VE FOUND SOME OTHER MAGICAL CREATURES TO SAVE...
A FEW...
THUS ENDS YOUR TRAINING, MAGICIAN GREGORY...
YEAH, I THINK IT'S THE END OF THE ROAD, PHIDIAS...

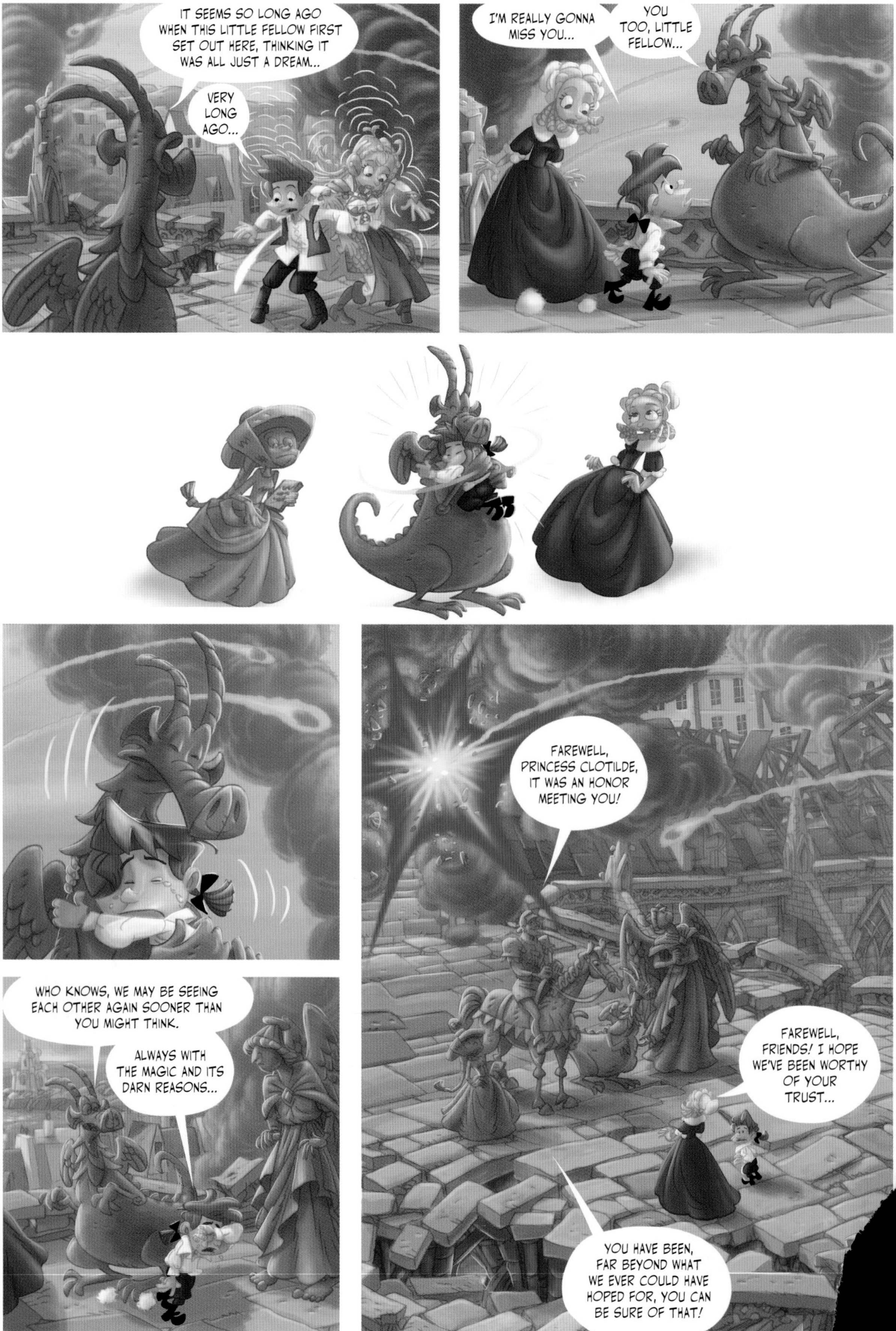
IT SEEMS SO LONG AGO WHEN THIS LITTLE FELLOW FIRST SET OUT HERE, THINKING IT WAS ALL JUST A DREAM...
VERY LONG AGO...
I'M REALLY GONNA MISS YOU...
YOU TOO, LITTLE FELLOW...
WHO KNOWS, WE MAY BE SEEING EACH OTHER AGAIN SOONER THAN YOU MIGHT THINK.
ALWAYS WITH THE MAGIC AND ITS DARN REASONS...
FAREWELL, PRINCESS CLOTILDE, IT WAS AN HONOR MEETING YOU!
FAREWELL, FRIENDS! I HOPE WE'VE BEEN WORTHY OF YOUR TRUST...
YOU HAVE BEEN, FAR BEYOND WHAT WE EVER COULD HAVE HOPED FOR, YOU CAN BE SURE OF THAT!

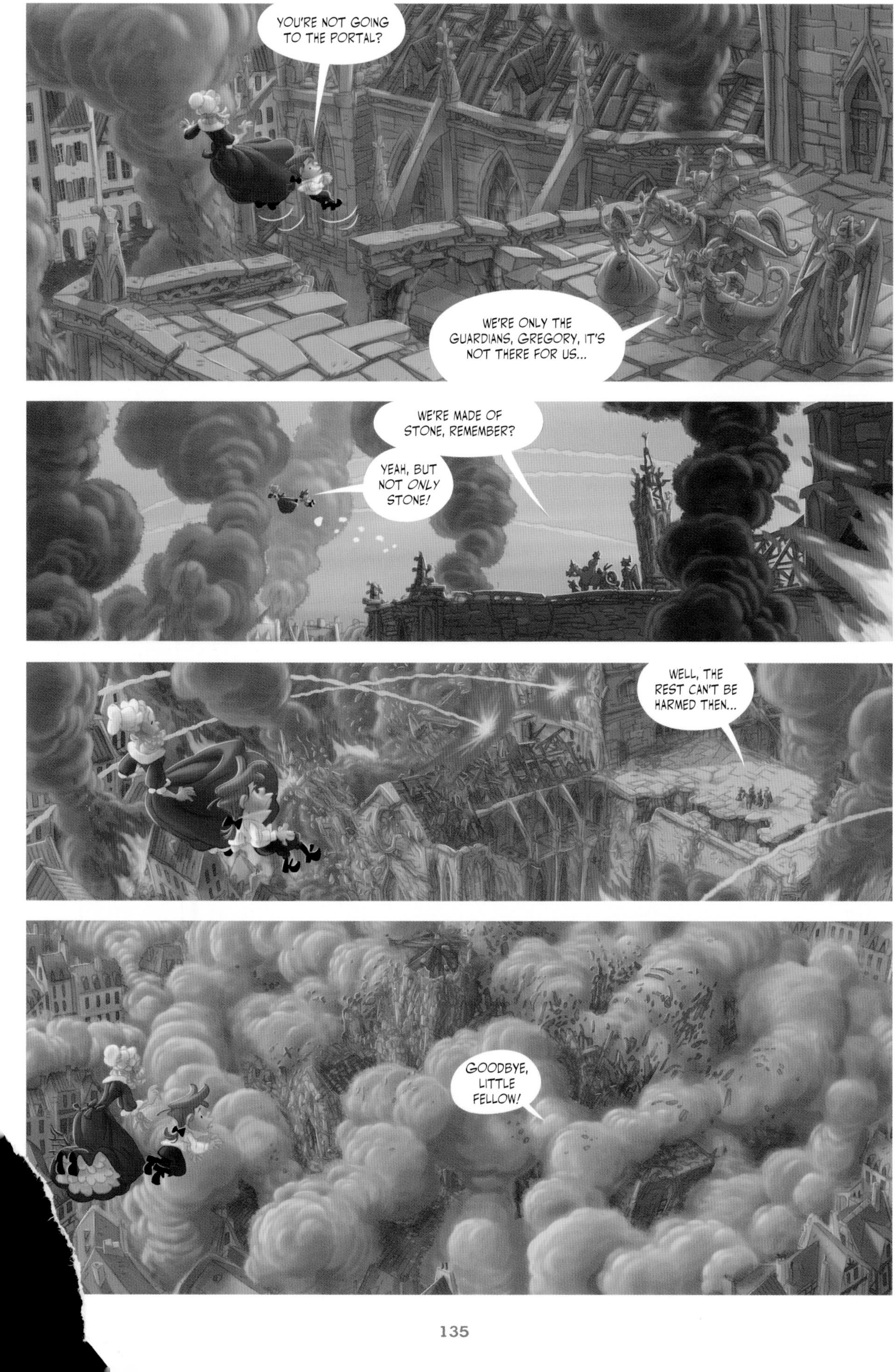
YOU'RE NOT GOING TO THE PORTAL?
WE'RE ONLY THE GUARDIANS, GREGORY, IT'S NOT THERE FOR US...
WE'RE MADE OF STONE, REMEMBER?
YEAH, BUT NOT *ONLY* STONE!
WELL, THE REST CAN'T BE HARMED THEN...
GOODBYE, LITTLE FELLOW!

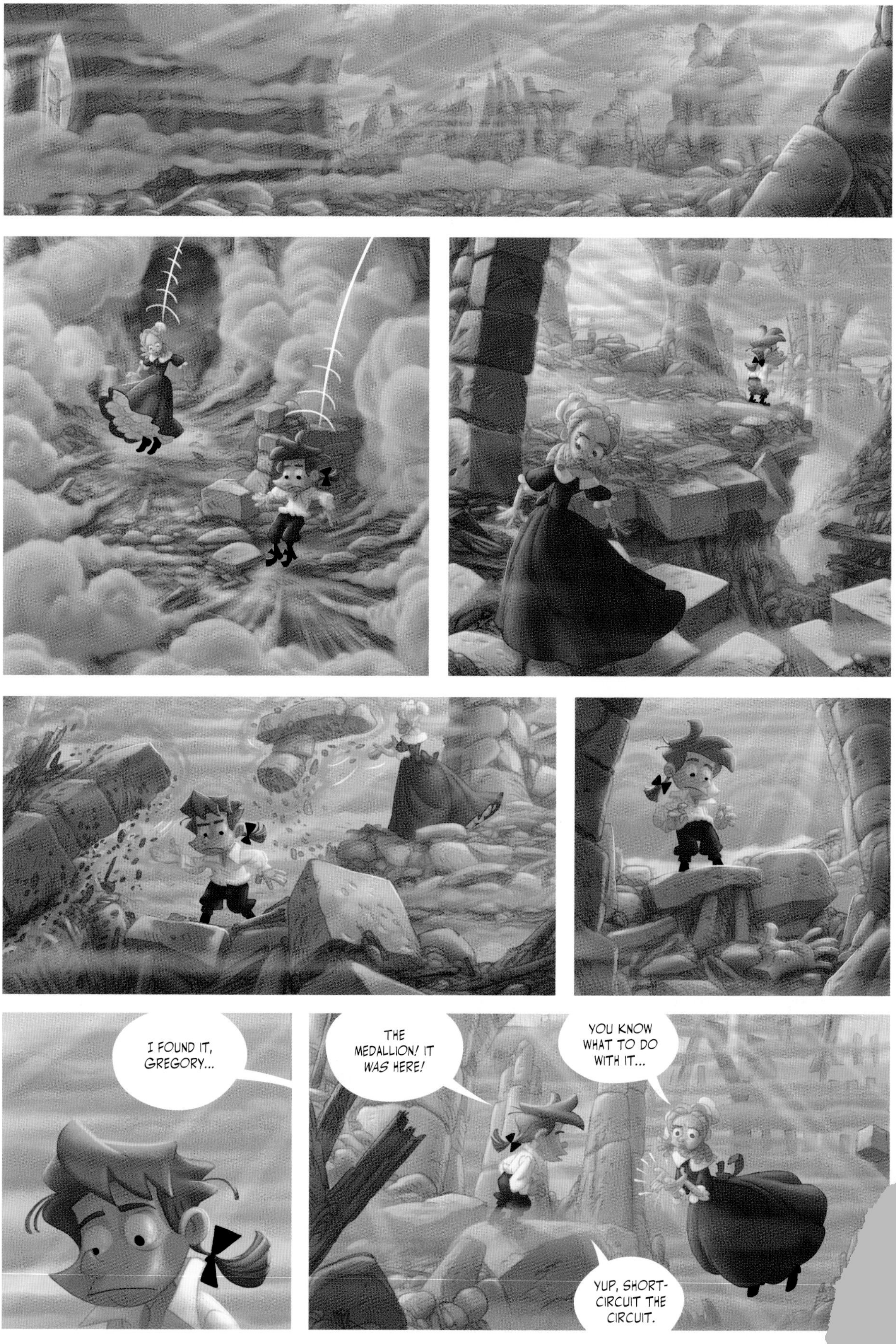
I FOUND IT, GREGORY...
THE MEDALLION! IT WAS HERE!
YOU KNOW WHAT TO DO WITH IT...
YUP, SHORT-CIRCUIT THE CIRCUIT.

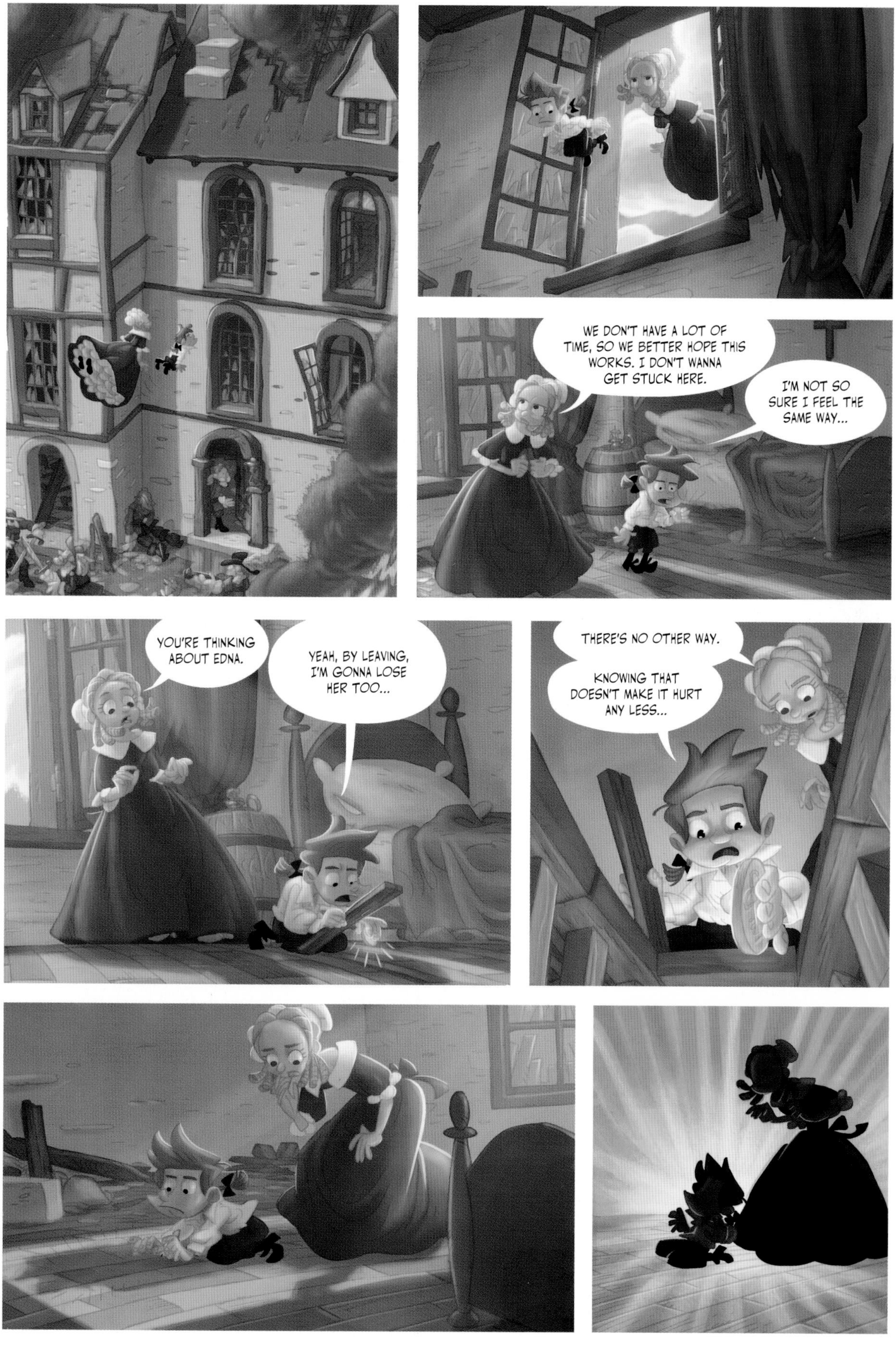

WE DON'T HAVE A LOT OF TIME, SO WE BETTER HOPE THIS WORKS. I DON'T WANNA GET STUCK HERE.
I'M NOT SO SURE I FEEL THE SAME WAY...
YOU'RE THINKING ABOUT EDNA.
YEAH, BY LEAVING, I'M GONNA LOSE HER TOO...
THERE'S NO OTHER WAY.
KNOWING THAT DOESN'T MAKE IT HURT ANY LESS...

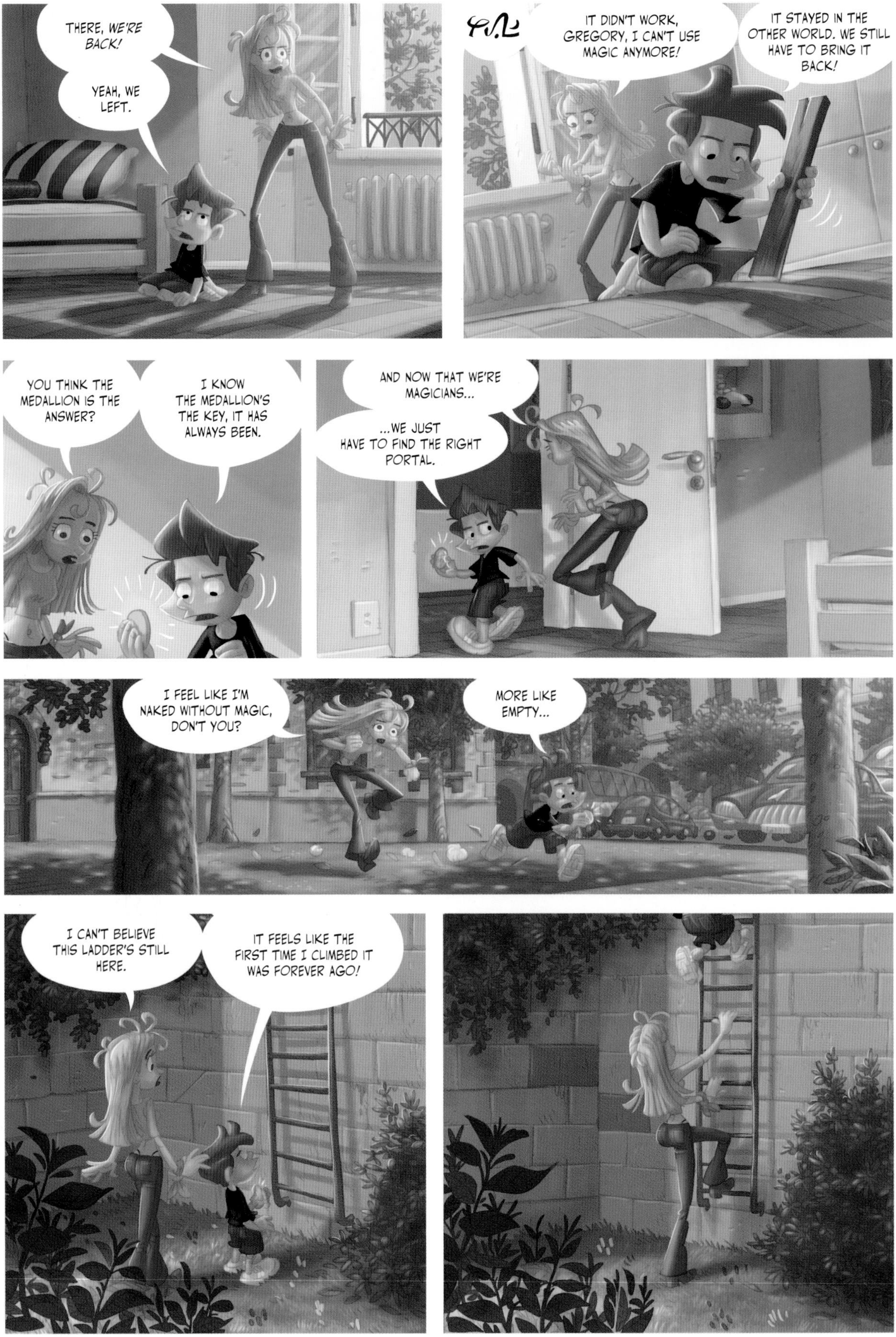
THERE, WE'RE BACK!
YEAH, WE LEFT.
IT DIDN'T WORK, GREGORY, I CAN'T USE MAGIC ANYMORE!
IT STAYED IN THE OTHER WORLD. WE STILL HAVE TO BRING IT BACK!
YOU THINK THE MEDALLION IS THE ANSWER?
I KNOW THE MEDALLION'S THE KEY, IT HAS ALWAYS BEEN.
AND NOW THAT WE'RE MAGICIANS...
...WE JUST HAVE TO FIND THE RIGHT PORTAL.
I FEEL LIKE I'M NAKED WITHOUT MAGIC, DON'T YOU?
MORE LIKE EMPTY...
I CAN'T BELIEVE THIS LADDER'S STILL HERE.
IT FEELS LIKE THE FIRST TIME I CLIMBED IT WAS FOREVER AGO!

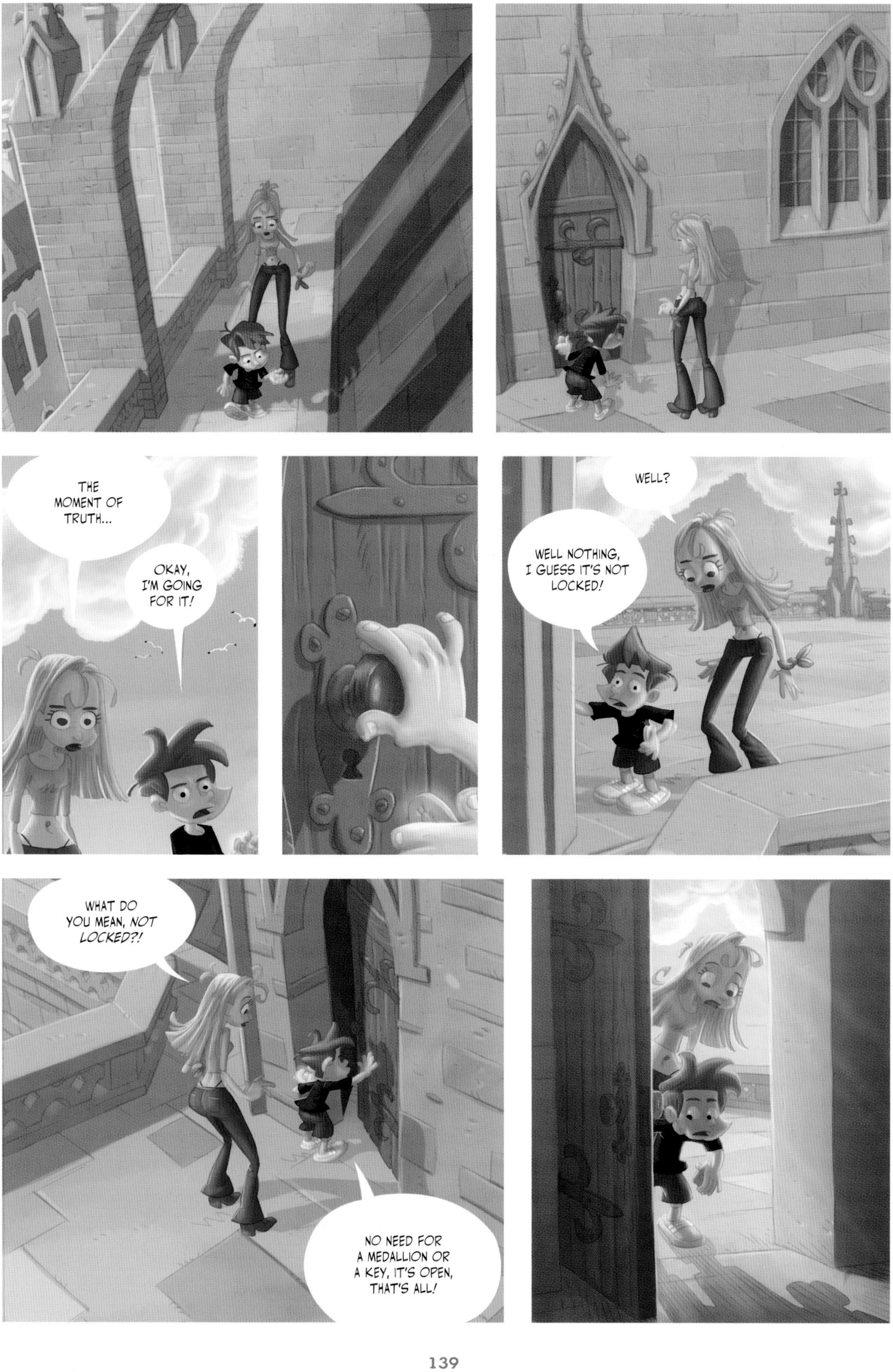
THE MOMENT OF TRUTH...
OKAY, I'M GOING FOR IT!
WELL?
WELL NOTHING, I GUESS IT'S NOT LOCKED!
WHAT DO YOU MEAN, NOT LOCKED?!
NO NEED FOR A MEDALLION OR A KEY, IT'S OPEN, THAT'S ALL!

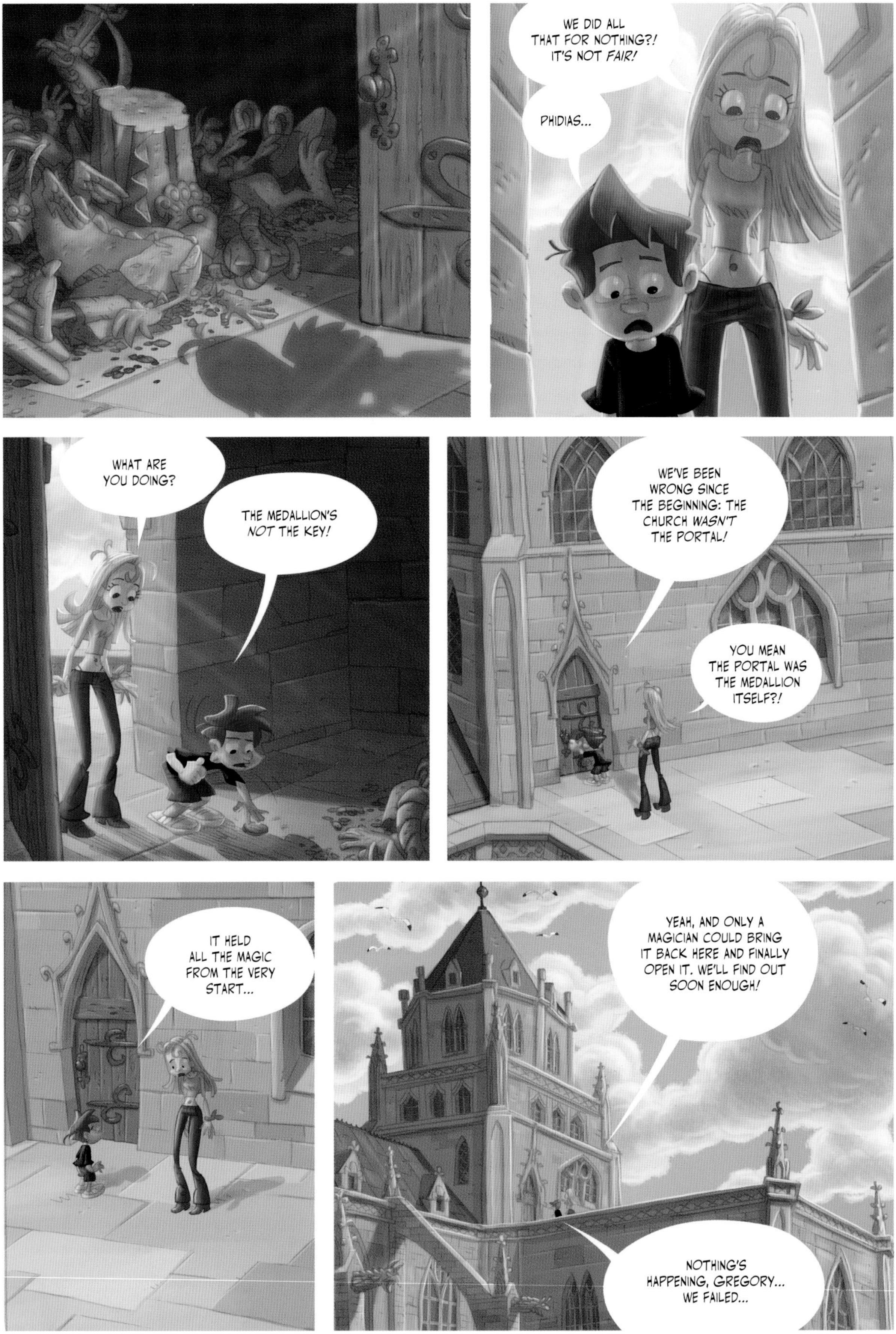
WE DID ALL THAT FOR NOTHING?! IT'S NOT *FAIR!*
PHIDIAS...
WHAT ARE YOU DOING?
THE MEDALLION'S *NOT* THE KEY!
WE'VE BEEN WRONG SINCE THE BEGINNING: THE CHURCH *WASN'T* THE PORTAL!
YOU MEAN THE PORTAL WAS THE MEDALLION ITSELF?!
IT HELD ALL THE MAGIC FROM THE VERY START...
YEAH, AND ONLY A MAGICIAN COULD BRING IT BACK HERE AND FINALLY OPEN IT. WE'LL FIND OUT SOON ENOUGH!
NOTHING'S HAPPENING, GREGORY... WE FAILED...

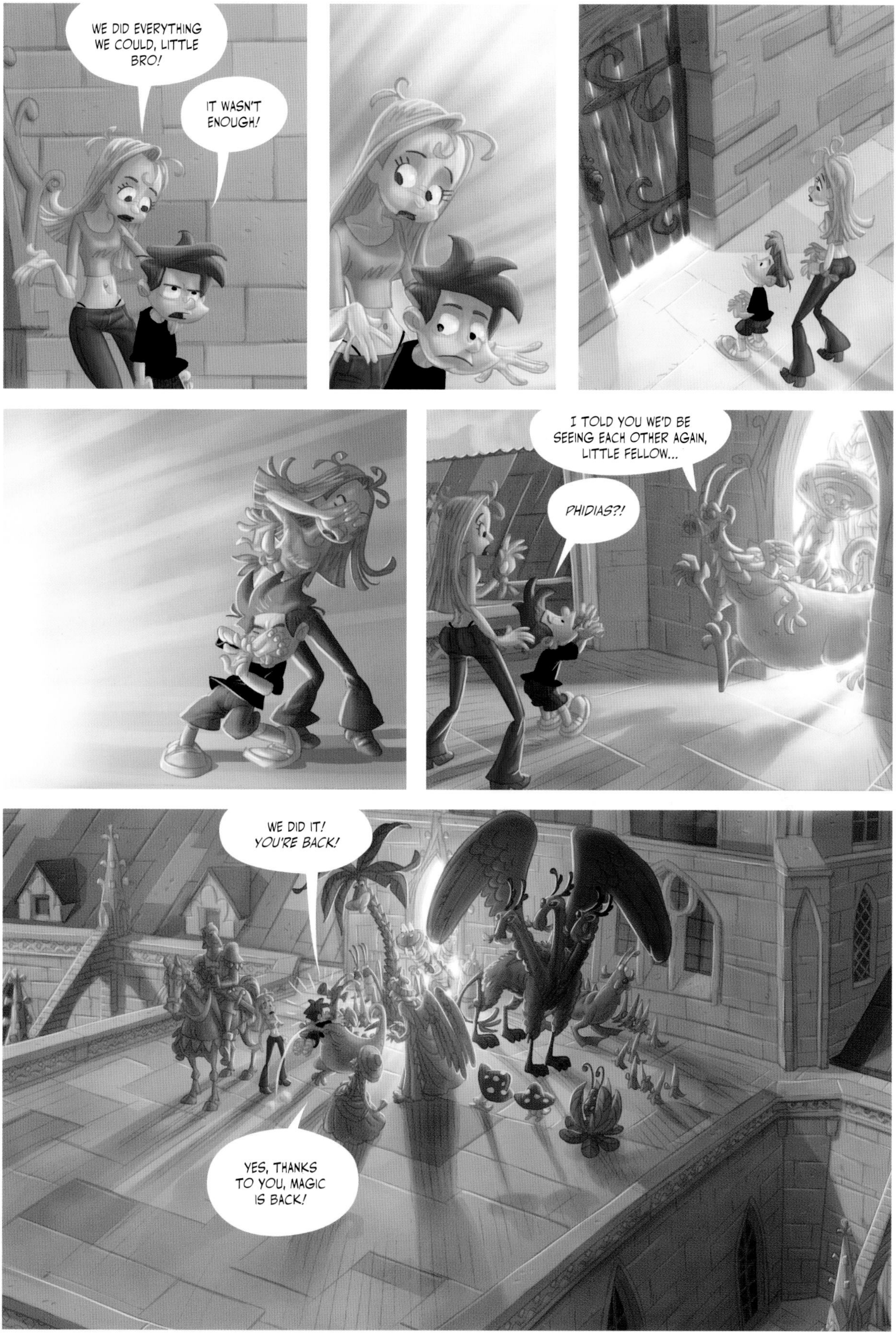
WE DID EVERYTHING WE COULD, LITTLE BRO!
IT WASN'T ENOUGH!
I TOLD YOU WE'D BE SEEING EACH OTHER AGAIN, LITTLE FELLOW...
PHIDIAS?!
WE DID IT! YOU'RE BACK!
YES, THANKS TO YOU, MAGIC IS BACK!

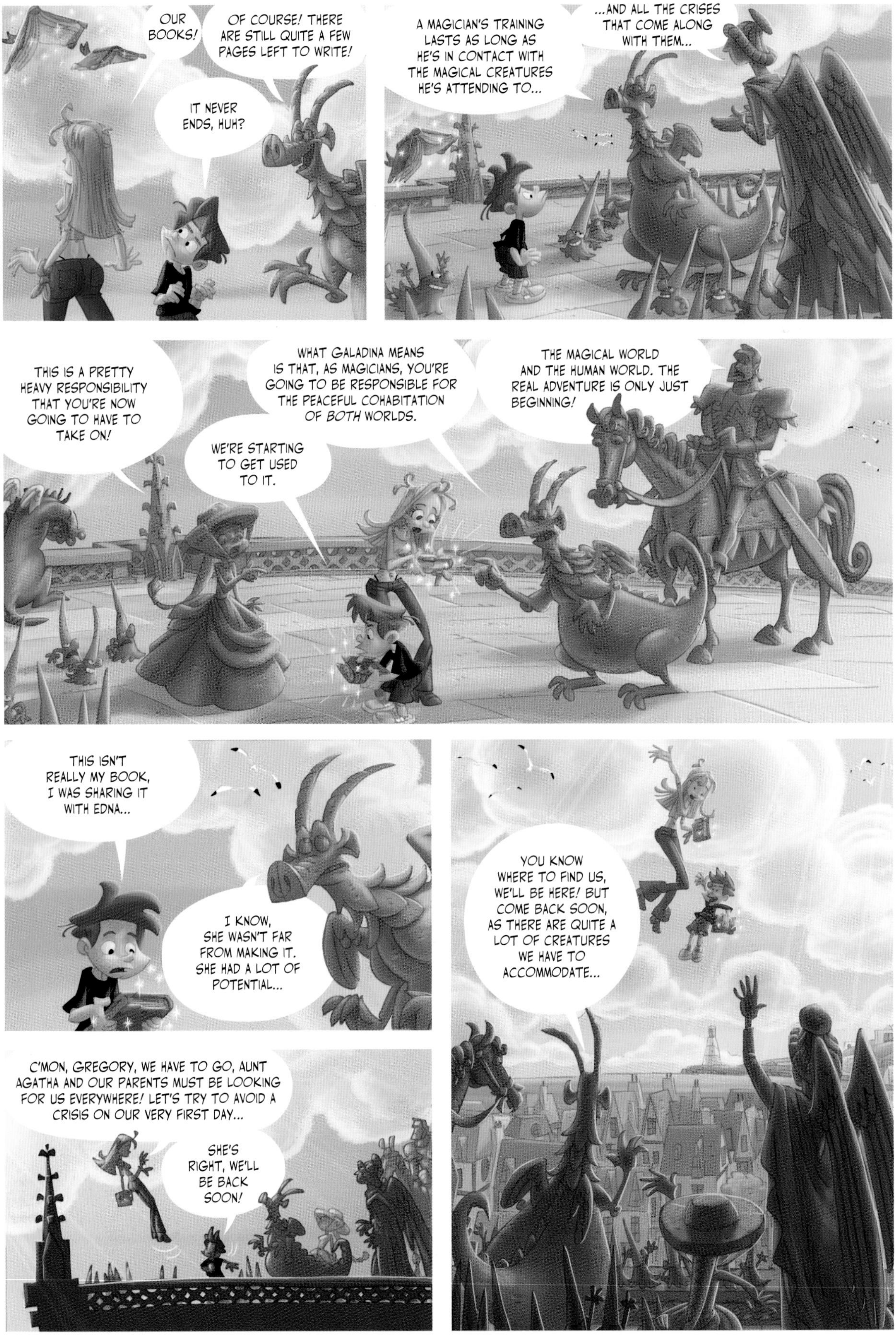
OUR BOOKS!
OF COURSE! THERE ARE STILL QUITE A FEW PAGES LEFT TO WRITE!
IT NEVER ENDS, HUH?
A MAGICIAN'S TRAINING LASTS AS LONG AS HE'S IN CONTACT WITH THE MAGICAL CREATURES HE'S ATTENDING TO...
...AND ALL THE CRISES THAT COME ALONG WITH THEM...
THIS IS A PRETTY HEAVY RESPONSIBILITY THAT YOU'RE NOW GOING TO HAVE TO TAKE ON!
WHAT GALADINA MEANS IS THAT, AS MAGICIANS, YOU'RE GOING TO BE RESPONSIBLE FOR THE PEACEFUL COHABITATION OF BOTH WORLDS.
WE'RE STARTING TO GET USED TO IT.
THE MAGICAL WORLD AND THE HUMAN WORLD. THE REAL ADVENTURE IS ONLY JUST BEGINNING!
THIS ISN'T REALLY MY BOOK, I WAS SHARING IT WITH EDNA...
I KNOW, SHE WASN'T FAR FROM MAKING IT. SHE HAD A LOT OF POTENTIAL...
C'MON, GREGORY, WE HAVE TO GO, AUNT AGATHA AND OUR PARENTS MUST BE LOOKING FOR US EVERYWHERE! LET'S TRY TO AVOID A CRISIS ON OUR VERY FIRST DAY...
SHE'S RIGHT, WE'LL BE BACK SOON!
YOU KNOW WHERE TO FIND US, WE'LL BE HERE! BUT COME BACK SOON, AS THERE ARE QUITE A LOT OF CREATURES WE HAVE TO ACCOMMODATE...

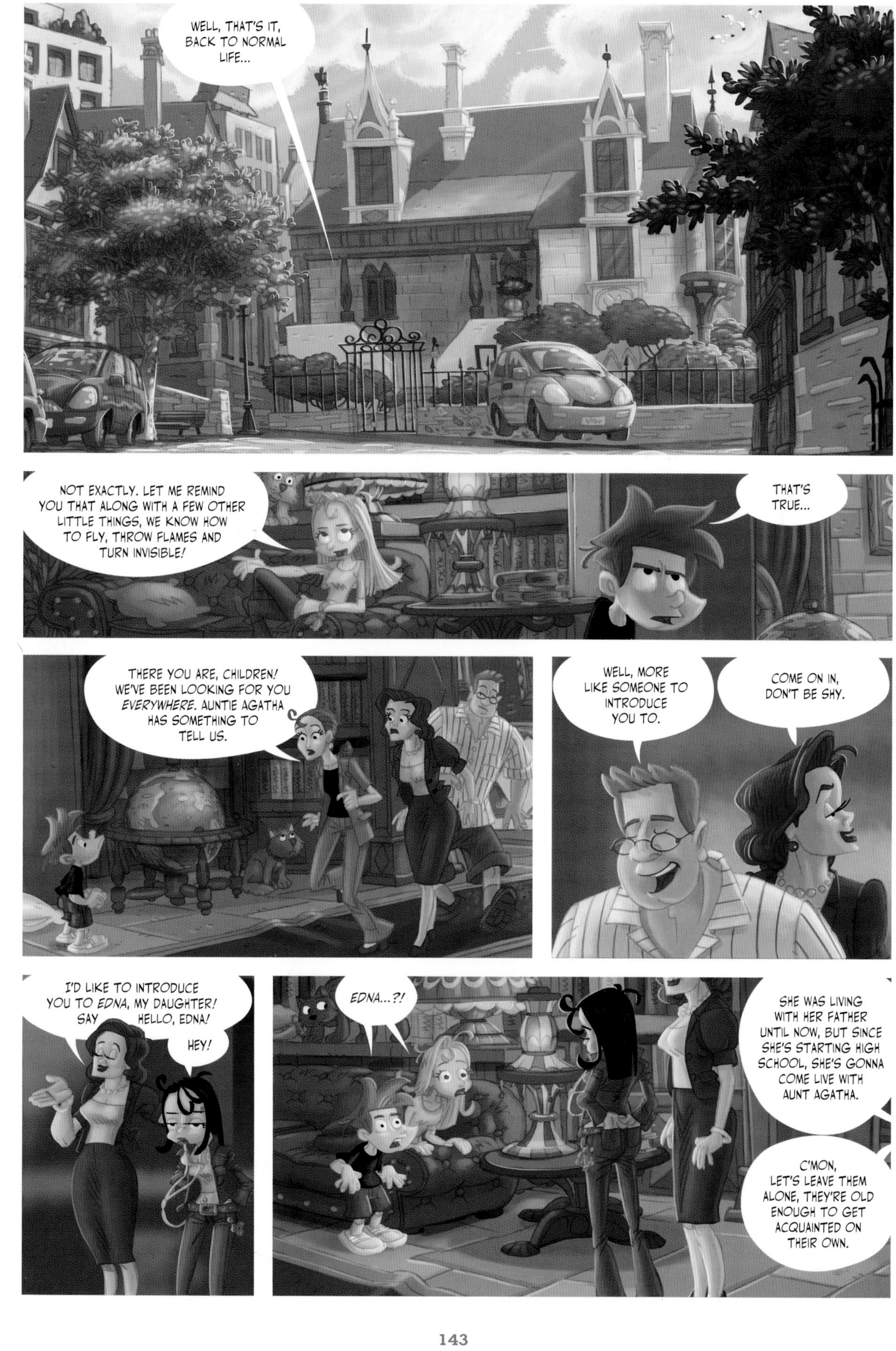
WELL, THAT'S IT, BACK TO NORMAL LIFE...
NOT EXACTLY. LET ME REMIND YOU THAT ALONG WITH A FEW OTHER LITTLE THINGS, WE KNOW HOW TO FLY, THROW FLAMES AND TURN INVISIBLE!
THAT'S TRUE...
THERE YOU ARE, CHILDREN! WE'VE BEEN LOOKING FOR YOU *EVERYWHERE*. AUNTIE AGATHA HAS SOMETHING TO TELL US.
WELL, MORE LIKE SOMEONE TO INTRODUCE YOU TO.
COME ON IN, DON'T BE SHY.
I'D LIKE TO INTRODUCE YOU TO *EDNA*, MY DAUGHTER! SAY HELLO, EDNA!
HEY!
EDNA...?!
SHE WAS LIVING WITH HER FATHER UNTIL NOW, BUT SINCE SHE'S STARTING HIGH SCHOOL, SHE'S GONNA COME LIVE WITH AUNT AGATHA.
C'MON, LET'S LEAVE THEM ALONE, THEY'RE OLD ENOUGH TO GET ACQUAINTED ON THEIR OWN.

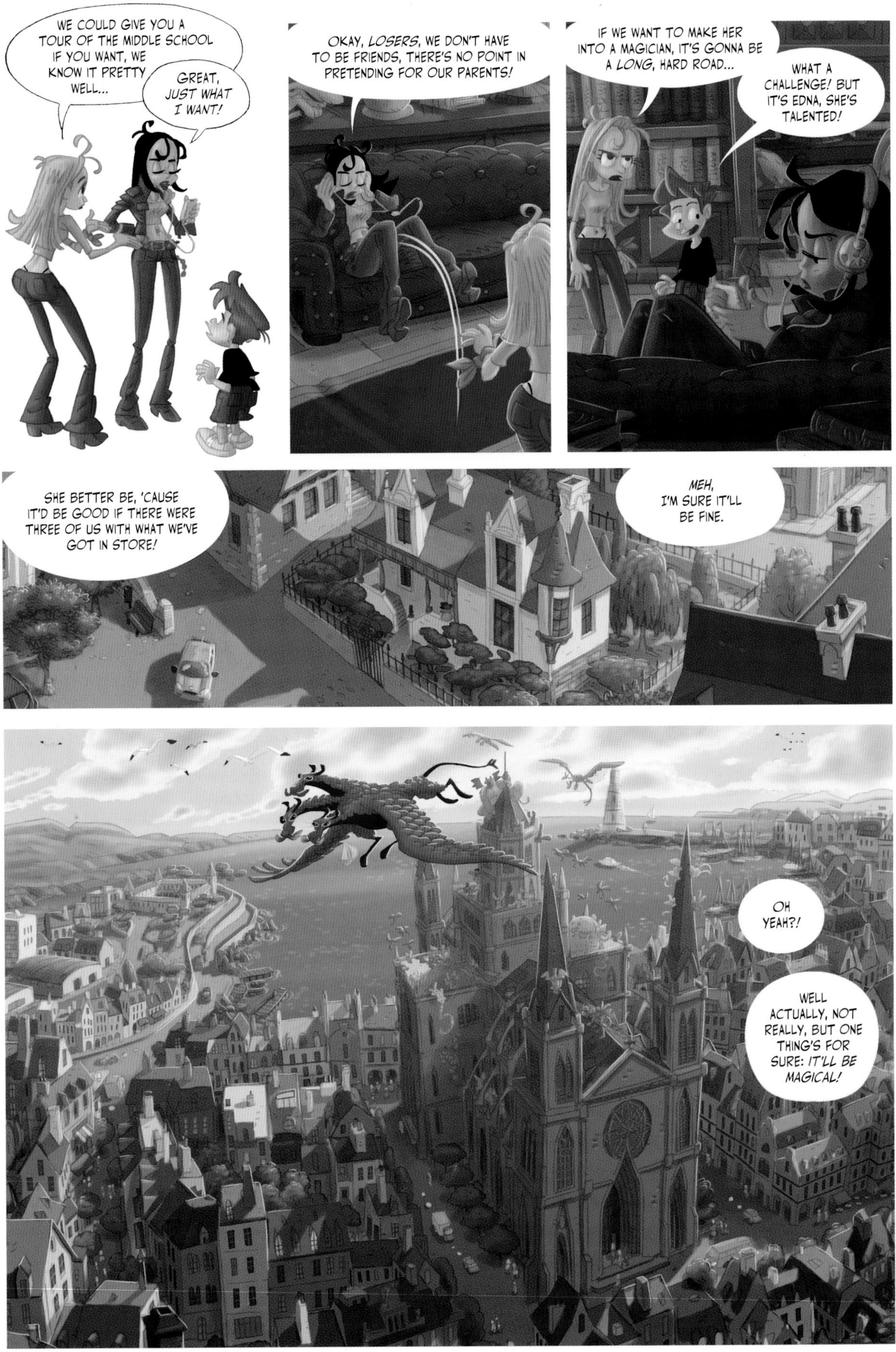
WE COULD GIVE YOU A TOUR OF THE MIDDLE SCHOOL IF YOU WANT, WE KNOW IT PRETTY WELL...
GREAT, JUST WHAT I WANT!
OKAY, LOSERS, WE DON'T HAVE TO BE FRIENDS, THERE'S NO POINT IN PRETENDING FOR OUR PARENTS!
IF WE WANT TO MAKE HER INTO A MAGICIAN, IT'S GONNA BE A LONG, HARD ROAD...
WHAT A CHALLENGE! BUT IT'S EDNA, SHE'S TALENTED!
SHE BETTER BE, 'CAUSE IT'D BE GOOD IF THERE WERE THREE OF US WITH WHAT WE'VE GOT IN STORE!
MEH, I'M SURE IT'LL BE FINE.
OH YEAH?!
WELL ACTUALLY, NOT REALLY, BUT ONE THING'S FOR SURE: IT'LL BE MAGICAL!

THE END... FOR NOW!